# A VAMPIRE'S GUIDE TO ADULTING

### VAMPIRE INNOCENT
#### BOOK TEN

## MATTHEW S. COX

DIVISION ZERO PRESS

ISBN (ebook): 978-1-950738-26-7

ISBN (paperback): 978-1-950738-27-4

# CONTENTS

# THE LAST MONDAY OF EIGHTEEN

Acceptance, as an emotional state, sometimes sits on top of a ledge way up a steep hill.

Not many people can make the climb, but vampires have claws. I can fly, too, but it ruins the metaphor. Seriously, though, if it's possible for the undead to find Zen, I'm there.

Maybe I haven't 'reached enlightenment,' but I definitely lack the motivation to be upset over where my life has gone. Technically speaking, my life *has* gone. I'm on phase two. As far as anyone looking at me goes, I seem perfectly alive—but it's a lie. However, unlike photos of fast food, the lie goes in the other direction. My reality is not a sad disappointment compared to the image presented, more of an unexpected surprise. Lies come in varying degrees from 'I didn't eat the last cookie' to 'no I didn't cheat on you with your best friend' to 'try peanut butter and pickle sandwiches, they're awesome' pranks. One can lead to tears, one fights, the other murder... results may vary with temperament.

I guess politics, has to count, too. They say anything a person can be gifted at evolves into a profession, and in the case of born liars, their path invariably leads to politics—or trying to sell pillows on cable. Okay, it's me. I'm the one who said it. Politicians lie more than used car salesman or kids when asked if they've finished their homework. Blame Professor Heath and going to philosophy class. He's got me thinking of all sorts of random stuff lately.

Back to the motivation thing. I've never been what anyone would call an overachiever. In fact, as far as school went, I ended up kind of lazy, doing only as much work as necessary to avoid getting in trouble. Considering my parents, it meant I scored mostly As and Bs but never did extra work or took AP classes or busted my butt on extracurricular things. Due to whatever fortunate circumstances surrounded my existence, school didn't require too much effort on my part to do well. For example, I didn't really need to take notes to remember enough to get decent grades on tests.

Presently, I'm applying the same lack of drive to my existence as a vampire.

Being upset over what happened takes effort and is pointless. Like if someone hit my car and damaged it, no amount of screaming at them would fix the dent. Nothing I could possibly do is going to give me back the future no longer ahead of me, so why bother letting it drive me nuts? Some vampires are caught up in politics—and not the governmental kind. I'm talking about society politics where people backstab each other to look cool for the 'in crowd'. Honestly, the only difference between vampire politics and high school politics is the amount of money everyone has—and the lack of homework.

We don't have vampires running for 'undead president' or mayor or whatever. Even if we did have an official power structure, there are so many Lost Ones around here any vampire trying to declare themselves the ruler would command about as much respect as Ollie Ziegler, my school's senior class president. Major nerd but not a bad guy. Problem was, he took things way too seriously. Walked around as if he had as much actual power as the principal. Everyone ignored him. If any vampire in Seattle declared themselves king or queen, they'd be laughed at exactly like Ollie.

No, the political structure—such as it is—among the vampires here reminds me of those old movies about Al Capone my mother used to watch. Arthur Wolent, a Fury, is basically the boss. He's not the oldest, not even 200 years a vampire yet, but Furies are weird. People are afraid of them and they seem far ahead of the power curve compared to others. He's essentially the de-facto boss of Seattle, but from what I've seen so far, he doesn't really feel as if he tries to tell everyone what to do. Vampires generally go along with him because he's got good ideas.

Works for me. I'm happy to merely exist and be as normal as possible. Can't say I'm trying to pretend the vampire thing never happened. It's far too major a change to ignore. No matter how introverted a person is, they won't spontaneously combust when exposed to sunlight. To be fair, I don't spontaneously combust either... it's more a slow burn like *Black Swan*. My bloodline is able to tolerate sun more than others at the expense of not having any really cool abilities. Like how Aurélie can charm an entire room at once or Furies can become so strong they're able to throw cars. According to rumor, some Old Guard can legit shapeshift into bats or wolves. Dalton, my sire, even suggested a few Academics wielded mystical arts.

No, it's not like wizards in the fantasy games Sierra and Dad love so much... real magic is far more subtle and usually takes a long time to do. And yeah, even the two-minute rituals are a long time when someone's trying to bash your face in. Sophia's one of those unusual mystics who can make magic happen simply by wanting it to. None of us are sure how exactly it happened. Magical talent like hers doesn't simply come out of the blue. It had to be in our family line, dormant for generations until a group of mystics stole her body to use as a spy. Oh, she got it back. They just punted her ghost out of her skin for a little while.

I guess having one's astral essence ripped apart from their flesh broke some stuff loose in her soul. If astral eavesdropping were a drug, the voiceover guy on the commercial would say something like: caution, use of this product may cause unexpected side effects such as temporal displacement, glowing kittens, and portal seepage. Use with caution.

So, yeah. I'm a vampire. My one sister, Sierra, has become a sword-obsessed warrior queen wannabe, my other sister, Sophia, uses magic… and my little brother, Sam, has a little imp he enjoys playing with. No, get your mind out of the gutter. I don't mean it in the way all boys have a little imp. I'm talking a *legit* demon, even if it is a minor one. Blix is pretty cool though, as demons go. Mostly, he and Sam play video games. The little guy goes with my bro everywhere. Kinda like a *Dora the Explorer* situation, only less educational.

I'd call my parents normal, but they're parents. At least they're not *supernatural…* as far as I know.

Neither are my friends Ashley and Michelle—or my boyfriend Hunter.

What *is* supernatural is the tangle of math in front of me. It's never been my favorite subject, but I'm not one of those people who moaned about how much it sucked. Sophia loves it. But she's basically a nerd disguised as Barbie. When she gets to high school, she's totally going to confuse everyone. I'm ninety-five percent sure she's going to be mistaken for an air-headed blonde cheerleader by looks, but she's whip smart. Sierra's more like me. Smart but unmotivated. Sam's scary smart, too. The reason he always seems to be playing video games is he gets his homework done in less than an hour every day. Seriously, I think he's almost one of those kids who could start college at fifteen. He's bored with school, but, like me, not motivated enough to push himself. He'd rather enjoy life.

Speaking of homework…

Calculus is being a pain in my ass tonight.

Normally, I'd complain about it being Monday because it's the American thing to do on a Monday. Given my circumstances, my leeway to complain about the first day of the work week is pretty thin. I've never held a traditional nine-to-five job, nor will I ever. The only way for me to even be awake at nine in the morning would be to go somewhere so far north the sun stays down for months at a time. Even then, I'm not sure if it matters. Vampire sleep might have time requirements beyond merely the sun being up or not. Then again, I *do* tend to fall asleep at the instant of sunrise regardless of what's on the clock at the time… so maybe going to bumfart Alaska would let me stay awake continuously for weeks.

Gah. Talk about a great way to go psychotic. After three months without sleep, Jerry Springer Show guests would seem well adjusted by comparison to me.

Tonight's problem focusing on calculus has nothing to do with it being difficult math. It's not truly feeling *hard* to me, more tedious. Every time I go over one of these problems, half the time goes toward questioning if choosing computer programming as my major was a mistake or if I'm merely allowing the whole vampire thing to distract me from school in general.

It has to mean something when every other vampire either laughs or 'awws' at me when they find out I'm trying to continue on with my life, academically speaking. Maybe it's my lazy side coming out. Undeath is a pretty strong excuse for not bothering to pursue a degree. What use could it possibly be beyond a hobby? There is literally zero chance of me ever having a traditional career. Computers and stuff are cool, but I'm not *that* kind of nerd. Programming came from me mentally throwing a dart at a list of ideas and thinking it's a job anyone can do from home. No need to expose myself to daylight.

But… I've been ignoring my complete lack of need to work, even before I chanced into a respectable amount of money in Ireland.

If I told anyone where it came from, they'd consider me completely crazy. Even most vampires would call me insane. Shocked me to find out how much real money gold coins are worth. It's hardly enough to live on for eternity, but if I stay modest—like in this house —I'm set for a good long while. Aurélie thinks she can set my money up to grow sufficiently to be self-sustaining. She's doing some kind of corporate banking stuff way over my head. I'd probably have an easier time learning magic from Sophia. Anyway, according to her, I have plenty to 'get started' and snowball into a self-sustaining source of funds. It'll be decades before 'living big' is even an option, but I don't care. It means I can't spend money on stuff like a fancy house or ridiculous cars or such. Luckily for me, I'm totally happy here.

It's pathological, really. What eighteen-year-old clings to their childhood home with literal claws?

Sometimes, homesickness hits me as bad as it gets Sophia on every family road trip, despite me still being here. Maybe 'homesickness' isn't the right word for it, but I'll be sitting here in my room and get hit with this sudden, intense fear like I really don't wanna lose my home. It doesn't last long, though. Honestly, it's most likely my brain processing my close call and the impermanence of everything. I'm basically a small dog who randomly gets super possessive of their toy and growls for no reason at everything. Only, no actual growling is involved and instead of a toy, it's my house and family.

I sorta have an excuse—almost died. Well, not so 'almost.' Maybe the same cosmic effect wherein ghosts can't help but haunt the place they died is making me abnormally attached to my house. Could be I'm not as adjusted to what happened as I've told myself. Then again, *death* is a big mental scar. It's a little beyond most traumas. Generally, people don't have to cope with the shock of their own demise. There's no support group for it. Not even self-help books.

Couldn't even find a Pinterest board dedicated to coping with involuntary resurrection.

After fifteen minutes vanish to me idly wondering if I technically died and came back or didn't completely die, it's pretty damn obvious there's too much on my mind at the moment for me to make room for calculus. Suppose I could try to focus. This calc isn't an immediate worry. It's not due until Wednesday. Still, oughta do it now when nothing else is in the way. Tomorrow could bring more work, and putting off a task only makes it suck more when I finally force myself to do it.

Ugh. I have English lit later tonight, just what a Monday needs— three hours of discussing the meaning of poetry written two centuries ago by someone mostly likely drunk or high as hell on laudanum. I bet the people who wrote this stuff couldn't even tell anyone what it means. Another nice thing about being a vampire... no matter how boring a class gets, it can't knock me unconscious. Wait, no. That's not a *nice* thing. Sleep would be a merciful escape.

Why is the idea of going to school bothering me so much now? Am I doing it for the education, because I want to feel normal like none of this supernatural stuff happened, or is it me wanting to make my parents happy? Doing it for them isn't the best motivation, but it makes more sense than wanting a degree for myself. It's not as if I'd ever use one to get a real job. Even if I did, how long would it be before time made me move? Professor Heath changes schools every thirty years or so. Office jobs seldom last anywhere near as long. Maybe it wouldn't be an issue. Office workers lasting six years in the same place are kinda rare.

Maybe, when my family's gone, I'll need something to do in order to beat boredom, but for now, a job is the last thing I want eating up time. Figure I've got maybe seven or eight years left before the Littles grow up and go off on their own. Need to enjoy having a family while we're still together as one.

Another thing killing my focus is what day it is.

Yeah, it's probably the date more than anything else.

Today is Monday. New Year's Day Eve or whatever they call the night of January first. Oh, duh. No class tonight, national holiday and all. Cool. No, I'm not wound up over it being New Year's. Tomorrow's my nineteenth birthday. You know what really sucked? My parents dressing me up as 'Baby New Year' for the first five years of my life. They still have the photos. Even one of me in the hospital hours after birth wearing a diaper marked 1999.

Embarrassing as hell. Dorky, too.

Those two words exactly encompass the enigma of my parents.

Maybe I should mess with them and dress up as Baby 2018 tomorrow.

Nah. Camera phones exist.

Grr. Now I know what's bugging me, why focusing on calculus is proving impossible. Should I still even have birthdays or would it be more accurate to consider my eighteenth year infinite? Assuming nothing destroys me along the way, Sophia doesn't do anything magically weird to me, and the toaster behaves itself, 200 years from now, my body is going to appear exactly the same as it does right now.

What do I mean by the toaster? It's developed a bit of an attitude. I suspect it has something to do with there being an imp living in the house. Dad called the toaster stupid for not turning on when he hit the button last week and it launched a flaming toast-jectile at his head. Hmm. Toast-jectile is a clumsy word. Toast missile? Incendiary bread bomb? Whatever.

Mom couldn't decide if she should put a nineteen on the cake or an eighteen with a little two next to it, as in second eighteenth. Sam rambled about it being eighteen to the power of two so she should technically put eighteen times two, but it would require hunting down an x-shaped candle, which none of us believed would be worth the effort.

Talk about feeling old before my time. Bad enough having nostalgia fits already, but women aren't supposed to start celebrating the 'anniversary of past birthdays' until they get super old, like thirty.

Argh! Getting emo over my birthday tomorrow is the exact opposite of trying to be normal.

I should be happy. If things hadn't gone crazy with Scott, I'd be living in a dorm in California now, majoring in who-knows-what and totally looking forward to a future without wasting any time whatsoever feeling maudlin about the end of my childhood. Hell, I'd have been revved up and eager to join the adult world.

People don't realize what a mistake it is until they're in their forties—according to Dad.

Sophia would probably *still* be crying over me leaving to attend USC.

Not sure if I'd have flown home for my birthday or made do with whatever friends I found down there. Back when I'd been trying to decide where to go to college, Mom made a remark about most people who go out of state to earn a degree tend to stay in the area of the school. Not sure where she got the statistic beyond the majority of her friends. The ones who attended out-of-state colleges all settled permanently in the area. She figured I'd go to USC and spend the rest of my life in California. If anyone asked me *why* seventeen-year-old me settled on going there, I couldn't come up with an answer. Seemed like a cool idea… maybe I'd say 'felt right.' Dunno. Definitely wasn't a desire to get away from home or anything specific about California. 'Which college do you want to go to' received the same amount of attention any other idea crossing my teenage mind did—which is to say, not a whole lot. Some decisions really do deserve more than forty seconds of consideration. A scarily large number of people don't develop the ability to really think things through until well into their twenties. For others, it takes much longer—this is why the *Jackass* movies are a thing.

Ashley thought homesickness would've reached critical mass in two months and I'd have come back home before even finishing one semester. Maybe she's right. Being a thousand miles away from home is a shock—not as big as being murdered—but it might've hit me anyway.

Whatever. No point dwelling on what-ifs. I have more important things to worry about tonight… like what to do with the three hours not spent sitting in English lit class. Life has settled back into our version of normal. The Littles aren't in cling mode anymore… except for Sophia. They're not going to want to spend hours hanging out with me. Hell, they don't really hang out with each other too much. Sophia's usually reading, Sierra's surgically attached to the PlayStation, and Sam's either in his room—also on a PlayStation—or hanging out with his friends Daryl, Jordan, and now Ronan.

Ooh, thinking about Ronan makes me think about Hunter.

It's been a while since we had some time together. Like both my friends, he's also working and attending classes. Between their full schedules and my weird hours, it doesn't leave us many opportunities to do stuff.

As if on cue, my iPhone rings.

It's Michelle.

I groan at the twenty-four remaining calculus problems awaiting my attention while reaching for the phone.

"Hey, 'Chelle."

"What's up?"

"Homework. Been trying to develop a mental power to make this calculus do itself, but it's not working." I lean back in the chair, staring up at the ceiling.

She laughs. "Wow, I am really hoping I don't have to take calc."

"Can't see a lawyer needing advanced math, except maybe to calculate bills."

Ashley's giggling erupts on the line, probably a conference call since they'd both still be at their respective jobs now.

"Ha. Ha. So, are you busy tonight?" asks Michelle.

I twiddle my pencil between my fingers, tapping the eraser end on my worksheet. "Just a little homework, but it won't take me all night. Don't have class, so…"

"No kidding. It's New Year's Day. Which means it's also the day before your birthday. Ash and I wanna take you to dinner for your nineteenth, even if it's a bit pointless."

"Ooh!" I sit up straight. "It's not pointless. Think of it as guilt-free calories. The point is spending time with friends. Hell yeah I'm up for it."

"Sa-wee-eet!" singsongs Ashley. "We'll head to your place as soon as we're out of the salt mines. You got a couple hours left."

"Cool!"

"See you soon," says Michelle. "Gotta go. Work and stuff."

"Right. Later."

I hang up.

Awesome. The motivation faeries have arrived. Birthday doldrums are dead. I take a quick look around to ensure no glowing kittens, random screams, or ghostly eavesdroppers are in my room. Seems as though I'm in the clear.

Time to finish this calculus.

# 2

## PACT

Normality has some downsides.

Relative normality, that is. As in, my relatives. Like most families these days, we don't always manage to sit down together for a family meal every day. In the wake of my death and return, Mom, Dad, and the Littles all scrambled to make it happen. Everyone has relaxed enough to where sometimes differing schedules once again turn meals into a series of microwave entrees at alternating times. For the most part, we still *try* to do family dinner whenever possible, but no one freaks out over unavoidable scheduling conflicts.

On the evening of January first, we make it happen since no one has to be anywhere.

Since Ash and 'Chelle want to take me out for my birthday, I don't eat here despite sitting at the table with everyone. Even though food goes right through me without contributing nutrition, I'm—usually—not a goose. Food takes about the usual amount of time to make its way to the other side. If I ate dinner here, I wouldn't be able to eat anything at Denny's.

They haven't said it's where we are going, but I know Ashley. We've been hitting Denny's for as long as we've been old enough to eat at restaurants. Every time my parents took us somewhere—Ashley tended to go with us a lot to museums and kid-friendly attractions— we'd invariably end up there afterward. It's become something of a sentimental place to us.

All three Littles are grumbly about having to go back to school tomorrow. It's so weird how the time off from school between Christmas and New Year's used to feel super long and awesome, but it's really only a week. As a kid, it felt like a month. Ugh, does not bode well. If time feels shorter the older we get, I'm going to lose years in the blink of an eye at some point. Like, do vampires as old as Aurélie spend months thinking it's 2004 when it's really 2017 the way normal people spend most of Thursday morning excited at it being Friday only to have their hopes cruelly smashed at lunchtime?

Can't really miss the sense of freedom from the Christmas-to-New-Year's week off from school, since my entire existence now is basically a break from normality. Reality is a video game and I've clipped outside the walls into the space beyond where people aren't supposed to go. It's liberating not to *have* to do anything. Sure, there are downsides like watching everyone I know and love grow old and die. No idea how my brain's going to handle it when it happens. From what I've heard thus far, my personality might be permanently stuck as it is. As in, I'm going to basically be a teenager forever, albeit an oddly philosophical mature one. Seriously, how many girls my age are already looking back on their childhood (which is all of like three years ago) with nostalgia? Doesn't happen. Girls my age should be entirely looking forward in the 'can't wait to adult' stage. Yay independence and so on. But they haven't died and gotten back up. Survival doesn't force them to put their lips on the necks of grubby pizza-delivery guys or old dudes who smell like cheese or men in suits wearing so much Old Spice my sinuses burst into flames.

No, I'm not bitter. Simply trying to convince myself my sanity hasn't shattered.

Anyway, my plan for the future is more or less to take things as they come and not waste time planning or hoping for anything too elaborate. I had at least the next four years mapped out for where my life would go, and all of it went poof in a split second when Scott stabbed me. For months, I'd stressed out over moving to California, getting accepted to college, wondering what sort of career would allow me to survive—now none of it matters. So much time wasted, so much stress for nothing.

Sigh.

Whoever said hindsight is twenty-twenty needs to be slapped… for being right.

But honestly, I'm not Coralie. No way to know any of this would happen before it did.

During one of our family summer road trips—wanna say the year I was ten—we stopped at this roadside place for lunch. Dad ordered one thing and got an entirely different meal, something he'd never have even thought of trying. He didn't even complain, just ate it. Said something about not wanting to waste food since they'd only throw it out if he didn't eat it… and sometimes life gives us stuff we don't ask for, but it doesn't mean the stuff is bad.

I ordered college and got immortality. Pretty good trade, honestly. Much better than that weird eggplant dish.

Ashley arrives a little after six and hangs out with us at the dinner table. Normally, Mom would try to feed her since she came straight over from work, but the 'rents know we're going out for food once Michelle gets here. The Littles complain about having to go to bed 'early' tonight due to school tomorrow.

"We shouldn't have to go to school tomorrow since it's Sarah's birthday." Sierra gestures at me. "Family stuff."

"Hmm." Mom shifts her gaze sideways to Dad, who appears to be mulling the idea.

Sierra's eyes widen with hope. Sophia's 'yeah right' expression morphs to 'wow, really?' Sam doesn't show any reaction either way.

"She's not going to be awake until a little while before you guys get home." Mom stabs some green beans on her fork. "Nice try, though."

"Nuts," mutters Sierra, slouching.

Sophia shakes her head in a 'yeah, thought so' sort of way.

"Almost had it." Sam grins.

"Sare could make the principal close the school for the day." Sierra elbow-nudges me.

I laugh. "Sure, but it wouldn't be worth the trouble I'd get into."

"What trouble?" She 'pffs.' "You can make the police leave you alone, too."

"You're forgetting Mom and Dad?"

"You're eighteen. Almost nineteen." Sierra thrusts her arms out to either side. "And a vampire. You're above petty mortal concerns."

Dad chuckles. "I'm not sure how to feel about being referred to as a petty mortal concern."

"Quite." Mom appears to be trying hard not to laugh.

"Dude, she'd get *so* grounded for mind-controlling your principal." Ashley snickers, then gives me a weird look. "If you had mind-control powers while we were in high school, would you have used them on anyone?"

Both parents look intently at me. Uh oh. Gotta watch what I say here. Honestly, a few times it would've been tempting to make teachers change their minds about surprise quizzes or erase their memory of assigning us a paper to write, but who knows where my head would've been if my life got turned upside down as soon as I started ninth grade. May not seem like it, but eighteen-year-old me is significantly more mature than fourteen-year-old me was.

Tactic one: attempt no self-incrimination by avoiding the issue entirely. "Other than the obvious problem of not being able to go to school in the morning."

"Ignore that. I mean theoretically." Ashley grins.

Crap.

"If Sare got turned into a vampire as a freshman, she'd look like a little kid." Sierra snickers.

I sigh at the ceiling. Bad enough being an Innocent made me appear a little younger than I am—mostly in the face—but she's right. If fourteen-year-old me ended up as a vampire, for sure I'd have been mistaken for eleven.

"Well, theoretically... I dunno. It's different facing an annoying situation while having the ability to simply ignore it versus being in a situation where there is no choice but to deal with it." I shrug. "Might've compelled Mr. Neece to get a better job."

Ashley laughs.

"The art teacher?" asks Dad.

"I remember him." Mom rolls her eyes. "I wouldn't have grounded you for dealing with him."

Heh, yeah. The guy was a trip, and not in a good way. He approached teaching art the way you'd expect an AP physics teacher to approach science. Every assignment, he'd put up on the board with this list of like twenty requirements, most of which made no sense. One time, we had to make vases out of magazine pages and he required a specific number of cords, every one of them a specific size, and so on. Like, what the heck is the point of *art* class when the teacher forbids any sort of creativity? He wanted everyone to make the exact same thing. That's training underage sweat shop factory workers, not teaching art. Plus, the dude thought he was like the world's greatest teacher. Prided himself on order and efficiency. Ugh. Art teachers are supposed to be *cool!* They're the ones who smoke weed after school in their cars and hope no one notices.

Ashley and I spend the rest of dinner talking about weird teachers, irritating classmates, and other situations in which she thinks having mind-control or vampire powers would've been cool. For the most part, I'd like to believe my conscience would've self-limited me to making the bullies leave the nerds alone and not coasting through school without having to do any work. Wait, I already did coast through school while trying not to do any work. Didn't have to be a vampire. Though, having mind powers could have changed doing minimum work to doing no work at all.

Nah. Follows Rules Girl would've been too afraid to get in trouble for being caught. Some schools expel kids for stupid crap like biting a Pop Tart into the shape of a gun. How would they react to catching me mind-controlling teachers? Well, I could've mind-controlled the principal to forget. It would have turned into a never-ending cycle.

Exhausting.

WHEN MICHELLE SHOWS UP AT 7:04 P.M., THE THREE OF US HEAD OUT the door with little fanfare, pile into Michelle's car, and drive to the Denny's in Woodinville. I fail at vampire. How many immortals still feel a little thrill about going out on their own, as in without their parents along? Our ability to pick up and drive somewhere whenever we want is still new and exciting. Wonder how old a person has to get before the awesomeness of independence wears off and being able to go places without asking for a ride or permission is no big deal.

Maybe I don't fail so much at vampire, since *driving* anywhere feels slow and tedious.

Not sure what makes me weirder between being able to fly or being eighteen and not really caring about having a car. Technically, I have one: Dad's old Sentra. Comes in handy for getting to school when my classes start before sunset. Speaking of which, the early dark of winter won't last too much longer. As soon as Daylight Savings hits again, I'll be stuck on the road.

Talking about all the mischief and trouble I could've caused in high school has us in tears with laughter by the time we arrive at Denny's. Being here with my friends feels so normal I stop thinking about supernatural stuff for a while and lose myself in feeling ordinary… at least until we stop acting like a pack of kids and start talking about real crap.

"It kinda sucks I don't have much free time anymore." Michelle swabs a french fry in ketchup. "Work and school are stressing me the hell out. It's not all bad. The challenge is exciting—but I'm definitely looking forward to being done with school."

Ashley makes a silly face at her. "If you wanted to avoid stress, you're picking the wrong career."

"Not *all* lawyers are stress factories." Michelle shrugs. "Some sit at a desk all day long going over contracts and stuff."

"But you're interested in criminal law, right?" I wag a forkful of my skillet at her. "You're diving headfirst into the chaos. Some lawyers are like the bacteria that thrive on consuming garbage—only you eat stress."

Ashley sprays tea on a sudden explosion of laughter.

Michelle frowns at me.

"No, dork. I'm not calling you—or lawyers—bacteria. Just saying you thrive on stuff other people can't tolerate. Garbage-eating bacteria is super useful."

"Stop while you're ahead." Chuckling, Michelle picks up another fry. "You don't think I know what's coming? Ain't gonna be bad when it's only one source of stress."

"Naw, it's gonna be easy." Ashley throws her arm around my shoulders. "If you're prosecuting a real creep, you can ask Sare to make the guy just plead guilty."

"Only if they really *are* guilty," I mutter.

"Girl, you know I can't." Michelle sighs into her cup before taking a sip. "Tempting as it might be, it's unethical."

"More unethical than letting a creep game the system and go back out there to hurt people?" Ashley tilts her head.

They both look at me.

I shrug. "If someone's a real threat to people, they shouldn't be allowed to exploit a legal technicality to get away with what they did. The legal system exists to protect innocent people mistakenly charged with crimes and to make sure those who are guilty of crimes aren't punished unfairly. But what do I know? I'm not a lawyer."

"Gonna try and make time when I can. I miss hanging out with you guys." Michelle leans back in her seat, gazing around at the place. "Damn. Feels like forever since we hung out here."

"It's okay. We know you're super busy now." I offer a reassuring smile. "It's kinda normal. Mom said she drifted away from her friends after high school, too. She hasn't seen most of them since she was our age."

"Aww. That's so sad." Ashley gives me this 'don't leave' look similar to the way she reacted when I told her about my plans to attend USC.

"Don't flip out. I'm not going anywhere."

Michelle snickers. "You guys are so cute together. When are you gonna just admit the two of you are perfect for each other?"

Ashley blushes. Yeah, she did sorta have a crush on me for a bit, but our relationship is somewhere between best friend and sister-from-another-mister.

Since we both know—or at least assume—Michelle is totally kidding, we burst into laughter at the same time.

"So what about you?" Michelle glances back and forth between us. "School and work kickin' your butts, too?"

"Nah." Ashley shakes her head. "I'm having a blast. It's gonna be a lot of work, but I'm totally set on going veterinarian. School's fun and I'm basically doing the same job as Michelle… crawling around cleaning up poop."

Michelle cackles. "Legal poop can be worse than anything you'll find in a kennel. But I'm not cleaning anything other than wastebaskets. I'm not even *in* law school yet, so I'm basically an office assistant doing random BS things like running messages, taking meeting notes, or running to Starbucks."

"Sare?" asks Michelle. "You made a face as soon as I brought up school. Something wrong?"

"Ehh." I shrug. "It's fine. Just being 'meh' about the programming thing. Not sure it's right for me. Haven't figured out what else to do yet, but it isn't too important. Even if I get a degree in a field with night shifts, I'll eventually have to disappear and reinvent myself before people start asking why this fifty-year-old woman still looks like she's eighteen."

"Try fifteen," says Michelle while stirring more stevia powder into her iced tea, not looking at me.

I toss a hunk of potato at her, bouncing it off her forehead.

She cracks up laughing.

"You should major in drama." Ashley crosses her eyes. "Since you basically already are."

"Hah."

Michelle scrunches her nose. "What about psychology or something? A therapist who can literally see into people's heads?"

"Oh, sure. I'll end up getting carted off by the PIBs for that." I whistle. "Need to stay low key. Might go for a generic liberal arts degree or maybe English."

"What about parapsychology?" asks Ashley, in a not-too-serious tone. "You can actually see ghosts."

"It's not a real degree… and it's kinda the exact opposite of trying to stay under the radar." I stuff my face with another forkful of eggs, potatoes, cheese, and sausage. So what if I got a breakfast skillet at dinner time? I always order these things here. Tradition should mean something, right?

"You should just relax and enjoy life." Michelle sips her tea and grimaces. "Ack! Too sweet."

"What did you expect?" Ashley laughs. "You asked them for raspberry flavor in it."

Michelle takes another sip, still cringing. "Yeah, but I think they put in too much."

I nudge her. "Maybe you put in too much of the magic powder."

"Oh, dammit." She glances at her little bottle of stevia—she brings it with her since no places ever have it—"I put it in twice."

"That'll do it." I wag my eyebrows at her.

"Going to school helps Sare feel normal." Ashley gathers up the second half of her burger. "Besides, she'd be bored otherwise."

I stare at my mostly empty skillet for a moment, trying not to feel guilty.

"What's wrong?" asks Ashley.

"You guys aren't jealous? I kinda feel like I'm getting away with something here. Cheating at life."

"Nah." Michelle frowns, shaking her head. "It's all good. Don't really agree with my parents' views on religion, but I do think my dad's got a point when he said everyone gets the life they deserve. Maybe it ain't a 'god' up there sending stuff people's way, but we all get what we get. Waste of energy being jealous about anything. You want something, then work to make it happen. But not everything can be worked for… good looks, who your family is, you know."

"Getting made a vampire," mutters Ashley.

"Oh, vampiness can totally be worked for. The hard part is learning it's real." I gather another forkful of egg-mageddon. "It's not even a lot of work. Admission's pretty cheap, too. Only costs death."

Michelle coughs on her food.

"Ehh, nah." Ashley scrunches up her face. "On some level, I am a little jealous of how you're never going to be forty wondering when you stopped fitting into the clothes we're wearing now, but I also want to have a family someday and I'm okay with growing older. Besides, people who *want* to become vampires probably turn into bad ones."

"Yeah." Michelle nods. "What's to be jealous of? She'll be eighteen forever, never get old or fat, never get sick. She can fly, make people do what she wants, and go places alone without having to be hypervigilant all the time. Totally sucks, right?"

We laugh.

"Total suckage." Ashley winks. "Though, that last one *is* tempting. I hate parking lots at night. Not sure it's worth giving up future kids for though."

"You could always adopt… or become a crazy cat lady." I grin.

"Crazy cat lady is happening either way." Michelle points at her. "She's going to have six cats, four dogs, and some form of rodent colony by the time she's thirty-five."

Ashley holds her hands up, head tilted to one side. "Guilty."

Random conversation about cats turns into Michelle and Ashley making a game out of guessing what I'm going to switch my major to. When Ashley abruptly gets up to go to the bathroom, I don't need powers of telepathy to know she's spotted our waiter and is about to tell him it's my birthday. Fortunately, Denny's doesn't really do the shouting, clapping, and embarrassing the hell out of people thing.

"So you are really enjoying running at 110 percent all the time?" I lean my chin on my hand, glancing sideways at Michelle.

"Yeah." She stretches. "Still not up for the kinda chaos chasing you around these days. I thrive on challenging stress. You're up to your eyeballs in 'oh hell no' stress."

I collapse forward on the table, laughing. "Just a little."

"Freakin' brownies?" She gives me a flat look. "Still ain't sure you're not messing with me."

"Ugh. Don't remind me. I'm trying to forget the whole thing. Vampires are weird enough."

"Glowing space kitten," whispers Michelle.

I snort-giggle. Ouch. Of course the sound makes me laugh even harder.

"Careful, don't choke." Michelle pats me on the back. "Don't forget to breathe."

If I actually needed air, I'd accuse her of trying to kill me. Fortunately, breathing is just something my body does to appear alive these days—so laughing myself into a choking fit is harmless.

"Honestly, Klepto is super cute. I don't mind her kind of weird."

Ashley returns with a smile to prove she's arranged some kind of birthday embarrassment, even if only a cake. I resist the temptation to peek at her head. Not long after she swoops into her chair, the waiter shows up with a small ice cream cake. The thing's about as big around as a DVD, maybe three inches tall.

"Happy birthday!" He sets the cake down in front of me. "Can I get you guys anything else?"

"A knife?" I blink at the confection in front of me. "I am not eating this entire thing myself."

"Be right back." He grins and hurries off down the aisle.

Michelle leans her elbows on the table. "So, I've been thinking."

"Uh oh." Ashley pretend cowers.

"Funny." Michelle tosses a napkin at her. "Anyway, we should make a pact to have dinner here together at least once a year. Probably on Ash's birthday since it's not so close to New Year's."

"Hmm." I shift my jaw side to side.

"Oh, damn. Sorry." Michelle cringes. "Never mind."

"Huh?" Ashley blinks. "What?"

"Yeah, I'm with her. What's wrong?"

Michelle exhales. "I didn't mean to be a downer, demanding you watch the two of us grow old."

I shrug. "I've already obsessed over you guys getting old plenty. Avoiding you won't help. Can't do anything about it, so I'm dealing."

"We've already established you technically *could* do something about us getting old." Michelle chuckles.

"You guys don't want me to, so I can't. Besides... I *can't*. It requires hurting you two." I gesture at Ashley. "Look at her. It would be like smothering a kitten. I couldn't possibly."

Ash laughs. "Okay, a pact then. No matter where life takes us, we'll all meet at this Denny's on my birthday until we die."

"Umm, I can't promise that. Already died," I whisper past a grin.

"You know what she means. Stop playin'." Michelle nudges me.

"Done," I say.

"Done." Ashley grins.

"Settled then." Michelle claps.

Hmm. Something's not right. I gaze around, surveying the room. Nothing appears unusual, which feels unusual.

"Umm, what are you looking for?" asks Ashley.

"The weird."

"Huh?" Michelle raises an eyebrow.

I chuckle. "The weird. A guy showing up to rob the place, or a ghost wandering by, or some bizarre new gremlin type critter showing up. Vampires Dalton pissed off trying to kidnap me... something *weird*. It feels so strange being this ordinary. Tonight feels like any other time we hung out here. It's kinda freaking me out."

Ashley rests her hand on my wrist. "Ordinary is what you wanted, right?"

The waiter returns, sets a knife down beside the ice cream cake, and hurries off.

I pick it up and start cutting the giant ice cream puck. Thirding it isn't too much of a portion for anyone who still has to care about calories. "Yeah, it is what I wanted... but I don't trust it to stay."

# 3

# THE BIG DAY

An odd, rubbery smell abruptly manifests in my room, smothering a faint essence of strawberry.

In most situations, random smells coming out of nowhere would worry me; however, I'm in bed. It means they didn't simply start spontaneously without cause. I've slept and come back to consciousness. Vampire sleep takes a lot of getting used to, as in it's been six months and it's still weird as hell. Before my Transference, I'd often lay in bed staring at the ceiling for an hour or so before passing out. Now, the instant the sun comes up, I'm out... and most of the time, sleep is dreamless. Since I spent my entire life struggling to fall asleep, it frequently feels like I'm lying here waiting to fall asleep but have already passed out and woken back up.

Honestly, the ability to zonk in an instant is awesome. Vampirism would've been worth it to me purely for that. Anyway, the sudden presence of smells means I've slept already. The rubbery aroma is intense and weird, and surprising since Hunter didn't spend the night here. Nor are we using protection. I mean, seriously, what's the point? My inner bits don't work and I'm immune to diseases. Can't suffer them; can't transmit them.

Not planning on having tons of intimate partners anyway. So far, it's only been Scott and Hunter—for however long it lasts. We're not having trouble, not even close... but me being an immortal and him not being immortal is going to eventually make things weird. Maybe it won't feel odd to me after being with him the whole time, but I'm not sure how to handle everyone assuming he's my father someday. Seriously, forty years from now, he'll look older than my father does now and I'll still be the same.

It's too weird to think about.

The faint strawberry scent is Sophia's shampoo. She must have been in my room while I slept. Considering the fragrance of cosmetics isn't hanging in the air, she didn't use me as a practice dummy again. Don't smell lipstick, so Sam didn't write 'happy birthday' on my forehead like he did last year. Despite taking a while to pass out, I used to be a heavy sleeper. Some things are still true. It takes a lot to wake a vampire up early in terms of noise. Takes much less to wake us up in terms of messing around with our bodies. If any vampire *ever* dares to question how much I love my family, all I'd need to do is tell them Sophia painted me up like a clown and it didn't make me stir in the slightest. Had no idea she did it until seeing myself in the mirror after waking up. The process by which we identify *who* is messing with us and their level of threat remains a mystery to me... but it works. Ask the guy Dad hired to fix the furnace last week. He walked into my bedroom by mistake. His merely entering the room woke me up at around eleven in the morning. Fortunately, my basement is dark enough for me to be online. I managed to erase his memory of me leaping out of bed to defend myself before my consciousness slid kicking and screaming back into the abyss.

Other ways to wake up a vampire before they're supposed to get up include exposure to sunlight or the death wails of another vampire nearby. If a mortal is stupid enough to stab, attack, or destroy an unconscious vampire in a place where multiple vampires are sleeping, the others all wake up. I've even heard rumors about once a vampire gets old enough, they can sense people near them even when asleep and, sort of like cats, can choose if they need to wake up or not. If they do, it usually ends pretty badly for the mortal, since most vampires awake when the sun's up are out of their mind feral—kinda like what happened to me in that motel room. One second, some guy opens the door and gives me a face full of bright sunlight. Next thing I know, there's blood everywhere and the door's closed. Total blackout. Somehow, despite killing a few people there, guilt isn't overwhelming. Having no memory of it whatsoever helps, plus it had been completely out of my control. Not like I made a conscious decision to hurt anyone.

Hmm. Aha! Balloons.

Upon finally recognizing the rubbery smell, I open my eyes to find a bundle of brightly colored balloons bearing a 'happy birthday' sign floating beside me. Despite not needing to, I stretch and yawn before crawling out of bed. Old habits die hard or some such thing. It's 2:39 p.m. according to my alarm clock. Slacker life. But hey, I have a good excuse. Short of having another stranger barge into my bedroom, I *can't* get up any earlier.

Sophia must've put the balloons here before she left for school. The Littles ought to be home soon, no doubt they're on the bus already. Keyboard clicking upstairs tells me Dad's working. Mom, of course, isn't home yet. As much as she might've wanted to, she didn't take my birthday off. As a kid, I used to have birthday parties here at the house, inviting a handful of friends from school. The parties gradually became less and less epic as I got older. What started as basically having my entire school class over became inviting maybe eight or nine sorta-friends from school... then trips to the movies with only Ashley, Michelle, and sometimes this other girl Paisley, but we kinda went in two different directions after eighth grade. No bad blood or anything, we simply stopped hanging out. She's way more of an outdoorsy 'go do stuff' type than me. You know, hiking, camping, canoeing, fishing. Paisley didn't really like the geeky stuff Ash, 'Chelle, and I are into.

I may not be anywhere near as bad as Sierra, but I'm still way more likely to play video games than randomly go biking on a wooded trail. Much less effort involved. Lucky for me, I have Dad's genes and never needed to exercise to stay thin. Granted, we are kinda *too* thin, but whatever. Can't be perfect.

After a quick shower, I throw on a tee and sweat pants. The Littles are already home by the time I go upstairs. Sam and Sophia appear to be doing their homework right away while Sierra's firing up the PlayStation.

"What?" She glances at me as I stroll by on the way to the kitchen.

"I didn't say anything."

"You looked at me like 'you haven't been in the house two minutes yet and you went straight to the game."

"So? You *haven't* been here two minutes yet." I grin. "I wasn't going to say anything. Are you okay?"

She plops down on the floor facing the TV. "Yeah."

I stop short, leaning over the back of the sofa. "Not a convincing 'yeah' there, kiddo."

"Don't read my mind."

"Boy issues?"

She gasps, then whirls to glare at me. "I said don't read my mind!"

"I didn't. Merely guessed. It's way too bright in here for me to be online anyway."

"Oh. Duh." She slouches. "It's not really a boy thing."

Hands up, I back away. "Cool. No worries. Don't want to pry. You know I care about you guys."

"Yeah." A little blush reddens her face. "Sorry for snapping. I fell asleep in class today, had a bad dream, and jumped awake looking like a dumbass trying to do kung fu while drunk. This boy I kinda like laughed at me."

"Ahh. Don't sweat it. Everyone looks like an idiot at one point or another. Besides, you're eleven and we don't live in a Hallmark movie. No boy you even know now is going to be the one you spend the rest of your life with. You're probably not gonna meet him until you're twenty-eight working the late shift at Starbucks."

She laughs, then gives me a dark look. "Hey, not cool. You think I'm gonna be slinging coffee when I'm old?"

"The amount of time you throw at video games compared to

school, probably. Either that or you're going to be a superstar game designer driving a Lambo."

Sierra groans. "Please. I'd never want one of those things. They're for stuck up jerks who want to wave their money in everyone's face. And seriously, what's the point? You can't drive one of those cars as fast as it can go without getting like *all* the tickets. Someone who spends more money than a house on a car two people can barely squeeze into is an idiot."

I snicker. "Sounds like you've got life all figured out."

"I dunno about life, but I've got *Call of Duty* down to a science." She grins.

"Those idiots still bothering you?"

"Not really, but I don't talk much on voice chat anymore." She sighs at the rug, uncomfortable and a little frightened.

I move around the couch to sit beside her on the floor. "Want to talk about the bad dream?"

"It's stupid. The giant five-headed tarantula thing chased me around the school."

"Ugh. Sorry."

Sierra stares at the screen, guiding her soldier down a narrow alley. "Umm, why are you apologizing? You killed it."

"Because the only reason you've seen any of this horrible crap—"

"Stop." She leans against me—which for Sierra is the equivalent of Sophia bursting into tears and clamp-hugging. "You're still here. I don't care about a couple weird dreams. I'm already nuts, so you didn't make me any nuttier."

"You are not nuts." I ruffle her hair. "Where did you get that idea?"

"Counselor at the school thinks I'm 'emotionally distant' because I don't have a billion friends and don't laugh at random stupid crap. It's fine. He's a tool."

I snicker.

"He is. He thinks everyone who isn't a copy paste of everyone else is broken."

"This guy Greg from my class always used to say schools were merely factories to produce people smart enough to run the machinery but dumb enough not to question authority."

"Are you quoting George Carlin?" calls Dad from his office. "Kinda sounds like it."

"Who?" we ask at the same time.

Her widening eyes function as a visible progress bar for her growing realization our father heard the entire conversation. She goes beet red and stares at me in a 'please erase his memory' way. Danger Wilhelmina Robinson—the parental unit has heard Child Two claim to 'kinda like' a boy.

"Ack. I have failed in my duties as a parent!" He laughs. "Okay, maybe his stuff is not exactly for little kids, but none of you are little anymore. I shall rectify this grievous failure of my parenting as soon as possible."

"Umm, okay." I shrug.

Weird purple light and a rushing noise come from the kitchen.

What the...?

I leap to my feet and run down the hall past the dining room. Upon reaching the kitchen archway, I skid to a stop, staring in awe at a three-foot-wide circle of dark purple glow hanging in the air by the cabinets. It kinda looks like a tiny version of a magical portal from video games and fantasy movies—however, it's a bit small to summon the Orcish hordes. A small demonic hand reaches out of the swirl, opens the cabinet door, and rummages for snacks. Within seconds of me seeing it, the clawed hand claims a bag of Doritos and recedes into the mini-portal, which promptly vanishes.

Oh... just Blix.

"What's on fire?" asks Dad from the hall behind me.

"Strange light. Nothing to worry about. The little demon wanted snacks."

Dad blinks. "Sam's got magic, too?"

"Not *that* little demon. Blix." I snicker.

He grins, then hugs me, his grip a little firmer than usual. "Happy birthday, hon."

I'm sure the 'rents are going to be dwelling on almost losing me all day, so I let him squeeze me as much as he needs to remind himself I'm still here. "Thanks, Dad."

"How's it feel to be nineteen?"

"The same as it did to be eighteen. It's only a year. Going from seventeen to eighteen is a much bigger deal."

"True." He releases the hug, leaving his hands on my shoulders.

"Aww, Dad. Don't go emo on me. You're getting your wish, way more than you ever wanted. I'm going to be in your hair forever. Never moving out."

He chuckles. "At least your mother and I won't need to end up in a care home when we're elderly. We'll have you to take care of us."

"Are you trying to scare me off? Not gonna work." My turn to get a little emo. "I'm kinda dreading watching you guys get older, but I'm definitely gonna be here for you."

"I'll help out, too," says Sierra in a quiet voice, right behind him. "Probably not gonna move too far away. I *will* be getting my own place as soon as I can though."

"Having your own place means *you* get to do all the cleaning." I fold my arms.

Sierra bites her lip. "Isn't that what husbands are for? Why else does anyone get married?"

Dad coughs into laughter.

True, he used to do more housework than Mom given the vast difference in their work hours, but I've been absorbing most of it lately. No big deal. I've got time on my hands.

Sam thunders down the stairs, trots up to us, holding his hands up like a surgeon after scrubbing. His arms are covered almost to the elbow in red sticky goop. "Guys, we have a small problem."

"You're not allowed to do sacrifices in the house," says Sierra. "You're gonna get grounded."

He shakes his head. "No. Not sacrificing anything."

"Why are your hands all slimy?" asks Sierra.

"If you don't stop, you're gonna go blind." I smile.

Sam looks at me like I spoke Greek. "I didn't do anything."

Dad snort-laughs. "What happened?"

"Ro got attacked by something in the mirrorverse on his way over. It tried to eat him, but Blix killed it." Sam points at the stairs. "He's covered in this gunk and can't move."

"The gunk paralyzed him?" asks Dad. "Why did you touch it?"

"No, this stuff is only mega sticky. It shot him with a quill." Sam cringes. "He flew out of the mirror and stuck to the wall. I couldn't get him down."

We rush upstairs to the bathroom.

Ronan, covered completely in raspberry jam—rather a substance surprisingly similar to it in appearance—hangs on the wall above the bathtub, upside down. Dark striations in the red slime kinda makes him look like a newborn foal mere seconds after falling out of a mare. He's still breathing, but looks far too pale. A six-inch porcupine-style quill sticks out of him, above his left collarbone. The poor kid is making a face like Freddy Kreuger offered him pickle-flavored ice cream. I'm sure he would've run screaming from whatever he saw if he hadn't been paralyzed.

Blix, perched like a gargoyle on the sink nearby, rambles incomprehensibly at Sam, who nods.

"He's gonna be okay. It'll wear off." Sam approaches the sink.

The imp glances at the faucet; the hot water turns itself on.

My brother begins trying to wash his hands, but the soap bar sticks to his hand.

Dad grabs Ronan at the hips and tries to peel him off the wall. He struggles for a little while, but gives up before the tiles—or the boy's jeans—fail. "Wow, this is... strong. Umm. Dammit."

"He can't let go, can he?" asks Sierra.

"Aha! Here it is." I snap my fingers. "This is the weird I'd been expecting. At least it's something relatively tame."

"Tame? He looks half dead." Sierra steps into the bathtub and crouches to eye level with Ronan. "Are you awake? Blink once for yes."

Ronan closes his eyes.

"He didn't blink." Sierra peers up at Dad. "He just closed his eyes."

"Ro probably tried to blink... and his eyes got stuck," says Sam. "I can't even wash this stuff off."

Sierra stands. "Are you gonna give him a bath?"

"Not sure how… I can't even let go of him. We'd have to throw him in the tub, clothes and all." Dad leans back, face reddening, but gives up trying to pull away in a few seconds. "I'm going to lose skin. Hate to say it, but he's probably going to have to hang out here until Sarah's strong enough to pluck him loose… and tile's going to break off the wall."

"Cover the window and close the door," says Sam. "She doesn't need sunset, only dark. Soap isn't working."

I lean out into the hall. "Soph?"

"Doing homework," yells my younger sister.

"Can we borrow you for a minute? It's important."

She peeks out of her room. "What's up?"

"An excuse for you to try doing magic that won't get you in trouble with Dad."

"Ooh!" She scampers over.

I point at Ronan.

Sophia screams and grabs onto me.

"Relax. He's okay. Just paralyzed. Can you get the goop off him?"

"Eww. What is it?" Sophia continues clinging to me.

Sam waves his hand, trying to get the soap bar to fall back into the sink. He waves his hand so damn fast I expect there to be *two* soap bars when he stops. But we're not in a Bugs Bunny cartoon. My life makes *less* sense. Alas, the soap bar is truly adhered to him. It's not going anywhere. "A giant slug thing tried to eat him in the mirrorverse."

"He's been using mirrors to go back and forth for months and nothing like this happened." I guide Sophia into the bathroom. "Did he do something careless?"

Blix shakes his little head, rambling at me.

"No," says Sam. "Stuff moves around in there. The slug got him before he noticed it. It wouldn't have been a problem if Ro understood demonic. He didn't realize Blix was yelling at him to look out."

The imp flails his arms and babbles. Pretty sure he said something like, "I *tried* to tell him."

"Open the window," says Sophia.

Sierra maneuvers around Dad, climbs up to stand on the toilet, and opens the small window behind it.

After a few minutes of making faces, Sophia raises her hands—a needlessly theatrical gesture from what I understand. The red slime undulates in response. She focuses on Ronan for a little while before pulling her hands at the air like she's peeling the wrapping paper off a giant present. The slime stretches forward, losing its grip on the boy as well as my father's hands. Dad keeps holding him so he doesn't fall straight down onto his head in the bathtub. Ronan's arms flop downward, his body as limp as a life-size silicone doll.

Sam runs over, holding his hands up. Sophia de-gunks him, too, adding the slop to the original mass she separated from Ronan, then sends the orb of foulness floating out the window. It hangs in space for a few seconds before rocketing off like a bullet. Ronan, no longer glued to the wall, flops into Dad's arms.

"Where'd you throw it?" asks Dad.

"Umm. Dunno." Sophia grimaces. "Sorry. It didn't want to be moved. I had to get rid of it fast before it did something bad."

Is it evil of me to daydream about it landing in Mr. Niedermeyer's backyard? Nah, it's moving *way* too fast to come down so close. Hopefully, it doesn't hurt anyone.

"Hey, his eyes are open." Sierra points.

"Yeah, the slime glued them closed." Sam looks his hands over, shrugs, and drops his arms at his sides.

"You had interdimensional slug saliva on you. Wash your hands." Sierra points at the sink.

My brother again examines his hands, shrugs, and decides to scrub them. "Ro had it all over his face."

Sophia gags. "La la la la la. Got more homework to do. Stop talking about slug spit." She runs out.

Dad shifts Ronan upright and eases him down to sit in the tub. After a moment of studying the quill, he plucks it out.

Blix mutters at Sam.

"Dad, can you put him in my room? Blix said he might be able to make the venom wear off faster."

"Is it going to involve blood?" Dad raises an eyebrow.

Blix shakes his head.

"Okay." Dad carries the boy out, Sam following.

"Excitement." Sierra exhales. "Think he's gonna start riding his bike here instead of taking the mirror?"

"Nah. We're talking about boys." I glance at the mirror. "It's gonna take more than one slug to scare them off from doing something recklessly fun. Walking here on the other side is like going one or two blocks. They live a few miles away."

"I'm not afraid of slugs."

"Not even ones big enough to swallow you whole?" I ask.

She mulls. "Nah. They can't be fast. But I also wouldn't risk going into the mirror world to skip a couple miles on a bike."

"Exactly my point about boys." I wink. "There's a reason girls live longer."

TWENTY MINUTES LATER, WE'RE ALL DOWNSTAIRS IN THE DINING ROOM playing the board game Descent. Dad's tossed a ham in the oven. Whatever Blix did for Ronan worked. The kid's back to normal and completely unfazed by his near-ingestion. He'd been staring at something shimmery in the air and didn't notice the giant slug until after it shot an envenomed quill into him. Blix mentions the quill flew about as fast as someone throwing a pencil, so he probably could've dodged it if he saw it coming.

Yeah, no one at this table would have any difficulty outrunning a five-foot flesh Twinkie.

And I really hope to death I never again hear or think those particular words in the same order.

A little after six, Mom returns home from work. She and Dad go to the kitchen to get started on dinner, plus whatever they're going to do party-wise for my birthday. Hopefully, they don't go nuts. Ashley shows up soon after, followed by Michelle and Hunter arriving almost simultaneously a few minutes after 6:30 p.m.

Hunter doesn't appear to care my parents are in the next room. As soon as he's in the door, he's kissing me. Naturally, this draws teasing and laughing from the Littles. It's only a tame 'I've missed you' sort of kiss, far short of what we'd rather be doing. But, not with an audience.

After about an hour, food chases the board game off the table.

Except for having extra people here, it feels more like an ordinary family dinner than like Christmas or Thanksgiving. As expected, Mom is upset, more visibly so than Dad, but I can tell he's every bit as misty-eyed as she is. Whenever she catches Hunter making lovey eyes at me, she chokes up. Not sure if she's mourning the grandkids I won't be able to give her or if she's happy for us.

It's a little early to worry yet, but hopefully, my birthday doesn't become a permanent painful memory for them. It's not like I died *on* or even close to it. This is only the first one since everything happened, so it's understandable for it to be a reminder of almost losing me. Next year, it shouldn't hit them as hard. Honestly, Christmas hit them harder than today emotionally. Neither one of them is openly crying tonight.

Fortunately, Ashley is like a beacon of positive energy. Between her, Sophia, and Sam, our house is painfully loud.

After dinner, Mom brings out a cake. Naturally, the Littles plus Ronan go ballistic. Ashley darts into the kitchen. Initially, I assume she's going for silverware or plates, until the scrape of the patio door opening proves otherwise. I sit there, eyebrow raised, wondering why she'd go out onto the deck in January. She comes back in right away, closing the door suspiciously hard—like she shut it using her foot.

I'm about to get up to ask her what the hell she's doing when she backs into view lugging a five-foot tall teddy bear.

"Happy birthday!" yells Ashley. "I'd have gotten you a bigger one, but they didn't have any."

"He's adorable!" yells Sophia. "Can I hug him?"

Ashley drags the giant teddy bear into the living room and sets him seated on the floor beside the sofa. "Sarah should get first dibs since it's her birthday."

"Okay, okay…" Mostly so Sophia stops staring 'please' at me, I get up and hug the bear.

Whoa. This thing is *so* soft. If I wasn't a vampire, I'd probably have been unable to get back up, lulled off into a nap by the awesome plush-ness.

"Did you enchant this guy with consciousness drain?" I ask. "It's trying to put me to sleep."

"Seriously?" Mom shakes her head. "What is Sarah going to do with a giant teddy bear?"

"Exactly what I'm doing right now. Hug him. Maybe sleep on him."

Sam laughs. "You gonna name him Hunter?"

Hunter's face reddens.

Dad finds his cake highly interesting.

To my horror, Mom bursts into laughter. Sophia and Sierra giggle conspiratorially.

Ashley stares open-mouthed at Mom. Ronan and Sam either don't understand or ignore it.

Right, so… I scrape the tattered bits of my dignity up off the floor and slink back to the table. Sophia saves me by leaping onto the teddy bear in a flying tackle while squealing in delight. Michelle gives me a little box wrapped in gold paper containing a couple cute bracelets. The Littles all present me with handmade birthday cards.

"Welcome to adulthood," says Dad, handing me a pink envelope.

Laughing, I open it to find an ordinary birthday card containing a Starbucks gift card—and a handwritten message under the printed 'Happy Birthday.'

*You were our first, and did such a good job we had to have three more. The calendar might say you're all grown up now, but you'll forever be our little girl. Every minute we have together is a precious treasure. Love, Mom and Dad.*

Okay… my turn to cry.

"Aww, guys. You got sappy."

"Lemme read it!" Sophia reaches for the card.

"All you got her was a card?" asks Sam. "It's her birthday?"

Dad coughs away the lump in his throat. "It's why I said 'welcome to adulthood.' All grown-ups get for their birthday is another year older. Maybe a gift card or a pair of socks."

Mom silently walks over and hugs me.

"But Sarah's not a grown-up." Sam flails his arms. "She's still eighteen. Like forever."

Mom squeezes me harder.

"Eighteen *is* legally a grown-up." Sierra adds herself to our hug.

"Depends on who you ask." Hunter shrugs. "Some people think thirty-year-olds are still kids."

Somberness hangs over us for a moment before Dad produces a gift-wrapped box. "Okay, I suppose she still has some kid left in her. Couldn't resist."

"Yay!" Sam cheers. "Presents!"

"Aww, Dad." I drag the Sierra-Mom hug over to him.

"Go on, open it." He smiles.

I take the box, slice the wrapping paper open with a claw, and peel it back to reveal a mini Nintendo NES. "What the heck?"

"It's got like 150 games in it. All the original ones from the Eighties." He beams.

"This gift is so Dad it hurts." I chuckle.

"Well, you are both immortal and have superhuman reflexes. You might actually be able to beat *Ghosts & Goblins*." Dad makes a weird arcane hand sign as if trying to banish demonic powers.

Sierra sets her hands on her hips. "She already has."

"We haven't seen goblins... yet." Sam wags his eyebrows.

I point at him. "Don't jinx me."

Everyone laughs.

"What do you want to do with the rest of your birthday?" asks Dad. "Movie? Party games? Board games?"

"Movie works. Anything really... just something we can do together." I squeeze Mom's hand.

Yeah, so what if I'm getting a bit emo. My parents need the feels tonight.

# 4

## TINY CAKE, BIG FEELS

We end up watching *Coco* on demand.

Maybe not the wisest choice considering the parents' mood, but it's more cute than sad—still, it gets Mom and Sophia crying at the end. Everyone kinda stays there hanging out for a little while after the movie ends. Once the Littles start yawning, Michelle grumbles about schoolwork. She hates having to leave so early (a few minutes after nine) but college is different from high school. Much harder to blow off homework when you're going into debt for it. Pass or fail, we're still on the hook for the cash. Good motivation to get it right the first time and not have to repeat a class.

The Littles head off to bed. Hmm. I didn't see Sierra do homework. She's got the same kind of laziness I had in regard to schoolwork, but completely ignoring it goes beyond. My lack of motivation did not extend into risking punishment territory. Hmm. Should I bug her about it or let the parents handle it? Don't want to start a fight with her—we've been getting along almost too well to believe ever since I technically died.

Okay, don't wanna be a pest, but if she's skipping homework, it could be something bigger going on, especially since she mentioned having nightmares.

I disentangle myself from Hunter, whispering, "Be right back."

He nods.

Upstairs, I find Sierra in her room, fluffing her hair out the neck of the nightgown she's changed into. She fires off three seconds of the 'what are you doing in my room' glower before softening it to a, "Hey, what's up?"

"Being worried and overprotective. Also, didn't say anything to Mom or Dad, but did you have any homework today?"

"Oh, wow, seriously?" Sierra rolls her eyes. "I thought you were freaking out over something actually important."

"I'm not as concerned with the homework itself as much as why you'd skip it."

She folds her arms. "I didn't. Finished it before I left school. I don't really do anything at lunch. Mr. Hooper put on a documentary in Social Studies, so I got my vocabulary homework done in class. It's the first day back after a long holiday. Teachers didn't give us much. I didn't wanna have to worry about doing homework today since it's your birthday. You can stop worrying."

"No, I can't." I grin. "Even when you're all grown up and can kick five men's asses in a sword fight, I'm still going to worry about you being okay."

Sierra blinks. "Wow. Umm, let's hope I never end up having to fight five dudes at once."

"Yeah, you won't. Maybe two vampires at once." I tap a finger to my chin. "If you see a troll, run."

"I won't see a troll because I'm not dumb enough to go through strange magic doorways." She sticks out her tongue.

"Touché. Okay, sorry for bugging you."

She shrugs. "It's cool. You didn't do it in front of anyone."

"On purpose. Night."

"Night." She ducks around me. "Old lady."

"Hah! Sure thing, kiddo."

"Bite me," says Sierra, not looking back as she heads down the hall.

"Okay." I extend my fangs and follow her.

She squeals and runs to the bathroom, slamming the door. "I didn't mean literally!"

Laughing, I head downstairs.

Hunter and the parents look over at me.

"Gonna grab a quick bite. Back in like twenty minutes."

"Cool." Hunter gives a thumbs-up.

"Don't bite anyone too grubby," says Mom. "You don't know where they've been."

Dad raises a finger. "She could know where they've been if she reads their mind."

She sighs at the ceiling, then looks at me. "Just be careful, okay? Don't start any fights with other vampires."

"Really not in my plans. If I got my wish, I'd never fight another vampire ever again." I step into my sneakers by the front door, then go outside. "If I'm not back in half an hour, send in reinforcements."

IF THERE'S ANYTHING ABOUT BEING A VAMPIRE I'D COMPLAIN ABOUT, IT'S eating.

Mostly because finding a blood meal is inconvenient. Normal people can just go to their kitchen or get delivery. I need to fly all the way to Seattle. Well, technically it's not *required*, but it's reckless to bite people too close to where I live. The increased population of a big city keeps it hidden. Little chance of me running into the same person twice. Also, people are too distracted with the chaos around them or the need to rush back and forth. In a place like Cottage Lake, there are only so many people around, plus it's quieter. Sooner or later, someone's going to start asking questions about large numbers of residents having episodes of brief memory loss and fatigue. I'm sure 'vampire' won't be the first thought on the minds of authorities, probably a radon leak or something similar... but it'll bring scrutiny.

Yanno, maybe I *could* technically order delivery. My family gets the pizza while I eat the driver.

Or bite the driver. I'm not one of those sick vampires who kills when they feed. Not only is it evil, it's foolish. Nothing attracts hunters faster than a series of exsanguinated bodies turning up in the same area.

Kill-feeding is also, according to Dalton, addictive. He's not speaking from experience though. I don't doubt his claim he's never fed anyone to death. Seriously, a vampire who'd feel sorry enough at being unable to save my life doesn't have the dark streak necessary to kill casually. Of course, I got a good close look at the kind of vampire who'd fallen prey to their vices: Ruben. From what Dalton told me, it sounds like kill-feeding is more addictive than heroin. Right up there with cigarettes or smartphones. Dunno if he's right about it mystically turning us dark inside, but even psychologically, it would have to. A person can't adjust to casually killing two or three people a month without changing inside. Unless they worked as a claim adjuster for medical insurance, then they'd probably end up killing *fewer* people after becoming a vampire addict.

Anyway, so yeah. I'm not interested in the supposed power one gets from kill-feeding. It doesn't bother me at all to 'miss out' on it. Vampires don't *have* to do it to grow in power, it's merely faster. And as far as power goes, I couldn't care less. It's inevitable my vampire self will become gradually more potent over the decades and centuries to come. Someday, I might feel well removed from the human I started as. Aurélie is sweet—well, as sweet as a vampire her age could possibly be—but there's no mistaking what she is. Dalton described her as a misericord wrapped in silk.

For now, feeding means I fly to Seattle, find a rando, and do what's necessary for continued existence. Blood-starvation won't kill a vampire, but it's like the absolute worst thing we can experience. Makes the idea of sitting through a forty-hour marathon of acapella disco music sound like fun. Even sun-death is better because the agony only lasts a few seconds. When a vampire isn't drinking blood, they wither away into a vestigial shadow of humanity, lacking reason, driven mad by constant wracking pain, unable to stop themselves from lashing out at anything around them and trying to devour it.

Kinda like Philadelphia Eagles fans whenever their team loses.

It's scary knowing I have the potential to be a threat to everyone around me, but at least it's pretty easy to avoid starvation. Not like we live in the middle of the desert or anything. Honestly, the worst part about feeding for me is looking into the heads of total strangers. I'm already over the creepy intimacy of biting people on the neck. Can't say there still isn't *some* bit of it left, since I generally try to feed on guys if at all possible. Sucking on a woman's neck is a bit uncomfortable for me, and I won't bite kids even if their blood tastes like candy or cake.

The whole 'blood flavor' thing is entirely in my head, by the way. Something about a person triggers my subconscious mind to assign them a flavor. Fortunately, I can smell it on them before biting so avoiding unfortunate taste assignments isn't difficult. Like the one guy in a green blazer my brain wanted to taste like pickles. Having hot dill brine gushing into the mouth is no one's idea of fun.

Back to the worst part. In order to feed, I have to mind-zap people into standing there dumbfounded for a few minutes. Much easier than trying to hold them down physically. Biting a person struggling to get away is usually a bloody process. It's the vampire equivalent of a kid in a high chair throwing their food all over the place. However, sometimes—especially with the people I find outside late at night—their thoughts contain horrible crap. Like the one dude trying to rush home because he couldn't wait to get his hands on his young daughter. Or maybe step-daughter. I've tried to forget the whole thing, so the details are foggy.

Shudder.

Thankfully, I haven't run into any more pedos... but I've found quite a few burglars, drug dealers, unfaithful husbands, and two murderers. Well, one murderer and one about-to-be murderer. Yes, I played vampire superhero again and stopped the guy from killing his business associate. Who knew plumbing contractors could be so cutthroat? Basically, my policy is... if someone's head contains crime stuff, and it doesn't really hurt anyone, I don't get involved. Not my circus, as they say. If they're about to hurt someone, I can't simply ignore it.

Really don't care if some people call it unethical. I'm sure the little girl who's no longer afraid to sleep in her own house doesn't give a rat's ass how 'unethical' it was for me to read the bastard's mind. Same with the plumber who's still alive because I randomly chose his former friend as a meal one night a few months back. Maybe it means I've put myself above normal humans already, but whatever. It's not my fault people are shitty. Their actions are their own. I'm merely a physical embodiment of karma at work.

And if I ever mentioned this to Professor Heath, he'd ask me if I thought the Universe coerced me into choosing those particular victims on purpose so I *could* be karma's avatar. Philosophy teachers and potheads are fairly close except for one major difference: professors get paid to ramble about 'deep thoughts.'

So, once again, I go cruising around Seattle after dark, keeping about 250 feet off the ground. There's enough artificial light at ground level to hide me in the air. Same way someone standing right in front of a campfire can't see too far into the dark. People generally don't look up unless they have a reason to. One of the many reasons I avoid sneakers with blinking lights. Sophia's suggestion I put on a faerie costume in case someone sees me flying was hilarious. Someone trying to tell their friend they saw a girl zooming around in the air would be implausible enough, but a giant faerie? They'd either get laughed at or wind up seeing a shrink.

Pity it's way too much effort for me.

After a few minutes of cruising around in search of a good candidate for biting, I spot a dude in a hoodie—with the hood up— suspiciously checking out a nice BMW. Either he forgot his keys, or he's about to break into the car. Car theft, or a smash and grab, isn't bad enough for me to get worked up over. Hey, I'm a good girl, but I'm not trying to play superhero over every little thing.

I glide in for a silent landing a few paces behind the guy—right as he pulls a brick out of his sweatshirt pocket and hurls it at the car window. The brick bounces off the glass with a dull *whud*, flying back into the dude's face. He crumples to the sidewalk, mostly unconscious. I blink in disbelief at seeing a YouTube fail video happen in real time right in front of me—then burst out laughing.

The guy's knocked himself so senseless he just lays there moaning while I recover from the unexpected hilarity. A quick look around confirms no one has come out to see what all the laughing's about. Good. I grab the guy, drag him to his feet, and pull him into the nearest secluded space between downtown high-rises.

As soon as we're out of sight, I dive into his head, giving him my usual derp command for feeding. His thoughts swirl back and forth between what he thought was a laptop sitting undefended in the BMW's passenger seat and utter confusion as to how a brick hit glass and bounced. The scent of his blood—generic fast food hamburger—surrounds us in a pungent cloud. His heart rate's way up from anxiety over his attempted burglary, making his face red and the veins in his forehead swollen. Or maybe it's because he just took a brick to the nose.

Miracle it's not bloody, really.

And no, nosebleeds are not like an open tap. It's still coming out of the nose. Eww.

I pull his hoodie out of the way, extend my fangs, and bite. Within the first few sips, the taste of his blood shifts from fast food to instant ramen. Ack. Yeah, okay, he does kinda have a pothead college student vibe going. Bleh. Whatever. Much the way people do with instant ramen, I suck it down purely for sustenance without bothering to taste it, and leave the guy staring into the fourth dimension.

Once I'm back in the air, it's tempting to laugh all over again at the idiot nailing himself in the face with a brick. Not wanting to draw attention to myself, I settle for a low chuckle. Hunter took the night off work to be with me, so I fly at my top speed, gripping the waistband of my sweat pants to keep them from disappearing. They're coming off eventually tonight, but I'd rather not have it happen to me in midair.

A few minutes later, I glide in to land on the deck behind my house. Despite it not *looking* dark to me, it feels dark. Not sure if I'm having some kind of weird phantom memory of my backyard being dark or this is simply my brain trying to let me know it's night.

"Hello, Sarah," says Glim out of nowhere.

I jump, yelp, and whirl to face him.

Oversized fangs stick out from a crooked grin surrounded by a greyish face made luminous in the strong moonlight. Yellow eyes glow like embers, sparkling with delight. He adores sneaking up on people, especially people like me who react in cartoonish ways to being startled. At least he's not recording me for a scare-cam video. Sam sometimes startle-pranks me—well, at least he used to before the vampire stuff. I'd scream, jump, sometimes fall over, but end up laughing. Sophia doesn't like scare pranks. After she's done screaming, she cries. Sierra usually punches him in the face if he makes her jump. He stopped pranking Sophia out of guilt, Sierra out of self-preservation, so it leaves me.

Seems he and Glim have something in common—laughing at people they startle.

"Hey." I grab my chest and take a few deep breaths to calm my racing heart. Yeah, it still reacts to emotions. And no, I don't mind. In fact, it's awesome. Makes me feel human. Can't imagine how bizarre it must be for other bloodlines because their bodies behave as dead as they are. Also, kinda strange for him to show up at my house. Hope he's not here to warn me Petra or St. Ives are planning to do something nasty. "What's up?"

He pulls his hand out from under his black trench coat in the theatrical manner of a stage magician. Seconds after his hand stops palm up in front of my face, a chocolate cupcake covered in pink frosting appears in a wisp of black vapor. A lone, unlit candle sticks up from the center of the icing. No, he didn't summon it out of thin air. His mind powers are based on illusions. He made me not see the cake until he wanted me to believe it appeared.

"Happy birthday." He grins. "Sorry if it's a bit small."

"Thank you!" I take the cupcake, then hug him. "It's not the size of the cake that matters, it's how you use it… or something."

He chuckles. "Forgive me for not lighting the candle. I'm not a big fan of fire."

"Yeah…" I cringe. Fire isn't a friend to *any* vampire, but Shadows are a bit drier than most. "I'm a little old to make birthday wishes anyway."

The patio door slides open, revealing Dalton. One of these days, I'll tell him the beige blazer over a T-shirt look stopped being cool in the Eighties. "Oy, luv. 'Appy birthday."

"Thanks. Wow. Didn't expect you guys would pay much attention to birthdays. I really appreciate it. Like having both of my families here." Grinning, I put an arm around their shoulders.

Glim still tenses up at being touched, but he's gotten better at it. He doesn't object to contact; he's simply not used to being able to show himself and not have people freak out. Even most other vampires shy away from Shadows—though it might be more from how powerful they can be rather than their frightening appearance.

"Eh, we mostly don't." Dalton glances off to the side, totally overacting nonchalance. "Don't rightly even remember what month mine was anymore, but you seem to fancy the notion."

"At least for now." I let a sad sigh slip out.

"Tonight is not the time for darkness." Glim lifts my chin on one finger.

"Funny to hear that comin' from you." Dalton chuckles.

I smile. "He's right. Gloomy thoughts can wait a few decades."

The patio door slides open again. Sierra pokes her head out. "Dalton, can I ask you something?"

He twists to look at her. "Aye, lass. Go on."

"Umm, like in private?" Sierra bites her lip.

"If she asks you to turn her, you will say no."

"Duh." Sierra rolls her eyes at me. "I'm at least gonna wait until eighteen. Being stuck as a kid forever would suck."

I whirl to stare at her. "You are not becoming undead."

"Chill. It's called teasing you." She makes a silly face. "I don't wanna become a vampire."

Hmm. Maybe she's trying to arrange some kind of birthday surprise for me. I shrug. Dalton and Sierra slip into the house. In the brief moment the door's open, Hunter's voice—in conversation with the parents about his classes—makes me feel a little less guilty about standing out here while he's waiting on me... but Glim is still uncomfortable hanging around the family. Neither Sierra nor Sam would bat an eyelash at his appearance. Sophia might scream if she didn't expect to see him, but she already knows about him from me telling stories, so even my 'delicate' sister should be able to handle having him around.

Glim chuckles when the door closes. "It's strange to me to see your siblings taking everything so casually."

"Did you let her see you?"

"Of course not. Isn't it obvious? She didn't scream."

I shake my head. "No. This is Sierra we're talking about. She'd think you are amazing. Sophia might flinch at first, but she's super brittle. Sam's got a freakin' imp living in his room. You wouldn't shock him."

"Perhaps." Glim glances at me. "Are you going to eat the cupcake?"

"In a bit. I just came back from feeding. Still kinda full."

"Ahh yes. Good call. Bad to mix cake and blood."

"I saw on the internet you can use blood to replace eggs in cake mix."

He laughs. "Do you believe everything you read on the internet?"

"Didn't say it's true. Just that I saw it."

"Technicalities." He flashes a toothy smile.

"Hey, do you think it's silly to care about birthdays anymore?"

"Not for you." He gazes off at the stars. "Personally, I gave up caring about birthdays around your age. Used to think they stopped meaning anything when it no longer became all about the presents. I wasn't a child anymore, so no point making a big production out of it. Didn't want to inconvenience everyone by making them feel like they needed to get me anything. Nowadays, I've come to realize birthdays aren't really for the person who's getting older. They're for everyone around them. You still have family. Of course you should care."

I lean against him. "Didn't you say I shouldn't be sad today? Grr. Is this a vampire side effect? Why do I keep thinking about a depressing future like sixty years away?"

"Teenagers don't normally think about the future so far away, but you've also cheated death. Tends to re-frame priorities. Besides, it's normal to lose one's parents. Happens to everyone for the most part. Except in tragic circumstances."

The look in his eye tells me he saw 'tragic circumstances' happen right in front of him while serving as a soldier in Iraq. Adult children go to their parents' funerals. It's the natural order of things, not the other way around. Dammit. There I go thinking sad thoughts again.

"Yeah. You're right. Birthdays don't really age well. Once you're no longer a kid, they're way less cool."

"Easy fix for that." He nudges me. "Don't grow up."

"Okay, I won't. I'll stay eighteen forever."

He laughs.

A flash of purple-blue light accompanies a *pop* and fizzle on the deck beside me. I look down at Klepto—Sophia's kitten 'familiar'—who's appeared out of thin air. She's got a large (compared to her) plush Siamese cat in her mouth... or as much as something six times her size can be 'in her mouth.'

"Mew," says Klepto.

"I believe she said happy birthday." Glim squats and skritches her behind the ear.

I crouch, pat her on the head, and take the plush. Klepto sits, peering up at me, her sparkling teal eyes overflowing with hope. At least, she looks as if she's desperate for me to like the birthday gift she got me. Probably reading too much into a kitten face, but damn if she doesn't give off serious hopeful vibes. Given her habit of randomly acquiring items from nearby homes, I'm a bit guilty over the possibility I'm holding some kid's purloined stuffed animal. However, this plushie looks brand new, so I'm hoping she yoinked it from a store. Yeah, it still smells like Target or Walmart.

It's still stealing, but depriving a giant corporation of a dollar or two doesn't bother me.

"Aww, thank you!" I scoop the real cat up and hug her.

She makes a tribble noise and nuzzles up to my neck.

Dalton re-emerges from the house. "Dear, you should probably head back inside. The young lad is about ready to mount a search party to locate you."

I chuckle. "Yeah. You guys are welcome to join us."

"Would, but I've got an engagement." Dalton winks.

He's not blowing me off. Being the one who gave me the Transference, he can see into my head. It's less mind reading and more like standing in the same room as my consciousness while it loudly narrates my life. He knows I am sincere about inviting him in, but also want some alone time with Hunter.

"As do I." Glim shocks me by initiating a brief hug. "You've still got a few hours of birthday left. Enjoy them."

"Oh, I'm sure she will enjoy it very much." Dalton wags his eyebrows.

Right. Time to blush.

Glim vanishes in a puff of darkness. Dalton salutes me before zooming into the air. Klepto licks my ear and teleports away— probably back to Sophia's bed.

Hmm. It's a little after ten. Pretty sure I'm going to keep Hunter up past his bedtime tonight. Oops. Oh well. Birthdays are once a year, right? Time to do that 'act my age' thing and be a little harmlessly careless.

# 5

# THE FINE ART OF THE AMBUSH

February brings a cold snap as well as the yearly financial exploitation of cuteness known as the Girl Scout Cookie Empire.

It's hard to believe an entire month went by without anything supernaturally crazy happening. At least nothing crazier than taking Sophia to visit the mystics so she can play around with magic. The Peters brothers—Cody and Ben—who I met on our family road trip last summer have been peppering me with questions about vampires via Facebook constantly. They're still 'investigating' their kooky neighbors. I swear the boys have vampire on the brain. Everyone they see who acts in any way slightly off normal they suspect of being a vampire.

Meeting me has resulted in two changes to the way they deal with undead—at least in their minds. They no longer trust daylight to infallibly protect them from being spied on by vampires, and they also no longer act like every vampire is completely evil. Okay, so I made them excessively paranoid in one regard (merely by existing) but also gave them pause. After seeing me able to go out in the sunlight—to a point—they think vampires could be spying on them all the time. This is also due, in part, to their drastically overinflated sense of self. As if a pair of boys their age would be so great a threat to the undead community, spies would be coming after them.

Cody and Ben Peters, names whispered fearfully in the shadows on the tongues of vampires from New York to Los Angeles… not.

They've glossed over the finer points of my relationship to the firey ball of ouch, though. As in, they ignore I can only tolerate *gloomy* days and how it's only one (fairly rare) bloodline capable of being awake before sunset. As far as they're concerned, any random vampire might be a threat during the day.

Another thing I learned from Aurélie: the vast majority of vampires *wanted* the Transference. Of the people who asked for the change, almost all of them would've been disappointed to get 'stuck' as an Innocent since our greatest 'power' is appearing lifelike. No shapeshifting, magic, mass mind control, Hulk strength or so on. All the cool 'Hollywood' abilities are way out of reach. Stands to reason someone chasing undeath for power would turn their noses up at Innocents. Makes me think there could be some manner of 'sorting hat' process going on where whatever mechanism the Universe has to choose bloodlines pays some attention to what the person wants. Innocent might be the default for anyone who's turned without having the vaguest notion of what's going on. Or maybe the Universe knows me too well.

Anyway, aside from Cody and Ben's thrice-weekly doses of neurotic paranoia via FB messenger, my life has, for the past several weeks, been more or less like it would've been if I hadn't become a vampire—with the obvious exception of my sleep-wake schedule and a giant teddy bear in the corner of my room. Can't do anything about the stupid sunlight shutting me down. Schoolwork, housework, helping the 'rents take the Littles back and forth to taekwondo (for Sam), sword lessons (for Sierra) and dance class (for Sophia) is a pleasant offset from worrying about old-as-hell vampires getting a bug up their butt about me. The hardcore ones who really don't like me remaining part of a mortal family appreciate me laying low. At least, I assume they do since nothing's happened and no nasty messages have shown up.

Okay, normality hasn't been entirely total.

Aurélie requested the Littles and I show up to sit for another painting, which we did the last Saturday of January. Sophia adored the elaborate dress. Sierra tolerated it. Sam got to wear shorts since she painted him as a faun. Honestly, I think Aurélie has taken a liking to interacting with them—to a point. Maybe it's the reason she's collected so many creepy dolls. Having some real children around who both know what she is and are cool about it has to brighten her existence. She's old enough to where most kids and animals instinctively sense her power and often want to run like hell.

Sophia also adores going to visit her since she's into the dolls. I don't know how the girl who gets nightmares at stupid movies can tolerate creepy-pocalypse of the doll room. Any rational person would take one step into a large room where all four walls are shelves containing a thousand dolls, many of which truly feel like they're staring at you—because they really are—and turn right the hell back around.

I don't mind covering for the 'rents as a limo driver so my sibs can get to after school activities. Feels normal and it doesn't inconvenience me at all—except for the occasional too-sunny afternoon. Two parents can't shuttle three kids to three different places at the same time. Driving's comparatively slow and tedious, but I can't fly when the sun's up.

And again, it feels normal.

Speaking of shuttling the kids around, as I said, with February comes Girl Scout cookies. Sierra's not part of it this year partly due to it being 'lame' and partly, I think, because the supernatural stuff going on in our lives is bothering her way more than she lets on. However, she still wants to come along to the supermarket while Sophia sells cookies by the door. She doesn't mind helping her little sister out as long as *she* doesn't have to wear a 'stupid uniform.' Bear in mind, to Sierra, most clothing other than T-shirts and jeans is 'lame'.

On a bleary Wednesday afternoon, the three of us show up outside the Safeway in Woodinville a little after four, joining two other Girl Scouts (Madison and Ariana) plus Madison's mom, Trish. They're both younger than my sisters. Madison is eight, her friend Ariana, nine. All four girls erupt in chatter while I unload Sophia's cookie inventory from the Sentra to the sidewalk, then go find a parking space. By the time I've walked back, my sisters have stashed the boxes under the tablecloth and set up their display. Madison and Ariana have their own stock. Even though they're in the same troop as Sophia, they're sorta competing here, but the kids don't really care who sells the most cookies. Some girls go completely insane trying to rule the sales charts and 'beat' the rest of their troop. Ninety percent chance those girls grow up to be middle managers whose employees daydream about setting their cars on fire.

Sophia's all smiles whenever someone enters or leaves the store. She's a little shy so she doesn't call out to anyone, rather hoping the supernatural allure of Girl Scout cookies does the work for her. Some people resent the ambush marketing by the Safeway door and refuse to even look at us. Others seem to appreciate her silent 'cookies are here if you want them' approach.

Sierra leans on the wall next to me, a few steps behind the table since she's not doing the Girl Scout thing anymore. "You gonna help her out again?"

"Can't until the sun's down." I shrug. "Might encourage a few sales if she's way under quota before we leave."

"Hmm." Sierra folds her arms, bracing one foot against the wall. "Is it technically stealing to *make* people buy cookies?"

No argument there. "Yeah, but it's not *quite* as bad as just stealing. I only gave people who almost bought them a little nudge. It isn't the same as forcing people who can't afford it to buy them."

"You'd make a lousy paladin." Sierra grins.

Dad's run a few D&D games for us, but it isn't exactly something we do all the time. "Notice I've never played one? They're more concerned with law than doing what's right."

"Depends on what god they follow." Sierra starts rambling about some of the different fictional deities, some of which would want their paladins to do what's 'right' rather than follow manmade laws.

Pretty sure mind-controlling people to buy cookies would still bother those gods.

See, she's way more into D&D than I am. Or Pathfinder. I forget which one they like more.

Maybe one in three people heading into the store stop at the table to say they'll be back on the way out, somewhat better than last year. Of people leaving the Safeway, roughly half pick up at least one box of cookies. Hmm. Way more than usual. Sophia's wearing a cat-that-got-the-canary smile. Ooh, is she using magic somehow? I mean, beyond her adorableness?

Probably because she's blonde, cute, and skinny enough to look like a starving orphan, she got the part of 'child Cosette' in her dance school's adaptation of *Les Mis*. The instructor coaching Sophia on how to make a sad, lost, alone, and begging for help face probably counts as being guilty of a war crime. It's as good as mind-control on anyone who isn't a sociopath. However, I suspect she's using magic beyond acting right now.

Madison and Ariana have no qualms over approaching people and asking them if they want cookies. In the moments when no one is close enough to tempt, they explain to Sophia some techniques one of the other moms taught them about the best ways to metaphorically pounce on people. Try getting their attention on the way in rather than out since people entering the store aren't in as much of a hurry to get home for example. Or when someone doesn't notice the table, don't say anything before they're too close to avoid it without being obvious. Some people might be self-conscious at being visibly rude to smiling kids in public. Apparently, the woman who spoke at the troop meeting about this works in marketing and came up with a bunch of advice on how to commercialize cuteness.

"Whenever someone buys cookies, you gotta be really happy and smile a lot," says Madison.

"Yeah." Ariana demonstrates the giant grin. "Old people like seeing kids smile."

Madison holds up a finger. "If someone keeps walking by, look sad.

It might make them feel guilty enough to come back when they leave the store. Try to make eye contact so they know you're sad at them."

"Wow," whispers Sierra. "They might as well skip right to pickpocketing."

I chuckle. "They're NPC merchants, not rogues."

Sierra snickers.

"The sad face doesn't really work." Sophia sighs. "Everyone ignored me last year. Some even gave me nasty looks. I ended up crying for real and it didn't help. This year, I'm trying to be as non-annoying as possible. If someone wants cookies, they'll stop. Everyone knows what Girl Scout Cookies are. Besides, you guys are talking to everyone anyway."

"Soph's playing 'good cop,'" I whisper to Sierra, who snickers again.

We hang out watching the girls sell cookies, chatting about random things like how weird it is she's too shy to talk to people walking by but will dance and (sometimes) sing for a recital. She's not a huge fan of being in front of a crowd, but evidently enjoys the theatrical part enough to cope. Helps it's kinda dark and she can't really see the audience in a proper theater. Far as I know, she's still wanting to go into cinematic cosmetics and/or special effects, so being around performers is somewhat related. Cookie sales are noticeably better than last year prior to when I decided to help. The day isn't terribly bright nor gloomy, but the covered sidewalk along the storefront is reasonably comfortable. Gazing into the parking lot is a little painful to my eyes due to the brightness, but at least I'm not smoldering.

The table gets a fair amount of business as well as the usual assortment of people who hurry by pretending not to notice us.

"That mom who gave the kids the marketing advice set up her daughter's table outside a pot dispensary. Kinda evil if you ask me." Trish glances at her phone to check the time.

"Evil would be putting a table outside a Weight Watchers place," says Sierra. "Waving snacks at potheads is smart."

"What's a pothead?" asks Madison.

Trish gives me a dirty look.

I shrug at her. "Don't look at me. I'm the older sister, not Mom."

"Oh, come on." Sierra sighs. "Your kid's talking about ambush marketing and you're gonna be upset with me for saying 'pothead'?"

A mild sense of warning comes over me for no obvious reason. Can't be anything supernatural since it's daytime.

"Umm. Shit," mutters Sierra.

I raise an eyebrow. "Huh?"

Sierra flicks her gaze to the left, indicating two people taking a shopping cart from the rows lined up by the store. They're in their forties and relatively normal looking. Danger doesn't click with me until the guy pulls the cart loose and turns so I can see his face: Mr. and Mrs. Deacon… Scott's parents.

Time feels like it grinds to a halt, the entire world stopping around us. Oh, awkward. As soon as he spots me, he freezes in place and goes from seeming annoyed at being dragged off to the store to giving me this glare like he wants to wring my neck. Neither of them move for a moment, entirely focused on *me*. Mrs. Deacon scowls accusingly, as if her son's death was my fault. It's like we're a pair of gunslingers having a showdown. A tumbleweed rolls by in the distance behind them.

Just kidding, it's a stray toddler. We don't have tumbleweeds in western Washington.

I swear Mrs. Deacon is a total 'Karen.' It's hilarious her name actually *is* Karen. She's even got the 'let me talk to your manager' hairdo with bleach-blonde tips. The only thing keeping me from biting her head off (verbally) is slight confusion about the extent of my responsibility. No, I don't blame myself whatsoever for him cheating on me. Breaking up with him was the right thing to do. My error came in not heeding the warning signs and ending it long before I did. Also, picking a secluded place turned out to be a mistake, too.

No, the confusion in wondering how responsible I am is coming from me smashing Scott's head open on a steering wheel then burning him to ashes inside a stolen Jeep.

Technically, he was already dead when I lit him on fire. Undead, rather. Dalton's the one who killed Scott while I lay unconscious, stuck halfway between alive and dead. Unfortunately, my sire hadn't been exactly thorough about finishing Scott off. He got back up as a Scrap, basically a half-vampire. I'd say they are base feral creatures driven by animal instinct and operating on a minimum of higher brain function, but the description would apply to Scott before he died, too.

It's no mystery how he ended up being an entitled bastard who couldn't handle me breaking up with him. His parents treated him like a prince who could do no wrong, spoiling him at every opportunity. Mrs. Deacon's the kind of mother who'd go to the school and yell at the teacher whenever her boy got poor grades rather than blaming her son's lack of effort. If Scott really had killed me permanently and been arrested for it, I can see her trying to tell a jury his 'momentary lapse of judgement' shouldn't ruin his future. Like so what if some random girl is dead, her boy's future is important.

And of course, to them, it's *my* fault their boy cheated on me, then murdered me, then died.

Granted, they don't know he actually did succeed in killing me. They also think he died in a car fire while attempting to elude police. The cops believe they chased him until he crashed—yes, Dalton and I played with a few brains. I'm not sure how the Deacons rationalize him stabbing me in the chest as 'deserved' beyond it being their son and anything he does, he must've had a good reason for no matter what. Maybe in their denial, they think I stabbed myself to make their son look bad.

Sierra returns the glare. Despite being a little scrap of a tween, she looks ready to spring straight into a fistfight with Mr. Deacon. Like Scott, he played football. College, too I think, but never pro. Don't remember what he does for a living, but it's got something to do with cars... half want to say he owns a dealership. I know they're well off financially. I'd say the Deacons pitied me for being 'poor' (by comparison to them), but it wouldn't be true. They never pitied me as much as regarded me with mild disdain. According to them, Scott should've aimed for a girl from a wealthier family than theirs. Princes marry princesses after all, not ordinary people. I hadn't even been one of the popular girls at school.

Right, so… judgmental jackasses.

Vampirism has the unfortunate side effect of making me *more* nervous during the sunlight hours than I'd been before death. Like most teens, I never used to think about mortality or waste too much time on consequences. I'd been a little more cautious than some, but for the most part, I didn't live in fear. It's different when screwing up is going to cost me centuries of existence compared to maybe eight decades. Even Aurélie hasn't been able to say for certain what would happen to me if something 'killed' me during the day when my powers are offline, but our assumption is permanent death.

So, yeah, being outside in the daytime as Grandma Sheridan always says, makes me feel like a long-tailed cat in a room full of rocking chairs. Considering Scott had the capability to stab me to death, I have to assume it's possible for his father to be every bit as potentially violent if pushed. Scott's opinion of a woman's place had to come from somewhere after all.

Maybe I should look down, break eye contact, and hope they go by without causing a scene. Might be the smart thing to do, but it irks me. I don't want to back down in front of them since none of this is my fault. No way am I going to give them any sense of victory they could interpret as me 'knowing I did wrong.' Screw that.

They don't appear to appreciate my 'yeah, I'm here, deal with it' stare. Sophia, Madison, and Ariana smile at them when they approach the table, though neither of Scott's parents look at them or the cookies for more than a few seconds. Okay, now I'm sure Sophia did something magical to attract people to the sweets. Only paranormal energy could break Karen's glower at me, even briefly.

"What are you doing here?" asks Mr. Deacon in a snide tone.

"Keeping an eye on my sister while she sells cookies." I fold my arms. Not gonna take the bait and get into an argument out in public. No matter what I say, they'll twist it around and play victim.

"How nice for you," says Mrs. Deacon. "It's ridiculous the police didn't charge you with anything."

Mr. Deacon sneers at me. "Shouldn't you be off somewhere getting someone else killed?"

Madison hides behind her mother, who gasps. Ariana stands completely still, perhaps hoping no one notices her. Both girls kinda give me this 'holy crap did you really kill someone' look.

Grr. Dammit. So much for ignoring them. Having two little girls look fearfully at me is too much. I can't resist the urge to clear the air. "Umm... last time I checked, being the victim of attempted murder isn't illegal. Your son tried to kill me, then crashed running away from the cops. How is that *my* fault?"

"You broke his damn heart," barks Mr. Deacon.

I point at him. "No. He broke mine. I didn't make him cheat. A boy is not entitled to have a side girl because he's a boy. Everything is not the girl's fault no matter what happened."

Madison and Ariana cover their mouths. Not sure if they're concealing gasps or giggles.

"We shouldn't have let him date a girl like you." Mr. Deacon's face reddens. "You killed our son."

"Hey, asshole!" shouts Sierra. "*Scott* is the one who cheated. Everyone *saw* him making out with another girl. The only thing Sarah did was fail to die when your butthead son stabbed her for breaking up with him. Maybe if you taught him how to cope with the tragedy of being told 'no' once in his life, he'd still be alive."

Sophia grimaces, looking around at everyone with her pleading face, trying to make the shouting stop.

Trish pulls out a cell phone, probably to call the police in case things escalate. Madison and Ariana scurry back to a safe distance, gawking at Sierra.

If the look on Mrs. Deacon's face means anything, she'd have slapped Sierra if not for having a table of cookies in the way. Offline or not, if that woman touches her, I'm going to lose my shit and this is going to end with police plus vast amounts of memory adjusting later on tonight.

Mr. Deacon narrows his eyes at Sierra, lets go of the shopping cart, and walks around the table up to us. I tense up since it looks like he's about to get physical. We don't exactly have anywhere to go, as our backs are literally against the wall. The guy's way taller than me and pretty muscular. Despite her whole body being only as wide as one of his legs, Sierra stares defiantly up at him.

Even though I feel vulnerable during the day, I don't hesitate putting myself between him and my sister.

"Scott tried to kill me," I say in my best attempt at a low, intimidating voice. "I'm alive only because he missed my heart by a quarter inch. The cops are going to think you're trying to finish what he started."

Mr. Deacon grabs me by the shirt—and starts reaching for Sierra. Swear, if I was online right now, I'd break his jaw. Not going to accomplish much as an ordinary mortal. Only thing I can do now is refuse to give him the satisfaction of letting him know I'm frightened. Doesn't matter if he hits me. It'll heal as soon as I'm online—as long as he doesn't kill me.

I ignore the hand bunching up my shirt and grab the wrist of the arm going for my sister. In dire moments, I can ease off my sun resistance to let a little vamp out. Basically, I'm still a vampire even during the day but *all* my power goes to resisting sunlight, leaving me effectively normal. I focus on projecting fear at him. "Think really hard about what you do in the next few seconds. I didn't kill Scott, but if you touch my sister, I'm going to arrange a reunion for you."

For a brief moment, the temperature outside feels as though it spikes up to 150 degrees.

"Go ahead." Sierra fearlessly slides out from behind me. "Lay a hand on me and see what happens."

The rage melts out of Mr. Deacon's face. He ends up staring at me in bewildered silence as though he experienced a brief flicker of inexplicable dread his rational mind can't process coming from a girl my size. He lets go of my shirt, his arm falling slack at his side, then shifts his gaze down to his right. The sight of a scrawny eleven-year-old not showing the slightest bit of fear at his looming over her snaps him back to being agitated. "Are you seriously threatening me?"

Sierra opens her mouth, but Sophia yells, "No, she's talking about the cop right there watching you. I'm sure he's gonna be mad if you try to hurt Sierra."

As soon as Mr. Deacon takes his eyes off us, I sneak a glance to my left. About thirty feet away from the cookie table, the Arnold Schwarzenegger of police officers stands by the shopping cart return. Seriously, this guy looks like he bench-presses other weightlifters—while they're lifting. He doesn't seem at all pleased at Mr. Deacon.

"Wow, they got here fast," whispers Madison.

Trish shakes her head. "I didn't call them… yet."

Scott's parents hastily scurry off into the store, firing off one final nasty look before they disappear behind the wall out of sight.

"Whoa." Sierra waves in greeting at the cop. "Totally didn't even see him. I meant he should be worried about what Sare would do to him if he touched me."

Trish gives her a 'say what?' glance while putting her phone away, then looks at me. "You're not carrying a knife or something, are you?"

Technically, I'm carrying ten knives… small ones. But I can't use them until the sun goes down. As far as ordinary weapons? None. "No weapons, but if he touched Sierra, I'd have like scratched out his eyes or something."

Trish gives a nervous laugh.

When she, Madison, and Ariana aren't looking, the cop vanishes into thin air.

Sophia appears overly pleased with herself.

Oh, son of a… I ruffle her hair. Just an illusion. No wonder the guy looked so ridiculously buff. Damn, she's getting better at realism. Dude looked real—except for no cop around here being so jacked. Once we have some privacy, I should talk to her about believability. Anyone familiar with the local cops would know Johnny Bravo doesn't work for the Woodinville PD.

"Nice," whispers Sierra, grinning. "You should jinx them, too."

"Nah." Sophia looks down. "They already lost their son. That's enough punishment. I bet they know it's really their fault, which is why they're so mad at Sare."

"Umm, not to pry," asks Trish in a low voice, "but what did the guy mean about you killing his son?"

Sigh.

I get she's worried since she doesn't want a killer anywhere near her daughter. Barring a sudden blast of bright sunlight when I'm trapped in a confined space, I'm no danger to anyone who isn't deserving of it. Still, I should settle her fears even if it is a little invasive a question. "I dated their son for almost two years. We got pretty serious, but he cheated on me with another girl at our school. The night I broke up with him, he snapped. Went all psycho and tried to kill me. Stabbed me pretty bad then left me for dead. He ended up stealing some guy's Jeep while running from the police. After a relatively short chase, he lost control, ran off the road, and died in the crash."

"Oh, wow… I'm so sorry." Trish cringes.

"Do you have a scar?" asks Ariana.

I nod. "Yeah, but it's kinda small. I got lucky."

"Yo," whispers a man. "Hook me up with some Thin Mints?"

Everyone turns to look at a twentysomething guy—clearly a stoner —in a long coat and wool cap. The dude's glancing around as if afraid someone will notice him trying to score cookies. He's either high as hell or being a goofball.

Madison scrunches up her face at Trish, confused, like 'why is he acting like we're doing something bad?'

"I got you covered if you got the cash. Just picked up a drop from my supplier." Sophia pats her stack of Thin Mints. "Can I put you down for five or ten boxes?"

# 6

# THE SKY IS FULL OF STARS

February is as over as my childhood.

Hmm. I guess it's kinda depressing to say. Been reading too much emo poetry for English lit. Hmm. What about: February is as over as my menstrual cycle. Okay, still unsure. Is that funny or gross? Whatever. It's the second-best part of being a vampire after flying. Not every vampire gets to fly, so for some, freedom from the monthly friend *is* the best part of undeath. Pff. Immortality, being able to lift a car, or shapeshift into animals has nothing on no longer being a victim of my anatomy.

Soon after my Transference, I made a promise to myself not to mess with Scott's parents. While the indulgent manner in which they raised their son ultimately led to my death, it's not like they meant me deliberate harm. However, based on what they did a few weeks ago, the self-promise needed a little tweaking. It might have been cruel of me, but to prevent any future situations from arising—and hey, the man *did* grab me, which is technically assault—I broke into their house and played around in their heads.

Nothing too complicated, merely a compulsion to stay away from me and my family. If they ever again see me out in the world, they'll have an urge to avoid me so blindingly powerful they might run straight into traffic. Kinda like the way some people dodge vendor tables outside Safeway or flee Mormon missionaries and Jehovah's Witnesses.

Sophia's been playing around with illusions ever since, spending the last two weeks conjuring random decorations around the house, making false faeries, tricking Mom into thinking Dad let us get a golden retriever (she was not pleased) and changing her appearance into various cartoon characters.

Her first use of illusion magic last year had been powered by—for Sophia—extreme desperation. A branch of the Aurora Aurea, the same mystical order we encountered here, from London tried to 'borrow' her using an apportation spell. Basically, teleportation is when someone moves themselves. Apportation is like teleportation, only the mystic is doing it to someone or something other than themselves. Unfortunately, the London mystics' attempt to grab Sophia using remote involuntary teleportation kinda missed and ended up yoinking her clothes right off her in the middle of a school day. Fortunately, she'd been in a bathroom stall at the time and no one saw her. Absolute embarrassment resulted in her creating a believable illusion of clothing so she could leave the bathroom stall without having to tell anyone she'd ended up stranded with no clothes. Unfortunately, she couldn't come up with a good enough excuse to go home early, so she had to slog through the rest of the school day wearing only illusions, paranoid the other kids all knew she didn't have anything on. No one realized. Teachers would've whisked her into a private room or given her something. Kids would've teased her mercilessly.

As traumatizing as it had been for her to be stranded naked at school, it's way better than her first *need* to use magic originating as part of her ending up in a life-and-death situation. Though, to hear her tell it, she 'almost died.' It seems her magic responds to severe situations by spiking in power. Case in point: when those two other mystics from the Serene Lodge kidnapped her, she managed to briefly turn day to night (in a small area) so I could go online and not die. It might not be necessary for me to worry quite so much about protecting her, but I can't help it. Sophia will always be my 'brittle' sister who I have to wrap in bubble packing.

Besides, as Sierra has pointed out more than once, mages start off weak. You know what's *really* stupid? Dad told us about the original version of D&D he played as a kid. Some genius decided to add housecats to the monster list, and gave their claws an actual damage value. According to the old rule set, a housecat could kill a first-level wizard in one claw swipe on a good enough damage roll.

Yeah, some roleplaying games have silliness baked into the rules.

Anyway, I'm once again in shock... and starting to become concerned.

It's March second and our lives have remained free of unexpected paranormal interference since Sophia and I returned from London back in December. Mom thinks because the Universe went *way* off the deep end over there, we're enjoying a lull. Once, not too long ago, I couldn't process seeing a legit troll. Granted, we'd been in some sort of parallel dimension at the time, but still—it had been *so* weird and unreal, my mind wanted to reject it. After everything in London, trolls seem kinda ordinary.

Really, vampires are a creature supposedly of myth. How is it possible for them to seem 'normal' but other magical stuff like trolls, brownies, and leprechauns is 'nah, those couldn't possibly exist?' Hmm. The only explanation coming to me is no one's made movies or written books seriously about fey creatures the same way vampires have become part of pop culture. Can't say I've *ever* seen a dryad in a movie at all. Leprechauns and brownies? If they're in a film, it's either a super cheesy horror movie or something made for kids.

Vampires are sexy, emo, trendy, hipster or whatever.

Great, we're basically the avocado toast of supernatural monsters.

So, yeah... it's past three in the morning. I lied before. It's not really March second. Friday ended at midnight. It's really March third now, to split a hair. As far as I'm concerned, it's still the second until after I sleep and wake up.

Had a bad meal after school, and I've been kinda feeling odd ever since. Not in a physical way like someone I ate gave me indigestion.

The guy I selected to feed from is stuck in a relationship he's not into, but staying because he's afraid his girlfriend would commit suicide if he broke up with her. Since I haven't looked into the woman's mind, it's anyone's guess if he's right. Only saw his thoughts, which aren't necessarily reality.

I ended up taking a seat here on a curb in downtown Seattle to debate getting involved. One thought led to another, and hours disappeared. Some time ago, my brain shut off. I've been staring up at the stars for a while, admiring them. It's nothing short of amazing, two whole months have passed where my life feels as normal as it can possibly be now. You'd think being killed would totally mess everything up, but it hasn't been too bad. What-ifs are a devil's pastime—something Mom says. I could spend years thinking about where my siblings and I would be if I hadn't become a vampire or died, and not all the theoreticals are good.

Total waste of time. Dwelling on the past won't change it. One could say examining the past helps us avoid the same mistakes in the future, but I'm not exactly worried about another asshole boyfriend murdering me. However, vampirism comes with confidence. At least, it did for me. I've never been as timid as Sophia, but I'm definitely more like Sierra now. This version of me wouldn't have quietly acted like she didn't know Scott cheated and spent months attempting to work up the courage to leave.

Wonder what he'd have done if I dumped him right in front of everyone?

Ehh, knowing him, he'd have gotten furious at the embarrassment but been too cowardly to do anything other than slink away after yelling something lame about how I'd regret 'doing that to him.' He'd definitely have come after me later, though. Exactly what I hoped to avoid by doing it somewhere private and quiet. Figured if no one saw him 'lose,' he wouldn't freak out. Yeah, really worked out for me, didn't it?

I exhale, fluttering my lips.

But, what-ifs aside, things right now are pretty cool. Surprisingly normal—at least they've been so for the past few months—and looking promising. All I have to do is keep my head down from a vampire politics perspective and enjoy being with my family while I can. Life almost feels ordinary. Except for the weird deep voice coming from Sam's closet at three in the morning.

Did I mention he's made a new friend? The boy's been sparse on details, only saying they had to ask *something* to help detox Ronan from the slug venom. When Blix mentioned the paralysis would wear off 'soon,' he spoke like a demon—meaning immortal, not evil. They don't have a real solid grip on the concept of time. Had they not sought outside help, Ronan would've been able to move again in about four years. So, yeah... Sam made the right call agreeing to let Blix call in backup.

Neither my brother nor the imp appear overly concerned about this new entity, so I'm not panicking about it... yet. Another good sign: Coralie hasn't shown up to warn me of calamity. So, my little bro has *two* demons in his room now, even if one is only a closet voice.

Staring up into the infinity of outer space gets me wondering if life exists on any other planets. My Dad thinks it's a mathematical certainty life exists somewhere else. Considering the size of the known universe, Earth is like a single grain of sand on all the world's beaches. Humans, our entire civilization and planet, are seriously insignificant in the grand scheme of things.

If there *is* life on some other world, would there be vampire aliens?

"Only in a Uwe Boll movie," I whisper.

Where did vampires even come from? If magic exists on Earth, it must exist everywhere. Our planet isn't the center of reality. It shouldn't sound so late-night-movie cheesy to think of alien vampires, but it does. Is that specist of me? Is specist a word? Species-ist? Bleh.

Some activities *are* a waste of time. Trying to understand where vampires came from is about as futile and pointless as searching for an answer to 'why are the Kardashians famous?' Worse, discovering the answer won't affect the world.

Despite me nearly dying nine months ago, my family is almost back to normal. The siblings and I have managed not to fall back into our old ways of bickering constantly, though the Littles do occasionally argue about typical kid things. We wouldn't really be considered 'normal' otherwise.

Sierra's enjoying the heck out of sword lessons. Admittedly, her interest came from the expectation she'd have to fight imps or vampires or some other real monster, but she's in a phase now where she's talking like she wants to make a career out of sword fighting. Aside from being a stunt person or actor in a medieval reenactment place, I have no damn idea how anyone *could* turn sword skills into a job. She's getting close to twelve, too. Still young. Good chance she'll change her mind about what to do for a living another dozen times before she truly *needs* to make a choice.

As far as Sophia goes, she's visiting the mystics twice a month in person as well as having an occasional video call. Weird, right? Studying magic via technology. She's not exactly cramming to become a master 'wizard' by the time she's out of eighth grade, but it's holding her interest. Well, duh. What kid wouldn't be enthralled by magic?

One of the weirder things to happen to me thus far is being given a sack of gold. Apparently, leprechauns *really* like it when you *don't* try to steal it from them or otherwise attempt to trick them out of it. Who knew? Mardle had been so astonished at me completely disregarding any mention of his having gold, he gave me some. In the interest of full disclosure, I will say the thought never occurred to me for him to have gold in the first place. Between my brain spinning in circles over Sophia's abduction and encountering such wild creatures, the only thought on my mind at the time had been getting my sister back and going home safe. I barely managed to accept the truth of what I experienced at all, forget trying to squeeze the little guy for money.

So, stuff happened.

'Stuff' being me acquiring a small fortune. It's not the sort of fortune where I could run out and buy a mansion, yacht, or whatever and forget ever worrying about money ever again. But, to a girl whose most outlandish future plans entail finding a way to live in my current house as long as feasibly possible, it's an astounding amount of money.

Enough for me to buy my parents a Christmas gift of a vacation to Iceland. During November and December of last year, Mom got stuck dealing with a truly demanding case at work. I basically ordered her to take a vacation before she cracked, and as luck would have it, the means to help her do it more or less fell into my hands.

I didn't think anyone would want to visit Iceland in January, plus needed to give the parents some time to prepare. They're leaving tomorrow. Originally, I signed them up for a one-week trip, but Mom worked out an itinerary after poking around online and ended up adding a few more days. So, they're flying back on Wednesday instead of Sunday.

Sophia's going to turn eleven on March twenty-second. The 'rents will be home on the fourteenth—assuming nothing goes wrong. For a little while, we'll have two eleven-year-olds in the house... until Sierra turns twelve in April.

I'm having a Schrodinger moment. Eleven feels simultaneously forever ago and only a few years. Eight years is, to a vampire, nothing. To a nineteen-year-old, it's a significant portion of my existence. I do kinda miss the way my life was uncomplicated back then. All the stuff I used to worry about as if it was the end of the world is laughably trivial to me now. Grr. If anything stinks about becoming a vampire, it's how I keep thinking about crap like this. When they tell people to 'act their age,' they're usually trying to get someone to be *more* mature. I need to act my age in the other direction.

Oh well. No point dwelling on anything. I'm going to enjoy my new reality. Being frozen at eighteen is cool. Definitely going to get weird in thirty or forty years, but I can mitigate problems by not doing dumb things—like interacting with people.

The crunch of tires on my right announces the approach of a car creeping around the corner.

I glance over at a police cruiser, the guy behind the wheel is— naturally—staring right at me. Good cue, it's about time for me to go home. He pulls around the corner, stopping right in front of me as I stand. Since he's facing the wrong way in the oncoming lane, he turns on warning flashers, then rolls his window down.

"Hey," says the cop. "Are you okay?"

He's thinking I'm sixteen, probably a runaway. Ugh. I really need to stop letting it bother me when people get my age wrong. Don't want to end up a monster a few centuries from now with a hair-trigger temper who rips people's throats out every time they call me a kid. Zen, Sarah. Try Zen.

"Yes, I'm fine. Thanks for checking on me. Taking night classes at SCC. Was just on my way home."

"It's almost three in the morning. A bit late to get out of class."

"Oops." I offer a cheesy smile. "Got stuck stargazing. Really, I'm fine."

A light mental prod convinces him nothing's wrong here and sends him on his way. No point wasting his time. Someone elsewhere in the city might actually need his help. I watch the police car go until he turns another corner out of sight, then wander into a dark patch away from any light sources. Confident no one's able to see me, I leap into the air and orient myself toward home.

I've done some wild stuff since becoming a vampire, but the next eleven days are going to be scary. For a little more than a week, I'm going to be the adult in the room.

Yay me.

We are so screwed.

# 7

# A MUCH-NEEDED VACATION

S aturday decides to play nice.

Meaning, it's overcast without actively raining. At least, according to my phone it is. I can't see much since I'm stuffed in a plastic cargo bin. Judging by the vibration and rumbling, I've been loaded into the back of Mom's Tahoe already and they're on the road.

Due to my schedule, my parents are taking an afternoon flight out of SeaTac. Takeoff's at 3:50 p.m. Seven or so hours later, they'll land at like six in the morning in Reykjavik. Flying across time zones is weird. Like, different places on the Earth all exist at different times despite time being a constant. If one could fly westward fast enough, it would technically remain the same chronological time as long as they kept going. The date would change, but it would, for example, appear to be 5:00 p.m. infinitely. Not sure how fast someone would have to go, but it's probably something ridiculous like a thousand miles an hour. A bit out of reach of a commercial plane, and *way* out of my personal reach.

It might make for an interesting experiment on vampire sleep, but no aircraft in existence could fly continuously past Mach 1 long enough to see if holding the sun hostage on the opposite side of the

Earth would keep sleep away. Also, it's really not worth it. Such information would never be practically useful.

Yes, I am a nerd. Or at least sort of a nerd. A true nerd would work out the exact requirements for the experiment and probably know off the top of their head how fast the Earth rotates.

Anyway, we need to be at the airport soon enough for my parents not to miss their flight... which meant I sacrificed comfortable sleep last morning. It's not much of a sacrifice since I take the idiom 'sleep like the dead' way too literally. Curling up in the cargo bin sucked for a few minutes, but once sunrise knocked me out, it no longer mattered. So what if I'm fully dressed, folded in half with my knees in my face?

A gentle push at the lid fails to move it. Not too surprised. These bins have plastic clamps to hold the lids on so they're weather tight. It's probably dangerous for a person to crawl into one of these, but I don't need air.

The entire point of the cargo bin was to allow my parents to leave the house early enough not to miss their flight. We all expected I would wake up on the way to the airport or shortly after arrival. Next Wednesday when they return, there's no need for us to stress out over my schedule. The 'rents can hang out at the airport after their plane lands waiting for me to get out of bed since they won't be chasing a takeoff deadline. Besides, it's extremely difficult to drive from inside a giant plastic storage bin.

I knock on the side. "Hey, I'm up. Unless it's nuclear, let me out."

A moment later, weight settles into the lid.

"What's it worth to ya?" asks Sierra.

"I didn't realize how desperately you wanted to enroll at Sophia's dance studio and wear pink unicorn leotards."

Sierra gasps. "You wouldn't dare!"

"Sarah," calls Mom. "Don't threaten your sister with mind-control."

"Kidding," I yell. "Please open the lid."

Clunking accompanies the six clamps popping open one after the next. The bin *is* plastic, so I could've broken my way out easily.

However, only an idiot destroys potentially needed shelter. Sierra pulls the lid away, exposing me to a blast of uncomfortable heat, then bonks me over the head with it when I sit up. It's not really 110 degrees out, merely feels like it to me.

"Dork. You know I'm only teasing."

"So was I about demanding tribute for your early release." She laughs, tosses the lid aside, then scrambles over the seatback.

I climb after her, squeezing between Sam and Sophia. He's the youngest, but the girls prefer being near windows and he doesn't care. The four of us fit in reasonable comfort. Once again, yay Dad genes. In another few years, we won't be able to share the back seat, at least not comfortably.

Mom's driving; Dad's watching traffic.

My timing is near perfect. Within two minutes of me waking up, we arrive at the airport. It is a little bright at the moment, but nothing a hood and sunglasses can't handle. Mom pulls up to the drop-off area. Dad and I unload their bags. The Littles unpack themselves, and we all stand there waiting for Mom to find a parking space in short term.

Sophia's clinging to Dad, which means she's upset at the idea of them going away for a week. The 'rents haven't taken any sort of vacation without us ever before—well, during the time any of us kids existed—so she's frightened at not having them around. Sierra is looking forward to what she expects will be a lawless twelve or so days where she can swear all she wants, stay up as late as she wants, and eat fast food every day. As far as Sam is concerned, it's Saturday. He isn't showing much of any reaction to the trip—except for wandering into my room the other night and asking me what we'd do if 'something went wrong' with the plane and our parents never came home.

Ugh. As if I needed *that* to worry about.

Eventually, Mom appears walking back across the lot. She hurries over to us and we go inside as a group. The parents check in, get their boarding passes, and we deal with the tedious process of going through the security screening to the terminal, arriving at 3:16 p.m.

Closer than Mom would've liked, but still plenty of time. The airline is probably going to start boarding soon. We actually made it through security surprisingly fast.

Yes, I splurged on first-class tickets.

I'll never waste money on a mansion or Lamborghini or anything ridiculous, but I couldn't justify not getting them nice seats. Not like I scraped and saved and barely afforded the trip. They deserve a nice vacation from the daily grind. Just hope there's a house to come home to.

Knowing my luck, all the normality of the past few months has been the proverbial calm before the storm. Sophia's going to sneeze in the middle of magic practice and teleport the entire house to Mars or something. Or the deep voice in Sam's closet is Mephistopheles, and he's going to drag us to the inferno.

One of the Eighties movies Dad showed us, *The Gate*, was about the parents going away for a few days. When they're gone, the kids accidentally summon demons, resulting in their entire house blowing up, only a giant crater where it used to be. This is too on-point. I'm a few years older than the 'big sister' in the movie, but our parents are going away and at least two literal demons are in the house. No dog, but we do have a cat. Sorta. Not sure it's possible for Klepto to die.

Ugh. Good thoughts. Think good thoughts. I am not going to fail so epically at babysitting our house ends up in Hell.

We sit in the waiting area at the terminal. Sophia's still being clingy but isn't acting upset. Sierra and Sam are both absorbed in portable electronics. I stuff my hands in my hoodie's pockets and hunker down against the seeming hundred-degree temperature in the room. Giant windows overlooking the runway area don't help. It may be overcast, but sitting here is as good as being outside from a daylight standpoint.

A few minutes into our wait, I notice a young guy—can't be older than twenty-five—suspiciously hovering near a bank of seats beside a column. It looks like he's hunting for a victim to rob. Curious to see what he does, I keep watching him. The guy pulls something out of his jacket pocket, crouches, and fusses at the column for a moment before casually walking a short distance away and taking a seat. It doesn't occur to me he did anything weird until he pulls out a cell phone and starts recording video of the column. Takes me a moment to realize why he's videoing.

The dude put a fake electrical outlet sticker up.

Wow. People really do this stuff?

I cover my mouth to hold in a laugh, and sit there waiting for his first victim. Airports are notorious for not having public electric outlets. A sticker is kinda cruel, but it's hilarious. It's not long before an Asian woman spots the fake plug and hurries over. She takes the seat closest to the column—and plugs her smartphone charger in.

Say what?

I gawk.

The prankster dude stares open-mouthed. If WTF had an entry in the dictionary, it would be this guy's face right now.

"What the hell?" I whisper.

"He's trying to play a mean joke," says Sophia.

I slow-turn my head toward her. "Did you seriously turn a sticker into a real outlet?"

She shrugs. "I dunno. Tried to. Not sure if it worked."

"The woman's still sitting there, so it must have." I'm not sure how to react. Did my sister do something wrong? Only the one guy who tried to play a prank has any idea something bizarre happened... but he's also recording video. "When she's done, you need to turn it back. The guy's making a video. You can't let anyone capture proof of weird stuff or the PIBs will show up."

"Eep." She covers her mouth and starts crying. "I'm sorry!"

"Shh... it's okay."

Dad chuckles. "Relax, Soph. You didn't notice the guy with the phone."

"We haven't even left the airport yet and already something strange..." Mom rubs her forehead.

Yeah, she is definitely in need of some sane time.

The prankster stands up, staring at the outlet.

"He's gonna go over there and look," I whisper. "Do something."

Sophia concentrates on the plug. The charger pops out of the socket as if by telekinesis, though the woman with the phone doesn't appear to notice it. Prankster boy wanders over, checks out the plug, and scratches his head, peering around in confusion. He seems to be searching for cameras like he's the one being pranked on TV.

Hard to tell without supernaturally sharp vision from here, but I think the sticker is once again a two-dimensional image.

"So..." Mom looks at me. "Last chance to chicken out, Sarah."

I grin at her. "It's fine. You guys really need some relaxation."

"You do understand why we've been pestering you about it, right?" asks Mom.

"She does, Allie." Dad squeezes her hand. "It will be fine. None of the kids are *too* young and they're all responsible."

I exhale out my nose. Mom's worried mostly about leaving me in charge because it's impossible for me to be awake before 2:30 (give or take, mostly give, a few minutes). I won't be able to help get the Littles out of bed in the morning, make sure they have breakfast, and shoo them out the door to school. On the upside, I will be awake before they get home.

"Ash is gonna stay over until you guys are back. She'll get the morning shift." I elbow Dad playfully. "You guys are totally freaking out over the trip. I told you Ash would be over like six times."

Mom does this weird meditative breathing thing. She is excited about the vacation but also fighting off feelings of guilt for 'leaving us.' At some point, I think she promised herself she and Dad wouldn't take a 'no kids' vacation until Sam was old enough to be home alone— maybe sixteen or seventeen. He's still nine until June. He'd only been nine for a couple weeks before my life got turned on its head.

I've been a vampire for three months short of a year. Wow. Not even a whole year yet. It feels way longer.

"Relax and enjoy your vacation. I got this." I smile at Mom.

"We did luck out having highly responsible kids." Dad pats us all on the head, one after the next. "Though, Sierra would probably sit on the PlayStation while the house burned down around her and not notice."

"Yeah, pretty much," says Sierra without looking up from her handheld.

"She wouldn't have to notice. If anything goes wrong, Soph will scream loud enough for the fire department to hear," I say, snickering.

Sophia sighs.

"Don't be mean," says Mom.

Sophia sighs again, louder. "She's not wrong."

I chuckle. "Between the four of us, plus Ash, plus Blix, we'll be okay."

"Don't forget we're back on Wednesday," says Mom.

"Yes, I remember." I give her the 'you've only told me this 472 times since you made the change' smirk.

Mom proceeds to go over an exhaustive list of 'emergency resources' including where she put the phone numbers for the grandparents and all sorts of worst-case scenario stuff. She also explains to me for the 504th time how she's planned out each dinner meal for us already.

"Allie…" Dad cuts her off when she starts worrying about if we'll be safe after dark without them there. "If anyone tries to break into the house, they're dealing with Sarah, Blix, at least one ghost, and Klepto. I legitimately feel sorry for the burglar."

The Littles and I laugh.

"Seriously, Mom. The only thing that might go wrong is Ashley oversleeping and the Littles being late for school once." I poke Sophia in the side. "But Sophia's always up early, so we should be good."

"You should worry about her summoning giant octopus tentacles," deadpans Sam.

"I only tried opening a teleport gate to school *once*," whisper-shouts Sophia.

Sam grins. "The wet slap was epic."

"Wet… slap?" asks Mom.

"Umm." Sophia fidgets. "Giant tentacle hit me in the face. Well, it kinda grabbed me."

Sierra pantomimes reaching around randomly. "It looked like some creature from another world stuck its tentacle blindly into a bag, realized it grabbed Soph, and didn't want her. Like, as soon as it noticed it had a human in its grip, it snapped back into the closet and slammed the door."

"Eww, this dimension has humans," deadpans Sam.

"I stink at apportation." Sophia hangs her head.

"Attention passengers," says a woman's voice over a PA system. "Icelandair flight 680 will begin boarding in five minutes."

The parents stand, forcing Sophia to slide out of Dad's lap to her feet.

Mom faces me. "Hold out your hand."

I do.

She pulls the Tahoe's security fob out of her purse, raises it up, and hands it over to me like she's passing on an ancient samurai sword to its next hereditary owner. "I trust you, dear, but there better not be a scratch on it."

"Gah! Mom!" yells Sierra. "Don't say that! Don't you watch *any* of Dad's movies?"

Mom blinks at her—Dad cracks up.

Sierra flails her arms. "Seriously. Every time someone says 'there better not be a scratch on it,' they come back to scorched wreckage."

"We're not in a movie." Sam shakes his head. "This is Sarah we're talking about. Mom and Dad aren't going to come back to the burning wreck of the truck. They're going to come back to a Tahoe with horns, a personality of its own, and an unhealthy obsession with *Pawn Stars*."

Mom laughs nervously. Dad's in tears. Even Sophia is giggling. Sierra unleashes the mother of epic eye-rolls.

"Seriously," deadpans Sam. "You think I'm joking. Only the *Pawn Stars* part was a joke. Demons aren't *that* evil."

Dad looks at him. "If you summon a demon into your mother's car, you're going to be grounded for a month."

"What if it's a nice demon?" Sam tilts his head.

"I can't believe we're having this conversation." Mom rubs her forehead. "I prefer my SUV demon-free, thank you."

Sam snaps his fingers in fake disappointment.

"If your mother wanted a demon-possessed truck, she'd have bought a Ford," says Dad.

Mom sighs. "What's wrong with Fords?"

"My father always used to pick on them." Dad shrugs. "Seemed funny. Not really sure what the deal is. Never owned one."

The airline calls for boarding of any passengers with special accommodation needs first.

We hug the parents in a group.

"Have fun, and try not to worry." I smile.

"What she said." Sierra yawns.

Sophia whimpers, clinging to them both.

"Don't get into any fights with Vikings," says Sam matter-of-factly.

"I'll try to remember not to." Dad pats him on the head.

We walk with them over to where the boarding line forms. Soon, they call for first-class passengers, and the parents make their way onto the boarding ramp. Sophia grabs onto me and cries like we're sending them away forever. Okay, maybe not quite *that* bad. She's not wailing, merely losing water rapidly from both eyes.

Sad movie music starts up out of nowhere.

The girls and I stare at Sam, who's holding up his phone—the source of it.

"What are you doing?" I ask.

He shrugs. "Our parents are leaving us. Soph's crying. The scene needed sad music."

Sierra punches him in the shoulder. "Stop. You're making her cry harder."

I squeeze Soph. "Why *are* you crying? They're only going away for like a week."

Sophia abruptly stops weeping. She wipes her face, then peers up at me. "Umm. I dunno. They've never gone away before. Wasn't sure how to handle it."

"She needs new software." Sam shrugs one shoulder. "Crying is her default response to unexpected errors."

"Drama queen," says Sierra.

"Oh, no!" whispers Sophia. "They're not gonna be here for my dance recital Saturday."

"Oh, the horror," mutters Sierra.

I palm her head and give a light 'don't tease Soph' shove. Sierra laughs at me.

Sophia looks down, sniffles once, then her lip quivers.

Before the waterworks start up again, I pull her into a hug. "Chill. I'll record the entire thing so they can watch it when they get back. And you just had the *Les Mis* one in February."

"Really? You're gonna go?" Sophia's blue eyes glimmer with happiness.

"Yeah. Wouldn't miss it if—"

"Stop!" yells Sierra. "Do not say anything else or you'll jinx it. Just say you won't miss it."

I point at her. "What she said."

I usher the Littles over to the window, clenching my jaw in response to the searing sunlight. No smoke at least, so I'm not in danger. "Let's watch them take off, then we can go home."

"Are we superstitious now?" Sam looks back and forth between me and Sierra.

"Yeah." I whistle. "Just a little."

# 8

# VAMPIRE MISTRESS... OF THE HOUSEHOLD

I t's surely a little too early to congratulate myself on not blowing up the house.

We haven't been back from the airport long enough for self-praise. The only thing scarier than the ride home—Tahoe full of kids when I can barely see due to sunlight was harrowing—is being the adult in the house. This has nothing to do with vampires or any of the supernatural stuff beyond how unlikely it would've been for the parents to take a vacation without us if none of the weird stuff ever happened.

I watched a cable movie with Mom a while ago where a girl younger than me ended up having to take care of her younger siblings after their parents died. Think she was seventeen in the story... not really sure how 'the authorities' didn't take them all into foster care, but whatever. They based it on true events, which for all I know only means the girl's name matched reality. 'Based on a true story' is code for 'the story was kinda boring, so we embellished a ton.'

Still, somewhere out in the world, a girl my age not only had to babysit, but work and go to school all at the same time. There are plenty of single mothers my age who survive much more harrowing circumstances than my life. I can handle things until next Wednesday.

After all, I made it to 5:13 p.m. the day the parents left and nothing's caught fire or triggered an interdimensional rift. One whole hour.

Almost.

Okay, so we've been in the door forty-six minutes.

Go me!

Hate to say it but without the vampire stuff, I might've spent most of my time hanging out with Ash or Michelle and letting the Littles run wild. Not quite the Eighties movie cliché of throwing a wild party when the parents are gone, but not exactly the most responsible thing. It's tempting to skip a week of classes so I'm home in case something happens... but Ashley talked me out of it. More annoying is having to drive again. Sunset's sneaking up on 6:00 p.m., so if I wait for it to go down before flying to school, I'm going to be late on Wednesday and Friday since my comp sci class starts at six. As soon as daylight savings kicks in on the eighth, I'll *have* to drive to school every night.

Ugh.

Okay, so I'm spoiled. Any person my age should be thrilled to have a car of their own, even a Nissan Sentra older than my little brother. And yes, I'm still intending to drive it. Not going to touch the Tahoe unless I need to transport the entire family somewhere.

So yeah, it's after five. Fortunately, it's still Saturday, so no class. I should probably start on dinner. Mom left me a list of meals, complete with every ingredient listed. If anyone looked at our fridge or cabinets now, they'd think we stocked up to weather a nuclear apocalypse.

At least Saturday night is an easy one: spaghetti with meatballs.

I'm a few minutes in to squishing ground beef between my fingers, mixing in breadcrumbs and such when Sam returns from Daryl's house. It's faster for him to cut across the backyard. He slides the patio door shut and stands there watching me knead the contents of the giant bowl.

When he doesn't say or do anything for several minutes, I glance at him. "What's up?"

He hugs me. "The definition of love is doing something for others when you get nothing out of it."

"Random." I chuckle.

"You're cooking food for us and don't have to eat."

I'd ruffle his hair, but my hands are covered in food. "I do get something out of it. I kinda like you guys. Letting you starve would make me feel bad."

He laughs. "Wow, you're making a lot."

"Yeah. Hunter and Ronan are coming over for dinner," I say, still mushing the meatball mix between my fingers. Is it weird to say this feels nastier than spearing my hand into someone's guts? Yeah, most vampire guts are cold, too... but not so slimy.

Pretty sure I'm warm inside when awake.

Hunter's never complained about coldness.

"When's it gonna be ready?" asks Sam.

"Like half an hour or forty minutes, I guess."

"Cool." He runs off to his room.

A PlayStation explosion shakes the house, followed by Sierra blowing up cursing in the living room. Grr. Should I yell at her or let it go? Bad words don't bother me the way they bug Mom and Dad. Honestly, when you've set up a perfect sniper position and some guy on the other team sneaks up on you, plants C4 between your legs, and sneaks away undetected, then sets the charge off, launching your character like a missile across the entire map—it's worth a few F-bombs. Can't fault her that. Even if scope-eye was her fault. Nah. The 'rents don't object to bad words as much as they object to her being eleven and using them. Mom's no stranger to swearing, especially when she's on a tedious case.

Time to take a passive-aggressive tack here. I'm not going to say anything about Sierra screaming swear words at the game. She'll probably get used to it and forget herself once the 'rents are home, then do it again and get in trouble. Saves me from having to be the bad guy. Don't care if not wanting to start an argument with her is a shallow reason to ignore her swearing. Not like coarse language hurled at a TV screen hurt anyone. She's not sending it over the voice chat, and better she shout bad words than break stuff. Sierra is still kinda nervous about revealing herself as a young girl over voice chat ever since those idiots made all sorts of sexually inappropriate comments at her. Could be another reason she's so into wanting to learn how to use a sword. Don't think it's legal to wear a sword around outside in the modern era, so I question the practicality of it, but whatever. She enjoys it.

Anyway, I have meatballs to squish. Gah, the noises coming from the bowl are disgusting. Like a pair of giant slugs mud wrestling.

TALK ABOUT SURREAL.

Everyone's at the dinner table and I'm in Mom's usual spot. Hunter's at the other end where Dad sits. The Littles, plus Ronan and Ashley are around the sides. Even Blix has a plate. It doesn't feel like I'm grave-jumping Mom, but the scene in front of me is giving me flash-forward to a daydream of an impossible future. Maybe I'm not so far removed from my age after all. The idea of Hunter and I having a family is squarely in 'yeah right' territory. Obviously, I can't have kids, but adoption's a thing. Still, I'm not ready for responsibility of this magnitude.

Ashley, I am not.

She can't wait to have kids. I don't mean that literally. She's not trying to get pregnant now, merely looking forward to when the time is right. Sitting in Mom's chair is like a preview, but nah. I'm happy being eighteen. Well, technically nineteen—but I don't feel any different. Probably because nothing about me has changed.

Sad thing is, we're in the minority having everyone at the table for dinner. Guess with Dad working at home for the past like eight years, it's been normal for us to have 'real' dinners more often than not as he had time to cook.

It's weird feeling like the mom. I'm supposed to be the adult in the room, but it feels like I need to ask someone 'higher up' than me for advice on every little thing. Did Mom ever feel like this? Did she call Grandma six times a day when she first had me? Is she *still* worried about screwing up? You'd think after dealing with a mess like what happened in London, the concept of being responsible for my siblings in the comfort of our house wouldn't be so intimidating. Like seriously. I can negotiate peace between multiple groups of supposedly mythological creatures, but enforcing bedtime is stressing me out?

Sigh.

The parents going away on vacation *was* my idea after all. They needed a break. Doesn't stop me from missing having them around. Oh, dammit. I understand now. This is like a tiny preview of fifty years from now when they're gone for good. Bleh. Short of turning them both into vampires, which neither wants, there isn't anything I can do about eventually losing them. I'm going to have to get used to the idea someday. Or not... maybe they'll haunt me. Honestly, even without the vampire stuff, the day would've come where I lost them. The normal course of events, as they say. Abnormal is parents losing their kids, like mine almost did.

Okay, now I'm angry at Scott all over again.

I distract myself by imagining a sitcom of me living here with my parents' elderly ghosts, occasionally visited by one of the sibs all grown up. I think Dad's going to be hilarious as an old man. Is it weird of me to *hope* they end up haunting the place? No idea what makes some people remain as spirits while others don't. I should say the majority do not. Whether it's reincarnation, Heaven, oblivion, or something else no one's ever even thought of, who knows. Darren Anderson, the leader of the local Aurora Aurea mystics, believes in reincarnation. He said the number of people alive at any one time capable of invoking real magic has been relatively constant for millennia. Makes me wonder what happens if an Academic vampire has mystical gifts. They'll hang onto it for way longer than a mortal. Is that cheating? Like the selfish kid hogging the toy at daycare?

Aurélie also thinks reincarnation is a thing, and vampires merely take much longer to go around for another spin. We last a long time but we're not immune to destruction. Honestly, it's all fairly pointless to think about. Even if death and rebirth is a way for a vampire to get mortality back, we wouldn't remember any past lives.

And no, I don't particularly want to give up being a vampire. It's cool.

Maybe I'd not be so happy about it if I'd been turned into a Shadow or a Beast. Some people might think being an Old Guard or Sybarite or something with wild supernatural powers later on down the line would be better than a little old Innocent. Not me. I'm content.

Blix levitates a portion of his dinner into a Flying Spaghetti Monster with meatball eyes and sends it floating around in circles over the table. Everyone laughs for a few minutes before I pull a Mom and ask him to stop playing with his food.

This, of course, makes everyone laugh even more.

After dinner, I hang out with Hunter and Ashley in the living room.

Sierra's monopolizing the living room TV on the PlayStation. Sophia is, as far as I know, in her room either reading, coloring, or fiddling around with mystic stuff. Sam's in his room as well, likely playing video games with Blix and Ronan. All in all, a reasonably normal Saturday night. Once the Littles go to bed, we'll probably throw on a movie. Ash and Hunter are discussing which Marvel film to stream.

Hunter is really into comic stuff. Ashley is more into it than I am. The two of them talk about the various characters' backstories—of which I am oblivious—but the movie is engaging enough for me. My boyfriend isn't one of those super-geeks who could tell you the name of each character's childhood pet, but he's a big fan of the genre. He's been trying to talk me into taking a trip to Comic Con so I can blow people's minds by dressing up as a character who can fly—then actually flying. Yeah, no. Opposite of subtle. The *last* thing I need to do is call attention to myself as a supernatural being.

Eventually, around ten, Sierra shuts down the PlayStation and heads upstairs. Hunter puts on *Thor: Ragnarok*. Not even twenty minutes into the movie, Ashley gets up and runs to the bathroom. I grab the remote to pause the movie. Hunter decides to take advantage of the break, going to the kitchen to make popcorn.

Sam thunders down the stairs like a herd of buffalo, runs across the living room, and tries the bathroom door, finding it locked. Before I can say 'Ashley's in there,' he sprints back to the stairs. Uh oh. Something bad is about to happen.

One… two… three…

"Get out!" screams Sierra upstairs. "I'm in the tub!"

"Gotta poop," says Sam.

Sierra shrieks, then yells, "I don't care! Get out!"

Ugh. This one I can't let play out. Gotta go play referee. Sierra keeps shouting at him, sounding more upset he's going to leave her trapped in a cloud of awfulness than he barged in on her while she's in the tub. She also complains about the 'rents policy of not allowing the Littles to lock the door when they're in the bathroom. You know, in case they slip or hurt themselves. They're probably old enough now where it isn't a big deal. Gonna bring it up with Mom when they get back.

I head upstairs, shocked to see a patch of light from the bathroom spread out over the carpet. Wow, he must've been in a serious hurry since he didn't even close the door. I jog down the hall, pausing in the doorway. Sierra's sitting in a foamy tub, curled in a ball at one end, glaring out from behind the shower curtain at Sam, who's on the bowl.

Sometimes, having a vampire's sense of smell is a handicap.

Fortunately, I don't have to breathe.

"Sorry," says Sam. "Someone was in the other bathroom and this couldn't wait."

"Sare! Make him get out!"

"I can't leave in mid-poo."

Good grief. I rub the bridge of my nose. Family, right?

Sierra gags. "Why did you even start? I'm trapped in here."

"Because I didn't wanna crap my pants," says Sam.

"Why can't you hold it a little bit longer?" Sierra coughs.

Sam shrugs. "Why do you have to take hour-long baths?"

"I do not take hour long baths." Sierra scoffs. "I've been in here for like fifteen minutes. What about the basement bathroom?"

"Oops." Sam cringes. "I forgot about it. Poop panic."

I pinch the bridge of my nose, trying not to laugh. Laughing would require air moving in and out of my head.

"Ugh. I'm gonna puke," mutters Sierra. "You're ruining my bath!"

Hmm. I have no idea if I should be angry with Sam or not. He didn't barge in on her specifically to be an annoying little brother. The boy simply has no concept of personal space and even less a grasp on embarrassment. I swear he could use an open toilet in the middle of downtown Seattle and not be the least bit uncomfortable. Hell, he could probably even listen to Justin Bieber in public without feeling shame.

Sophia walks in. "What's everyone screaming about?"

"Argh!" yells Sierra, water sloshing. "Does anyone realize why bathrooms have doors? It's because taking a bath isn't supposed to be a spectator sport! Why is everyone in here?"

"Ashley, Ronan and Hunter aren't in here," says Sam. "It's not technically everyone. Want me to get them?"

Sierra growls. "You're ruining my bath. It's horrible in here. I can't breathe!"

"If you yell less, you won't need to breathe as much," deadpans Sam.

"C'mon, hurry up." I gesture at him in a 'get on with it' manner.

Sophia waves her arm in a grandiose sweep. "Begone, foul demon."

"Whoa." Sierra blinks. "You got rid of the stink."

"Yep." Sophia smiles.

I test sniff. The air smells a bit like flowers. "Nice..."

"You need to do this whenever Dad explodes," says Sierra.

Sophia cringes. "Sorry. My magic has limits."

"Heh. Okay, c'mon, Sam. Hurry up and get out so your sister can finish her bath."

Sierra ducks completely behind the shower curtain out of sight, still huddled in a ball. Yeah, there's going to be retribution for this. Hopefully, it doesn't involve blood.

Sophia returns to her room. I stand guard with my back turned while Sam finishes up, mostly to make sure the door gets closed when he leaves. Wow. This is the kind of situation Mom and Dad had to deal with for years.

They totally need more than a week's vacation.

# 9

# SCRAMBLING

M onday March fifth starts off like any other Monday in recent memory.

I float out of unconsciousness around the usual time, about twenty minutes to three in the afternoon. A lack of heaviness in my limbs tells me it's a gloomy day. No point rushing anywhere. The Littles aren't home yet and all my schoolwork is caught up. So, I lay here in bed enjoying Hunter's scent.

With Ashley sleeping over—since she's crashing in my room—Hunter and I couldn't do much more than cuddle. I wasn't expecting Ash to handle my appearance during sleep as well as she did. It's not something I like to think about since it's way too much of a reminder of how dead my body really is. Though I'm nowhere near as ghoulish as a Shadow when I'm sleeping, my body basically turns into a freakin' mummy. Grey skin, kinda sunken features, like if a hiker way up in the mountains dropped dead and froze within minutes. It could be far worse, but no one looking at me would have any doubt they found a corpse.

Mom totally can't handle it. She won't go anywhere near my room during the day. In fact, she only goes to the basement long enough to drop off laundry baskets.

Alas, Hunter had to leave Sunday before I woke up. Ashley did, too, for her job at the vet hospital, but she tag-teamed her mother into stopping by to watch the Littles until I woke up. Mrs. Carter knows what I am and is surprisingly okay with it. We haven't told Michelle's parents. They couldn't handle it. Still not sure if they'd have a worse reaction to discovering I'm a vampire or finding out Ashley is bisexual. Either scenario would likely result in them trying to ban Michelle from seeing us—like she's still fourteen and can't be friends with people her parents choose not to like.

Is it technically lying not to tell people like them the truth about one's identity?

I dunno. It's not as if her parents are outspoken against any groups. They're highly religious and in the privacy of their home, have commented to Michelle they believe gay people are ungodly. They'd never go out and protest or even say anything unkind to someone's face. We're all assuming their religiosity guarantees they'll hate Ashley. Maybe they wouldn't. Could be they'd merely try to talk her into being 'normal,' as if someone's sexual orientation has anything to do with wants. It's also possible they'll say nothing at all beyond quietly grumbling about 'the state of the world' to each other when no one's around to hear them.

Ash doesn't want to risk it, though.

At least in my case, I *am* a supernatural monster. There's way more going on with me than love taking a path some people say it shouldn't be on. Vampires really can be dangerous, evil monsters. The worst thing Ashley would ever do to anyone is make a snarky comment about the tackiness of their curtains. So yeah, I wouldn't take it personally if they freaked out about me being a vampire.

They won't, because they're never going to know.

Eventually, I get out of bed and grab a quick shower in the basement bathroom. With Mom not here to collect dirty laundry, it's on me to make the rounds. Might as well keep up the routine. The Littles return from school, along with Megan and Nicole while I'm in the midst of emptying out the hampers. Sam must've noticed me collecting clothes and has his laundry waiting for me in a basket by the time I come back upstairs from carrying Sierra's basket to the basement. He's engrossed in homework at his desk while Blix is on the PlayStation.

Swear the little demon is totally addicted to video games.

"Thanks." I grab the basket.

Sam gives me a thumbs up without looking away from his work. "Welcome."

Maybe an hour later, I'm emptying the first completed load from the dryer when Sam yells, "Hey, Sierra, Soph summoned brownies in the kitchen!"

Ugh. Seriously? You'd think the girl had quite enough of those little monsters after being held hostage by them. Grumbling, I hurry toward the stairs, prepared to yell at her for reckless use of magic—only to find Sam's being a dork. The scent of brownies—as in baked treats—fills the stairwell at the top even before I open the door. Whew.

Sierra, Sam, Megan, and Nicole gather in a group by the counter, ogling a baking tray.

Sophia stands between them and the treats, waving in a shooing motion. "We gotta wait a bit. They need to cool off before we can eat them."

I lean on the doorjamb, surveying the damage. The kitchen isn't *too* messy, but a ten-year-old can only be *so* careful. Her birthday's in like two weeks, so maybe she's closer to eleven now, but still. Should I be freaking out over her baking brownies totally on her own without Mom or me in the room, or should I be impressed she appears to have done it properly without burning the house to the ground? How old does a kid have to be before they shouldn't have to ask permission to use the stove?

Somehow, my parents managed to produce three kids who are more responsible than their ages would imply. Any one of them would probably act in a reasonable manner, except Sophia's easy to rattle and gets scared at the drop of a hat. If the stove caught fire, she'd want to do the right thing but panic too much. Sierra has a bit of a short fuse. She'd probably get angry at a stove fire for existing and attack it herself. Sam would calmly Google the best way to put out a grease fire while it burned in front of him.

I'm a mix of all three, only I wouldn't need to use Google. Grease fires and me have prior experience. Tried to make breakfast in bed for the parents when I was ten. Bacon happened. Too much in a pan at once. Hey, everyone likes bacon.

Oh hell. As long as she cleans up the mess, I won't freak out.

"Don't forget Sophia's gotta go to the dentist tomorrow," says Sierra. "Maybe she shouldn't be eating brownies now."

Sophia whines at her, annoyed at the reminder. Yeah, she's afraid of the dentist. Sierra's not a big fan of having her teeth cleaned, either, but she's more embarrassed at seeming weak than afraid... so tolerates it.

"It's tomorrow. Doesn't matter. I'll brush my teeth tonight." Sophia waves her hand back and forth over the brownies, then carefully cuts one out, defiantly chomping it at Sierra.

As soon as the kids start scrambling for control of the knife, I zoom over and confiscate the deadly implement. "Back off. Don't be idiots around a knife."

They quiet down.

I cut mega-brownie into normal-sized squares and toss the knife into the sink. Might as well have one since I'm here. It's so nice not to be worried about calories. Know what? I don't care about calories. Why not go all out? A little bit of cold vanilla ice cream is the perfect complement to a still-hot brownie.

A LITTLE BEFORE FIVE, I DRIVE SAM TO TAEKWONDO CLASS.

While I'm signing him in, the guy behind the counter at the dojo points at his computer screen. "Your membership's going to expire next month. I can process the renewal for you now if you want."

Sam peers up at me. "Can you sign me up for another six months?"

"Umm." Well, I am technically a legal adult. Might as well try. I nod at the dude in the karate uniform. "Sure, he's into it. What do you need in order to renew the sub?"

"Consent, a signature, and a credit card. Wow, you look super young to be his mother." The guy hands me a form.

I laugh. "Because I'm not. Older sister. Yes, I'm over eighteen."

"Really?" He studies me, skepticism in his eyes but not enough to argue. "Cool. Good genes, I guess."

Got the feeling this place isn't particularly concerned about making sure I'm old enough to sign a contract. We're not exactly talking big money on the line. Whatever. I fill the thing out and hand over my authorized-user card for Mom's Visa. The parents won't have any problem with it since they'll renew this as long as Sam is interested in going.

While I'm filling out the paperwork, my phone rings. I'd ignore it except for the cute cartoon music ringtone telling me it's Sophia. Her calling me means only one thing: the house is gone in a fiery cataclysm of runaway magic and exploding kittens. I practically throw the phone at the taekwondo place dude in my haste to get it out of my bag and answer it.

Sam stares at me like I'm nuts.

I swipe to accept the call. "Soph? What's wrong?"

"You're not here."

Ugh. Please tell me she's not having a cling attack now. "Yeah, you know I had to take Sam to karate."

"Taekwondo," says Sam and the dude behind the counter simultaneously.

"You forgot I have dance class." Sophia's voice rises in urgency. "And I still need to get a costume for the recital on Saturday."

"Isn't the dance place providing your costumes?" I ask.

Sophia laughs. "Are you serious? We have to buy all our own stuff."

"Umm. Okay, we can get the costume before Saturday." How expensive can a leotard be? "Plenty of time left."

"What about class tonight? I'm gonna miss it."

"I'm at the taekwondo place with Sam. He's gonna be a while. How the heck does Mom manage this?"

"Dad usually drives Sam to karate."

Grr. Being in two places at once is not part of my vampire power set. "I can't leave him here... what about Ashley?"

Sophia pauses a few seconds. "Are we going to leave Sierra home alone?"

"Grr." I eye the dojo guy, smile, and back off a bit to whisper out of his earshot. "Can Blix mirror you there safely?"

"How should I know?" asks Sophia. "I don't wanna be covered in slime and stuck to the wall like Ronan."

"He wasn't paying attention to his surroundings. Either take the mirror or ask Sierra to go with you if Ashley's able to drive you there."

Sophia exhales hard. "Okay."

"Call me if anything weird happens."

"Umm, going into a mirror doesn't count as weird anymore?"

I chuckle. "It does, but you know what I mean. If you mirror there, call me so I can pick you up after Sam's class."

"Okay."

We hang up.

I stare at the phone, wondering what genius decided to schedule everything. Monday, Wednesday, and Friday, both Sophia and Sam have their respective activities, pretty much at the same time. Unless Blix helps Sophia mirror there, she *will* be late. At least Sierra's sword lessons are a Tuesday / Thursday affair. No surprise she's the youngest person in the class, the only non-adult.

After finishing the signup for Sam's six-month renewal, I take a seat among the parents watching the kids go through the motions of taekwondo class. The place is pretty low key. Seems like their focus is more on giving the kids a workout than making hand-to-hand combat a second nature instinct. As Sam once said, it's 'yoga with more screaming.'

Lots of screaming.

Thankfully, I can't get headaches anymore.

# 10

# FEAR MANAGEMENT

I picked Sophia up from the dance studio on the way home from the taekwondo place, dropped them at the house, then rushed to Seattle for class. Ashley is my angel. She took care of dinner. By the time I got home from school, any place selling the kind of leotard Sophia needs for the recital already closed. Online is an option, but not a great one. No guarantee it'll get here on time, and what if it doesn't fit?

Reading for English Lit ate a few hours, but I waited until after the Littles went to sleep. Since Ash cooked, I cleaned up. She totally adores helping me out since it feels like a practice run for the day she has kids of her own. It's not fully accurate though. My siblings are all well into the fun ages. Dealing with infants and toddlers is way more work. And considering how exhausting it is keeping up with three tweens, ugh. I can't imagine having three toddlers in the house at the same time. Sure, I lived here when my siblings were all super little, but it wasn't my job to take care of them. I was only eight when the 'rents summoned Sierra.

Anyway…

Tuesday is on me before I'm ready for it.

As soon as the Littles get home from school, I metaphorically abduct Sophia and whisk her off to the dentist's office. Mom would've picked her straight up from school, but doing so requires being awake earlier than I can be.

Also, Tuesday sucks majorly.

Nothing against the second day of the week in general, merely *this* Tuesday. The sun's being a bitch. It's almost enough to make me reschedule the appointment as I'm not fond of driving while it feels like I've applied habanero eye drops. Jeans, a hoodie, and sunglasses mitigate the oven factor to a point. Still, it hurts only somewhat less than being microwaved but not quite as much as watching someone take Dr. Phil seriously.

"You want me to drive?" asks Sophia.

"I can't tell if you're serious or joking." I shut the door and fumble the key into the ignition.

"I'd rather get in trouble for driving too young than have you crash us because you can barely see."

"The cops pull *me* over for looking too young. We'd never make it with you behind the wheel. Besides, I've seen you play Mario Kart. You'll drive straight through the front door of Starbucks."

She sticks out her tongue.

"Are you honestly worried or making excuses to avoid the dentist."

"Yes."

I chuckle, then spend a moment evaluating my ability to see. It hurts, but if I drive like a little old lady we should be okay. The dentist's office isn't too far. No need for major highways. She whines as I back out of the driveway.

Sophia gasps. "Dude! You're on fire."

"Shit." I slam on the brakes. "Seriously?"

"Yeah, there's smoke. I don't see actual flame though."

"Damn."

"I appreciate your willingness to put yourself at risk to take care of me, but my teeth can wait."

"Nice try."

She snaps her fingers.

Like a high school kid behind the wheel for the first time, I baby the Sentra through the streets of Cottage Lake on the way to the dentist's office. It must absolutely suck to be a vampire in a place where the sun's always strong, like Arizona or California. At least, suck to be an Innocent. Other bloodlines don't really care since they *can't* go outside until dark. Doesn't matter how bright the daytime is when you're invariably unconscious. Seattle has to be the best possible location for me, short of maybe London. It rains a lot there, too.

It takes longer than it should, but we make it on time without causing an accident—though some dude behind me about had an aneurysm because I wouldn't do sixty in a forty zone. Sophia said the truck had New York plates. I couldn't tell—the outside world's a blurry haze to me at the moment.

At least the inside of the dentist's office is dim enough to reduce the ouch factor. I no longer feel like I'm body surfing a hibachi grill. More like I'm standing by the pit of molten metal they used to melt down the terminator. Honestly, whatever aspect of the Universe designed Innocent vampires needs to go back to the drawing board. You'd think if tolerating sunlight was our major power, it wouldn't be so damn painful. Like, hey, here's this neat ability… but if you use it, we're gonna punish you for it.

Hmm. Vampires tend to get more powerful with age. Wonder if it applies to my sun tolerance, too. Maybe in sixty years, I'll be able to walk around on a bright day and have no problems. Fingers crossed.

We approach the receptionist.

"Hi. Sophia Wright here for a checkup." I gesture at her.

The woman nods, gives me a weird look. "Do you smoke?"

Sophia stares up at me, making an 'ack! She knows!' face.

I shake my head. "Only when I go out in the sun."

She laughs. "You don't look like one of those goth kids."

Heh. "Nah. Just joking." I wince internally, forcing a smile.

Maybe it's dumb of me to crack jokes about being a vampire or allergic to sunlight. On the other hand, people who deny things too fervently are usually guilty. Might be better to make vampire jokes. Dalton floated the idea—his guess, not actual knowing—real vampires are responsible for the surge in Hollywood vampires. The more people think of us as fictional creatures, the less likely they are to take our existence seriously.

After checking her in, we move to the waiting area and sit. At least, I sit. Sophia keeps standing.

"Sit down. We'll be a few minutes."

She tugs on my arm. "Sare… make me not be scared."

"There's no reason to be afraid."

"Duh. Irrational fear isn't rational. You can't talk me down. Please?" She bounces on her toes.

Sigh.

"Okay." I go with her to a small bathroom adjacent to the waiting room. A sign on the door says 'patient use only.' Guess Sam couldn't use this toilet. He always rush-poops.

We're in luck. The tiny bathroom has no window. As soon as I close the door, I'm online. The abrupt shift to wonderful cool air is enough to paralyze me in relief. Oddly, as soon as my powers activate, I sense malevolence in the air. Though the sun is a hell of a distraction today, I didn't pick up any such feeling while offline. The dentist's office seemed pleasant and welcoming—as much as a dentist's office can be. Now, though, all the little hairs stand up on the back of my neck.

Whoa. I gaze around at the walls. "You've always been scared in here, huh. This office in general, not the bathroom."

"Yeah." She nods, her whispery voice echoing. "Ever since I was little."

I continue studying the walls—and mirror—but nothing stands out as unusual. "Something is definitely out of whack here."

"Seriously."

"Heh. No, I mean… I feel something here. Paranormal badness."

Sophia hugs herself. "Really?"

"Yeah. I think maybe you've been sensitive to it for a long time. Do you see any ghosts?"

"No. C'mon, hurry up. People are going to think we're doing something weird being in the bathroom together. Especially in the dark."

"Are you sure you want me to poke you in the brain?"

Sophia nods. "Yeah. Don't like mind-control me. Just help me not be afraid of the dentist. It takes longer when they have to hold me down."

"Hold you down?" I blink. "Seriously?"

"Usually, it's Mom or Dad, but yeah… as soon as they start scraping my teeth, I try to get away."

"Umm. Wow. I didn't know that."

She blushes, looking down. "I hate being a scaredy cat."

I stare into her eyes, opening a mental door to her thoughts. Wow, yeah, she's inches from panic-running out the door. "You're not. Something is here and it feels kinda pissed."

"Did you do it yet? I still feel scared."

"Not yet. You know I don't like messing with you guys."

"I'm *asking* you to." Sophia tugs on my arm. "It's like giving me a shot for pain, only in the head."

Fine, whatever. I implant a mild compulsion not to be afraid of the dentist simply for being the dentist. Her posture relaxes. And yeah, while in there, I notice her subconscious sense of an otherworldly presence here. As far back as she can remember, the dentist's office has scared her in the same way most people are afraid to go into the boiler room of an abandoned mental hospital. Yes, she's already on edge about the dental cleaning. The supernatural stuff makes it ten times worse. She's come to associate the paranormal dread with the dentist—not fair to him at all. Crap. My sister's been picking on paranormal stuff her whole life but never realized it.

"Cool. Thanks."

"Keep your eyes open. There's something here."

We leave the bathroom, pretending we'd been dealing with a stray lash in her eye. As soon as the door opens, I once again feel like I'm standing in an oven and the weird creepiness disappears. Neither the receptionists or the two older women in the waiting area pay any attention to us. Sophia's fidgety but more bored than nervous.

Maybe twelve minutes later, a hygienist calls Sophia in. She insists on me going with her. The office staff appears to expect this since

Mom usually does so. The few times I remember coming with them when Sophia had an appointment, they let me stay in the waiting room.

I take a seat in the extra chair by the wall as Sophia hops in the main dentist chair. She and the hygienist make small talk as the exam-slash-cleaning starts.

"You're doing well today. Braver than usual." The hygienist, Carol, pats her on the hand before looking at me. "Usually, she needs to hold Mom's hand the whole time."

"Our mother's in Iceland on vacation. I'm filling in."

Carol nods. "That's nice. I hear it's quite beautiful there."

"So they say." I shrug. "The parents liked the idea."

"Sarah is it?"

"Yep."

Carol resumes working on Sophia's teeth. "Been a while since we've seen you."

Poor Sophia clutches the armrests of the chair, squirming. For once, I'm glad to be offline. The scratch of the metal pick on her teeth is a bad enough sound *without* vampire-boosted hearing. Practically feels like the woman is scraping it down my spine.

"Yeah, I've been super busy lately."

Carol 'pffs.' "Aren't we all? The whole world's running on eleven. Well, if you can find the time, you really ought to make an appointment. Gotta keep your teeth healthy."

Sophia balls her hands into fists for a second, then slaps the armrests back and forth. Ooh, she *really* wants the scraping to stop. Poor kid. Maybe I should've given her a prod to pass out in the chair. Nah, Carol would've freaked and called an ambulance.

Screw it. I move closer and take Sophia's hand. She squeezes hard, giving me a 'please help' stare.

Carol keeps working. "Your teeth look nice and healthy, but I can tell you're not flossing like you should. This scraping part you dislike so much wouldn't take nearly as long if you flossed."

The expression on Sophia's face has a lot to say about Carol and the horse she rode in on.

I'm not sure it would be wise to come in for a dental exam, even if it keeps up the illusion of normality. What would an x-ray show? Normal people do not have retractable fangs. Yeah, bad idea going anywhere near diagnostic equipment. Vampires don't get cavities. Even if we feed on pastry chefs.

Sophia gives up trying to talk while she's got the vacuum hanging out of her mouth, but she seems much less squirmy for the polishing than the scraping. All of a sudden, her eyes go huge, focused on the corner of the room in front of her on the left. At first, I don't notice anything, but a few seconds later, a transparent figure coalesces into being under the wall-mounted TV. His clothes look kinda old, but not ancient. If I had to guess, I'd say he died in the late Seventies. Sophia continues staring at him as Carol buzzes the electric tooth polisher around her mouth.

The ghost doesn't say or do anything more than glare at us. He reminds me of a younger Mr. Niedermeyer. Not from looks, but his body language and attitude. Like he hates people and is only barely managing to hold himself back from physically throwing us out the window. Carol totally ignores him. I glare right back at him, not the least bit worried about what a ghost might do to me. He's no scarier than a high school English teacher. Kinda looks like one, to be honest. Or maybe history.

Since I'm not intimidated and Carol ignores him—bet she's used to the weird energy here or simply unaware of it—the ghost focuses primarily on Sophia. Japanese hibachi restaurants almost always have this fake soy sauce squeeze bottle loaded with black yarn. It's meant to trick people into thinking the chef is squirting them with soy sauce. They'll *always* go for the youngest child at the table who isn't *too* small, or the youngest-looking woman. Chefs tend to single out the person they think has the highest chance of jumping. For example, they always target Sophia and ignore Sam even though he's a year younger. They used to go after me until Sierra turned about six.

Point being, the ghost probably thinks Sophia is a prime target for scaring. Normally, he'd be totally right. The girl has screamed at a winter coat hanging out of her closet she forgot about. It does *not* take much to give Sophia nightmares. *The Gate* kept her up for two weeks, and most people think of it as super campy and not the least bit scary.

"Okay, go on and rinse," says Carol. "I'll go get the doctor to have a look at your teeth. You should be out of here pretty soon." She pats my sister on the shoulder before leaving the room. "I'm really proud of you today, Sophia. You were incredibly brave."

"Thanks." Sophia glances at me. "Had some help."

Carol wags her eyebrows at me. "You should come with her every time."

"Not a bad idea." I smile.

As soon as Carol leaves the room, Sophia sits up, glaring at the corner. "Why are you scaring people? Yes, I can see you."

"He probably thinks you didn't finish your homework," I mutter.

The ghost gives me a dirty look.

"What?" Sophia glances sideways at me while sipping water.

"He looks like a teacher. Gotta be the sweater vest."

She rinses her mouth out, spitting in the drain beside the chair. "A ghost... no wonder I've always been afraid in here. What's wrong with you?"

"They tore down my house and put up this damn office." The ghost glares.

Sophia shakes her head. "I'm sorry... but it's not a good reason to mess with people. The dentist is scary enough already. Scaring people here isn't going to make them put your house back up."

"I know," snaps the ghost. "I'm trying to shut this place down."

"You're haunting this office with mild anxiety, like looking at a Rubik's cube where one square on each side is out of place." I fold my arms. "Scaring Sophia and being pleased with yourself is like a grown man feeling accomplished for beating her at a weightlifting competition."

"Hey!" Sophia glares at me, struggling not to smile.

"Go away and don't come back." The ghost leans at her.

"No." She points at him. "You need to stop trying to scare people. Don't make me cast a banishing spell and kick you out of the building. Be nice."

Grumbling, the ghost walks into the wall.

"Oh, yay. That's not gonna bite us in the ass." I gaze at the ceiling.

"Relax." Sophia leans back in the chair. "He's not powerful at all… and he's stuck here."

The door swings open, admitting the dentist. I don't recognize the guy, Dr. Ross according to his shirt. Must be new here. He looks at Sophia, then me, then Sophia.

"Older sister," I say.

"Aha." He offers a handshake. "Nice to meet you."

"Same."

He faces Sophia. "How are you feeling today, miss? Anything bothering you?"

"The scraping."

Dr. Ross chuckles. "No one likes it. Okay, let's have a look."

Yeah, seriously. I think the average person would choose to be bitten by a vampire rather than go to the dentist.

Hey, works for me.

# 11

# THE PERKS OF UNDEATH

Had to rush home from the dentist so I could drive Sierra into Seattle for her sword-fighting class.

It's mostly similar to Sam's taekwondo lessons other than there being only six students—all adults—two instructors, and about eighty percent sparring to twenty percent technique instruction. Sam's class rarely spars each other. They tend to do forms or hit those reusable breakaway boards. Granted, these guys aren't trying to knock each other's heads off. They use rattan training swords and pads, attempting to make contact rather than 'do damage.' It's basically the 'touch football' version of sword fighting.

Obviously, with Sierra being eleven, her sparring partner is going easier on her than they would against another adult. Considering she's only been doing this for a few weeks now, it's kinda surprising to see her keeping up with them. The rattan sword is a little big for her, so she's using both hands on it.

Dalton shared some of his experience using blades over our mind link, giving me something of a basic competence. Well, basic according to Dalton who's 162 years old. He's been getting into knife or sword fights since age twelve. Not so much lately. The modern world doesn't offer many opportunities to do so. Anyway, if he thinks I'm 'decent' at it, I must be.

However, he's never fought with an enormous sword requiring the use of two hands. Watching Sierra swing her practice sword around makes me itch. I can see her trying to use techniques intended for fast one-handed weapons and they're not quite working out as well. She is, however, scoring more points than the woman they paired her up with—the only other female student, a late-twenties dye-redhead. Or an alien. If her shade of magenta is natural color, I'm the reincarnation of Winston Churchill's groundskeeper.

Both the woman—I think her name is Danae—and the head instructor, Gene, seem surprised at Sierra's score. It's kinda fun watching the woman shift from 'going easy on the kid' to really trying to beat her. I don't mean 'beat' her as in physically wallop her, merely score more points.

By the time the sparring period is over, Sierra's up by two points but neither one of them hit the ten necessary to 'win' and stop their match. Meanwhile, the two pairs of men plus one male student sparring with an instructor have finished multiple ten-point rounds. My sister's thrilled with herself, grinning broadly as she shakes Danae's hand.

"Gah, she's so frustrating." Danae fake growls. "Shortness is an unfair advantage."

Sierra laughs.

A tallish bearded guy gestures at me. "Don't feel bad. The other kid over there'd probably beat ya without any lessons."

Danae glances at me, then him, and gives him the finger. "Oh yeah, Jim. How about we have a rematch?"

"Whenever ya want, dearie," says the guy in a fake Irish accent.

"My sister could probably beat *him*," says Sierra.

I laugh in a 'yeah right' way.

Jim frowns at Sierra. "You're a little young to be talking smack."

"I'm not 'talking smack.' Just saying." Sierra grabs her water bottle and chugs half of it.

At this point, Jim notices everyone else in the room is looking at him. He points at me. "Hundred bucks if you score even one point."

Ugh. Sierra. Really? Getting me into situations like this is the exact opposite of being low key. During the day as a 'normal' person, I don't expect I'd mop the floor with him—or even get ten points before him. However, I for damn sure would score at least one point. Probably within three seconds since he'll be expecting me to be clueless. Dalton didn't give me sword techniques designed to look good on camera by knocking blades together for ten minutes while going around in circles. His style is all about managing large groups of attackers by killing them as fast and neatly as possible.

I wave him off. "Nah. Wouldn't be fair."

Jim grins, shaking his head at me in a 'yeah, thought so' manner. Whatever. I don't have anything to prove here.

Rick interrupts, setting the class up for drills where they repeatedly perform the same attack-defense-counterattack pattern to drill it into muscle memory. It strikes me as basic, which is intellectually confusing but makes sense. Direct brain download of skills—which is basically what Dalton did to me—is *so* bizarre. Much easier than spending years training. Though, I'd be way more effective with practice. Knowing theory and feeling it work are different.

Maybe Sierra and I should spar at home. We could use pool noodles.

"You'd totally have beaten him," says Sierra in the car after the class is over.

"Maybe. Maybe not. You do realize I'm trying to *not* draw attention to myself?" I smile. "How should I have explained why he didn't totally kick my ass?'

Sierra blinks. "Why bother explaining?"

"Because it would seem strange. They don't know me. Some random girl comes in off the street who's never had a single lesson and keeps up with a guy who's been doing it for years?"

"I dunno. Say you were captain of the fencing team in high school."

"Hah. The school doesn't even have one. Only rich schools have fencing teams." I snicker. "Places where everyone wears those snooty jackets with a coat of arms on it."

Sophia's about to say something, but stops to peer out the windows. "Umm, where are you going? This isn't the way home."

"We're stopping to get you some fast food then I'm going to class."

She gives me a 'say what' stare.

"It's not dark enough for me to fly yet. My bio class starts at seven. Sunset is right around then. I'll never make it without being late."

"So, make the teacher forget you walked in five minutes late."

I fidget at the steering wheel. "Dunno. Can't use my abilities to cheat at every little inconvenient thing."

"Making a teacher ignore you being a few minutes late is not inconvenient. Me sitting for three hours bored out of my mind in your biology class is inconvenient. Besides. You don't get out until ten. It's after my bedtime."

I laugh. "Wow, you fail at kid."

"I do not."

"What kid in the history of kids has ever used their bedtime as a positive thing?"

"Kids who don't want to drool on themselves for three hours."

"Okay. Fine. You're right. Sounded better in my head. Not sure they'd let me bring you with me into class anyway."

She grins, triumphant. "Are you still getting fast food?"

"Nah, you can eat at home."

"Poop."

"What's it gonna be? Burgers and sitting in bio class with me or going home and eating whatever Ash put together."

"Home, please."

Thought so. Okay, maybe I can do this 'mom' thing after all. Negotiating with the kids is a mom skill, right?

YANNO, THAT JIM GUY'S 'I THOUGHT SO' SMIRK ANNOYS ME MORE THAN I thought it did.

Maybe I should've sparred with him. Nah. Wouldn't be worth it. Arrogant people *do* annoy me, but there's no reason for me to rub every idiot's face in fail sauce. Besides, technique is fine and all, but I don't know how my offline body would react to sword fighting. Still think I would definitely have scored *one* hit on him, tap really, but bleh.

Turns out I didn't have to mess with Professor Connolly's head. The sun went down far enough to let me fly at 6:57 p.m. It's roughly a seven-minute flight normally from home to Seattle. If I 'rush,' I can shave almost a minute off. Pushing flight harder is a drain on my energy reserves or whatever, similar to using superhuman speed or strength. Not a huge deal. Only makes it necessary for me to feed more than twice a week. Easy enough to grab a bite after class. So yeah, I got there three minutes after seven and blamed traffic. Professor Connolly didn't even mind—and I wasn't the last student to arrive.

So, no big deal.

Bit a security guard in an office building on my way back to Cottage Lake.

It's about quarter after ten when I arrive home. The house is fairly quiet. Ashley's at the kitchen table doing homework. She looks up at me as the patio door slides open.

"Hey. How was class?"

"Okay. Bio. Much more interesting than comp sci or calculus." I chuckle. "Everything good here?"

"Yeah." She flashes an impish grin. "You should probably check your bedroom. I think I heard a little ol' mouse snooping around down there."

"Uh oh." I wag my eyebrows at her, resisting the urge to cheat by looking into her thoughts.

Don't really have to. There isn't much capable of making Ashley *not* talk endlessly. If she's encouraging me to go downstairs, it can only mean Hunter's down there. He's probably hoping for some alone time with me due to a rare moment of having an open schedule.

Awesome!

I hurry down there to find him stretched out on my bed reading a textbook. As I walk in, he closes it, jumps to his feet, and hands me a bundle of realistic fake roses. The cloth petals are quite obvious to vampire eyes. Not a problem, since I'm not superficial. It's all about the gesture.

"You're probably wondering why they're satin." Hunter leans in to kiss me.

"It's not a problem. I actually like these better."

"I know. Killing flowers bothers you. And, these remind me of you."

There are numerous ways to interpret that line, none of which are good.

Hunter flashes a roguish smile. "They will stay beautiful forever and never die."

Aww. Yeah. I… wow. Gonna keep them forever. I peer over the roses at his face, willing this moment to burn into my consciousness. A century from now, when I look at these roses, may it take me right back to now.

"Thank you. I love them."

"Oh. Got you this too." He holds up a box of chocolates. "I know… I know… but got the roses, so I figured might as well go full cliché."

Laughing, I fall into his arms. "It's cute. Things become clichés for a reason, you know."

We make out for a little while, but it doesn't take long for things to escalate. I push him down flat on my bed while straddling him, breaking the kiss only long enough to pull my shirt off. Somewhere in the background of my awareness as we start kissing again, the ping of Facebook messages sound from my computer. Yeah, as if I'm going to stop everything and go see who sent me a stupid meme.

Hunter's hands sliding up my back trigger explosions of mental fireworks all over my body, almost setting off my bomb merely from the caress of his fingertips. It's *so* weird how much more sensitive I am to touch in general as a vampire. Like my entire body is as sensitive as my nether bits used to be, and down below is an instant derp button. As soon as he touches me there, I'm tasting colors, so to speak.

He rolls over on top of me and sheds his shirt before going for the button on my jeans.

No, it's not like I'm a walking sex organ. Intent has everything to do with it. Hunter caressing my arm in a romantic way is totally different from one of the Littles tugging on it or clinging. Honestly, them grabbing me doesn't feel any different from before. I could probably sit bare-butt on a quarter and tell if it's heads or tails up, but ordinary life doesn't drive me crazy with touch overload. Same for idiots. If someone grabs me in the middle of a fight, I don't fall to pieces having an instant orgasm. It's only when I'm in the mood the hypersensitivity goes *there.*

Gotta be a defense mechanism.

You know what *isn't* a defense mechanism? The rippling, paralytic waves of ecstasy shuddering through me from the sensation of Hunter pulling my jeans down over my hips. This is totally not fair— to him. I've 'gotten there' like three times already just from his hands on my arms, legs, and back.

Being a vampire is *wild.*

At the risk of being too bawdy, I am super glad I'm not the kind of girl who makes tons of noise in bed. Admittedly, we are trying extra hard to be as quiet as possible considering the Littles plus Ashley are upstairs. I really don't want to explain to the sibs why 'those noises' came from my room. I suspect Sierra would probably guess their meaning. Sophia would freak out, believing I'm in trouble or pain and come running down here to check on me—yeah, super awkward. Not sure what Sam would think. Probably assume I'm being a dork and trying to talk to whales or something.

Hunter slips out of his jeans and pounces on me.

We roll together, still kissing and pawing at each other. He's noticeably more aggressive—no, not the right word. Confident. Yes. He's way more confident and into it than usual. Like someone replaced my shy, cute boyfriend with some character played by Zac Efron. Oh, eek. I hope this isn't like the thing Aurélie did to Ashley.

I still can't believe my best friend and my vampire patron (matron?) had sex. It's one of those things I try not to think about except always do. After their session, Ash turned into this overamped sex fiend for a few weeks. If I'm totally honest with myself, all Aurélie did was pull down the 'cute and innocent' mask Ash wears. My friend really can be a bit of a kinky freak sometimes, but it embarrasses her, so she hides it from everyone except whoever she happens to be in the bedroom with.

Always the quiet ones, right?

Hunter is totally 'driving' tonight, taking the lead—which is rather unlike him. At first opportunity, I arrange eye contact and check on his thoughts. He thinks I have beautiful eyes. They're brown like the majority of people in this country. Hardly remarkable. But he's staring at them like they're the most precious gems in the world. Aww.

No sign of weird supernatural effects in his head. He's just missed me due to his crazy schedule.

Whew. Okay. Carry on.

Maybe Aurélie affected Ashley the way she did because she fed from her in the middle of it, or perhaps because she's been a vampire for almost four centuries, not to mention an Old Guard heavily steeped in charm powers.

Me? I'm Innocent.

Notice the capital i. What Hunter and I are doing right now? Yeah, I'm not so innocent.

MY EVERYTHING TINGLES.

Hunter and I lay in my bed, somewhat sweaty, still naked, staring up at the ceiling. Well, I'm staring at the ceiling. He's staring at me. Swear, a housefly could land on my nipple right now and I'd go off again. Last time we had sex, my senses weren't this over-tuned. Guess he's not the only one who needed it bad.

In between feeling lucky to have found him and mildly guilty for taking him away from a live girl, my nerd brain decides to go off on a tangent contemplating why, exactly, a vampire would have any desire for sex at all. Everything I've learned so far indicates we are incapable of reproducing. Biology drives animals to mate to ensure survival of the species. No such thing applies to vampires. Then again, our mere existence relies on magic, which isn't well understood by science. Sex drive must be a ghost from our human side. It's so deeply embedded in the human psyche it would be almost impossible to delete. I mean, sure, some people are asexual. I'm sure turning them into vampires wouldn't change it. If Ash became a vampire—bite my tongue—she'd still be into both women and men. Going vamp didn't make me start liking girls. No, nothing about it changes us, but it is weird we still have any carnal drive.

Perhaps it *is* an evolutionary thing. An argument could be made about intimate contact being a perfect opportunity for feeding, but it's also not difficult to mind fog a random stranger on the street. Even a child turned vampire would have no problem overpowering adults or mentally influencing them so they can feed.

"What's on your mind?" asks Hunter.

"All sorts of stuff. My head is still spinning. Kinda wondering why vampires still want to make love, but I think it's one of those questions no one will ever be able to answer. Tonight was *amazing*. You literally shut my brain off it was that good."

He chuckles. "*You* were amazing. I couldn't stop thinking about you. Sorry I've been so busy."

"It's life." I smile. "If not having the chance to be alone together for a month ends with a night like this, it's worth it."

Hunter threads an arm around me, pulling me into a cuddle. "Gonna try not to let it be a month until next time."

"Good plan." I rest my head on his shoulder.

Honestly, it escapes me when I'd last felt so happy and content as in this moment here and now. Junior and senior years of high school, anxiety over the future dogged me as well as the constant pressure to keep my grades up, what college to go to, what career to work toward, and so on. Add in the disastrous relationship with Scott and, yeah… it's been a long time since I felt true peace. Having a boyfriend should be all about wanting to be with them, not constantly hoping they'd be too busy and forget to call you. Yeah. So many red flags I ignored.

Sure, there's still a chance vampire BS will give me grief, but it would mostly be reactionary. I'll stay out of everyone else's way and hope they ignore me as the triviality most of them consider me to be.

For now, I have a Hunter to cuddle with, and the world outside my room doesn't matter.

Two days into the parents being away and things are going well. Yeah, I think I can pull off managing the house until they get back, even if the idea of being responsible for the Littles is scarier than Petra.

At least, with her, I know exactly what form the crazy will take.

# BECOMING OFFICIAL

L eave it to me feeling secure to dare the Universe into throwing a curveball my way.

Wednesday comes with the expected scramble to get Sam to taekwondo and Sophia to dance class. It's also raining like hell, which makes going outside nice and easy on me, except for the water. I decide to chance it and trust Sierra to stay home alone for an hour. Ashley takes Sam to his dojo while I drive Sophia to the dance studio. She insisted *I* take her because she wants me to peek at the head of this other girl, Veronica, who she says has been giving her weird looks and stares at her all the time.

Sophia's too innocent to suspect the girl might have a crush on her, and wonders what about her is 'wrong.' Being stared at makes her feel as though she's got a giant booger hanging out of her nose she hasn't noticed.

Easy enough to settle my sister's anxiety. Mission accepted.

I pull up by the curb in front of the shopping center to spare Sophia a longish walk through the rain. She darts inside while I park. Considering the weather, it's dark enough outside already at five for me to be online. Wow. Serious storm. Fortunately, no thunder.

If not for having to be around people, I would've worn a bathing suit. If I'm going to get soaked, might as well dress for it, right? Alas, I do the umbrella thing and resign myself to sitting in the waiting area in damp jeans and a T-shirt for the hour-long class.

The cougars are back, still talking about some theoretical pool guy they fancy. No, I haven't been tempted to eavesdrop on their thoughts to see if the man is real or not. Don't care. They're much cuter to listen to when I imagine they're having fantasies.

Speaking of eavesdropping on thoughts... I look for Veronica. She's easy to spot, being only one of three black kids in the dance studio. The girl's pretty, like she could legit do photo shoots for clothing catalogs or end up in TV commercials. And yeah, she does seem to be staring at Sophia whenever she can.

Interesting.

I peek at her thoughts. She's mildly jealous of Sophia being so thin. Oh, damn. Almost another Alexis situation, except it's not Veronica's parents overachieving. The kid's doing it to herself. I think the poor girl is in danger of becoming anorexic. She's obsessed with her weight. Sure she's thicker than Sophia, but so is everyone considered normal. My sister—well our family in general—are twigs. Again, thanks, Dad.

Grr. I spend the bulk of the dance class period watching the girls go through their routines while grumbling in my head about the pressure put on us—girls that is—by society to be thin, pretty, and perfect. At least the instructors and other kids here are awesome. Megan is a big girl, little bit chubby even. Other than the unavoidable situation where Sophia was physically unable to hold the girl up over her head—physics doesn't care about feelings—no one here pays any attention to Megan's size.

Well, this one stuck up girl named Lindsey did, but I sorted her out.

Speaking of sorting out... I decide to give society a middle finger and completely ignore ethics. When the class ends, I wander into the group of kids, ostensibly heading toward my sister, but veer into Veronica's path. As soon as she makes eye contact with me—an involuntary reaction to nearly colliding—I dive into her head.

A simple compulsion to be satisfied with her body as it is should be enough.

Her distorted opinion of herself as being fat—absolutely untrue—already resulted in her having a mild eating disorder. No doubt it would've worsened as she hit her teen years. Hopefully, this mental zap is enough of a Band-Aid to get her through it. Hmm. Just in case, I add another compulsion to remove her inhibition about talking to her mother. If she starts feeling insecure about her body again, she's going to confide in her mother about it.

There. Fingers crossed.

"Sorry..." I step around her, trying to make our almost-collision look like a navigation error on my part, and collect Sophia.

Veronica stands in place, gazing into the fifth dimension.

Sophia's eyes ask me what the deal is with her, but I don't say anything until we're outside in the privacy of my car.

"Nothing's wrong with you or your outfit. Veronica was jealous."

"What?" Sophia blinks. "Jealous of me? Are you kidding? She's *so* pretty. Like a model."

"You are, too."

"Am not. I'm a stick figure. Models have more shape than a drinking straw." She laughs. "I should be jealous of her, but I'm not."

I grin. "Pretty sure she'll be okay now."

"Cool. What did you do?"

My explanation turns into a brief conversation on body image. Sophia's been teased occasionally for being 'too thin,' but doesn't let it bother her. My timid little sister admits to having gotten into some arguments at school recently when the popular girls decided to pick on Megan for being thick. Soph's turning into quite the 'mouse who roared.' Heh. Guess we both are.

Time to surrender my 'Miss Non-confrontational' crown.

It's amazing what being immortal does for confidence.

I SCRAMBLED TO GET SOPHIA BACK AND FORTH TO DANCE CLASS AND PUT some food on the table for the Littles before I had to rush out the door for school. Wednesday is comp sci and calculus, so one of my early nights. First class is at 6:00 p.m.

Cheating happened in two ways: I ordered pizza for dinner, leaving Ashley to manage distribution to the kids when it arrived… and I did the bikini-in-the-rain flying thing to make it to school. Being drenched is irritating, but the ability to fly to class in like eight minutes versus a thirty-five-minute drive is totally worth it.

Still, I had to dry off and change in the parking garage so I ended up being a few minutes late. Professor Garcia didn't seem to mind too much. Then again, college isn't like high school. No one's going to get in trouble for skipping class, merely waste money and fail.

So, anyway, back to the curveball.

Aurélie called me at 9:45 p.m., a few minutes after I left calculus, to inform me I needed to attend an event tonight. Ugh. Vampires and their soirees. Two things I can't say no to are another season of *Firefly* and anything Aurélie asks me to do. Alas, I think even vampiric mind-control isn't powerful enough to make the first one happen. I'd have to attack network executives, and mind-control only works on creatures with brains.

Okay, no big deal. The soiree isn't starting until midnight, well after the Littles are in bed.

I fly home, not bothering to change out of my bathing suit since I'm going back out soon. A long T-shirt over it is good enough for the hour or so I plan to be in the house. Few things in life are as unpleasant as putting a cold, still-wet bathing suit back on. Much better to stay wearing it. Yeah, it's still raining hard. According to the weather app on my phone, it's not going to stop until like two in the morning.

Except for Blix playing video games with my brother in his room, the house is shockingly mundane tonight. Sophia's reading on her Kindle and Sierra's doing her usual Vulcan mind meld to the PlayStation in the living room. Only the existence of an imp in the house gives away my family is no longer normal.

I'm in the middle of explaining to Ashley—who is curled up on the couch reading something for school—about my need to go to a vampire thing tonight when Sam comes running downstairs in a panic.

"Sare!" He zooms up to me, bouncing on his toes, eyes wide in near panic. "I'm outta food for Edgar and Allen."

"Huh?" I blink at him.

"My frogs."

"I know. I processed what you said. The 'huh' was reflexive." I rake a hand up through my hair. "It's almost ten at night. There isn't anywhere we can get dried crickets at this hour. Can they wait for tomorrow?"

He bounces harder. "Not really. They're starving."

I'm sure he means 'starving' in the way a kid who hasn't eaten anything since lunch time is starving ten minutes before dinner time. Not literally starving. Still, he's really upset so maybe the poor guys *will* be hurt if they don't eat. Ugh. What do I know about frog care?

"Umm. I understand, but the stores are closed. Are you asking me to break into a pet store and steal bugs?"

Sam stops fidgeting. "Oh. Good idea." He runs back upstairs. "Soph, I need your cat!"

I face-palm. "Did I just initiate the commission of a crime?"

Ashley cracks up. "Felonious cricket acquisition by means of a kitten with a loose relationship with physical space?"

"Something like that." Nothing to do but laugh. "Can you imagine the police report? Teleporting kitten steals $2.00 worth of freeze-dried bugs."

She giggle-snorts.

It occurs to me Sierra's playing a fantasy type game instead of *Call of Duty*. Either Ashley spoke to her about screaming curses at the screen, or Sierra wanted a change of pace. I still don't understand how she can play the same game so damn much and not get sick of it. One good thing about this one at least. When she's doing a single-player game, she stays much calmer. She only gets screaming-pissed at other human players. She's more Zen than me there. Sierra understands the computer is only doing what it's been programmed to do when it 'cheats.' Unlike an AI, other human players take satisfaction when they kill her character. Their mockery is what sets her off, not the character blowing up.

Anyway…

I make the bedtime rounds, taking care to ensure Sophia and Sam appreciate using Klepto to acquire needed items should be reserved for emergencies where everything is closed and a frog will die or get sick if we don't act right away. I don't see either of them resorting to thievery as a matter of routine, but still, I feel the need to play mom even if I am a co-conspirator and have no plans to tell Mom about this.

Considering Klepto's thievery came in *way* handy for dealing with the vampire hunter problem I had a few months ago, it would be completely hypocritical of me to complain too much about the Littles asking the kitten to help them out when needed. I don't want them thinking it's okay to send her out to fetch a new video game or whatever on a whim. It doesn't escape me I've been using paranormal means to take what I need from random people (blood) against their will for months, but basic survival is different. Okay, maybe tweaking people's heads to improve their lives or 'helping' Hunter's mother get a better job isn't exactly ethical.

Whatever. My life is morally complicated.

It's not wrong of me to demand my siblings at least turn eighteen before they take advantage of people via paranormal means. The Kitten of Acquisition is a valuable friend and she shouldn't be used willy-nilly.

Once the frog food crisis and bedtime are dealt with, I resume filling Ashley in on the need for me to attend a social meeting with Aurélie. Ash gets a little weird whenever I mention her, no doubt thinking back fondly on the memory of the best time she's ever had—or will likely ever have—in a bedroom. Ack. I can't even maintain eye contact. It's as cringey as thinking about close family getting intimate with someone.

"All right," says Ashley. "Have fun. Hey, is it okay if my mom joins us for dinner tomorrow? She's kinda lonely in the house all by herself."

"Of course. You know you didn't really even have to ask."

"Cool."

I wave and head to the kitchen, draping my long T-shirt over the back of a chair before stepping outside into the downpour. No point bringing any clothes beside the swimsuit. Aurélie always insists on me getting dressed up in one of her super elaborate gowns to the point I even wear period-accurate underwear. Considering how hard it's raining tonight, I'd be less wet if I swam to Seattle.

Sigh. Might as well get the ice bath over with. It's only freezing for a minute or two.

LUCKILY, THE BUILDING AURÉLIE LIVES IN HAS A PARKING GARAGE, AS does the hotel the local vampires use for these meetings. As far as I've been able to tell so far, they don't follow any set schedule. Three months has been the longest gap between them, two weeks the shortest. Guess it depends on factors outside my visibility.

Again, don't really care.

I'm happy to go with Aurélie when she asks me to, but at least for the time being, I wouldn't complain about skipping these parties. Maybe when the Littles are all grown up and fully established out on their own and our parents are gone, I'll want to more fully immerse myself in the vampire world. Sitting alone at home *will* drive me nuts. However, for now, I deal with the 'underworld' so to speak only when necessary.

As expected, I end up wearing a puffy peach-colored gown with all the underpinnings. I'm halfway between a Victorian courtier and one of those paper dolls some old people put in the middle of their table during fancy dinners. Pretty sure Aurélie's wardrobe room could fully supply a theater company performing any play set in the 1700s... at least the women's clothing.

We take her limo to the hotel, arriving at the soiree a few minutes past midnight. 'Fashionably late,' as she says. It's embarrassing to feel like the kid hanging on Aurélie's sleeve or being the demure little woman not making eye contact with anyone… but I'll deal with it instead of setting off an argument.

Some of the elders really don't like my decision to try living in two worlds at once. Without Aurélie's protection, it's almost guaranteed I would've been forced to abandon my family or watch them be killed to keep secrets. At least, it's the impression I get from Stefano Bianchi and Paolo Cabrini, the two elders who have the biggest problem with me. Her protection isn't completely foolproof, either. A big enough screw up on my part could force her to leave me to suffer the consequences of my dumbassery.

A 'big enough' screw up would involve me exposing the existence of vampires—which I'm trying hard not to do—or attempting to destroy other vampires, deliberately mess with their affairs, and so on. Obviously, humanity—to some extent—is aware of the truth, or the PIBs (persons in black) wouldn't exist. They came calling the day I returned home from the morgue to inform me they knew what I was and they'd be keeping an eye on me.

So the CIA (guessing) is aware of vampires. No surprise there, really. Dick Clark and Keanu kinda gave us away. Heh, just kidding. No idea if either of them are vampires… but you gotta admit they're kinda ageless. Makes me go 'hmm' at those photos from the 1800s where someone looks exactly like a modern celebrity. Used to think it coincidence. Now, I'm not so sure.

But yeah, I don't mind being Aurélie's companion for the night. Our relationship is so strange it doesn't really fit into a neat category. I'm somewhere between her proxy daughter, apprentice, cousin, some poor girl she took under her wing, and whatever they called those girls from lower-class backgrounds who essentially got hired to be companions or friends to wealthy women. One minute we have a highly 'sensei-student' sort of relationship, another moment it's as though we're at the same level—just friends hanging out. Sometimes, she even throws off vibes like she loves me in a familial way. There's zero romantic spark between us, despite what some of the vampires around here whisper.

No one looking at her would guess her true age. She looks about eighteen or nineteen, a delicate French waif or a porcelain doll brought to life. Her skin is inhumanly white, like literal chalk, as is her hair. I think in her era, women of a certain social class actually wore white face paint, so undeath merely saves her the trouble of bothering with outdated cosmetics. Seriously though, as innocent as she appears on the outside, she's quite far in the other direction, and I don't mean evil. She is 'adventurous' as they say.

I suppose most people would consider a woman who could casually lop a guy's head off evil, but really, the dude *was* trying to kill me.

So, yeah. To any outside observer, we look like a pair of young women close in age. She got turned at twenty-two and appears somewhat younger. Only, being an Old Guard, her vampiric nature isn't what shaved a few years off her face—genetics for her, unlike me. The supernatural change made her alluring rather than cute/harmless. Vampires generally develop something of a specialty power when they become old enough. Hers is charm. At her age, she needs to actively concentrate on *not* enchanting an entire room by merely existing. Fortunately, her abilities tend not to work passively on vampires unless they're significantly younger than her.

As always, the vampire event is taking place in one of the large convention type rooms. Most of the left wall—compared to the door we enter from—is a spread of tables bearing snacks for the snacks. I still have no idea where the normal people come from who mill around waiting to be bitten. They're all out of their heads on mind-control fumes. It's doubtful any of them will remember being here. For all I know, they're hotel guests borrowed from their rooms upstairs. Nice, convenient, and self-contained. No need to transport what are essentially kidnapping victims around outside.

Still haven't decided how much it bothers me, or why it bothers me when ambush-feeding out 'in the wild' doesn't. How is it any different? Well, I'm not sucking two hours out of people's lives by forcing them to stand around like a zombie during a social meeting of higher-order predators. Then again, if they *are* sourcing these people from the hotel, they'd otherwise be sleeping.

Whatever. I'll cling to a tiny island of moral high ground by not availing myself of their blood.

We make the rounds, me mostly staying quiet while she talks to everyone. The usual cattiness comes from Vanessa Prentice, a Fury with some envy issues regarding beauty. Aurélie is quite proud of her looks, but she's so damn pretty, she knows she doesn't have to call attention to it. It appears outwardly as humility, but it's actually the opposite. And no, I'm not judging. A world-champion athlete has every right to be proud of their accomplishments. One might say it's a bad comparison since athletes work for years to get where they are while looks are a roll of the dice. In Aurélie's case, however, looks *are* the product of effort. *Supernatural* perhaps, but still effort.

Jennifer Ruiz, a 'California blonde' Sybarite, has nothing to be jealous of, but still gets a little weird around us. In her case, it's not so much envy of Aurélie but disappointment at no longer being the prettiest woman in the room.

Again, don't care. I stay out of it.

I do pick up a few snippets of conversation among the Old Guard about my recent trip to London, specifically about me meeting Peter Corley. Apparently, no vampire from the Pacific Northwest has officially made contact in any sort of diplomatic sense with the London vampires before. Questions have arisen regarding what, if any, political ramifications may come from me being there. Of course, Wolent already got the entire story from me within days of my return to the US. Nothing political happened. But among vampires, things are never taken at face value. Especially in my case. Because I'm so new at this, some might think I missed a subtle undertone of displeasure or failed to do something properly to prevent an international incident of the undead kind.

Considering no wars have started, it's most likely safe to assume we're all good, but 'safe to assume' isn't a hundred percent certainty. Great. I get to spend the rest of the night on edge, waiting for the hammer to drop. If the inner circle is *still* whispering about me being in London three months later, something's up.

Remember the curveball thing? Yeah. Here it comes.

When we reach the group containing Arthur Wolent, he breaks off his conversation with the woman next to him and smiles at me. "Ahh, Sarah."

Eep. Okay, this is beyond weird. For one thing, he reacted to us right away. Usually, he does the Mafia don thing where he doesn't act at all like he's noticed anyone's standing there waiting for his attention until he's ready to give them attention. Secondly, he acknowledged me before Aurélie. There isn't any social rule—as far as I know—requiring him to address other vampires in age order. He's not technically any sort of legitimate 'ruler' of the Seattle vampire community, even if everyone more or less regards him as such.

We're basically like a tenant's organization and he volunteered to be the leader.

Good thing, though. Much better him than Stefano or Paolo. Honestly, the majority of the vamps around here think those two guys are a bit *too* old school. They'd probably try to make it illegal to sleep outside of coffins. Really, though. No one does that. It's as douchey as going to a concert wearing the T-shirt of the band you're going to see.

Since Aurélie doesn't visibly react to him acknowledging me before her, she must have been expecting it. No one is throwing off vibes like I screwed up, so it's possible for me to stay somewhat calm. Never did like having to go see the principal, so to speak.

"Hello, Mr. Wolent." I freeze, unsure if bowing, curtseying, or something else is appropriate.

Turns out, he's happy with a handshake.

After letting go of my hand, he faces Aurélie. "Good evening to you, Miss Merlier."

"A pleasure, Arthur."

He ceremonially kisses her hand. Yeah, I'm totes cool with the shake. His small group of hangers-on still make faces at me in varying degrees of pity, mockery, or 'give me a break.' It's the outfit, mostly. This dress is so totally extra.

"Sarah," says Wolent, approaching me again. "I'd like you to do a slight favor for me, bring you into the community in an official sense. You've had six months to get a feel for this new life, and it's time for you to be considered a full member."

Unicorns and bunnies!

"Okay. Great." I manage a brittle smile, concentrating on cute things so neither Wolent nor Aurélie catch me being underwhelmed at what should probably be a big deal.

Maybe I shouldn't be unenthusiastic about this. Becoming a 'full-fledged' vampire is an entirely political thing having no bearing on my abilities. I'm not a character in a video game where achieving 'full-fledged' status unlocks some new power. No matter what I do, it's not going to change the truth of what I've become. I've spent so much energy focusing on the human-slash-family side of my life, I can't really claim to be trying to walk in *both* worlds.

In all honestly, it's been like eighty-twenty. I don't dislike or resent being turned, so perhaps I ought to pay a little more attention to the other part of my reality.

Stefano and his group, likely in a constant state of eavesdropping on everything Wolent says whenever they can, edge closer. They look as though they're contemplating a demand for me to disassociate myself from my mortal family in order to claim 'full' status among the vampires. I'm sure Wolent knows I'd have no problem remaining on the sidelines, especially if the price of admission to the 'cool kids club' is breaking off contact with my parents and siblings. Hell, the area has plenty of Lost Ones who couldn't care less about vampire politics.

Case in point: Dalton never goes to these soirees.

Though, I'm not sure he counts as a 'Seattle vampire.' He tends to move around a lot. Though, after the recent problems in LA, he's been sticking close to enjoy a presumption of Aurélie's protection. She hasn't said anything officially about him. Dalton's hoping anyone who might give him a problem will assume by virtue of his being connected to me, Aurélie would be upset if anyone messed with him in her territory.

"Of course," I say. "Hopefully, you're not going to ask me to hurt anyone."

A few of those watching us 'aww' at me. Unlike Sophia, I don't adore being thought of as cute and harmless. Yeah, as vampires go, I'm overly squishy—as in I hate hurting people or animals. One of Paolo's cretins actually called me a 'social justice vampire' a few weeks ago because I actually have empathy for humans and don't get off on being crappy to people who are different. Whatever. Sure, every group has those who take things too far, but anyone who uses 'social justice' as an insult is almost certainly a selfish, entitled prick. I'm not out there screaming at people because plastic straws make seagulls cry. I just think people shouldn't be shitty to each other, and humans —despite what some vampires think—are still people.

Oh, the horror. Seriously dude, go punch a kitten or something if it bugs you so much I care about people other than myself.

Wolent chuckles. "Nothing of the sort. I'd like you to deliver a message on my behalf to Cassandra Upton. She is, for lack of a more official term, the vampire in charge of the San Diego region."

Whew. Just a Fed Ex run? No problem. Oh, wait. How many other angry vampires are going to want to intercept this message?

"You seem nervous." He raises an eyebrow.

"Wondering how sensitive the message is and if I should be on guard for problems."

"Ahh." Wolent nods once. "A wise thought. Truly beyond your apparent years."

"Nah. I just watch a lot of movies." I flash a cheesy smile. "Figured you were sending something sensitive if you didn't want to e-mail it."

A murmur of laughter goes around the vampires close to us.

"It is a traditional message which is hand-delivered." Wolent turns to retrieve a scroll from a younger man standing behind him, like something straight out of the *way* old days. Wax seal and all.

"Oh. Wow." I accept the scroll. It's about the size of the cardboard tube paper towels come on. "This is seriously old school. Are you going to warn me not to try opening it or a demon will pop out?"

Wolent grins—good sign. Speaking with Furies is always a nerve-wracking experience. Sometimes, the slightest wrong thing can set them off in anger. It doesn't necessarily mean instant doom. If I can survive long enough for their rational mind to take over again, I'll be fine. Better still not to poke the sleeping bear in the first place. "No demons. It's a simple yearly catch-up message. Think of it as a long-distance handshake. Routine political make nice type stuff."

I nod. Great, I've been promoted to undead intern. No point arguing. Even if this means I'm technically becoming part of Wolent's 'crew,' better to have allies than be alone right? He wouldn't be giving me a task unless he meant it as an overture of invitation. Not sure why I keep reaching for Mafia comparisons, but this totally feels like the first little job someone gets to show loyalty to the Don. My future invariably involves associating with vampires. Might as well make it official and align myself with Arthur Wolent.

"I'll deliver this message for you." Say one thing, mean another. Yes, I'm taking my place in 'vampire world' and accepting the invitation to your... for lack of a better word, political party. I watch too many movies, don't I? This is probably far less formal than the scenario playing out in my head. "You said bring it to Cassandra...?"

"Upton. It is unlikely you'll meet her directly." Wolent waves for the man who brought the scroll to step forward.

The guy approaches, handing me a purple business card for 'Delirium,' a night club in San Diego. Someone wrote a phone number in sharpie marker on the otherwise blank back.

"Look for an Old Guard named Jermaine Warwick. That's his number." Wolent gestures at the card. "He's Cassandra's... what is the term they use nowadays? Personal assistant?"

The other vampires around us chuckle again. Can't tell if they're humoring him or amused at how society has changed the term 'secretary' to personal assistant. One annoying part of being among vampires is having no idea how old anyone really is. The face of a handsome twenty-year-old guy might conceal an attitude like my Uncle Hank. Seriously, I hope never to see someone who appears young use the term 'whipper snapper.' I'd lose it and laugh in their face.

And yeah, I still have trouble wrapping my head around Aurélie's true age.

"I can do that." I bite my lip. "Would it be too much of a problem if I did it this weekend so I don't miss classes? San Diego is kind of a haul."

The idea of me trying to 'be normal' by attending college doesn't bother anyone the same way staying at home does. Aside from temporary mind-reading, becoming a vampire doesn't allow a person to instantly obtain knowledge. Several of the people around me have, at one time or another, partaken of university courses or even inserted themselves into corporations. It does, however, garner another murmur of 'aww how cute' from the older ones. It's more pity than derision, since they know I'm only doing it to feel normal. Most of them think I'm in denial, pretending to be human.

Maybe they're right. But… if the opposite to pretending humanity is turning into an arrogant asshole like Paolo Cabrini, I don't care what they think of me.

Wolent smiles. "Yes, of course. I understand you've been left in charge of your siblings."

Paolo frowns at me. Yeah, he's butthurt I'm 'getting special privileges' for having mortal family aware of my existence. Normally, if Arthur Wolent asks someone to do something, they go do that something right away. Vampires shouldn't have mortal attachments, and so on. Whatever. Despite his fearsome reputation, Wolent's a decent guy. At least, he's being quite decent and friendly to me. Then again, he's from the old world and I'm a young woman, so it's normal for him to treat me a certain way. Even better, I'm a young woman with zero political aspirations and no desire to do anything to get on his bad side.

"Thank you. I'll make sure Jermaine gets this message as soon as possible."

He smiles, then proceeds to make routine small talk, asking me how things are going. It's pointless to leave out details when speaking to a guy who's easily capable of seeing the contents of my head. I'm not terribly comfortable talking about Sophia's gift and Sam's new friends with Stefano and Paolo—and worse, Eleanor St. Ives— listening in, even if any of them could mine the information straight out of my head if they really wanted to. It might be naïve of me, but I don't have a problem with Wolent knowing about them. For one thing, he'd find out anyway. For another, he doesn't seem likely to try using them... at least not until they're adults. Besides, I don't think Blix would be of much use to a serious vampire trying to do serious things. Dalton might use him in a manner similar to an old-timey burglar throwing a bag of marbles at the cops chasing him, but yeah... an imp's 'serious' applications are limited. Fortunately, the last three months have been painfully normal. Nothing for the 'forces of evil' to use against me. I've been doing exactly what I promised: staying under the radar.

Our conversation shifts from my recent lack of interesting existence to the war between the Aurora Aurea and Serene Lodge over in London. Curiously, Eleanor St. Ives walks right up to me, asking numerous questions about the conflict. This woman is talking to me like we have no prior history, and by that, I mean, she's acting as if she never sent vampires to kick my ass, threaten my sister, and steal some special spyglass Dalton stole from another group of vampires— long story. Could probably write a whole book about the spyglass affair.

St. Ives appears to be a few years shy of forty, with short blonde hair and the completely mirthless presence of an East German research scientist. She looks like the host of a TV talk show trying to make people feel *bad* about life or conducting random painful experiments on the studio audience.

Her approach puts me instinctively on guard, but there is no way in hell she's going to try anything in person right in front of Wolent and Aurélie.

Whatever. She's an Academic. According to Aurélie, most of them have an emotional range somewhere between Spock and a Fabergé desk lamp. She came after me months ago because she wanted something, not due to any anger, jealousy, or contempt. Probably the same reason she hasn't pursued any revenge for me refusing to give her the old telescope. Tonight though, she's behaving as if none of it happened. The instant being cordial with me can get her what she needs, she's cordial. So damn creepy, like an AI. Again, whatever. I much prefer neutral parties to enemies, so I deal and talk to her. She's probably doing the Jane Goodall thing and wanting to study mystics. As far as I know, she's at least two centuries old and *not* in possession of any mystical skills. Generally speaking, when vampires possess magical talents, they're Academics… but it's rare.

For the better part of the next twenty minutes, I explain as much as I can remember about the mystics without mentioning Sophia doing actual magic. As far as Eleanor gets to know, my sister broke a soul jar and the mystics needed her to be part of the ritual to get rid of the angry spirit.

I've definitely got the feeling Aurélie wanted me here tonight specifically so Wolent could ask me to deliver his message. Such a trivial thing, I can't understand why almost everyone attending this event paused to watch him give me this scroll to carry. It's probably akin to a vampire's coming out party, though—despite my outfit—I'm hardly a debutante being introduced to society in hopes of securing a husband from a powerful family.

Since I don't have pockets—or a purse at the moment—I have no choice but to hold the scroll like a fashion accessory for the rest of the night.

They say small revenges taste the best, and in one case, it's literal truth. Stefano and Paolo can't bear to watch me pluck a few macarons from the actual food set up for the mortals. The faces they make, you'd think I ate cat poop off the sidewalk. Heh. It's *so* petty, but making them squirm feels awesome.

Hey, if I'm going to officially join this club, I might as well enjoy myself.

# 13

# UP TO NO GOOD

I make it home from the vampire social a few minutes shy of three in the morning.

Thankfully, the rain stopped at some point during the event, considering the scroll didn't come with any sort of protective covering. This thing is totally like the way people sent letters back in medieval times. Guess I'm the young scout sent off on horseback to a foreign land, carrying the king's words. Sounds much cooler to think of basically running a Fed Ex quest in terms of epic fantasy, right?

The Littles are fairly good about not invading my room and rummaging. I mean, they freely come in here whenever they want, but they're not a destructive force. Still, it's probably a good idea to put this letter in something to protect it. A Pringles can would be ideal, though perhaps greasy. If delivering old timey messages becomes a habit, I might have to make a scroll carrier out of PVC.

For now, I stick the letter in my desk drawer and get going on homework. Ferrying the Littles all over the place has cut into my study time, resulting in a fairly tall pile of work in need of doing. Since comp sci and calculus are coming up again Friday, I need to get their work done first. Everything else can wait until next week. The weekend should offer me enough—aww crap.

I'm going to burn the entire weekend delivering a damn message. San Diego is roughly 1,100 miles as the crow flies away from Cottage Lake. Flying myself there will consume one entire night. According to the GPS on my iPhone, my normal max flight speed is about 120 miles an hour. I can strain myself and get up to 150 or so, but it's tiring. Basically lasts as long as I could sprint before as a mortal. Cruising at 120 is as tireless as walking.

There is no way in hell I'm going to ask Sophia to attempt teleporting us to San Diego. For one thing, neither of us have ever been there before. Second problem: I don't want to be face-groped by a giant black tentacle again. Long story.

Hmm. Internet time. The sun's going down close to six at the moment, at least until this Sunday when Daylight Savings shifts it forward an hour to seven. Grr. So sunset on Saturday is at like seven minutes after six. According to the web, sunrise in San Diego is going to be 6:05 a.m. That gives me about twelve hours of darkness, though more realistically eleven or ten. I need to factor in some time to find shelter. Good chance the San Diego sun is not going to be as forgiving to me as Seattle weather.

It's tempting to charm my way onto a commercial flight. Jets fly *way* faster than vampires. Of course, using mind-control powers to get on an airplane potentially exposes my existence as a vampire to ordinary civilization. I could purchase a ticket, but airlines viciously screw people buying tickets the same day as the flight. Even if I bought them today for a flight Saturday, I'd pay through the nose.

Do I feel ethically challenged about using mental powers to get on a plane? No, not really. For one thing, the flight is happening whether or not I'm on it, so it's not as though I'm costing them anything at all. Second, what airlines do with their fares is worse. Like, one time, my mother needed to fly to Colorado on short notice for work. Same-day ticket was over $1,000. If she'd booked it months in advance, it would've been closer to $280. I mean seriously. They might as well straight up rob people while holding a gun to their head.

Anyway... A commercial flight is a little under three hours.

Hmm. Tempting, but risky.

Heck with it. I'll fly on my own and sprint as much as I can. Sacrifices an entire night to getting there, but at least it'll give me enough time to find a hiding place before sunrise.

Right then. Homework time.

I dive into the comp sci book, reading the suggested chapters. The more I read, the more it's obvious to me my major is going to change. It's not overly boring or complicated. Honestly, programming is possible for me to do, just not anything I'm in love with like Sierra adores video games. I can totally see her turning into one of those reclusive programming geniuses who develops groundbreaking video games and becomes a household name among the geek community. Or maybe she'll do a one-eighty and end up working as a stunt person for fantasy movies. She's really taking to the sword class. Of all the things she could study… sword fighting is about as useful as getting a PhD in Aramaic.

Maybe slightly more so. It would be really damn impressive if she could use Aramaic to kill vampires or imps attacking us. I mean useful in terms of earning a living.

After comp sci, it's calculus time. Yay. I'm so excited.

Again, it's tedious rather than impossibly difficult. Nothing I can't figure out with a bit of back-and-forth to the textbook and Google. Math has never been my favorite subject, but I don't hate or even fear it. It just kinda is. Sophia loves it. Sierra dislikes it. The wail is going to be epic the day she realizes computer programming, even for video games, is like *all* math.

I manage to finish the calculus homework by 5:49 a.m., roughly an hour before sunrise. Given how crazy my schedule is at the moment, I keep right on working, getting started on the short essay due for philosophy class tomorrow. Since this is entirely coming out of my head—based on opinions and personal mental ramblings—it requires no research and I can write supernaturally fast. Clearing 2,482 words in forty minutes is probably superhuman, even if it is somewhat rambly BS. Then again, philosophy *is* generally composed of rambly BS punctuated by the occasional profound sentence.

Maybe I *will* make it to my bed before the sun knocks me out this morning.

Right before I get out of the chair, I decide to take a quick look at Facebook.

The '36' on the messenger icon for Cody Peters catches my eye. Ugh, really? Only out of concern they're going to do something stupid, I open the window and catch up on messages. He's freaking out about the strange people living down the street from him. He and his brother are convinced the neighbors are 'evil vampires' and need to be stopped. A long string of comments like 'someone's carrying a suspicious bundle into the house' or 'he's outside again, I think they're dumping a dead body' proceed in a tone of escalating panic. According to the timestamp, they sent me those messages the other night while Hunter and I made love.

The text barrage stops around midnight, probably because their mother or father caught them awake. Hmm. They're fourteen and fifteen—possibly fifteen and sixteen now, no idea when their birthdays are—so their bedtime might be midnight. Probably earlier. Heck, their parents seemed kinda laid back, so they might not even have one.

More messages start up today:

4:03 p.m. ‹No activity at the house during the day. Gotta be Vamps.›

4:08 p.m. ‹Do you know any vamps down here?›

4:11 p.m. ‹Sorry to blow up your messenger. Are you mad at us?›

4:23 p.m. ‹If we're bugging you, say something and we'll stop.›

4:40 p.m. ‹One creepy old man is trimming the bushes. We think he lives there. Possibly not a V since he's outside in the sun.›

4:43 p.m. ‹Duh. Sorry. You were probably sleeping.›

6:19 p.m. ‹Operation Vampire Watch complete. We have eyes on target.›

6:21 p.m. ‹Activity inside the house. Camera mic picked up a scream. Ben thinks it's a movie.›

6:22 p.m. ‹Thinks the scream came from a movie, not that we are in one.›

9:07 p.m. ‹Two big guys just left in a van. We're going to check on the house.›

9:39 p.m. ‹Old dude almost caught us. I think he heard us, but he didn't see us. We're safe.›

10:03 p.m. ‹Sarah! Deffo vamps. They're grabbing people. The news is blowing up with missing persons around here.›

I whistle. Those two are going to get themselves hurt or arrested. I totally should've removed the idea of vampires from their consciousness. Ugh. This is partially my fault. Hmm. What's the best way for me to respond? Don't have much time to carefully craft a reply. Here goes nothing.

‹Hey, guys. I'm still here. Sorry for not responding to you. My parents are on vacation so I'm juggling everything right now. Super busy. Not ignoring you and you guys haven't made me mad. We're cool. I'm just swamped and haven't looked at the computer. Look, be careful. Don't get involved. Your neighbors are most likely weirdoes, but I doubt they are Vs. No way would multiple Vs buy a house together and drag people back there. Too much risk.›

‹Hey! Wow, you're up late… or early. Sun's almost out. This is Ben btw. Cody's not up yet.›

I glance at the clock. Got maybe five minutes before I face-plant my computer desk. ‹Yeah, just about to go to bed. Had a sec to look at FB. Can't talk long now, need to zzz.›

‹Cool. Did you see the news? Thirty-nine missing people over the past four months within a fifty-mile area around here. It's crazy. We're totes sure vampires live at the end of our street.›

‹You guys have any real evidence?› I type so fast the keyboard makes a buzzing sound.

‹Not really. Just seeing weird stuff going on at the house. Looks like they're carrying bodies inside.›

I sigh. ‹Why would vamps bring dead people *into* their house? They don't eat people.›

‹Might be unconscious, not dead.›

‹You saw them lugging actual people inside?›

‹Not exactly. Suspicious bundle over the shoulder. Hard to see at night. Large dark things. Looks like bodies wrapped up. Unless they're buying a ton of carpet at night, what else could they be carrying but people?›

Sigh. Come on… come on… I need to go to bed. ‹You guys don't have any real evidence, do you?›

‹Umm, no… not really. But this family is really sneaky. Their butler dude is hella creepy.›

‹Being creepy and strange isn't proof they're vamps. You guys went through a weird experience at the L&C Caverns. Trust me, if a pair of high school boys caught onto them, they aren't vampires.› I stare at the screen for a second before hitting send. On the remote chance the people the Peters brothers are spying on *are* vampires, they'd have to be the absolute most careless idiot vampires on Earth.

‹We'll try to get better evidence. Can we send u pix?›

‹Don't break the law. And you guys shouldn't get involved. Probably only some crazy people, and you're going to get in trouble. On the one-one-thousandth of a percent chance they really are vampires, you and Cody are going to get yourselves killed. I can't see vamps being this obvious or reckless, but if they are, it will attract the attention of experienced hunters. Please be careful and don't do anything stupid.›

‹Okay.›

‹GTG. Feels like daytime's coming.›

I fling myself out of my chair using flight, and crash face-first into my pillow.

Don't even have time to roll over onto my back before I'm out.

# 14

## SOFT SPOT

Not sure if being responsible for my siblings is stressing me out, but it feels like I went to sleep on Wednesday and woke up on Friday. Yes, I'm aware my schedule makes me 'go to sleep' the following day compared to when I get out of bed, but I consider one period of wakefulness to be entirely the same day of the week.

The morning I chatted with Ben started off Wednesday afternoon, so it had been my Wednesday until sunrise knocked me out. Thursday went by fast, probably due to the lack of craziness. I took Sierra to her sword class again. No one got into a smack talking contest at least. I'd been half tempted to claim Sierra gave me a few pointers and duel Jim, but nah. Better for me to remain unassuming and forgettable. Can't make myself stand out in anyone's memory.

When we got home, I found my brother in the kitchen covered in mud. At first, I thought he wore jean shorts in March, but they'd been full-length jeans when he put them on. He needed an emergency trip to the store for new sneakers. I have no idea what happened to the old ones beyond him saying *something* chased him through the little patch of woods he cuts across between home and Daryl's house.

Whatever ran him down managed to shred his pant legs and

sneakers without causing serious injury. Don't have the faintest clue what the hell happened to his socks. They simply ceased existing. Probably went into the same vortex that steals them from the dryer, but I dunno. Socks only commit suicide one at a time, not in pairs— certainly not straight off someone's feet. He only has a few cat scratches on his legs, which may have actually come from his running bare-legged through the underbrush. Figure it's about time for the weird to rear its head again. We've had a good three months of quiet. I couldn't come up with any explanation for why anything would go after Sam or how it destroyed his pants and shoes without hurting him. He said it felt like a man tackled him and held onto his legs as he struggled to crawl away. When he finally escaped and twisted to look back, his jean legs and shoes were in tatters, but no giant creature or person remained in sight.

Something capable of exploding sneakers like they'd gone through a wood-chipper grabbed him and Sam's only got a few scratches?

Does not make sense.

At least, it doesn't make sense in any way but one I'm hesitant to think about. Something came to 'play' with him. His description of what happened sounds way too much like a giant dog unaware of its own strength trying to play a little rough. Only, I'm sure we're not dealing with a dog here. Can I have a nervous breakdown yet, or is there a minimum age requirement on those? His total calm about the situation made me even more anxious.

Anyway, we ran to the store to get him new sneakers. Replaced the jeans, too. Hey, why not? We were already out.

Thursday night meant philosophy. Since the class starts at eight, I had time to fly in, so I made dinner. Once my parents are back, I really should do something super nice for Ashley as she's been such a huge help.

Right, so it's Friday afternoon.

I'm not as fried and panicky as expected after an entire week pretending to be Mom, but it will definitely be cool when my parents are home. Speaking of them, Mom has been sending me a steady stream of photo texts updating me on their vacation. They are having an awesome time. Well, at least awesome for them. Mostly relaxing in hot springs, checking out historic sites or beautiful landscapes. They don't really do the adrenaline vacation thing. However, serenity is exactly what they—mostly Mom—needed. Dad's a pretty sedate dude already, and a work-at-home programmer doesn't have a quarter of the stress my mother deals with.

I don't think either one of them has truly relaxed since before having me. Probably not terribly smart of my mother to bring her cell phone into the water with her at Nauthólsvík geothermal beach, but she did. Seriously, it's *so* pretty over there I may have to check it out myself sometime.

Alas, there is no time for me to sit around being a blob today. I pop out of bed, shower, and do a bit of cleaning around the house. Something had to give, and since leaving the Littles to reenact *Hunger Games* for food is bad, and I didn't want to take a week off school, housework suffered. Might as well try to catch it up a bit. My siblings return home from school while I'm scrubbing the downstairs bathroom. Sierra jogs up to the door to see what's up, realizes I'm cleaning, then emits a belabored sigh while plodding off.

Sophia pops into the doorway right after. "You do the kitchen yet?"

"No."

"I'll get it." She zooms down the hall.

"I'll grab trash." Sam chases after her.

Okay, now I *know* aliens have abducted my siblings and replaced them with not-quite-perfect copies. It's not *too* bizarre for Sophia to voluntarily help out with housework, but both Sam and Sierra need to be asked. Sam will help sans complaining *after* Mom asks him to. He doesn't mind chores, merely never thinks to do them on his own. Sierra will help with a side order of grumbles and mild delay. Of course, I'm assuming she trudged off to clean the upstairs bathroom based on the face she made at me. It's possible she's hiding in her room to avoid being conscripted. However, the rattle of an empty bucket going by followed by non-thunderous footsteps heading upstairs (way too soft to be Sam) surprise me.

Okay, seriously... did whatever the deep voice thing is in Sam's closet legit swap my siblings out for demon clones? Sam pops into the room with me long enough to change the bag in the wastebasket. Once I finish up in here (the downstairs bathroom is more of a toilet closet) I head to the kitchen to help Sophia out. The floor's kinda wet and she's presently wiping the countertop down with Lysol spray. Wow, the kitchen appears perfect already. How in the heck—oh… she must've used magic.

My life has 'gone to plaid.'

Sophia twists around to smile at me. "Sare, is it cool if I go with Megan and Nicole in a little while?"

"What's up?"

She swaps bottles and spritzes glass cleaner on the stove door. "Meg's mom is taking us to the mall. A nail spa. Girl time, you know."

I chuckle. "As long as a mom's going to be there, sure. How long are you going to be?"

"Right after dinner. I think it's like forty minutes. Not *too* long."

"Okay. Sounds reasonable."

"Sierra doesn't want to go with us. Too girly." Sophia laughs.

"I fail at girl." Sierra enters, carrying an empty bucket. "Upstairs bathroom is clean."

"No, you don't." I turn to keep facing her as she passes by on the way to the closet. "You rule at 'girl.'"

Sierra stows the bucket and gloves in the closet, then gives me this 'yeah right' smirk. "I'm totally not a Barbie doll like Soph."

"As if." Sophia looks down at herself, her pink dress making no secret of the non-shape under it. "Maybe a Barbie made out of popsicle sticks."

Heh. "Sierra…" I walk over and grasp her shoulder. "It's total bullshit about there only being one way to define 'girl.' Sitting around at home in sweat pants kicking ass in *Call of Duty* is as girly as overdosing on pink and unicorns and faeries like Sophia. Writing a hundred thousand lines of computer code or becoming a doctor or whatever is all 'girly.' The only thing that makes something 'girly' is a girl doing it."

"You should work for Hallmark." Sierra play-punches me in the side.

"I'm being serious. Don't get down on yourself for not living up to what other people think you should act like, dress like, or enjoy doing."

Like something straight out of a Bugs Bunny cartoon, a floating mass of trash bags sprouting small legs goes by on the way to the patio door. Sam emptied every wastebasket, trash can, and recyclable bin in the house and is taking the whole load outside at once. What the heck is it about boys? Dad's the same way carrying groceries in from the car. He claims not to be a real man if he takes more than one trip to bring everything inside.

The Littles retreat to do homework or whatever while I get going on dinner, following Mom's planned meal guide. It's kind of like a paint-by-numbers, only with food. Tonight is baked chicken with green beans and mashed potatoes. Hmm. I don't mind cooking. What about culinary school? I could taste test everything as much as I want and not blow up into a walrus. Nah. Bad idea. Might be a fun diversion, but if my future is going to involve any sort of 'real job,' it can't be one requiring frequent interaction with people. Well, interaction with the *same* people as a matter of routine. Randos I pass on the street won't realize my age isn't changing. Going to work every day among the same group will force me to relocate or change surroundings every few decades like Professor Heath.

Works for him, but I don't want to bounce around the country. At least not yet.

Scary to think about in a way. If what Aurélie believes about vampire psyche is true, it means I'm not going to 'mature' past where I am now. This clinginess to home is who I am. Guess she would know. After all, she's spent a few years as a vampire. If her personality is largely the same as she'd been centuries ago, it's a fair bit of proof. Obviously, *some* changes happen. Not so much in her case, but the world has plenty of vampires who seem to have forgotten ever being human and regard people like farm animals—expendable food.

I spend the time preparing dinner debating how much effect our bloodline has on personality. Like, if a kid got turned into a vampire and became an Old Guard, would they have a higher chance of turning into a tiny adult than if they ended up as an Innocent or a Sybarite? Don't look at me like that. Not all Sybarites are succubus-like sex fiends, merely super passionate about something. Like, I could see Sierra going Sybarite and becoming obsessed with video games.

It's too sad to think about child vampires, so I force myself to change course and wonder what sort of creature chased my brother home yesterday. Believing it meant him no harm is the only reason I'm not out there hunting for it. Coralie didn't pop in to warn me about it, either. Maybe I'm getting lazy and shouldn't rely on a ghostly oracle warning system so much. Spirits are flighty. As much as she may want to help me all the time now, she might poof on a whim and I'd never realize it.

At least the Universe waited for me to finish high school before the vampire thing happened. It would have been a real pain in the ass otherwise—though if I had the ability to be awake early in the day, vampire powers would have been so damn fun there. Oh, there's a stupid thought. I can easily pass for sixteen. Someday maybe when my family is all gone from old age, I'll reinvent myself and pretend to be a high school student in some other town for a while to kill boredom. Gee, that sounds like a lame Eighties movie, doesn't it? *Vampire High* or something. Dad would love it.

Sigh.

Bad Sarah. Stop thinking sad thoughts. I bonk myself over the head with the canister of bread crumbs.

⟫⟩ ———————— ⟨⟨⟪

DURING DINNER, SAM ASKS IF HE CAN SLEEP OVER DARYL'S HOUSE tonight.

He's done so before, usually on a Friday, so I'm fine with it. Ashley hasn't come back from her job at the vet clinic yet, though she did text me to ask if she could go on a date tonight. She met a girl at school who wants to bring her to a party. No, she's not asking for *permission* to date per se. Ash committed to helping me out until the 'rents came home, so she wanted to make sure going on a date won't mess things up here. Can't begrudge her the time after she's been helping me so much all week. Megan's mother is taking the girls to the mall after dinner... which leaves Sierra.

Hmm. I have classes tonight.

How wise or dumb is it to leave an almost-twelve-year-old home alone? I'm not at all worried about what she'd get into. We're in a nice area, but nowhere is perfectly safe from bad stuff. All it takes is one news story about some eleven-year-old kid home alone when burglars kick in the door, and parents freak out. Worse, Sierra probably wouldn't be the kid who hides in a closet on the phone to the police. She'd grab the real sword Dad gave her for Christmas and be a dumbass. Fierce as she is, she's only so big.

I could drag her to school with me or maybe insist she goes with Sophia and the girls. She'd grump the whole time and ruin it for them, though. Rolling the dice by trusting her home alone for the three-ish hours I'm at school *might* work, but it's difficult enough to concentrate on calculus while being serenaded by the wails of the thousand bodily functions of my classmates. Add worry about Sierra to it and I'd learn more skipping class to stay home.

It shocks me initially when Sierra self-appoints to dish detail after dinner. She's totally aware of the situation and probably attempting to show responsibility so I don't insist she go on the girly spa trip with Sophia.

Not much time left before I have to go out the door or decide to skip class. As in, I need to be on the road within the next three minutes. Grr. Stupid cars. So inefficient. The world would be a much better place if everyone could fly.

"So..."

Sierra, elbow deep in dishwater, glances at me through a curtain of light brown hair. If 'whatever' had a picture in the dictionary, she'd be it. "I'll be okay while you're at school. Keep the doors locked, don't open them for anyone. I know the drill."

"I'm not worried about you doing something bad, more like something out of your control—especially if it's weird."

"Little green men weird?" She raises an eyebrow.

"More like angry Los Angeles vampire weird." I sigh. "Maybe I should stay home."

"Sure." She faces me, arms dripping suds and water. "It's been months and nothing's happened. Don't be paranoid. The forces of evil aren't going to magically sense the two or three hours you're away and I'm here by myself."

I rub the bridge of my nose. "Nothing happening over a period of time is not proof it can't ever happen."

She starts to roll her eyes into a heavy sigh, but stops. "Ask Dalton to come over."

"It's not dark yet."

"So? It'll be dark soon. You can leave me alone for twenty minutes or whatever." She resumes washing dishes. "I'm basically twelve."

"Your birthday is in April."

"Right. Notice I said 'basically' twelve, not 'I am twelve'?"

"Argh. I don't have time to argue."

"So don't argue." She smiles over her shoulder at me. "Talk to Dalton as soon as it's dark. If he can't stay with me until you get home, send me a text and I promise I'll go to Ashley's and ask Mrs. Carter if I can stay there. Besides, Blix is here. If anyone *does* try to mess with me, he'll keep them tripping over themselves enough for me to get away."

I groan at the clock. Ugh. Am I being overprotective or reasonable? In the ten seconds I have left before I'm guaranteed to be late to school, I cave in. "Okay. Fine."

Sierra smiles to herself like she got away with something, but I don't have time to grill her over it now. Odd she brought Dalton up out of the blue. Dammit. She better not be attempting to wheedle her way into getting him to turn her into a vampire. More so than me, I don't think she wants to grow up. Being able to sit at home all the time playing video games without having to worry about school or a job is exactly her paradise. Also, staying eleven would mean she avoids any drama involved with boyfriends. She always made fun of me for 'having drama' and used to brag how she wouldn't deal with it. Granted, this came out of her mouth when she was like nine, so we thought it funny. Probably harmless. She's not really planning to beg my sire to turn her, too. This is purely my worst fear haunting me.

Okay, maybe not worst fear. My *worst* fear is the Littles ending up dead. Their becoming vampires would be far better than gone. Still, though. Not copacetic. Sierra said she has no interest in being a vampire, and it didn't come off sounding fake. I trust her.

Right. School.

Megan's mother pulls up outside while I'm throwing on shoes. Sophia and I leave the house at the same time.

"Whoa, you're really letting Sierra stay home alone?" Sophia gawks at me.

"Only for a few minutes. Dalton's going to swing by and keep an eye on her."

Sophia grins. "Ahh. Yeah. She's totally got a crush on him."

Oh, hell no. I didn't even think of that. Still, nothing to worry about. Dalton would never take advantage of her, and it's not unusual for tween girls to have crushes on roguishly handsome guys with British accents. Though, to be fair, Dalton is a little more Monty Python than Hugh Grant.

Ack. I'm being an idiot. She's not crushing on him. Sierra probably wants him to teach her how to fight with a sword. Makes sense now. And yeah, I'll suggest the two of us break out the PVC 'blades' sometime. Wouldn't hurt for me to stay in practice.

"I think she's more crushing on the idea of sword lessons."

"Oh. Yeah." Sophia laughs. "Good point. See you later!"

She hops in the car with Megan, Nicole, and Megan's mom.

I get in the Sentra and end up sitting there staring at the house for a moment. A house containing only Sierra—plus Blix and Sam's new closet voice. And oh, maybe a new sneaker-eating monster in the backyard. Ugh. This better not bite me in the ass.

A FEW MINUTES AFTER I TAKE MY SEAT IN COMPUTER SCIENCE, I GO online.

The instant it happens, the relative quiet of the classroom erupts in audible chaos. Fabric 'scraping' over itself, fingernails tapping, gut rumbles, and so on. Someone chewing gum sounds like ten sumo wrestlers stuck in a swimming pool full of Jell-O. Ugh.

Unfortunately, Professor Garcia happened to be looking almost right at me when my eyes flared bright red. Easy enough to zap her brain and make her forget seeing the glow. Easier still to give her the notion she saw a retinal flash from my eyes catching the overhead lights at a momentary perfect angle.

First things first.

Dalton? Are you out there listening? I concentrate on trying to get his attention. As my sire, he's permanently connected to me on a mental level.

*Aye, lass. Just waking up. Not as spry as you. Give me a tick, what?*

Any chance you'd be willing to stop by the house and keep an eye on Sierra until I'm back? I think about the situation of her being alone, a much faster way to convey information to him than words over a phone.

*Handsome, eh?* He chuckles in the back of my mind. *Pretty sure I'm closer to Hugh Grant than the Python crew.*

Grant? No. Hugh Laurie maybe. You're like half him, half David Tenant, and a bit of the guy from *Shaun of the Dead*... with Pink Panther's luck.

*Happy to see you're in a good mood tonight. Reckon I can stop by and keep her company.*

Wow, really? Wasn't expecting him to agree. It's kinda funny to pester a vampire about babysitting, though he does have a soft spot for kids—it's why I still exist. He couldn't bear to watch a 'kid' die in front of him. Guess, to him, I looked younger than eighteen even before becoming an Innocent. Aurélie would definitely have watched Sierra, too, but we'd have had to go to her. Not a complaint, just saying.

*Aye, sure. Why not? You've gotten my arse out of a fix or two way worse than a stray sibling needin' not to be alone for a few hours.*

Thanks.

Whew. Minor crisis averted.

*Good heavens, there are entirely too many letters involved in that mess,* says Dalton reacting to the math on the whiteboard behind the professor. *Are they adding numbers to English or is it some banjaxed form of math?*

It's calculus.

*Good on ya, luv. I'd rather take on another warehouse full of idiots. Right, I'll leave ya ta concentrate on summoning Cthulhu. Let the little one know I'll be there in a tick.*

Awesome. Thank you!

All right, so Sierra will only be alone for about a half hour. Not *too* worrisome. I'm not overreacting at all considering Sophia ended up being kidnapped three times inside one week back in December. I haven't made any new enemies, but don't know how much of a grudge Petra might carry. Her fear of Glim (and the other Shadows) exacting revenge plus Aurélie's protection of my family have so far stopped her from coming after me. It really is irrational on her part to be angry with me for saving some dude she had her sights set on. Mentally tormenting people into suicide is super wrong, even if she does consider it 'art.' The woman reacted like I walked up to a masterpiece painting she'd been working on for weeks and slashed it to pieces.

Whatever. Fingers crossed she stays away.

Dalton watching Sierra has to be better than leaving her by herself. Nothing's going to go wrong having the two of them together, right?

# 15

# EACH STEP PROGRESSIVELY WEIRDER

D riving home from class Friday night should have felt like a victory.

It didn't for two reasons. One, the parents extended their vacation a few days so I still had Monday and Tuesday classes getting in my way of watching over my siblings. The second metaphorical thorn in my backside is Wolent's request of me to serve as his messenger. I do not have the entire weekend free from obligation to spend watching the Littles.

The entire drive home, I argue with myself about asking him if he'd mind me waiting until my parents are back. I'd rather miss two days of classes than skip out on my oath to Mom and Dad to keep Sam, Sophia, and Sierra safe. Stefano is a large part of why I'm hesitant. Anyone with a functioning sense of humanity wouldn't question family being more important than a routine 'hi, how are you doing' message being late. It's not like a vampiric war is going to break out if the message isn't rushed down there as soon as possible. However, Stefano lacks such a grasp of empathy. To him, I'd be putting 'mortal concerns' over vampire concerns. He'd find a way to flip it around and make me sound like a threat to all vampire kind, which in turn puts my family in danger.

My internal argument screeches to a halt as soon as I turn left onto the cul-de-sac in front of our house. Mom's Tahoe is gone. Dammit. I knew the instant my mother uttered the fatal words, 'there'd better not be a scratch on it,' the stupid truck would explode. Fate took it as a dare. Great. I really am in one of Dad's movies. Parents go away, tell the kid 'not even one blade of grass out of place' before they leave… and come back to a giant smoking crater where a house should be.

I pull into the driveway a bit fast, chirping the tires when I slam on the brakes. The absence of flaming wreckage is somewhat reassuring. Will Mom be upset with me for someone stealing the truck right out of our driveway? I hadn't even been home at the time. Sierra and Sophia are yelling inside, lots of 'I have no idea' and worry coming from Sophia.

Dalton sounds as though he's trying not to die laughing.

Calm, Sarah. Calm. Find Zen.

I take a few breaths and go inside.

The girls and Dalton stand by the dining room table. As soon as I walk in, Sophia bursts into tears. Sierra face-palms. Soph is guilty about something. I hurry over to them, the words forming in my brain evaporating at the sight of the Tahoe sitting on the table. It's about the size of a guinea pig.

There is only one thing I can possibly do—stare in bewilderment.

"I didn't mean to shrink it!" yells Sophia past tears.

"I've been trying to tell her it's an accident." Sierra rubs Sophia's back. "But she's too upset to concentrate on undoing it."

"What the hell?" I grasp the truck like a toy, surprised to find it light enough to lift. It's unusually heavy for its size—but then again, most toy trucks are made of plastic. This thing's as heavy as an old-school iron. Clearly, the laws of physics have decided to take LSD, too. So much for constancy of density. "Dammit. Mom's going to freak out. She told me not to put a single scratch on it."

Dalton grins. "Nothing to worry about then. It isn't scratched."

I smirk at him. "She's not going to appreciate the semantics. What happened?"

"Cheap sword," mutters Sierra.

"Huh?" I set the Tahoe down on the table.

Sophia clutches her hands at her chin, sniffling, giving me this 'please don't be mad at me' face. I get the distinct impression she tried to help fix something and lost control.

"Umm…" Sierra grimaces. "Dalton was showing me some sword stuff on the front lawn and my sword came apart. Blade flew right out of the handle. It kinda smashed the driver door window on the Tahoe. Total accident."

I examine the 'toy' truck again. All the windows seem fine.

"Soph fixed the window." Sierra laughs. "But the truck got small, too. She freaked out and can't undo it. Like, her magic stops working if she's too upset to concentrate."

"Aww, c'mere." I hug her. "You're not in trouble."

She mumbles into my chest.

I let go.

"It's not you I'm scared of. Mom's gonna ground me 'til I'm thirty. She's like super sensitive about her truck."

"We still have four days to sort it out before they're back. Calm down and think about how to undo the shrinking magic." I squeeze her shoulders, then realize what Sierra said and gawk at her. "Umm. Did you say the sword *blade* broke, and it smashed the window? Were you two sparring with real weapons?"

"Not completely real." Dalton holds up a relatively short one-handed blade composed of a blunt-edged ingot generally fashioned in the shape of an arming sword. "Metal, yes, but slugs. Not sharp in the least. The place she's been going to has her working with a rattan longsword, which is a two-handed weapon for her. Better she gets a feel for the proper weight and balance. Didn't expect these to be quite so cheap. I should pilfer from more respectable suppliers next time."

Sierra chuckles.

He really is like the wild uncle who shows up once a year at holidays, lets the kids try beer and does reckless things for amusement. Stealing practice swords… or props for a ren fest. Oy. "I hope you at least didn't take her with you for the burglary part."

Dalton tugs at his lapels. "Of course. The entire point of me being here was not to leave her alone."

The *only* reason I don't freak out is Dalton's supernaturally sneaky. Cameras don't record him, motion sensors don't pick him up, and so on. Perks of his Lost One bloodline. It's kinda like how Glim conceals himself from people by forcing their brains not to see him. If he brought Sierra on a B&E, he'd have asked her to stay close enough to hide her, too.

"Help me calm down?" asks Sophia.

"I can't use mental prodding for everything. Your brains are going to make less sense than a David Lynch screenplay if I keep doing it."

Dalton cracks up. The girls stare blankly at me.

"Just you being here is enough." Sophia exhales. "I feel safer."

"Are you almost eleven or almost five?" asks Sierra.

"Yes," whispers Sierra in a fake-scared voice before giggling.

Everyone stands around making 'okay, now what' faces at each other for a few minutes.

Finally, Sophia puts a hand on the mini-Tahoe. "Umm. I think it's unstable. It's probably going to wear off on its own."

"Great idea putting it on the dining room table then." Sierra wags her eyebrows. "What happens if it wears off right now?"

"You'll need a new table." Dalton glances at the front door. "And likely have to cut a hole in the wall to get it out of here." He winces. "Good chance it'll end up scratched."

"I didn't want to leave it outside. What if someone steals it?" asks Sophia.

Dalton cackles. "Then they're in for an extremely rude surprise whenever it goes back to normal."

"Wait…" Sophia picks the 'toy' truck up and clutches it to her chest. "Blix!? Bliiiix? Are you here?"

The imp glides down the stairs, swoops into the dining room, and lands clinging to my back. His needle-like claws poke me in the shoulder—it's enough to make me clench my jaw tight, but not so painful I reflexively swat him off.

Sophia smiles at him. "Can you do something to the Tahoe so no one notices it and takes it?"

The imp nods, making his ears flop around.

"Cool!" Sophia runs outside carrying the truck.

Blix leaps off me and follows.

It's a really damn good thing I have no choice but to fall asleep when the sun comes up. Until Mom's truck is back to normal, my nerves will be on fire. It's bedtime for the Littles already, but Sam's sleeping over his friend's house tonight. The girls head upstairs. Dalton and I hang out for a while, talking. He finds the whole messenger thing hilarious, and he's also sure Wolent doesn't care so much about the message itself but intends the task as a statement.

"So that's it then, you've thrown your lot in with them?"

"As opposed to?" I raise an eyebrow.

"Being a free spirit like me." He flashes a used golf cart salesman smile.

"Hah." I snicker. "Knowing my luck, better to have as many allies as possible. You know I don't care about their politics. And it doesn't matter if I put down roots here. I'm in no hurry to go anywhere."

He fusses at the broken dummy sword, repetitively sliding the blade into the handle and pulling it out. "It's never so simple. Do it for him now. Next time, he's going to ask you to spy on some other vampire, maybe kill someone."

"Says the guy who took a contract to firebomb a whole lair." I raise an eyebrow at him. "Wolent's not an idiot. He knows what kind of person I am. Really don't think he's going to ask me to do wet work."

Dalton coughs. "Since when do you know the term wet work?"

"You truly underestimate the scope and breadth of Dad's movie fixation."

"I could say the same regarding your trust of Arthur Wolent. Men like him seem nice on the surface, but they're capable of doing anything to get what they want."

"Yeah. I know." I twirl my hair around one finger, let go, then do it again. "Already assumed as much about him. Luckily for me, I don't have any political goals. Besides, they all think of me as some harmless kid."

"Exactly why he's interested." Dalton points the dull sword at me. "He knows you'll be underestimated. The day will come he wants you to do something when your seeming harmlessness works to his advantage. Though, in all probability, he's mostly interested in your ability to be up during the day."

I fidget. "Are you warning me not to become part of their society?"

"Bollocks. Who knows? Feels bad to me, but it's in my blood to be on the outside. Not so for you. Maybe it'll work out. Just saying be careful."

"My plan exactly." I give him side eye. "So, how did those swords break?"

"Cracked them together a little too hard. They're not made for sparring. Renaissance festival props. The plastic bit holding the tang in the handle cracked."

"Oh. So, umm, how is she?"

"Taking to it quite well."

I continue fidgeting at my hair. "She's really into it. More than anything else she's tried as a hobby. Is there anything to worry about here? What's driving her?"

"You assume I've looked into her mind?"

"I do."

He laughs.

"You'd look for the same reason I'm tempted to. You'd want to make sure she's okay. And you haven't promised her you wouldn't peek."

"Aye. Little bit of jealousy. She feels like 'the normal one' in your family. No magic, no pet imp, no fangs—and no, the lass does not want to be a vampire."

I breathe a sigh of relief.

"So she thinks becoming a master sword fighter is going to..."

"Give her a sense of not being helpless if bad vampires or other strange things try to hurt your family." Dalton lets a long, slow—somewhat worrisome—sigh out his nose. "The girl's honestly more upset over not being able to help protect you, Sophia, or Sam than afraid for her life. She doesn't want to be forced to hide somewhere and watch everyone else."

Wow… umm… okay. Saw a bit of it in her while she fought the imps off Sophia in the mirrorverse. "She's not going to be able to keep up with a vampire, especially as a kid."

"I know. Sierra's not training to go hunt supernatural things. It's mostly for confidence. Ideally, she'll never need to fight 'monsters.'"

I lean back against the sofa, staring at the ceiling. Yeah. Ideally is right. At least she's still ordinary. No magic. Mystics won't be after her. Being ordinary won't shield her from any vampires *I* piss off, though. Not second guessing my decision to go home, but it's definitely why I'm playing nice with Arthur Wolent.

Gotta protect my family.

———————————————

Saturday afternoon, I wake to the chaos of multiple tween girls in the house.

From the sound of it, my sisters, plus Nicole, Megan, and another voice I don't recognize are upstairs. A hint of mustard hangs in the air, no doubt from lunch two-ish hours ago. Thanks, Ashley. At least, I assume she fed them.

Speaking of Ashley, almost the instant I think of her, she screams.

Uh oh. Not good.

Still wearing the long T-shirt I slept in, I drag myself out of bed and go up to the kitchen, opening the door at the top of the stairs before thinking to check the weather. Luck is with me—it's a bright day but not *too* bright. As in, I don't begin emitting smoke right away. Ouch. Okay, focus. Vampires grow in power as they age. Aurélie didn't start off being able to knock an entire room into Derpville. Years ago, she'd have needed to concentrate to charm one person.

Charm is her primary vampire power.

Sun tolerance is mine.

Maybe I can work on it. Build it up. Treat the sun like iocaine powder. Surely I cannot trust the daystar in front of me. Never start a land war in Cottage Lake when vampires are involved—or something. I doubt walking around the Sahara Desert in broad daylight will ever happen for me, but maybe the day will come where I can tolerate Seattle being sunny.

Unlife goals.

I stagger across the kitchen and down the hall to the living room, the source of the shriek. Ashley's standing in the open front door staring out at the driveway… where her little VW Jetta is sitting *on top of* the Tahoe. At least Mom's truck is back to normal size—and the windows aren't even smashed. Can't say as much for the roof, though. Pretty sure it's well past being 'scratched.'

The unknown voice belongs to Veronica. Apparently, Sophia invited her over. Nicole and Sierra barely look away from the PlayStation at the fuss outside. The other girls appear to be doing stretches from dance class. Snacks, nail polish, phones, and tablets litter the living room. Two tablets and a phone all play different movies or TV shows. I have no idea how anyone follows any of it. It's like the destructive aftermath of a party from every Eighties college movie, only 'tween edition.'

"Sarah!" yells Ashley. "I don't know what happened."

Shit. I stagger over and lean on her, muttering, "Soph shrank the Tahoe by accident. It was sitting in the driveway. You probably didn't notice it, parked on top of it, and the magic wore off during the night."

"I swear I didn't see it."

"Yeah. You had some help not noticing it." Thanks, Blix. Not sure this is better than some kid stealing it as a toy. "Uhh, Soph? Is there anything you can do about this?"

She's balancing on one foot, left leg up behind her, both hands gripping her ankle. She holds the pose for a few seconds more, then relaxes and walks over, completely calm until she looks outside at the Jetta perched atop the Tahoe—at which point, she gasps, covering her mouth with both hands. "Eep! Oh, no!"

Please don't be one of those situations where every attempt to fix a problem only makes it progressively worse. Please. I cross my fingers, making wishes upon wishes.

"Umm. I got an idea." Sophia steps outside, then whispers, "close the door so the others don't see."

Ashley and I follow her.

Sophia raises her arms toward the automotive mess. "Ash, if what I'm about to try works, hop in your car and move it fast."

Remind me to hug Blix. If not for whatever he did to make people not notice the Tahoe, I'm sure the police would've been here already. Especially with Mr. Niedermeyer on the lookout for every possible thing to complain about.

It's good Sophia is so humble and self-deprecating. It's impossible to pick on her for stuff like her appearance. She laughs at herself for being 'twig Barbie.' Not to sound too condescending, but when she gets angry, she's adorable. Sophia knows it too, so she doesn't stay angry for long before she ends up laughing at herself—the growling hamster, as Sierra calls her.

She makes an angry, determined face while focusing on the Jetta humping Mom's Tahoe.

Weird pink-purple light erupts around us, globs of darker glow whizzing around like comets. It looks the same as when she rewound time after messing up the conversation with Mom about keeping Klepto. Loud rushing swoosh noises come from the loose globs of raw magic energy. Ashley might be screaming, hard to tell.

The Tahoe abruptly shrinks out of sight, allowing the Jetta to drop back down onto its tires.

Ashley bolts forward, jumps into her car, backs it to the end of the driveway, and ducks down out of sight behind the steering wheel for some reason.

Sophia drops her arms at her sides; the magical weirdness vanishes in an instant.

Mom's truck blows up like one of those inflatable emergency rafts with a ripcord, springing up to full size so rapidly it bounces a few inches off the ground. Cool. No damage. Only… we have a new problem.

Ashley's gone. She doesn't seem to be in her car anymore.

"Ash?" I call.

"This is not cool!" yells a little girl voice from the Jetta.

"Oops," whispers Sophia.

The car door opens. A little red-haired girl of about six, wearing Ashley's sweater like a dress, climbs out, then leans back into the car to grab a skirt and underpants off the floor. The child furiously shakes the clothes at us. "Are you freakin' kidding me!?"

Sophia stares at her. "Is that what I look like when I get mad?"

"Kinda."

"She's adorable."

"Yeah."

"Like seriously." Sophia blinks. "She's super angry but it's making me wanna just hug her."

Ashley stomps up to us, bare feet clapping on the driveway. "Don't laugh at me. Why am I so small? What happened to my boobs?"

"Umm, you're a little kid." I pat her on the head.

She growls. "Really?"

"Something went screwy with the time fabric." Sophia taps a finger to her chin. "Mr. Anderson warned me not to monkey around with time haphazardly since odd things can happen. But this doesn't count as haphazard. Mom would've been super pissed if Ash's car crushed the Tahoe."

"Grr!" yells mini-Ashley. "How long am I going to be stuck like this?"

"Damn, I hope it wears off before I need to go to San Diego. Ash is supposed to be babysitting you guys, not the other way around."

Mini-Ashley punches me in the hip. "Not funny!"

"Aww, but you're adorable." I scoop her up.

She taps her foot on air. "This is totally messing up my plans. I can't work or go to college this small."

"We can't let the others see her like this." Sophia backs toward the front door. "Smuggle her in though the kitchen. I'll meet you downstairs. Give me a sec to distract everyone." She darts inside.

Ashley's anger gives way to nervousness. "Please tell me I'm not stuck as a little kid again. It's not fair! I *just* got done being a kid. I don't wanna go back to not being allowed to do anything. I'm so little, Mom's gonna make me go to bed at seven."

"Relax. Your mother's not dumb. Your mind is the same, right?"

"I dunno. I'm about to start crying uncontrollably."

"Yeah and? That doesn't mean you're mentally six. It means you're mentally Ashley."

She raspberries me.

I set her on her feet and lead her around the house to the backyard, up onto the deck. After a momentary delay, Sophia runs over to unlock it, letting us inside. We hurry down to the basement. Unused to being the size of a six-year-old, Ashley trips on the stairs, but I've got her hand, so she doesn't fall far, dangling from my grip by one arm.

"Dammit this sucks!" wails Ashley.

We retreat to my bedroom. I can't help myself and take a few photos of her. Gawd she was an adorable kid. Sophia stands there watching Ashley run around trying to grab the phone away from me, attempting not to laugh.

"Okay." Sophia claps once to get our attention. "I got it."

Ashley stops chasing me, twisting to look up at her. The 'I'm going to wallop you with a pillow' glare is so Ashley it hurts.

"It's gonna wear off on its own. Time is an amazingly strong force with a bunch of self-correcting powers." Sophia nods. "Mystics have been trying to make themselves younger for like ever, and it doesn't usually work."

"You are forgetting the first fundamental law of magic," I say.

Sophia blinks at me. "Don't use it for anything I can easily do by mundane means?"

"No, the other first fundamental law." I smile. "Maybe it's *Murphy's* first fundamental law of magic. Nothing works as well as a screw up. People have been deliberately trying to make themselves young again, so it didn't work. This is an accident. Kinda like how they invented floating bar soap. Tons of awesome things are really the products of errors."

Ashley face palms. "Are you seriously telling me I'm legitimately little again? Ugh. That's horrible."

"Not exactly. Could be worse."

She smirks. "I'm not dead?"

"No… you could end up being frozen at this age forever."

Ashley falls over backward dramatically, then wails. "Noooooo!"

"She is totes adorbs," says Sierra.

"Yeah."

Ashley snarls.

Sophia and I giggle, causing her to snarl again. I'm sure she did it on purpose, so we laughed. That's Ashley. She loves doing cute, silly things to make people laugh.

"It's incredibly unlikely she's frozen and not going to grow up." Sophia grimaces. "She *might* be stuck having to grow up again, but I don't think so. Just like the Tahoe, she's gonna pop back to normal soon."

Ashley sits up. "How soon is soon?"

"Are we about to do the 'when will then be now' routine from *Spaceballs?*" I ask.

Sophia laughs.

The red hair wildly draped over her face, the sweater-turned-dress, the expression of such a little girl being completely done with the world is *too* much. I take another picture of her.

"Stop it!" Ashley whines at me.

"Chill." I take another pic. "We'll tell people it's a filter or something."

"Not fair. I want embarrassing pictures of *you* as a kid. You have an unfair advantage."

I fold my arms and raise one eyebrow. "You forget my father took *gigabytes* of photos."

"Umm." Sophia shifts her jaw side to side. "Sometime between any minute now and like three hours, she should go back to normal."

"Three *hours?*" wails Ashley. "Augh!"

"But you *shrank* the Tahoe." I scratch my head. "You didn't really 'shrink' Ash as much as rewound time in a highly localized manner."

"No. I rewound time around the cars to a point before Mom's Tahoe blew up to normal size, so Ashley could move her car *before* either one of them got damaged. Then I let time snap back to where it belonged. I don't know how it affected Ash. She probably got slapped in the face by a temporal ripple when the time stream crashed back to normal. But... time's gonna fix itself. She just needs to be careful because it'll happen fast and she won't have any pants on when she gets tall again."

Ashley blushes.

"Wrap yourself in a blanket or stay in Sarah's room." Sophia looks at me. "I don't want to risk trying to undo it in case I make it worse by accident."

"Wow." I snicker. "Okay. Umm. So the babysitter's become the babysit-ee."

"No way." Ashley shakes her head. "My body is small but I'm still the same inside."

"We can't let Nicole, Megan, or Veronica see you like this, though. If this doesn't wear off by sunset, we'll have to figure something out for when I run to Cali."

Sophia gasps, lip quivering. "You're not going to my recital tonight?"

"Oh, dammit." I rake a hand up through my hair. "I forgot to take you to the store—and forgot the recital was today. Ack!" I pull her into a hug. "Of course I'm going to your recital. The message can wait." I sigh out my nose. Screw it. I'll fly commercial. No way will I have enough time to attend her dance recital and fly ten hours under vampiric power in the same night before the sun burns me out of the air.

"I kinda wanted to go, too," says Ashley.

"You still can go. My old dresses and stuff are in the attic. We can find something for you to wear." Sophia grins.

"Eep!" Ashley blushes. "What if I go back to normal?"

"Then you pull a Hulk smash and rip out of the dress." I laugh.

"Umm. No thanks. I'll hide in your room until normal returns." She shivers.

"You're going to be waiting a long time." I wag my eyebrows.

Ashley flops flat on her back again. "Ugh. Why is life so crazy?"

"Are you sure this is going to wear off?" I ask.

Sophia nods. "Yep. Eventually."

"At least the cars are no longer messed up. I think Soph's right. Better to wait this out. Each time we try to fix things, they get weirder." I grab a unicorn plush from my bed and hand it to her.

"Seriously?" She stares up at me. "Are you setting me up for more embarrassingly cute pictures?"

"Yes, but I also know you *still* cling to unicorn plushies to feel better."

Ashley makes the cutest 'I'm mad at you for being right' face while hugging a plush almost as big as she is now.

*Click.*

"Oh, pose with the giant teddy bear!" chirps Sophia. "It's bigger than she is!"

Ashley narrows her little eyes at me. "Only if you swear you'll never blackmail me with these."

I hold up a hand. "Promise. Besides, once you go back to normal, no one will believe it's you. You're not six."

"Fine." She stands, turns to face the bear, and whistles. "Wow, it's huge!"

A 'that's what she said' joke almost happens. But I can't. She looks too innocent.

# 16

# LAST-MINUTE RUSH

S ome psychiatrist would probably have a field day analyzing me squeeing over Ashley.

We more or less grew up together. She's always lived just down the road from here, but we didn't go to the same school until fifth grade after she transferred—got kicked out—of Catholic school and ended up in my class. It's not like I've never seen her as a kid before... but it's totally different being little together. A six-year-old doesn't think of another kid the same age as adorable. They're just another kid. Wow. No wonder my parents used to let us get away with so much stuff. The way mini-Ashley is giving me a 'please fix this' stare almost causes physical pain because I can't wish her back to normal right away.

I'm sure the Littles wielded the same powers of cuteness at this size, too, but I hadn't noticed back then.

Sophia can't help herself and conducts a brief experiment to determine the nature of the effect by tempting Ashley with dolls. She doesn't behave like a kid, merely has the appearance of one. So we're not dealing with a 'simple chronological upheaval.' As if a chronological upheaval of any kind would be simple. My sister's official opinion on what happened here is 'no damn idea.'

Ash might be teeny, but she's still got the brain of an eighteen-year-old. I don't need to worry about leaving her on her own even though it does kinda feel weird to do. However, she needs to stay out of sight and can't reach anything in the kitchen, so I end up scrambling to arrange dinner for everyone while simultaneously helping Sophia, Megan, and Veronica get their hair ready for the performance. The girls wanted to eat a little early so they don't end up having gas or getting sick during the recital.

Nothing ruins a dancer's career like poorly timed flatulence in a pin-drop-silent theater.

While Ashley safely hides in my bedroom, Sophia and I gather the horde into the Tahoe—sorry, Mom, but the Sentra's out of the question unless I strap two kids to the roof like dead deer. Something tells me the police would object. Pretty sure the kids would object, too.

My three siblings plus Nicole, Megan, and Veronica pile in for a trip to the store. Meg and Veronica are already wearing their costumes, leotards divided diagonally down the chest, the left arm and upper part jet black, the bottom and other arm grey, a metallic silver stripe separating the two. They've added white leggings, metallic silver ballet flats, and gossamer frilled skirts. Fortunately, Sophia's online search found the leotard and trimmings she needs for the recital already at a store specializing in ballet and dance costumes, and even called to make sure they had it in stock. The silver ballet flats, she already owned.

This is, after all, a kids' dance school. The instructors aren't going to have an aneurysm over slight variations in shoe style.

Withering heat from an uncooperative sun coupled with the sheer volume of six children makes for a grueling trip. Worse than either of those problems is me constantly thinking about *having* six children in a five-thousand-pound death machine I'm responsible for controlling. I don't know how Megan and Veronica's parents would feel about their daughters getting in a car driven by a teenager who can't see well in bright sunlight, but I can't exactly leave them at the house with a child-i-fied Ashley to watch them.

The girls tease me a little for driving like grandma, but it doesn't bother me.

Getting them to the store in northwest Seattle safely is easy compared to trying to keep tabs on them once we arrive. It's like letting mice loose in a maze full of cheese bits. Yeah, I know mice aren't really as into cheese as cartoons claim. But for metaphor purposes, I'm sticking with it. Sophia goes right to the counter where a purple-haired woman a few years older than me leans against the wall, talking on the phone. I can't help but stare at the huge nose ring she's wearing. It's damn near a door-knocker.

"The Gates of Az-Muradin shall never be opened for as long as I draw breath," mutters Sierra.

I whirl away and laugh, making Sierra smile. Sophia takes a second longer to catch the reference, then blushes while laughing. Last year, Dad ran a D&D game for us where we went into this old underground maze and ended up having to fight a minotaur guardian. It said the same line right before our characters fought it. Sierra's saying this girl looks like a minotaur with the huge nose ring.

Oh, so wrong. But so funny.

Sophia coughs. "Umm, hi. I called a little while ago to ask if you still had the starlight leotard in stock?"

The woman mutters, "Gotta go" at the phone, hangs up, then smiles at my sister. "Hey, sweetie. Sure. I remember. Pulled it aside for you."

"Awesome! Thank you." Sophia bounces on her toes, takes the package from the clerk, and zooms off to the changing room.

Sam hovers beside me, not having any interest in looking over girls' clothes. This place carries mostly dance costumes and frilly dresses. I catch Sierra eyeing a gown in her size. The girl *does* have a fancy side, but keeps it in a locked trunk most of the time. Hmm. Maybe she didn't hate sitting for the paintings at Aurélie's as much as she claimed. Veronica and Megan run around checking out various cute outfits.

Sophia scurries out of the changing room, runs to the shelf of frills to select a gauzy skirt, then approaches the counter. The leotard's a perfect fit. Surprising, since almost nothing ever fits her right. She's both at an awkward age for sizing plus rail thin. Clothes where the fit is right aren't tall enough. Anything tall enough is baggy on her. I suspect magic happened to the leotard in the changing room. Duh. We could've ordered it online. So what if it didn't fit? She'd fix it.

I pay the clerk, round the kids up, and hit the road again.

We make it to the theater at 5:22 p.m. The routine is supposed to run for about an hour, starting at six. On the way inside, I notice Sam's wearing a backpack with the zipper open. It appears empty but the shape suggests otherwise. Blix. Gotta be. Not sure how to react. Sam isn't exactly bringing a dangerous, uncontrollable pet creature into his sister's dance recital. Blix is rather intelligent. He may, however, fail to resist the urge to mess with people in a crowded theater. Fingers crossed he only picks on audience members. Considering Sophia is in the show, I'm sure he'll leave the performers alone.

Sophia, Megan, and Veronica rush off to the backstage area while I take Sam and Nicole down the hall to the normal theater entrance. Nicole, never having been to any sort of live performance, gazes around in awe, asking a dozen questions every minute. I'm hardly an expert on theater, but I do my best to answer her questions.

Eventually, the lights dim. The curtain parts to reveal Lindsey alone on stage. This is the girl who made fun of Megan for being a little chubby, total alpha. No surprise she got the 'lead' part. At least, I think there's a lead. The instructors at the dance school love to 'adapt' popular plays and turn them into routines without words. Not sure they're going for 'interpretive dance' or anything artsy, merely something fun for the kids.

If whatever the kids are doing on stage is inspired from a movie or Broadway show, I am totally clueless as to which one. For the *Les Mis* adaptation, they did some of the songs but no dialogue. Tonight is pure dance, no words. The two boys, Ryan and Darian, are wearing all black outfits. Kids ranging in age from like nine to fifteen fly around the stage doing some fairly impressive moves considering their ages. Predictably, as one of the lighter students, Sophia's got an 'aerial' part. She's easy to lift and toss around. Drives Mom nuts with worry, but Sophia adores it. Tonight's routine isn't dangerous, merely a lift over the head and spin around type deal. They don't do wire work. Parents would object and I'm sure the insurance company would freak.

You know, I never thought watching a bunch of kids dance would hold my attention, but they are kinda mesmerizing. It's totally not the clumsy-funny-awkward sort of thing one would expect from a school talent show. They're surprisingly good, as are the student musicians from a local music academy the dance studio partners with. The hour goes by fast. And yeah, I recorded the entire performance to show Mom and Dad when they return.

SAM, NICOLE, AND I WAIT OUT IN THE FOYER ALONG WITH A BUNCH OF other parents.

I assume the dance instructors are having a post-recital meeting, party, or something. Eventually, the dancers, most of whom are wearing coats over their costumes, spill out of a steel double door and rush over to their respective families. Sophia zooms up to me, practically vibrating from excess energy. She's thrilled, excited, and nervous. Poor kid's having an emotional short circuit. She's frightened of being on stage in front of a crowd, but also had a blast tonight. Being so exhilarated at the performance despite being terrified of getting up in front of an audience is causing her to tremble. She's not sure how to process the conflicting emotions, so she settles for bouncing around and squealing in delight.

The drive home is much less nerve-wracking for me since I'm online. It's after seven and dark. Yeah, I'm still in a constant state of reminding myself this vehicle, being higher off the ground, has a greater chance of rolling, so no sudden swerving. Nonetheless, Grandma Wright gets us home in one piece. The kids—even Sam— spend the ride talking about the show. For the most part, he sounds serious saying they did a great job, but he can't resist teasing Sophia about Ryan 'grabbing her butt' when he held her up over his head.

Predictably, this makes Sophia turn bright red.

I get to deal with "It's not like that!" shouted multiple times before she realizes Sam saying "sure it isn't" over and over again is entirely meant to mess with her and not a serious accusation of her having a new boyfriend. The other girls find this hilarious, mostly since Ryan is—according to rumor—sweet on Alexis.

Anyway…

I drop Nicole off at her house, bringing Megan and Veronica with us back home. Veronica's parents are both working and couldn't take her to the recital, or attend it… so she's going to get a copy of the video I took. Megan's mother is also stuck working. Her father's in the Navy, presently out on a ship somewhere. Both girls are expecting to stay at our house until their parents pick them up here.

Ashley—back to normal—is sprawled on the living room floor surrounded by her school work. Yes, she still has my unicorn plushie nearby.

Sophia looks at her, glances at me, and pantomimes wiping sweat from her forehead.

Sierra and Sam run to the kitchen on the hunt for snacks. Megan flops on the couch. Veronica stands inside the door awkwardly for a moment before realizing she doesn't have to ask permission to take a seat on the couch.

"Ash!" I rush over.

"Oh, hi there. I didn't notice you walk in," she says, doing an impression of Tommy Wiseau. "Things have worked themselves out. I feel fine now."

I laugh. "Good."

"Talk about weird," She says, dropping the impression. "This is going down as one of the strangest days in my life."

"At least it's back to normal." I bite my lip. "Umm, I really hate to do this, but you know I have an unavoidable errand I need to take care of. Would you mind holding down the fort here until I get back?"

"Sure, no problem. How long do you think it'll take?"

"Uhh, good question. It's too late now for me to, uhh, 'walk' there, so I'm gonna go commercial. Figure three-ish hours each way plus whatever time I lose waiting on a flight schedule. Once I'm down there, it could be as fast as 'here ya go, bye' or I might get pulled into an hours-long meeting." I shrug. "Whatever happens, I'm going to try to be as fast as possible."

"Okay. You have my number. As long as your sister doesn't turn me into a Pikachu, we should be good."

"Sorry!" yells Sophia from the kitchen.

Megan and Veronica laugh, probably assuming we're talking about a video game.

Right. Time to do this.

I head to the kitchen and bring the Littles—who are presently foraging for munchies—up to speed on my need to fly a message. They're cool with it. Perhaps a little *too* much so. Sierra wants to come along, but fortunately doesn't put up a strong argument when I ask her to stay here and be safe. The 'rents are probably going to be annoyed enough at me for running this message before they come home. I can't bring Sierra *into* the world of vampire politics needlessly.

After hugging through the 'back as soon as possible' thing, I run downstairs to grab the scroll and head out the patio doors to the deck behind the house. Shit, I forgot shoes. I look down—at my sneakers. Oops. Been walking around the house in sneakers. Sorry, Mom. Somewhere, far away in Iceland, my mother's probably spent the past half hour or so attempting to figure out why a mysterious sense of wrongness came over her. Yeah, she has a sixth sense about people wearing shoes in the house.

I'm about to leap into the air when I catch sight of a large paw print in the backyard about twenty feet from the deck. Oh, hell. What now? Sometimes having superhumanly sharp eyesight can be a curse. A quick hop-flight lands me next to the print. It's the size of a bear track but more canine in shape. The faint hint of 'wet dog' smell hangs in the air, along with a sense of something watching me. No malice, though, but perhaps a little more intelligence than animal.

I'd ask Ashley out here to look at the print, but it's too dark. She wouldn't be able to see it. Besides, she's only seven months into her first year of college, hardly an authority on all things animal yet.

"You're probably the critter who tried to play with Sam the other day…" I look around, seeing nothing. This animal is either invisible or gone. Oh, great. Did Sam attract a freakin' hell hound? Do hell hounds even exist outside of D&D or general mythology.

Is it weird to say 'oh, it's a demon, no big deal; that's on Sam'?

Whatever. Let me deal with this message crap first.

I do know flying at 120 MPH is not going to get me to San Diego before sunrise thanks to the dance recital. No problem. No way could I have missed it. Sophia is only going to be a kid once. 'You blew off my dance recital to run a message for your vampire overlord' sounds like a shouting argument from an episode of Jerry Springer brought to you by meth… or Florida. Wait, same thing.

Anyway… into the air I go.

It's really easy to spot SeaTac from the air. Being easy to see from high altitude is a good quality to have in an airport. It doesn't take long for me to find a shadowy place to land and slip inside. No point bothering with a fake ticket since it's only me this time, no Sophia needing to fly, too.

A little brain surfing for information leads me to the terminal where the next direct flight to San Diego Airport is leaving. Alas, the flight isn't taking off until 9:15 p.m. I've got a little over an hour to kill. Might as well go eat someone. The airport isn't big on secluded areas, and bathroom feeding—especially in a big public airport—is disgusting. Sierra thinks she had it rough trying to take a bath in the room after Sam blew up. Hah. Her sense of smell is normal. A vampire trying to *eat* in the presence of similar fumes is… no. Just… bleh.

I ambush a guy in his younger twenties, basically someone who wouldn't raise too many eyebrows if seen making out with me in public. We're not actually making out. I'm feeding, but I position us so it looks as though we're having a PDA. Feels like I'm in a CIA movie. Stealth isn't about not being seen at all. Sometimes, it's easiest to hide in plain sight. Let people see you, but make them see something other than what's really going on.

An ominous narrator type voice rambles in my head.

*Young couple kissing by the wall. Innocent. Harmless—or so people think.*

Go figure, his blood tastes like avocado toast, extra tomato.

"Blaze!" shouts a woman. "You bastard!"

Uh oh. I hastily slurp down a few more mouthfuls before retracting my fangs and cleaning up the wound. Girlfriend's coming in hot, going to grab my hair and yank me away from her man. She's not at all prepared for my speed and stops short when I whirl to stare at her. Rage melts out of her expression as my mental power overwhelms her mind. A minute later, she doesn't remember seeing me and Blake thinks he's spent this whole time making out with her. I leave them sucking face and hurry back to the terminal.

A few minutes before they're ready to call for boarding, I get up and approach the ramp door.

Any airline employee who looks at me gets a mental prod to see me wearing a flight attendant uniform or simply ignore me. I make my way onto the plane, surprised to see the flight crew before they close the security door to the cockpit.

Hmm. Idea. There's a little fold-down jump seat behind the left pilot's chair. I could totally avoid being seen on this plane and bypass a potential argument with a passenger from taking an occupied seat by staying in here. Nice. I zap the flight crew into thinking I'm close family of the pilot and erase their hesitance at letting me ride up here.

Cool. Works for me. Scary how easy it would be for a vampire to cause serious damage, but airplane crashes tend to be fiery affairs. It's highly improbable we'd survive. Though, I suppose any vamp who could fly could bail out before impact.

Dammit. Stop thinking morbid thoughts.

The jump seat isn't exactly comfortable, but the view is amazing. I've been in cockpits before, but never of a production plane and certainly not while it flew... only halfway built ones at the Boeing plant. Pretty sure this is a 737. All digital screens and stuff. Pretty cool. This is my first time having a view out the front windows of a functional airplane.

I am—other than forcing my way onto the plane—my old alter ego, Follows Rules Girl, for the entire trip, keeping to myself and not interfering or getting in their way. It occurs to me on the flight down to San Diego I could've also hidden in the cargo hold with the luggage. Thin air or deadly cold won't bother me. Still, a baggage handler seeing a girl climb out of the underbelly would be the opposite of subtle. Easy enough to erase memories, but airports usually have security cameras on baggage areas. I'd have no way to know how many people saw me slip out and run off.

Grr. And really... running a physical letter by hand like some sort of Pony Express carrier? Haven't vampires ever heard of email? Wolent is so old, technology probably stops working around him. Maybe his fingers don't register on iPhone screens because he's too dead or something. Sigh. I'm sure sending me is some ceremonial thing, like, 'Hi, check out my new baby apprentice.' Maybe he wants his friend, this Cassandra Upton person, to meet me. Wait, no... he said it would be unlikely for me to see her. Oh, well. Might as well go through the motions and keep everyone happy.

While I don't mind doing the guy a favor, 1,100 miles is a complete pain in the ass. It's only bothering me because of the parents-on-vacation situation. I hate leaving the Littles on their own while going off to do 'vampire stuff.' And yeah, it's not like the four of us are still super clingy over my near death and always spending every minute of the day together. We've processed the guilt and almost-grief enough to return to normal. Mostly, I want to be there in case they need me.

*Ping.*

The co-pilot looks back at me. "Sweetie, you gotta turn your phone off."

"Ack. Sorry." I take it out of my bag and notice a text from Ben previewing on the lock screen: ‹The crazy neighbors have...› but can't get into a back and forth now. Gotta shut the phone off. No idea if a cell phone really can threaten an airplane, but Follows Rules Girl is not willing to take the chance.

AFTER WE'VE LANDED, TAXIED IN TO THE TERMINAL AT SAN DIEGO Airport, and the pilots have finished all the end-of-flight checklists, they get up and open the cockpit door, standing there to interact with disembarking passengers. I stay hidden behind in the jump seat, legs up, curled into a ball, more or less out of sight from people going by.

When the pilot leans back in to collect 'his kid,' I emerge from the cockpit, taking a moment to blank myself out of their memories. Anyone inside the airport is going to mistake me for a straggler passenger getting off the plane late.

Great. Wonderful. I'm in San Diego and totally lost.

It's easy enough to find the airport entrance. Once outside, I turn my phone back on. The trip might have been long, but I'm still in the same time zone. It's a little after midnight, leaving me approximately six hours before sunrise. Being caught in California during the day is going to be painful. Can't risk it. But six hours is a lot of time. Meeting vampires to drop off a message couldn't possibly keep me out past sunrise. No matter what, I'm not making it home tonight and will need to spend at least one morning sheltered here before going back to Washington. Still, if I can get done everything I need to do now, tomorrow is all mine.

No texts came in from the Littles or Ashley during the time in the air. I do, however, have another barrage from the Peters brothers. They've decided to go spy on the neighbor's house against my advice. According to Cody, they saw the two big guys dragging a live person inside seemingly against their will. I swear those two are going to get in trouble. They most likely saw them helping a drunk buddy. Honestly, if a pair of teenage boys observed a 'kidnapping,' the bad guys didn't make any effort whatsoever to be subtle. While it could potentially mean they're vampires capable of erasing the memory of witnesses, the most likely explanation is the Peters boys are seeing something innocent and imagining it dark.

Sighing, I shake my head and pull out the business card for the Delirium night club so I can plug the address into my GPS app.

How the hell did anyone find places before smartphones? Seriously.

# 17

# LOOSELY ORGANIZED CHAOS

I stop at a hover maybe 250 feet off the ground, observing Delirium.

The night club, not the mental condition.

It's an ultra-modernist industrial orgasm of burnished steel and sleek black lines, the exterior walls covered in one of those mind-warping illusion patterns where the spiraling dashes appear to move if you stare at it too long.

Wow. Merely looking at the place makes me feel a touch woozy. I'm not sure if the designer was going for East Berlin circa 1989, techno-dystopia, or what. No line waiting to get in, but the parking lot has a decent number of cars, mostly Lexus, BMW, Audi, and Mercedes. Good chance my jeans-and-T-shirt outfit isn't good enough. Don't care. If anyone tries to give me attitude for not wearing expensive clothing, they can spend an hour clucking randomly like a chicken.

No one stops me at the door, which is strange for more reasons than simply my overly mundane attire. Everyone keeps telling me how I look closer to sixteen than eighteen. Last I checked, the minimum drinking age remained twenty-one. Oh, maybe this isn't an alcohol club? The few windows on the outside appeared dark, so it might be a nude bar. Unsure what to expect, I pre-cringe on my way across the foyer to the second set of doors.

Inside, it looks like a trendy bar—or a movie set for a trendy bar in a science fiction world. At least there aren't any nude dancers. Whew.

Not saying I'm an expert on bars or anything. In fact, it's a true statement to claim I never set foot in a bar my entire life. The few times I've been inside them all happened after my Transference. A blonde woman standing at a small cashier station on my left gives me a 'what are you doing here' disdainful look. She's wearing a shockingly bright purple dress with weird silver hoop things in the shoulders—basically a fashion show experiment from the Jetsons.

I make eye contact. She's mortal, so I 'encourage' her to ignore my plain clothes and insert a command to tell me where the guy I'm supposed to meet—Jermaine Warwick—is. Mentally inserting the name into her consciousness triggers a reactive thought. He's in a VIP area accessible via a short corridor on the other side of the room. An image of him forms in her mind in response to my question as well. I'm looking for a black guy in his mid-twenties with an old-school afro as if he hasn't realized the Sixties are over. Heh, maybe he hasn't. Dude's wearing a loud-as-hell pinkish blazer, so he ought to be reasonably easy to spot... from orbit.

Careful to shield the scroll from bumps or the wait staff zooming around carrying trays of drinks, sushi, overpriced hot wings, and whatnot, I make my way across the club to the hallway. Naturally, I catch a few looks. Guess places like this rely on a person's sense of shame to keep everyone up to dress code. Good thing for me, I don't care what anyone here thinks of me. I walked halfway across Woodinville bare ass naked. Wearing jeans into a fancy club doesn't bother me at all. The people here might *look* trendy, but I'm comfortable. Hmm. Maybe I should exploit Sophia's illusion powers so I can stay in sweat pants all the time and hide it.

That'd be the life, right?

Anyway, I'm not planning to be here long, so it doesn't matter. It'll take me longer to go find 'nice' clothes than drop off the damn scroll and leave. Do they make delivery people dress up before dropping stuff off here? Well, they probably don't walk in the front door, either. Whatever.

A guy in a white suit steps in front of me, raising one hand and an eyebrow when I attempt to enter the VIP area. His attitude is somewhere between keeping a little kid out of a bar and making sure the peasants don't stray into the nice parts of the building. Lots of Dad's Eighties movies have the 'Kent' character. Rich parents. Handsome. Jock. Gets a brand new Mercedes the day he turns eighteen… and a total douche. He hasn't said a single word, and he's totally 'Kent vibing' already.

Not sure what exactly put me in a bad mood—other than being away from home when I really ought to be watching my siblings—but the idea of hearing his sanctimonious voice infuriates me even before he opens his mouth to tell me I'm not worthy. Fortunately, he's a normal human, so there's no need for me to talk my way past him.

One mental jab and he stands there staring into the fifth dimension. No need to make him forget I exist, only ignore my presence. Yeah, this is totally not the atmosphere I expected. No pounding music, no packed dance floor full of young adults slathered in neon baubles, and probably more a restaurant than the term 'night club' implies. If the local vampires use this place as a meeting-slash-feeding area, it makes sense to provide food for the blood donors.

The carpet in the VIP hallway has a similar mind-warping illusion pattern. Thin blue lines on black harken back to mid-1980s video game box art, but also create the appearance of pits and hills due to the way the lines bend and warp. Yeah, this is *not* the place to walk when drunk. Following the Jetsons' fashion model's thoughts, I head to the third door on the left.

The room is basically set up like a lounge with wingback chairs, a few small coffee tables, more chairs, a sofa, fireplace containing a neon squiggles pretending to be flames, and a ton of burnished steel décor. It's a complete clash between a stuffy old English sitting room and something out of a noir corporate dystopia where it's 300 years in the future but the décor somehow feels retro.

Jermaine's reclining in a wingback chair near the fake fireplace, one elbow on the armrest, hand supporting a wine glass of alcohol-infused blood. The smell is obvious from here. The guy's smaller than I expected, kinda reedy. Between his Sixties hair and supremely relaxed posture, he makes me think of a Vietnam-era soldier who deserted, crawled into a hole deep in the underworld, and started a little opium den.

Hi, my name is Sarah and I watch far too many movies. I'm an addict.

Seems I've interrupted a conversation. Three other vampires in the room all give me the same 'who is this bitch' look. A super pale woman in a frilly goth dress lounges on a sofa to the right of the false fireplace, her bare feet up on the cushions, boots on the floor nearby. She's probably around my age, meaning eighteen or nineteen, though she looks it. Goth Queen rolls her eyes at me, holding back the urge to laugh. I'm not feeling hostility, more of a 'how did they let you in here like that' vibe.

To the left, a pair of guys in their apparent thirties sit on either side of a little round table about the size of a dinner plate. The one on the left has Italian or Mexican features and appears to be going for the cowboy aesthetic via fringed jacket and snakeskin boots. His friend is almost as pale as the girl, but oozes a sense of 'I've got money' in a black suit over a neon purple dress shirt—the top four buttons open revealing his hairy chest. Multiple silver chains hang at varying lengths from his neck, some with charms, others plain. He's totally got Alice Cooper hair but looks nothing like him facially. Head's too narrow, face is too young, and a big Adam's apple. His week-without-shaving aesthetic gives him a presence somewhere between renegade music producer and laid-back rock star.

Jermaine narrows his eyes, no doubt wondering what the heck a girl like me is doing walking into this room uninvited. For the most part, vampires can sense each other—as vampires—on sight, even from behind. I say 'for the most part' due to my stealth technology. Other vampires need to look me square in the eyes—when I'm online—to get the same read on me. Offline, no one can tell. Duh, it's kinda stupid to point out since when I'm offline it means daylight, so no other vampires *could* be around to see me.

As I'm both online now and making eye contact with Jermaine, he obviously knows I'm a fellow vampire. Also, unless they're way older than me, they won't be able to read my mind—another big clue as to my being an undead. It takes roughly an eighty-year age gap for a vampire to be able to force their way into another vamp's head, not counting the mental link to one's sire.

Jermaine makes no move to speak or do anything.

Okay... before my death, I'd have stood there awkwardly waiting and probably thinking I did something wrong. Now? I don't care. Just want to go home as fast as possible, so I walk up to him. "Hi. Don't mind me. Just dropping off." I hold up the scroll. "You're Jermaine right?"

"Oh, wow," says the woman. "Who turned you so young? Poor thing."

Ugh. This again. Foreign city. Need to be polite and all, so I resist the urge to sigh. "I'm eighteen. I have resting kid face."

"Girl, you is a walkin' fashion apocalypse." Jermaine flails one hand about in a parody of a priest dispelling a curse, making a face like I'm wearing an outfit made of anchovies. His tone is unabashedly flamboyant. "If you're goin' to be spendin' any time 'round here, we need to get those rags sorted."

I'm about to laugh when it hits me he might have a point. Crap! Wolent sent me here officially. I'm like an ambassador or something. Maybe jeans and a *Death Note* T-shirt is a bit too informal.

"Sorry." I flash a weak smile. "Totally my fault. I should've dressed like an emissary."

The other two guys laugh.

"Aww, just teasin' ya." Jermaine cracks a smile. "We ain't formal. Welcome to San Diego."

"Thanks." Whew. Always a good thing not to start a vampire war for being too casually dressed.

He gestures at the other vampires. "Allow me to introduce Wednesday Muir, Dusty Molina, and Shaw Kimball."

Wednesday nods as he says her name. Dusty—the cowboy—makes a hat tip gesture despite not wearing one, and Shaw tilts his hands up in a 'what you see is what you get' manner. Or maybe he's making an 'it's here if you want to ride' offer. Ack. I pretend to ignore it since I'm not sure what the heck he's trying to say.

I almost laugh at the girl having the name Wednesday given her looks. Naturally, she senses me wanting to laugh and does it for me.

"Hi." I wave at everyone. "I'm Sarah."

Jermaine flicks two fingers in a beckoning manner at the scroll. "Lemme see that."

I hand it over. Gah, feels so weird acting in an official capacity as a representative of Wolent. Great. I'm like the vampire version of student council president: technically here in an official capacity, but the janitor has more power—and respect. Maybe I should invest in some professional attire for any future social situations Wolent might send me on or require my presence for. Good chance no one warned me to dress nice for this because they saw me in the ridiculous gown Aurélie loaned me and assumed I adored overdressing. Seriously, the one she wore the other night had enough room under the skirt to conceal an operational merry go round for brownies—the little one-foot tall dudes, not pre-Girl-Scouts.

Jermaine sets the scroll on the table to his left, then gestures at the other wingback chair opposite his. "Please, have a seat. Relax. You look like you're ready to run right out. Socialize."

"Yeah, well…" I sit where indicated. "I kinda was. Got a minor situation at home."

"Sorry to hear that. Hope it ain't too bad." Jermaine offers a warm smile.

"No, I meant 'minor' literally. I'm responsible for three kids."

All four vampires give me curious looks.

"Actual kids or are you chaperoning newly turned vampires?" asks Wednesday.

"It's a complicated situation. Actual kids."

Dusty and Shaw fidget uneasily, seeming concerned.

"No, they're not for biting. They're my siblings."

"Oh, honey, this I have to hear." Jermaine leans forward. "Please indulge my curiosity."

So much for a quick drop off and run. "I had a mild panic attack after my Transference. The guy who turned me lost track of my body so I ended up in a morgue having no idea what happened to me. Didn't know vampires existed…" I share a brief version of my first few days as a vampire, focusing on my snap decision to go home to my family and refusal to let them believe I'd died.

Dusty gets a far-off 'wish I thought of that' look. Wednesday 'awws' at me while Shaw doesn't show any particular emotion on his face.

"Cool. Cool. I can respect." Jermaine sips blood. "Long as you keep discretion."

"Wish everyone thought the same way. I'm all about keeping my head down, but there are some traditionalists who aren't happy." I explain the situation with Stefano and Paolo. "Arthur Wolent doesn't object at least, as long as I'm careful."

Jermaine's expression says 'ahh, no wonder you fell in with him.' Yeah, true. Can't argue. Forces gathered against me, so it would be stupid to ignore a powerful ally. "Politics are a bit more relaxed down here. Certain situations make alliances more valuable. We have an ample font of other issues so have no need to look for reasons to get pissy at each other."

"Uh oh. Sounds bad." I whistle.

"Mexico's pretty much lawless as far as our kind goes." Jermaine sips blood. "Unless you go down by Mexico City or anywhere big. Tijuana's a damn murder amusement park. Only thing stopping them from makin' San Diego untenable to us is they're so disorganized they rip each other up as much as anything else. They often head our way since we're so close, tryin' ta extend their territory. All up by Los Padres Forest is almost as bad. Ventura, Oxnard, Lompoc, all them places there are pretty wild in terms of vampires. We're caught between it and the freaks in LA."

I chuckle. "Yeah, I had an issue with the freaks in LA once before."

Dusty and Shaw go on for a while about vampire gangs and how idiotic they think the fools are. Fortunately, the 'gang' vampires in LA spend all their time fighting each other and don't often leave the city.

"Were you serious about me being underdressed? I really should've worn something a bit nicer for an official visit to like the 'mayor' of San Diego."

Jermaine and the others laugh.

"Cassandra basically calls the shots around here," says Jermaine, "but she's not officially in charge of anything. She and Wolent go way back, like to the 1800s."

"Wow…" Impressive, but not enough to shock me. Aurélie experienced the Transference in 1643.

"They're long-time friends." Jermaine makes a suggestive eyebrow motion. "Rumor has it they might'a been more than friends at one point. But then we'd be talkin' all 'unsubstantiated rumor' and all." He picks up the scroll. "This here is basically the old-as-hell version of a 'what's up, not much, cool' text exchange."

I laugh. "Really? Guess it's more to send me down here to meet you guys then? Announce myself to Cassandra?"

"Eh, something like that." Jermaine swishes the last of the blood around his glass before draining it. "Nothing so formal. Ain't like it is in Europe, or even the East Coast. Damn New York vamps waste too much damn time on formality. Bunch of elitist fools, ya ask me."

"Like London? They kinda got mad at me for not presenting myself to their leader right away."

"Oh, wow. You went to London?" Wednesday sits up. "What's it like?"

I shrug. "Basically a shadow monarchy. Vampire king. Got the sense of it being formal and organized, but I didn't get too deep into it. Had no reason to stay there long."

"We're a lot less caught up in the details of politics here," says Dusty, his voice deeper than his appearance implies. "Some cities have a strong vampire who takes the time to establish order, gather underlings, and enforce their power. Like Chicago back in the twenties."

I can't tell if this guy's trying to sound like he's from a 1950s western movie, he lived in the actual fifties, or it's merely his voice.

"Yeah." I chuckle. "I've kind of been thinking of it like the Mafia without the crime part."

"Don't let 'em fool ya, honey." Jermaine winks. "They're inta plenty of crime. Just not the same kind. Big money white-collar stuff, not prostitution, drugs, and protection."

"Every so often, ya get two such 'kings' too close to each other." Shaw wags his eyebrows. "Then the fireworks fly. Fun to watch. Not so fun to be caught in the middle."

"You should avoid Florida," says Wednesday. "It's crazy."

Jermaine refills his glass from a large wine bottle, then holds the bottle toward me in an offering manner. Sure, why not? I nod. He smiles, takes a clean glass from a cabinet under the table between our chairs, and pours me a drink.

I go to sip the blood but stop short at a whiff of alcohol. Darn. Forgot. I smelled it on the way in. "This isn't pure blood."

"Course not, dear." Jermaine smiles. "Why be boring?"

Whatever. One drink won't hurt me. I sip. The blood hits my tongue like atomic cherry. Can't tell the type of alcohol other than it being strong enough to taste like I'm swallowing flames. Whiskey, vodka, or something along those lines. Maybe even moonshine. Eek. Not sure whether to sip it gradually to minimize discomfort or get it over with. Tiny sips are more polite. I'm still here as a representative, after all. Not the time to go all Sarah of the North, Barbarian Queen, and chug ale. Besides, this stuff is so damn strong if I slug it down in one gulp, I will cough, gag, and look like an idiot.

"What's up with Florida?" I ask after the flames in my throat die down.

Wednesday makes a 'you have *no* idea' face and waves dismissively at me. "Sweetie, as if the sun, heat, and bugs weren't bad enough, picture Florida Man with vampire powers."

Dusty flares his eyebrows. "Yeah. Gets powerful weird down there."

I cringe. Facebook's had some bizarre 'Florida Man' news stories…

like some dude getting himself killed while trying to have sex with an alligator. Don't even want to imagine the vampire equivalent. "Wow. Okay, yeah…" Eight sips into this spiked blood is starting to give me a little buzz. Better stop at one glass.

"How's it up in Seattle?" asks Shaw. "You got any crazy ones up there?"

"Nothing even close to 'Florida Man' type stuff, but I do kinda keep to myself."

"Probably why the old man sent ya down here." Shaw winks. "Whenever he or Upton get some new blood, they send 'em over to say hi."

Wednesday approaches us, holding her empty cup out to Jermaine for a refill. "I think they're collecting followers and having a friendly competition to see who can get the bigger team."

"Great, I'm a Pokémon." I chuckle.

The others look at me as if I'd started singing in some foreign language. Guess they're too old to get the reference.

"I'm a new pet critter he wants to show off." Heh. Here's hoping Wolent and Upton don't make their minions fight random duels.

Wednesday tilts her head. "I don't think they're 'collecting' us, but who really knows how the really old ones think?"

"Yeah, seriously."

Jermaine leans closer, studying me like I'm a bug under a magnifying glass. "Damn, girl. You're an enigma."

"Umm, okay?"

He smiles. "Never saw anyone put so much effort into their face while pullin' a total 'screw it' on the wardrobe."

"I'm not wearing makeup."

Jermaine lets out a sassy sort of sigh. "I mean your *face,* not your cosmetics. Honey, you be tryin' way hard to look like you're still alive. Not knockin' it, just find it odd for you to be so concerned about appearances and ignorin' the most important part—the wardrobe."

"Oh. Can't help it. My body does it on its own."

Sigh.

A conversation about being an Innocent—I avoid mentioning my sunlight tolerance—plus finishing my spiked blood eats far more time than expected. At least these three don't pity me for being a weak strain. Wednesday embraces her paleness due to—or perhaps in spite of—her name. For all I know, it's a 'character' name she adopted after turning into a Goth queen post-Transference. My guess about Dusty proved reasonably accurate. The guy used to be a film actor in the later Fifties. No one famous, mostly played random henchmen or ranch hands who ended up on screen for a few minutes before taking a bullet. Shaw doesn't share much of his background other than to say he became a vampire in the early Eighties. He and Dad would probably get along. Both of them are frozen in the same era.

Finally, they realize time's short. I hadn't really expected to be able to fly home tonight, but it's still mildly annoying to have lost hours here. Oh well, not really a big deal. Being friendly to the locals is the nice thing to do and it's not as if the sibs would be awake now anyway.

After our little party breaks up, I make my way outside via the back door at the end of the VIP hallway. Conveniently, the Delirium night club doesn't have any lights on behind the building. Almost like they do it on purpose for us to have a secluded place. Works for me. I leap into the air and fly around in an expanding circle, searching for a good place to weather the morning.

Tonight, I'm the 800-pound gorilla in the fourth-grade joke.

Where does a vampire sleep?

Wherever she wants to.

# 18

# SPEAKING OF CRAZY

S helter takes the form of an abandoned house a mile or so away from downtown.

Maybe abandoned isn't exactly the right word. Vacant works better, since it's not in bad shape and a 'for sale' sign stands in the front yard. Place has a weird energy inside. Can't tell if it's haunted or the odd feeling is coming from my unease at legit breaking into a place. Yeah, Follows Rules Girl engaged in a little casual B&E.

I rationalize it away as not a big deal due to it being a matter of survival. Not as if I'm kicking in the door to steal someone's crap, trash the place, or even go exploring for stupid teenage curiosity. My ass needed something between it and the California sun. The house doesn't have a basement, so I squeezed into the closet containing the hot water heater. Only spot free from windows.

It bothers me to be away from home on Sunday while my parents are out of the country. I don't like sitting in a little closet over a thousand miles away from the Littles when Mom and Dad aren't there for them. Ashley's doing a great job helping me, but she's still Ashley. There's a reason I couldn't tell if she mentally turned six when Sophia's magic went wonky. The differences in her personality aren't terribly manifest. About the biggest change in her is no longer believing Santa is real. Otherwise, she's still pretty much a kid at heart —which is good. Ashley is sweet, innocent, kind, loving, and puts herself wholly into everything she does.

But I'm not a hundred percent confident she'll hold it together in a serious crisis.

Then again, she did attack the wannabe vampire hunter the one time. Maybe I underestimate her. Sometimes the cute ones are the deadliest. Also, Blix and some large dog-like creature are at the house. No idea if the mysterious canine is friendly or merely present, though.

Argh! I wanna go home.

Totally don't mean it the way it sounds. I'm not homesick. I'm worried about my siblings.

I call Ashley since it's the only thing I can do from a hot water closet.

We talk for over an hour. Once the initial 'is everyone still alive' stuff is out of the way, it feels like we're fifteen again and stuck at home after it's too late to go outside, killing the last hour before bedtime by talking about random nonsense. She teases me by saying the Tahoe should be back to normal before I get home and won't admit if she's kidding or something happened.

My assumption is she's kidding. Anything serious, she wouldn't avoid telling me.

I can't quite get out from under the feeling 'something weird' is imminently about to happen. Hopefully, it's only my guilty conscience needling me for going off on a vampire errand while my siblings needed me. Maybe they don't *need* me quite as much as I want to believe. It's not as if they're five and six years old, though Sophia might still be afraid of the closet monster. Sam actually *has* a closet monster.

"Ash, do you think I should've waited for the 'rents to come back?"

"Before going to Cali?"

"No, before dying my hair blonde."

She squeals. "You did not!"

"No, dork. I didn't. Of course I mean running the message to Cali."

"Uhh, maybe. I guess something was important for you to do it."

I twirl my hair around my finger repetitively. "Worried using family as an excuse to delay doing something for them would give the idiots ammo to use against us. I can just hear Stefano whining to Wolent about how I'll always put my family ahead of vampire matters and demanding I make them forget me—or someone kills them."

"Well... you will put them ahead of everything. And you should," says Ashley.

"I know. But waving it in their faces right now isn't smart. Besides, what he asked me to do is fairly trivial and it's not like the Littles are four-year-olds. Plus, I have you to save my ass. Better to hold off on getting into an argument with elder vampires for when it's important. Gotta protect you guys. Don't want the buttheads having any reason to get more upset at my family."

"Guess it makes sense then. Like I said, all quiet here. Sam's friends are here. Up in his room. The girls went to Nicole's house."

"Okay. Sounds good. I'll be home in a couple hours. As soon as the sun lets me out."

"Cool. Any idea what time?"

"Probably not going to get there until at least ten, unfortunately. Unless I buy an actual ticket... which I might do just to hurry it up."

She laughs. "Let me know what happens, okay?"

"Definitely."

I can't even sit still for ten full minutes after we're off the phone before worry gets me again. How long it will take before my expectations of supernatural badness affecting my family lessens? We're way overdue. Then again, mystics magi-kidnapped Sophia across the ocean, then other mystics kidnapped her, then freakin' brownies nabbed her. Such craziness ought to satisfy the Universe's need for weird for a few more months.

At least a couple weeks.

Right?

Hmm. Don't wanna sit here. I crack the closet door open to test sun levels in the house. It's pretty damn bright as none of the windows have curtains. Almost too painful for me to leave the space beside the water heater. But, if my ability to resist—

somewhat—sunlight is technically a vampiric power, it stands to reason I can develop it and get better at doing it. Innocents can't be as rare as we seem to be. I'm guessing the apparent scarcity is a combination of vampire society not thinking us significant enough to study/document much, plus a little embarrassment. Some vampires might not want to admit being Innocents the same way people in the 1800s attempted to conceal being left-handed.

You know, since using the 'wrong' primary hand meant Satan owned you or some nonsense.

I clench my jaw and extend my hand into the sun until it smokes, then recoil, watch it heal, and repeat the process a few times. Damn this is painful. California sun is not messing around. This shit hurts. The only way I'm leaving this closet at the moment is an epic Hollywood style running-on-fire charge because I need to save one of my siblings from being hit by a car... or grab the last skinny mocha before the Starbucks ran out of sugar-free chocolate syrup. I might end up a smoldering ruin of bones and leathery flesh, but... the coffee... my precious.

Yeah, no. Developing my sunlight tolerance is not happening in five minutes. If it's even a possibility at all, I'm looking at decades. Furies don't wake up from the Transference strong enough to throw vending machines right away.

Right. Stuck in jail for now. Grr.

I pull the closet door shut, rest my chin on my knees, and make faces at the wall while rubbing my poor, tender hand.

MAYBE AN HOUR LATER, IT'S GOTTEN FAR ENOUGH INTO THE AFTERNOON where I'm able to leave the windowless space.

Outside still isn't happening without spontaneous Sarah combustion, but my cage got bigger. This house has no electricity. Can't charge my phone. No TV. Gah. Mega bored. I spend another forty minutes or so wandering empty rooms playing chicken with patches of sunlight. As long as I don't stand in them, I'm not in too much pain. So weird playing 'the floor is lava' for real.

The eerie feeling is gone from the house, or maybe my senses are so damn dulled by the daylight I wouldn't notice a box truck running over an army of mimes twenty feet away from me. Would a mime getting hit by a car scream for real or just make faces?

Hour drags into hour. So bored.

I'm half tempted to clean the place purely for something to do, but the cabinets are all empty. No cleaning supplies. Yes, I checked. Every cabinet. Crawled into them too like a six-year-old. This place has a lazy Susan inside the corner cabinet in the kitchen. Am I pathetic for thinking it's a cool use of otherwise inaccessible space?

No, I'm bored.

Lazy Susans are not mic-drop cool unless you're elderly or pathologically into home design. It's a sickness.

Bored.

I kill an hour 'painting' a flock of doves on the wall in what I think is the dining room by making handprints in the dust. It's tempting to take a shower despite the lack of hot water, but... the water doesn't work either. Must've been shut off. Speaking of... what evil genius found a way to charge people money for water? The Earth is covered in it. How can water be monetized? I bet the same bastards are working hard to monetize air if they can. Some places make it illegal to collect rain water. Probably so the bastards can charge people for water. They don't want anyone off the grid.

Bleh.

No, I'm not a conspiracy wonk. I'm bored.

Argh.

I bang my head into the wall, adding to the dove artwork—not hard enough to damage anything. If I didn't want to go home so bad, the time wouldn't be so maddening. Screw it.

At 5:19 p.m., I walk out the front door—and burst into flames.

I peer down at myself, on fire. "Well, that didn't work."

Ouch.

The flames go out as soon as I jump inside and slam the door.

Okay, I didn't exactly pull a Sarah Connor clinging to the fence during a nuclear blast, only a few flickering candle flames. Still. Owwie. No one likes to be on actual fire. It sucks. I do a stupid little dance routine starting off by swatting the smoking patches of my clothes and ending by giving double middle fingers to California and the sun. Nothing against the state or its people, just its geographical location and relationship with the firey ball of 'screw you.'

I count the rooms again.

Except the attic. It's the house of nope. Too hot. And it's got one of those little pull down folding ladder things. Never liked those. I'm afraid of the one in our house, too. Sane people don't go to attics. Attics are where the ghosts and scary stuff live. House builders know this. It's why they put in those idiotic deathtrap contraption ladder things as a warning to keep people out.

No, I'm not having a mental breakdown.

Bored.

Phone's at twenty-two percent charge. Screw it. Don't have too much longer to wait. Oh, craprabbits. Daylight-Mess-With-Sarah's-Life-Time kicked in overnight. Sunset isn't until 6:53 p.m. Best case scenario, it takes me a few minutes to fly to the airport, there's a plane leaving for SeaTac between 7:15 p.m. and 8:00 p.m., and I'm home around eleven. Littles will be asleep. I could also fly on my own straight home, in which case I'll get there closer to four in the morning. Littles still asleep. Going commercial gives me more time to deal with house stuff or throw at the homework I need to complete for Monday's classes.

Okay. Commercial it is. Maybe I can speed things along.

Could take an Uber to the airport before sunset so I'm there on time to catch the earliest possible flight based on when my powers come online. It's probably not worth it though. Won't exactly take me forever to fly from here to the airport after dark.

Bored. So bored I make 'dust angels' on the floor.

The worst way to make time pass is to want it to pass.

I know the layout of this house as well as anyone who lived here for ten years—except the attic. Could be a pile of money on the floor and I still wouldn't go up there. A magical portal to teleport me home is about the only thing capable of tempting me to scale the rickety folding ladder, and I'd still have to make it past the evil ghosts.

Figured I passed the point of desperation when I got annoyed at not being able to clean a stranger's house. Cleaning isn't fun, but it's *something* to do. I make more dust angels on the floor. Good thing Ashley isn't here or the dares would've gotten out of hand. There would've been bare boob prints on the walls. Some realtor is going to be highly confused when they show this place. Yeah, crap. I better do something about fingerprints. One downside to being an Innocent, I might still leave them. Most vampires don't since their bodies no longer produce skin oil.

One might ask how mine does, considering I'm as dead as any other vampire.

I can fly. Explain *that* with science. Who cares about minor bodily functions?

"It's magic!" I yell, doing an impression of Eddie Izzard.

Pacing.

Grumbling.

Ugh.

FINALLY! THE SUN WEAKENS ENOUGH FOR ME TO GO OUTSIDE.

Can't fly yet, still too daylight-y, but screw it. I'm walking to the airport. I have an iPhone and a navigation app and I'm not afraid to use them. Don't care if the distance covered on foot is minuscule compared to flying, it's something to do other than rattle around an empty house. At least I busied myself wiping down fingerprints for a while.

As soon as I go online—like twenty minutes after leaving the house—it's tempting to hurl myself right into the air. But... pedestrians and traffic exist. Worse, they exist in places where they can see me. To avoid a 'girl flies into the air' video appearing on

YouTube, I duck into an alley behind a convenience store for some cover.

An instant before takeoff, the crunch of shoes on pavement stalls me. Someone's coming up behind me. Great. Figures I pick a spot where a mugger's waiting for a victim. For an instant, I tense up, bracing for attack. It's not easy to disregard six or so years of hypervigilance. Ever since Mom gave me 'the talk' around twelve, being anywhere alone is scary, worse at night. Don't have to worry about it anymore—provided my attacker isn't a vampire—but the scenario still triggers an instinctual response.

Does it mean I'm still mentally human or just a chicken?

The dude continues walking toward me at an unhurried pace. Probably thinks I haven't noticed him. Most people can't hear the noise sneaker soles make on blacktop. It is a pretty bizarre sound, honestly. Similar to slowly biting down on a rice cake plus a little bit of rubbery squeaking.

When he reaches about six feet behind me, the smell hits. Oh. My. God.

An ammonia fire scorches my nostrils. He stinks like he threw whiskey vomit up all over himself, crapped his pants, then sunbaked in the same clothes for several days. Good thing I can hold my breath forever.

Don't even want to know what his blood would taste like.

"Round here somewhere," mutters the guy. "Lizard man stashed it. Where ya at?"

I turn my head, peering back over my shoulder at him. Guy's only a little older than me. His long, unkempt brown hair is down to his waist, almost touching his grungy jeans. He doesn't seem to notice I'm here. His thoughts are all over the place. The only thing even close to a coherent theme rattling around in his brain is a six-foot anthropomorphic talking lizard man who told him he stashed some meth behind this 7-11 to keep the CIA from finding it. Whoa. This guy's on something pretty damn strong. Or he's legit nuts. Maybe both. High *and* crazy.

Wow. Okay, he's *not* a creep coming to assault me.

My fear shifts entirely to pity. I back out of his way, letting him go on about his night hunting for the imaginary drugs and the lizard prophet. Good luck dude. Hope you find your crystal myth.

Speaking of crazy, I wonder what's going on with the Peters brothers. No, not calling them nuts, but 'crazy' made me think of the bizarre neighbors. After flying up to about 200 feet, well out of sight from anyone on the ground, I pull out my phone and check the texts I forced myself not to look at before. Have to save battery in case home calls. Answering one non-essential text would've suckered me into burning my battery away on texting for hours. When trapped in an empty house, even talking to Cody and Ben about their nutty conspiracy theories would've been welcome.

Some poor realtor is going to walk into the place, see my explosion of dust doves on the wall, dust angels randomly on the floor, and have a complete WTF moment. I laugh to myself at the imagined scene and open the window to Cody's messages.

Hmm. They heard screaming coming from the creepy house down the street from them. Ben insists a male voice yelled for help, but Cody didn't hear it. They talk about watching the video camera, thinking someone's being chased around inside … and going to check it out in person.

Their last message came in over an hour ago.

‹Hey guys. What happened?›

I wait a minute.

Two minutes.

‹Hey, you guys there?›

Another two minutes, no response.

Dammit!

I flip to Ashley's messenger window. ‹Something might have come up. Peters boys are like lemmings. Think they ran off a cliff. They're right around here in SoCal… gonna pop over there and check on them. I shouldn't have let them remember.›

Meh. Those two would have 'gone after vampires' anyway. It's probably not my fault they are in trouble. Most likely, the cops picked them up for trespassing on the ordinary—but weird—neighbor's lawn. If so, I should let things play out normally. Maybe they'll learn. But, I have to at least go look to satisfy my guilty conscience.

Ventura, California isn't too far away from here according to Google Maps. Oh, look. It's right next to Los Padres Forest... the area full of wild lawless vampires according to Jermaine.

Oh, shit. Could the boys be *right*?

# 19

# VAMPIRE COMMAND CENTER

San Diego to Ventura is about 140 miles in a straight line.

I must be having a mild freakout since it takes me less than an hour to fly there. Not *much* less, but fifty-six minutes is still less than an hour. Between the exertion of flying faster than normal and spending the day playing chicken with intense sunlight, I can't resist the urge to pounce on the first person I see below me.

Sorry, random guy walking across an enormous field alone at night.

It's probably a farm or something. Whatever. Sometimes a girl would really kill for a cheeseburger. Fortunately, while my diet has the potential to be more than metaphorical in terms of killing someone to eat, I am not crazy hungry, merely super hungry.

Anyway, this poor farmer happened to be in the right place at the right time. All alone out in the middle of the field. Headlights stream by on a road off to our left—East Harbor Boulevard according to my phone. We're too far away for anyone to notice me drop out of the air, knock the guy flat to the ground, and climb on top of him.

Dude puts up a bit of a fight at first, screaming and trying to throw me off while yelling in Spanish about Chupacabra. He does manage to toss me aside—hey, I don't weigh much—but the instant we make eye contact, he's mine. Dude goes limp. I climb on top of him again. Another thing I have to thank Scott for... whenever my brain doesn't concoct an opinion of a person before biting them, their blood tastes like cheeseburger. The first blood meal I ever consumed came from him—via thermos from Dalton. Scott's death probably put at least one Burger King out of business considering how often he ate there.

When I'm done drinking from the guy, I leave him a memory of a dog running out of nowhere, crashing into him, and taking off to explain why he's going to come back to his senses lying on the ground.

Into the air once more I go.

The boys mentioned they lived in Ventura soon after we began Facebook chatting. When we met at the Lewis and Clark Caverns campsite, they'd only told me they lived in Southern California. This place has palm trees. Vampires should not be here. At least, vampires capable of being awake before sunset should not be here. Nuclear sunlight isn't an issue when it's impossible to be awake unless it's dark.

While they told me the city, they never gave me an address. Honestly, why would they? I live a thousand miles away. Even them popping up on Facebook surprised me. I never expected to see or hear from them again after our road trip ended. Of course, now I'm worried sick they've gotten themselves into trouble. Jermaine talking about the vampiric political system—or lack of it—in this area has me on edge, and not only for the boys. By my thinking, any vampire who would want to live in an area where no organized effort is made to be civilized is probably prone to violence. Not nice people. I don't feel like being the target of a random sport attack or end up kidnapped by a gang of wild Lost Ones.

Yeah, good chance I'm panicking and worrying too much.

Half the time this crazy shit happens in my life, it feels like I've fallen into one of Dad's Eighties movies. Depending on cheese factor, I'm going to end up forced into a combat skateboard event for my unlife or wind up chained to the front end of a post-apocalyptic doom wagon. Yes, Dad has a movie about post nuclear vampire gangs. I don't remember the name of it but it exists. Also, yes… it's every bit as lame as it sounds. How lame? The main bad guy is named Nuke Fang.

Right, so I'm in Ventura. I've got the city part down, but have no idea where in said city to find the Peters clan. Suppose the best way for me to find out is to mentally influence a cop to look them up in the system. If I *was* in one of Dad's cheesy movies, something impossibly convenient would happen right about—*ping*.

I blink, then look down at the phone in my hand.

Facebook chat message from Ben: ‹Hey, we're back. What's up?›

Oh, son of a bitch.

Another freaky cool thing about being a vampire. I can thumb-type as fast as normal people can speak. Wait, that doesn't make me a vampire. It makes me a tween girl. ‹You guys scared the hell out of me. Thought something happened to you. Already in Ventura to check on you.›

‹Oh, wow. Cool! You really came down here?›

‹Yeah. Other issues brought me to SoCal. Was about to go home when you didn't answer texts after saying you were gonna go snooping around.› I exhale hard, most of the concern I had for them having morphed into irritation. Mostly at myself for panicking, not so much at them.

‹Sorry. Parents made us go shopping with them. Left the phone in the truck. Hey can you help us out since you're already down here?›

‹You guys are nuts. Your neighbors are not vampires.›

‹Can you tell?›

I stare at the stars. Ugh. Here we go. Whatever. I'm already here. ‹If I come over and tell you these people are not vampires, will you believe me?›

‹Totally. Swear. As long as you like actually check and don't just say it.›

All right. The least I can do is stop these two guys from ending up in juvenile detention for breaking into a house or whatever other trouble they get into. ‹Okay. I'm by a farm. What's your address?›

They send the address, all the way at the east end of the city, about a mile and a half from where I landed. Easy peasy. They describe their house as being a small two-story, powder blue, covered in 'strange crap' like giant dreamcatchers and mystical crystals their mother thinks wards off bad energy.

Hmm. Sunflower Street. Sounds like something straight out of a movie. One of those seemingly innocent 'horror but not really scary' movies that kids think is lame or funny but ends up giving them nightmares for years. It isn't too difficult to find despite the relative sameness of the houses in the suburban neighborhood. I slip out of the air, gliding straight down between two houses across the street from theirs, a nice spot too dark for anyone to see me land.

The boys are waiting for me out on their porch. And wow. They *look* older. It's only been like eight months since I saw them and they're both taller. Ben's a year younger than Cody. I distinctly remember his eyes being an inch or two below mine. We're now the same height. Other than getting taller, they haven't changed much. Still the same kinda-long light brown hair and overacted 'vampire hunter' bravado. Ninety-eight percent chance Cody has a camouflage bandanna in his pocket. Speaking of pocket, something I'm not entirely comfortable with is hanging out of his jacket. No, nothing dirty.

It's a fluorescent orange gun, and not a super-soaker.

The whole thing is bright orange. I've seen enough movies to recognize a flare pistol. Of course, he's carrying one of those thinking it will ignite a vampire like a dried-out Christmas tree. Considering Glim's feelings toward a single birthday candle, a flare gun might actually be a threat... at least to Shadows. I *think* my body is 'moist' enough not to immolate in seconds.

"Uhh, what's that?" I point at it.

"Insurance," says Cody, trying to do an impression of an action movie tough guy. Note, the 'trying.'

"Flare gun." Ben slaps him on the shoulder. "He picked it up at a garage sale last summer. Figure it'll one-shot a vampire. Cody thinks you're hot, but are you flammable?"

Cody blushes hard.

He's gotten over his crush on me, but he is embarrassed by his brother's joke, worse because neither of them have girlfriends. Two boys who spend most of their time 'hunting vampires' and reading vampire comic books haven't managed to find girls yet. Surprising. There's gotta be a girl or two their age out there who's into horror comics and can't wait to sit in the bushes spying on someone's house for hours at night. She might not be in this state, but she's gotta be out there. Statistical probability.

I spent most of my time in high school being relatively invisible. Not too popular, not too nerdy. These two let their freak flag fly. Most of their friends think they're 'out there,' believing in monsters and space aliens and healing crystals. They don't, by the way. Believe in healing crystals, I mean. Mrs. Peters does. Oh, boy does she. There's an eight pound one in the front window of the house like *the lamp* from *Christmas Story*. There for all the neighbors to see in its gleaming amethyst glory.

Anyway – nothing too abnormal going on in their heads. Cody is no longer daydreaming about me rising out of a pool in a string bikini and swinging my wet hair over my head. I'm 'one of the guys.' Part of their 'vampire hunting team.' Ugh. These two are totally going to get themselves killed if they run into a real vampire. On the plus side, they're not afraid of me.

"I don't think I'm any more flammable than a normal person. But we are also not testing this. Please be careful. Those things are dangerous."

"It's a weapon. It's supposed to be dangerous," says Cody, still trying to do Arnold Stallone or Sly Schwarzenegger. Can't tell what he's going for. Oh, wait. I think he's attempting Charlie Sheen as an action hero. Works, since he's definitely more *Hot Shots* than *Rambo*.

Heh. I can't help but grin. "Right... so what—"

"Check this out." Ben grabs my hand and drags me in the front door.

I could resist, but I gotta see where this goes.

Mr. Peters is in the living room watching some manner of sports. He pays us no attention, mostly because we cross behind him to the stairs and go up. Other than the excessive amount of quasi-mystical stuff (talismans, more dreamcatchers, crystals, pendants, moon symbols) everywhere, the house seems pretty normal.

The boys' bedrooms stand opposite each other not far from the top of the stairs, a bathroom and the parents' bedroom farther off down the hall. Ben leads me into the door on the right. Yeah, wow. I'm totally in a cheesy movie. His bedroom is so stereotypical it hurts. I gaze around in stunned disbelief at comic posters, band posters, two Sports Illustrated swimsuit posters, various models of military planes, ninja weapons, two swords, combat knives hanging on the walls, a set of nunchakus, and a gradually collapsing bookshelf littered with soda bottle caps and GI Joe figures he probably hasn't touched in years. And yes, piles and piles of comic books stacked wherever he can put them. About the only thing missing is the bed shaped like a spaceship or race car. Bet he had one but outgrew it.

Something smells strongly of grape. I don't see any obvious source, so I'm going with spilled soda on the rug from months ago.

A single, small dreamcatcher on the inside of the door *has* to be his mother's demand.

He rushes over to his computer desk, which boasts an impressive three flat-panel monitors as well as a laptop. None of the gear looks brand new, most likely all hand-me-downs from Dad or bought used.

"Welcome to vampire command." Ben gestures at the screens.

"This is where the magic happens." Cody wags his eyebrows.

"Yeah, I'm sure." I whistle. Not gonna ask what kind of magic goes on in the bedroom of a teenage boy.

Ben sits in the chair and taps the keyboard. The monitors flicker to life. Two have a Windows desktop over wallpaper based on a horror comic I don't recognize. Monitor three is full-screen showing video from a camera in bushes facing a huge, white house in a style completely unlike all the other houses in the area. The place looks older, as if it had been built in the early 1900s. White siding, black roof… totally the setting for a scary movie. Okay, now I understand why they're going nuts about these neighbors. Anyone living in a micro-mansion and acting creepy is going to inspire overactive imaginations. Worse for Cody and Ben since they *know* vampires exist.

Two relatively large guys in dark coats emerge from a side door into a small paved lot—wow, this house has a driveway so big it's more of a parking lot—and get into a black van. The pair do look shady. Both are older, in their fifties or sixties, tall, broad-shouldered, kinda dark complexions with unibrows. Maybe Greek or Sicilian. Neither man appears to be in a good mood, as if they've been called in to work on a day off or are on their way to break someone's legs for not paying a debt.

"They go out together like this about once a week." Cody points at the first screen. "Pull up file thirty-six."

"Oh, yeah." Ben opens a video player app, scrolls down a file list, and double clicks one. "We recorded this Wednesday."

Another window opens showing the same view out of the bush as monitor three, again at night. Ben fast-forwards to the nineteen-minute mark. The same black van rolls into view from off camera, parking in roughly the same spot where the two men found it tonight. The guys exit the van, stroll around to the back end, and drag a bundle out.

Okay, I gotta say... it really *does* look like a person wrapped in a blanket. The somewhat younger looking of the two carries it away to the house effortlessly, like it's a fake Halloween prop made of empty plastic bottles in the shape of a dead body while the other guy shuts the van doors before following him. Hmm. Anyone seeing them wouldn't think it's a real body purely due to how easily the man carried it. Dead humans are much heavier than most people think. Not only are they literal dead weight, they're cumbersome. Even strong people transporting a body appear to be exerting effort. Not this guy.

Two possibilities. Either he's a vampire—or werewolf—and incredibly strong, or the boys are paranoid and the bundle didn't contain human remains or an unconscious person. Transporting dead bodies doesn't fit anything a vampire would do, at least not transporting them *into* their residence. So, either they went for takeout and brought an unconscious meal home, or something else is going on here.

Hmm. I fold my arms. "It does and doesn't look like a body."

The boys stare at me.

"How can it be both?" asks Ben.

"Schrodinger's corpse?" Cody laughs.

I chuckle. "Shape matches, but it doesn't look heavy enough to be a person."

"Duh. They're vampires." Ben flexes his arms. "They're crazy strong."

Cody nods. "Yeah, and we never see them taking any corpses out of the house. Only in."

"Whoa. What are they doing, stacking them up?" I shift my jaw side to side. "Assuming they really are carrying bodies, or people."

"No idea. We haven't gotten into the house." Cody narrows his eyes. "Yet."

I raise my hands in a 'wait up' gesture and head over to the window. "Okay. Fine. I don't want to spend all night here. My sibs need me. Be right back."

"What are you doing?" asks Ben, spinning in the chair to face me.

"I'm going to go down the street, wait for those two to come back, and see what they're thinking." I open the window, letting in a nice breeze, then the screen. "If they aren't vampires, I want you guys to ignore them... or send your video to the police."

"What if they are?" Cody folds his arms, chin held high in confidence. "What then?"

I pause, one leg out the window. "Honestly? Same thing. You two stay away from them. If they hurt you, I'm going to feel responsible for it. Now, wait there. I'll be back in a few minutes."

Not waiting for any reply, I dive out the window and cruise into the air.

Quick trip down to the end of the street—well a bit past—and I can go home.

I'd say 'there's no way these people are vampires,' but if I do, they're definitely going to be.

# 20

# VALID CREEPY

The street the boys live on curves gradually to the left.

While they said the strange neighbors lived at the end, in truth, the big, white house isn't at the end of their street as much as a short distance outside this suburban development on the other side of maybe sixty yards of open scrub desert. Yeah, the eerie white house definitely existed here long before this residential area popped up. I glide down to land among the houses where Sunflower Street curves away from the open dirt and walk the remaining distance. The residential area is pretty desert-like. All palm trees and weird bushes. Not many places to hide in the neighborhood. Even less cover out in the field surrounding the strange house.

There are, however, giant bushes arranged as sort of a hedge-wall around the property. Ben's camera appeared to be concealed inside one of them. The house is even more eerie in person, without the separation of electronic video. As soon as I look at the building, it's beyond obvious *something* supernatural is going on here. The giant house gives off a dark presence strong enough to where I almost mutter 'nope' and walk away. But if this is a horror movie, I'm the dumb teenager, so I keep going.

All the other homes in this area share a common aesthetic,

seemingly built within the past twenty years. Nice little lawns, attached garage, some single-story, some two-story, a few with a partial second floor, but generally they're all the same basic design.

This place is completely different. Pretty sure it's got wood siding even. It's large, two stories and a full attic, so basically three stories tall. The attic level's ringed with dormer windows, six on the front face. All dark, even to my eyes. Like straight out of *The Amityville Horror*, it feels as though the house itself is staring at me.

Okay, what the hell? I am a creature of the night. I'm not supposed to get the willies from creepy houses. I may be a Starbucks-sipping plushie-hugging version of a creature of the night with an appreciation for cute, but I'm still a darn vampire.

Grr.

I step around the hedge and come face to face with a possible answer for the weird vibe in the air—an old wooden sign at the corner of the property. The words 'Stillwell Mortuary' stand out in faded gothic lettering above 'est 1908.'

Whoa. Old funeral home. Explains why there's a small parking lot next to a house.

The relatively deteriorated state of the sign suggests this funeral parlor is no longer operational as a business. Or is it? Could be a reason those men would be carrying bodies into the building. However, I don't think it's normal for bodies to be brought in slung over a guy's shoulder, is it? Yeah, sure, if they're coming right from the hospital where they died, the bodies wouldn't be in caskets yet, but at least use a gurney. Some dignity? Don't throw people around like a sack of dog food. The dark 'blanket' might've been a body bag. A mortuary is like any other business, right? Some can be shady, cut corners. If there's a working undertaker here, I understand why bodies could be going into the place, but wouldn't they have to come out eventually? I don't see any sign of a hearse or limos or flower car. The boys would surely have noticed funerals taking place. Neither one of them said anything about it being a mortuary.

Who in their right mind buys an old funeral home to live in?

According to Ben and Cody, the people here are not in their right mind, after all. But vampires? I dunno. Seems too on the nose for vampires to live here. But, reality is often far stranger than people think. Windows too dark for me to see through, stark white walls, black roof... yeah, this place is totally un-creepy. Not. Tint is the most mundane explanation for the windows being impenetrable. Might be shadow people blowfishing the glass, but unlikely. Could be magic, too. Also, unlikely. Mystics are even rarer than vampires.

Know what's funny? Most vampires I've met don't believe mystics are real. Talk about ironic.

I'm annoyed at this place for having the gall to make me nervous, so I sneak onto the property for a closer look. It's weird the boys didn't say anything about the serious creep factor hanging over it. I'm guessing my supernatural senses are able to detect something ordinary people can't read. Admittedly, becoming a vampire has made me somewhat of a spiritual medium. I can see ghosts, but it's hardly unique among vampires. Almost all of us can with one surprising— and one not surprising—exception. Furies often can't see them due to their diminished ability to concentrate on stuff. They don't do well with tasks requiring quiet focus. Give a Fury a Rubik's cube and something's going to get smashed when they can't solve it in two minutes. The surprising exception is Academics. According to Aurélie, their inability to see ghosts has to do with their near-complete lack of emotion. Ghosts are creatures of pure emotion—and a dash of electromagnetism.

Anyway, if this place is teeming with spirits, it would definitely throw off gobs of creep.

Something else is here, though. And I really don't like the way it feels—mostly because it feels similar to Aurélie. Vampires of a certain age have so much power other vampires can sense it on them. Like how people can feel heat coming from an element on an electric stove, only one where it takes two centuries to heat up. Depending on the elder's personality, the energy takes on different moods.

Oddly enough, Arthur Wolent doesn't have it yet. He's relatively young, a decade or two away from being 200 I think. Paolo Cabrini does, unfortunately. And his radiance is definitely of the 'do not F with me' variety. Aurélie's is of the 'don't you dare use the wrong fork with the salad' variety. Kidding, she's also a 'cross me and die painfully' type, though *I* don't get the vibe from her. For me, her aura makes me feel simultaneously reassured and terrified of doing something stupid in front of her.

Anyway, the vibe wafting from this house is 'leave me the hell alone.'

No. Can't be. The freakin 'Frog Brothers' can't be right about the people who live here. No way are they actually vampires. Something else is going on and my brain is misinterpreting. I haven't been a vampire for a full year yet. Why am I trusting my senses and assuming because the mood in the air from a creepy former funeral home kinda feels like the mood hanging in the air around elders, it's a vampire.

I have to be wrong.

Annoyed and curious, I sneak onto the property and head around the side toward the back of the house. An odd grilling smell in the air, initially appealing, rapidly turns disgusting once I recognize it. They're not flame-broiling steaks… it's the smell of a burning human body. Thanks, Scott. He taught me what burning human smells like. Least he could do for me after I lit him on fire.

Burning bodies here? Curiouser and curiouser, as they say.

I spot multiple basement-level windows big enough for me to slip through, but going inside the place is a bad idea. No reason to, plus if there *are* vampires here, breaking into their home is definitely going to result in an ass kicking, and I'm the one who's going to end up with shoe prints on her butt.

Bizarre chimney work sticks out of the roof near the back-left corner, nothing I've ever seen before. A hunch tells me it's the source of the charred human smell. I stand there for a minute staring at it, trying to make sense of what I'm seeing… until a flash of headlights washes over the side of the building. Tires squish on pavement, accompanied by the creaking of automotive springs.

Like a cat being snuck up on by a cucumber, I spring into the air faster than the speed of conscious thought, taking cover on the roof. The strange chimney gives off a constant low roar. I'm guessing they don't have a blast furnace in their basement, so... duh. It's a crematorium oven—a functioning one.

Okay, talk about scary. There aren't too many guaranteed ways to permanently kill a vampire. The sun and fire are the two main ones. A few other bizarre options exist—like strong acid baths or throwing us into volcanos, but technically speaking, lava and fire are pretty much the same. Anyway, a crematory oven would certainly do the trick.

I flatten myself out on the roof and crawl to the far edge so I can watch. By the time I get eyes on the parking area, the two men are both out of sight behind the van, unloading something. It doesn't take the younger dude long to toss a squirming body bag over his shoulder and walk out into view.

He's in his early fifties by appearance, curly black hair, thick eyebrows, and has the physique of a guy used to manual labor. And... son of a bitch. He *is* a vampire. As soon as I look at him, even without eye contact, it's obvious. Worse, he's radiating power. So, he's at least two centuries old. Dammit. Why was I right? My senses shouldn't be so accurate. Stupid instincts.

The second guy closes the van doors and follows. They could be brothers since they have a strong familial resemblance, though might be father and son. Weird things can happen with vampires, as in the younger-looking dude could be the dad. Though, something about them strikes me as brothers. If I had to guess, they experienced the Transference at the same time. There's an inexplicable sense of connection between them. Not gonna question it.

I'm also not going to question how neither one of them noticed me. Of course, who notices a one-battery flashlight during the day? I'm so weak compared to them, the ambient creepitude of this house is perfect camouflage for their senses. Assuming, of course, elders can feel other vampires around them. Not sure they can. Newbies don't give off dread auras after all. It's also something only vampires can pick up. Like, ordinary humans wouldn't think twice about those two guys. They'd look like a couple of amicable dudes who probably work for a moving company.

Crap. Elders.

I have about as much chance of winning a fight against one of them as a two-year-old beating an MMA champion in a boxing match. Being an Innocent doesn't matter too much at this age. A nine-month-old vampire of any bloodline would get their ass handed to them by an elder. If I were a Fury, it would still be like a two-year-old trying to fight an MMA champion, but someone gave her a knife. Doesn't change the odds much.

Yeah, there is no way I am messing with them directly. There's even less of a way the Peters boys are going to destroy them.

But, dammit.

Normally, I don't mind math. Sometimes, I really hate math. Like now. Vampires plus squirming body bag plus people going in but never out plus crematorium equals massive guilt trip. These vampires are addicts. Kill-feeders. There is no reason whatsoever for vampires to collect dead bodies. Every suspicious bundle the boys saw had to be a live person. Vampires have about five minutes after someone dies before the blood inside the corpse turns rancid. Don't believe the folklore about tricking a vampire by feeding us dead blood. Once it goes, it *goes*. Smells horrible.

The only reason vampires would have to bring body bags into their home is the people inside them aren't dead yet. And the only reason they'd be firing up the crematorium is they're murdering their meals. Holy shit, the boys are right. They mentioned a spike in missing persons cases around this area lately. Wow. These guys aren't being at all subtle. Sooner or later, someone is going to notice what's going on here. But... elders. I'm sure they expect it will happen and already planned their next home. Everyone within a quarter mile of this house will probably forget them ever being here, and the elders will move on to some other quiet town.

I have a damn strong suspicion whoever is in the body bag is going to be dead soon. Yes, I realize this makes me the vampire version of a vegan, feeling so sad about our food being hurt, but I have to at least try to help.

The *thud* of a door startles me. I freeze in place, trying not to make the slightest noise.

"How many more do you think we need?" asks a relatively normal male voice. Not super deep. Not creepy. No weird accent.

I lean up ever so slightly to peek at the two brothers walking back to the van.

"Eh, at least one, preferably two. Always good to have a few snacks in the pantry."

"I agree." The older one hops in the driver's seat.

Okay, stopping these elders from running around on murder sprees is not happening by any stretch of my imagination. Bad things I don't see happening in front of me won't cause insurmountable guilt, merely guilt. However, I watched them carry a victim into the house. Damn my oversensitive conscience, but if I don't at least make an effort to get the person out, I won't be able to live with myself.

Or un-live with myself.

Whatever.

# 21

# CAMPY EIGHTIES HORROR MOVIE

The Brothers Grim drive away.

Now's my chance, such as it is, to be a reckless bleeding-heart dumbass as my Uncle Hank would say. I'm going to assume other vampires are inside the house, possibly at least one elder as the place still feels like one is here. All the blackout film on the windows makes sense now. I can't imagine the basement of a former funeral home built in the early 1900s is luxurious. Good chance they spend the night hours upstairs in the house proper. Fingers crossed.

If I get caught, things will become interesting and terrifying fast.

Since I'm so damn young, elders can force their way into my mind. Heck, Wolent can read my mind and he's only like 175 or so. Pff. Only. Right? Point being, if I get caught, they're going to know exactly why I snuck into their house—to free their prospective meal. Hopefully, they will think of me like some idiot kid trying to steal a loaf of bread from them. Or maybe find me adorable like some little girl trying to talk her parents into going vegetarian 'for the animals.' Of course, I might also end up locked in a cell or—worst case— thrown into the crematorium oven. This is, after all, a lawless area for vampires quite far away from Seattle where Aurélie has zero political influence.

Someone really ought to stop them entirely before they attract an army of hunters, but I'm not tall enough to ride this ride. I am, however, short enough to sneak in and out. Once the noise from the van's engine is completely out of my awareness, I slide from the roof and float to the ground on my feet.

Predictably, the side door they went in is locked. While I might be able to break it open, doing so would *not* be quiet. Any hope I have in avoiding the notice of any vampires in the building depends on me being silent—and them not being in the basement. My plan kinda also hinges on the body bag occupant being in the basement. Hey, searching around, finding nothing, and running away is still 'doing something.' It'll still make me feel bad, but nowhere near as bad as not even trying to help.

I make my way from the side of the house to the back, heading for another door. I'm so convinced it's going to be locked a gasp almost flies out of my mouth when the knob turns. I ease the door open, peering in at a kitchen covered in dust. The fridge, one small area of counter, and a space at the table are clean, suggesting one person— probably the elderly man the boys saw on camera—is not a vampire.

Doubt any of the people they carry in here are given food, at least nothing requiring cooking.

Faint feminine grunting and a chain-on-metal clatter comes from behind a small door at the opposite side of the kitchen beside a series of tall, narrow cabinets. Yeah, sounds like they put their victim in the basement and she's struggling to escape whatever they tied her with. I make it two steps across the kitchen before a creak comes from the hall beyond an arch about ten feet to the left of the door I need.

Crap!

Someone's coming.

I leap into the air, flying across the kitchen as fast as I can go in the limited space—and press myself against the ceiling at the top of the arch. My hair drapes down for a second, but I grab it and hold it to my chest.

A moment later, the old man walks in, passing obliviously below me on his way to the counter near the fridge. Eep! If he turns, he's going to see me. Like some weird human Ouija board planchette, I slide across the ceiling, zipping back and forth to stay behind him out of his field of view as he makes himself a cheese sandwich. After several tedious, nerve-wracking minutes, he carries his sad dinner out of the kitchen on a plate.

Whew.

I sink down to my feet, fighting the urge to exhale in relief—too loud—and pull open the door to reveal rickety wooden stairs down to the basement. Another creak comes from the corridor. Grr! Damn old man! Screw it. I duck into the stairwell and pull the door shut before fly-gliding down to stay silent.

Hah! Take that, conveniently placed creaky stair I know is here but aren't sure which one you are. You won't get me caught!

The old guy re-enters the kitchen grumbling about forgetting his tea. Apparently, it's a serious problem to eat a cheese sandwich sans tea. Whatever, dude. You do you. Concrete floor at the bottom is far more trustworthy than century-old wood not to make noise, so I stop hovering.

And… I've just drifted onto the set of a bad Eighties horror movie. Okay, not really. The room is full of old timey mortuary gear like embalming stuff from the last century, tubes, huge needles, giant jars, and hand-cranked machines I can't even begin to guess the function of. I'm fairly certain huge surgical saws, machetes, and sickles aren't normal tools found in funeral homes. It doesn't look like a procedure room, merely storage. But wow. So damn creepy.

We are definitely not in Kansas anymore.

I haven't been this uncomfortable anywhere since my first OB/GYN visit. Wait, no, being inside Petra's house beat it. Freaky bitch. This is pretty damn close, though. What is it about old quasi-medical equipment? Tweaks every nerve in exactly the wrong way.

Yeah, stop being a dumbass. No time to gawk. I hurry across the room, following the sound of struggling to another door. It leads to a hallway straight out of a haunted insane asylum. Filthy white tile covers the walls like in every creepy hospital from a hundred years ago. Six rooms, three per side, give me the willies. I know this is a funeral home, but it looks like where they used to take people for lobotomies. Two ancient gurneys stand against the wall on the left. Eek.

Sorry, lady, but if ghosts in straitjackets pop out of those side rooms and come after me, I'm out. I can only handle so much freaky at once.

The woman's argument with the chain is coming from the far end, an open doorway at the end of the hall into another dusty, large area. I am a creature of the night. I should not be afraid of ghosts or creepy rooms. I'm already dead. A ghost can't do anything to me unless they happen to be carrying a flamethrower.

Refusing to look left or right into the doorways, I run to the end, entering a large basement area containing a huge steel tank painted a dull brick red, connected to a mess of pipes and valves. A short conveyor of metal rollers sticks out from one of the narrow ends like a tongue. Latent heat wafts off what can only be the crematorium oven. It's not roaring anymore, so it's obviously been shut down. Not long enough ago for my comfort, though.

Seriously, there is something about old boilers and crematory ovens the human psyche is vulnerable to. I'm terrified like this thing is going to come to life and eat me even though on an intellectual level, I know it's impossible. Too many damn movies. Okay, Sarah. Focus. You need to be more Sierra now and less Sophia.

Not too much Sierra, though. She'd try to fight the elders.

Yeah, there's blood on the floor—dribbles, but still blood. Another gurney nearby still holds the scent of a person, no doubt the poor bastard presently collecting in the ash receptacle. I'm stunned to realize Ben and Cody got it right.

Wow... their neighbors really *are* the damn Klopeks. I'm legit in one of Dad's movies.

The struggling noises come from behind a door in the wall a short distance past the oven. I bite back my childish fear of an inanimate object devouring me in flames. Honestly, going headfirst into a crematory oven would be much more merciful than other forms of torturous death—like being a guest on the Dr. Phil show.

'My daughter's become a vampire and she won't listen to me anymore.'

Quiet as can be, I approach the door. Okay, ninety-nine percent chance this woman is going to scream when I open it. She is making a reasonable amount of noise already, so she might not notice me if I'm quiet. Really should get on with this before the Super Vampire Brothers come back. Dammit. Now I'm going to think of them as Count Mario and Count Luigi.

Ugh.

I pull the door open.

The windowless room looks like it had once been used for storage. It's entirely empty except for four somewhat rusted support columns propping up the ceiling and a relatively young Hispanic woman. Don't wanna be too judgey, but the tiny skirt, low cut top and gaudy platform heels makes her look like a prostitute. She's locked to one of the support columns by a pair of handcuffs connecting her wrists together, hugging the pole. The woman's taller than me by like four inches, but her height advantage is almost all coming from those shoes.

We are lucky. She's got her back to me and is so absorbed in trying to escape, she hasn't noticed the door open. Perfect. In all the history of vampire kind, I doubt many of us have ever used supernatural speed to ambush a woman from behind with the intent of *saving* her life.

I pounce on her blurrily fast, clamping a hand over her mouth to hold in the scream she reflexively tries to set loose.

"Shh," I whisper. "I'm here to get you out. Make noise and we are both going to die."

The woman nods.

I let go of her. She twists to look at me, squinting. "You're free? Go get the police." She yanks at the handcuffs. "These creeps think no one will miss me, but I got parents and two brothers. Hurry. Get outta here 'fore the old man gets you."

"Don't need the cops," I say, reaching for the cuffs.

"Stupid. What you gonna do? These people are freaks. Saw 'em kill this other poor bastard they locked in here with me."

"Wait…" I blink. "Didn't they just bring you inside?"

"No, girl. I been here two damn days. Get the police. My name is Ava Marquez. These freaks killed two people. They used ta be in here, then they took 'em out. Then I see 'em out there dead, goin' straight into that big ass oven." She pulls at her arms, giving a teary whine. "C'mon, stop standin' here. You gotta go get the cops before they kill me, too."

Crap. What the hell are these vampires doing?

I mean, obviously, I know *what* they're doing. How can they be so damn reckless and cruel?

Sigh. This is over my pay grade. I grab the cuffs and snap them apart like cheap plastic toys. Can't do anything about the vampires, but I can help Ava.

"You… You…" She gawks at her wrists. "How the f—"

I stare into her eyes. "Be quiet and follow me."

# 22

# A PERFECT SCENARIO FOR AN F-BOMB

Breaking those cuffs destroyed any chance of me avoiding involvement here.

The vampires at Club Abaddon got seriously pissed off at me for 'stealing their food,' and they didn't even murder their victims. No telling how these crazy ones will react if they catch us before we get out of here. The best plan I can come up with at this point is 'run like hell.'

Whoever happened to be in the squirming body bag either went straight upstairs to be dinner or is in another cell down here. While Ava stands there gawking at her wrists, I listen. Her breathing is damn loud, but not so much it hides the presence of three voices coming from upstairs. A man who sounds like a Texan, neither old nor young, appears to be discussing *Game of Thrones* with a woman who has to be in her early sixties, speaking in an unfamiliar accent. It doesn't sound foreign in terms of nationality, more like time. It's as if I'm watching a movie set in colonial Boston or something. Shit, she's gotta be old. Another man occasionally speaks. He sounds older, too—like late fifties—and has a posh British accent. The three of them find the deaths and tortures on the show 'unrealistically tame but hilarious.'

Okay, they're messed up in the head. When the woman says she hopes they 'kill that little girl soon, she's annoying,' I immediately dislike her. Not sure which character she's talking about. Honestly, I haven't watched the show. Too dark for me. Dad warned me about it. Sometimes, I can be a bit too 'Sophia.' The deaths of fictional characters, especially ones I really like, hit me almost as hard as real people.

Anyone who finds *GoT* 'funny,' is a damn psycho.

And speaking of deaths, I really need to get my ass out of here.

In addition to the creepy 'hospital' corridor I came in from, another passage heads out from this room catty corner to it on the next wall. Looks like more 'patient' rooms. Old buildings like this often went through multiple incarnations. Before it became a funeral home, this could've been a hospital or even a tuberculosis sanitorium. Who knows? The weird stuff you learn from watching ghost hunter shows.

Getting *bad* vibes from the other hallway... so I don't go there.

Gonna chance the kitchen. Wait. No. Basement windows. The crematorium room has four of them. Old style lever-handled latches make it impossible to re-secure the windows from the outside, so unless the vampires who live here are really unobservant, they're going to know someone opened it. Yeah, but they're already going to notice someone was here because Ava's missing. Or not. Maybe they'll think she simply escaped on her own. Here's hoping.

Hell with it.

I grab Ava's wrist—and hesitate. Those plastic bricks she's got strapped to her feet are going to make a ton of noise. Damn, we can't go running around the house. The faster we can get outside, the better. I lead her over to the nearest window, a narrow rectangle near the ceiling. Looks big enough for us to squeeze through. Sometimes, Dad's genes come in handy. Ava's got more of a butt than me, but she still looks capable of fitting. The bottom edge of the window is higher than the top of my head, the opening only barely as wide as my hips. It's super awkward to climb out such a tight opening with nothing to stand on and most likely nothing to grab outside, but I plan to cheat.

After reaching up to open the latch and shove the glass panel outward, I face Ava. "Do not scream or make noise."

Her eyes flutter under the weight of mental compulsion. While she's dazed, I grab both her wrists, float off the ground, and glide backward, sliding feet first out the window and pulling her up after me, dragging her out onto the pavement. She lays there dazed while I dart over to shut the window, then pick her up, draping her over my back like a cloak. The instant we fly straight up, she snaps out of the fog and clamps on—but doesn't scream. Having the weight of another adult on my back does not make flying fun. It's about as ungainly as carrying a person the normal way. My speed is crap, maneuverability worse, and it's tiring. To be fair, it's much easier for me to fly Ava out of here than it would have been for mortal Sarah to carry her away on foot.

From the air, the development of suburban houses to the west looks like some kind of weird doodle. No two streets follow the same shape. Zero pattern. I keep flying past streets of private homes for about a mile to a small shopping center, where I land near a UPS store and a massage therapy place.

The instant Ava's shoes hit the sidewalk, it's like a reset button for her brain. She screams as if only now realizing we'd been a few hundred feet in the air.

I stab her in the brain—using mental powers.

Time for thought surgery.

Okay, let's see. Yeah, the woman *is* a prostitute. The Super Vampire Brothers compelled her to get into the van when she walked over to solicit business from them. She wasn't lying about having parents and brothers, but she hasn't spoken to them for over a year. Ava's hoping they'd have somehow magically known she ended up in trouble and come looking for her. The two days she'd spent locked up in the basement, she'd been making all kinds of promises to God about going home, getting off drugs, changing her life, and so on if he didn't let her die. Ugh. This poor woman thinks her abduction happened as some kind of divine punishment for being a prostitute.

Okay, I'd never personally do it... but sex work is valid work. It's wrong to vilify the women but not the dudes paying for it. And really, how is giving someone a pleasurable time a bad thing? Whatever. Don't have time to philosophize. She's gonna do what she's gonna do. If going home to her parents makes her happy, do it. Worked for me. Good chance these vampires won't find her there, though I doubt they're going to try to hunt her down for escaping.

Like any self-respecting serial killer, they're certainly looking for victims no one will miss.

In her admittedly confused memory—probably drugs or just sheer pants-staining terror—she vaguely remembers being locked in that room for two or three days with a pair of homeless guys, both of whom the vampire brothers dragged off while leaving her there. She later watched them load the men's remains into the crematory oven when the elderly dude entered the cell to give her a few pieces of bread to eat. Good. She has no idea about vampires. And wow, dick. Couldn't even give her a cheese sandwich? Just plain bread.

Okay, so. Back to mind surgery. I erase myself entirely. As far as she will remember, she slipped out of the handcuffs on her own, climbed out the window, and ran to this shopping center. She can find any random person here and ask them to call the police for her. Slightly mean of me, but I don't want any electronic trails. If those vampires get mad, I don't need them mind-controlling the cops and telling them who called 911. Oh, yeah. Also, better to prevent any cops from being killed. I make sure Ava doesn't remember where she was held captive. She didn't have the best recall of the house or location to begin with, so it isn't too difficult to muddle it up more with a fake memory of wandering for a few hours after escaping. Her bringing the police to the old funeral home would end badly for the cops.

Probably end up being like a scene out of *Grand Theft Auto* after the player's all leveled up. Waves and waves of police showing up and just getting torn apart—in this case by elder vampires. At least until the National Guard shows up. Nah, these vamps aren't being subtle but I don't think they'd quite push it into open war with humanity.

They'd most likely kill the first cops to show up, then relocate before any others came looking.

So, no. Ava Marquez is *not* going to lead the authorities into a deathtrap.

Memory tweaking done, I glide into the air and wait.

A minute or two later, Ava blinks, screams, and sprints off like the vampires are right behind her. And yeah, those bricks she's got strapped to her feet sound like wooden blocks banging together as she runs. I keep an eye on her until she's safely surrounded by a bunch of people near the Grocery Outlet supermarket. Gee, minimum effort on naming the place, dude. Whatever. She's in good hands now, so I swing around and race back to the Peters' house.

⁓⁓⁓ —————————— ⁓⁓⁓

I SWOOP IN THE WINDOW, LANDING IN THE 'VAMPIRE COMMAND CENTER' bedroom.

Ben yelps, jumping so hard at my sudden appearance he kicks the desk while attempting not to fall out of his chair. Cody, seated on the foot of the bed, throws a comic book he'd been reading over his head and yanks the flare gun from the pocket of his coat draped over the bed next to him. He clutches the orange gun to his chest, making such a derp face I wish I had my phone out to take a picture.

To make a point, I dash forward, grab the flare gun out of his grip, and go back to where I landed too fast for the boys to react.

"Careful with this thing." I hold it up.

"How the heck?" Cody looks down at his hands, back at me, and down at himself again.

I stroll over and set the flare gun down on the bed, within his arms' reach. "Trying to show you something."

"Huh?" He glances at the gun.

After walking back to stand by the window, about ten feet away, I point at the flare gun. "Ben, count down from three. Cody, on the count of one, try to grab the gun before I can."

The boys exchange a glance, then shrug.

"Three... two... one," says Ben.

Cody appears to be moving in slow motion, his fingers creeping toward the flare pistol. I rush over and swipe it out from under his hand, leaving him to grab a fistful of comforter.

Again, Ben nearly jumps out of his chair. "Whoa."

Cody frowns. "Yeah, whatever. So you're fast. "Your point?"

I hold up my right hand and extend my claws. "My point is, I'm not even a year into being a vampire and look how fast I can move. Any vampire older than me could sink their claws into your neck so fast you'd never see it coming. I'm trying to scare you guys into staying safe and alive."

"They're vamps, aren't they?" asks Ben. "The neighbors..."

"Yeah." I let my arm drop to my side and retract my claws. "And, we have a big problem."

"Bigger than us having a vampire nest on our street?" Cody reaches for the flare gun.

Against my better judgement, I chuck it to him. "Yes, bigger. The two guys you keep seeing on the video? They're definitely vamps. And they're old."

"No kidding, they're like fifty." Cody chuckles.

"Don't be a dork. I mean vampire old. They're elders. I want you guys to stay away from them."

Ben points at his middle computer screen, a Google search. "But they're killing people. Look at all these stories about missing people."

"Most of those probably have nothing to do with this." I lean on the back of his chair, skimming the webpage. "Some of them could be, but the vamps are going after victims society either won't miss or will take a long time to notice. Homeless people, prostitutes, gang members..."

"Like a serial killer." Cody nods. "Doesn't mean it's excusable."

"Argh." I stand away from the chair, grabbing my hair in both hands out of frustration. "I'm not saying it's excusable. Recognizing a problem we can't do anything about isn't the same thing as liking it. *One* of those vamps would twist me into a pretzel before I could even react, and there are at least five of them. You guys are only going to get yourselves killed."

"We have to do something." Ben twists back and forth in his chair, sneakers skimming over the carpet. Guess their parents don't have a thing about shoes in the house. "Ignoring it is the same as saying it's okay."

I pace. "Not saying we do nothing at all. But direct confrontation is beyond stupid."

"So, what then?" Cody sights over the flare gun at the wall. "This should take care of one."

"*If* you could hit him. And it's still an unknown if a signal flare would even ignite a vampire on contact. Also, I told you before, it holds one shot at a time. Even if you did ash one of them in an instant, the others would shred you before you could reload."

The boys stare at me like I've got the answers.

Grr.

Maybe I should try to get in contact with Damarco? He's closer to being a legit vampire hunter than these two. Doubt he's tangled with an elder at all much less five of them. A vampire calling in a hunter on other vampires also feels kinda weird, like I'd be breaking some unwritten rule. Sure, I'm Follows Rules Girl, but keeping my head down and being a narc are totally different. Yes, this group of psychos needs to be stopped, but if other vamps start thinking of me as the vampire who hates vampires, it's not going to end well for me—or my family.

Am I applying the Mafia comparison too much? No, not really. As far as Stefano or Paolo are concerned, me calling Damarco in on this is no different from a made man working with the FBI—and the Mob doesn't kill traitors in nice ways.

Sorry, Mom, but some situations deserve the F-bomb. I'd shout it, but the boys' parents are downstairs.

This is over my head. I blink. Exactly. What does the kid do when they see something over their head? They tell Mom or Dad. No, not going to my parents… they can't help with this. Mom will panic and

Dad will tell me to wear a headband. Dammit, I left the one he got me back home. Whatever, I'm not at all planning to get into a fight.

Time to talk my way out of a problem.

"Got an idea. Going to talk to some people I met who might be able to help."

"More vampires?" asks Cody, frowning.

"Duh," mutters Ben. "Who else would she call, the FBI?"

I chuckle. "Oddly enough, there *is* something… not sure if they're FBI or CIA, but… no. Not gonna involve them yet."

The boys exchange a 'whoa, holy crap' stare.

Out comes my iPhone. Let me see what Jermaine thinks.

# 23

# THE WILD WEST

Mostly to cover my butt, I give the boys a mild compulsion to stay quiet until I'm off the phone.

Don't want Jermaine or anyone who might be listening in on the call to hear me talking about vampire stuff while boys too young to be turned are in the room. No, I have no plans to turn them, but some vampires get their panties in a wad if certain topics are discussed openly in front of mortals.

I call the number on the back of the Delirium business card.

"Mammoth Erections Contracting," says Jermaine by way of answering. "No job too hard. You need it up, we'll get it up."

Takes me a moment to control my giggling enough to speak. "Jermaine? It's Sarah, we met last night."

"Oh, hey, darling. Couldn't stop thinking about li'l ol' me? Hate to break your heart, but you're not my type."

Heh. "You're unforgettable. Had a question. I'm still in the area and ran into a situation I'm not equipped to deal with."

"Do tell."

"There's a house in Ventura, former funeral home. A group of vampires, pretty sure they're elders, are using it as a kill factory. They're abducting homeless people, prostitutes, and anyone else they can get a hold of, draining them dead, and cremating the bodies."

"Ooh. Sounds like they're being a little melodramatic, but what did you expect for Ventura? You probably ought to get gone sooner rather than later, honey."

I blink. "Umm… what did I expect? Vampires not being so obvious about it. The local news is blowing up with missing person stories. Someone needs to do something here."

"Doubt anyone in San Diego's goin' ta get involved. It's the vampire Wild West. All the wackos end up there one way or the other eventually—or Salem. Ain't your problem. Why you makin' a deal of it?"

I stare down at the rug. "Because kill-feeding is wrong. And more than the simple evil of it, they're eventually going to attract the attention of hunters. These vamps are pretty old and have obviously done this before. They'll know when it gets too hot and move on to somewhere else, leaving all the non-insane vamps to deal with the invasion of hunters. It's the exact opposite of what we're supposed to be doing."

Ben and Cody look at me like 'more hunters? Awesome. What's the problem?'

Sigh.

"We're on the same page, baby. I agree it's not optimal, but this is San Diego and that's Ventura."

Grr. I furrow my brows. "Are you saying vampires have jurisdictional limits like cops?"

"Nah. More like the way you ain't terribly inclined to clean up dog poop in your neighbor's yard." He chuckles into a sigh. "But, I suppose this be the kinda dog poop what explodes and gets on everyone. All right. You do have something of a point. Meet me at the club and we'll go talk to Cassandra."

I swallow. "Umm. You want me to meet Cassandra? Should I find some nicer clothes?"

"Nah. Don't worry about it. She won't care. And you look more earnest in jeans."

"All right. I'm about an hour away."

"Cool. Cool. See ya in an hour then."

"Okay." I end the call, ending the condition of my command for the boys to stay quiet.

They explode into a flurry of questions. When they stop and stare at me, I hold my hands up in a wait gesture.

"This problem is not one we can do anything about directly. I'm going to speak to the person who's politically in charge around here. Sorta. Ventura is kind of outside their territory. Still, it's the best option."

Cody thrusts his arms out to either side. "You said hunters are going to show up. How many more people have to die before they notice? Can we contact them now?"

"Guys…" I sigh at the ceiling. "This house has at least three elders. There are five vampires total. Dunno if the three who haven't left the place are all elders. One, five, or ten in the same place feels the same. This is the kind of situation where it would take a large group of multiple hunters to have any chance of winning, and they'd probably still lose a lot of people."

"Whoa. You've seen this before?" asks Ben.

I fidget. "Only in movies."

They both smirk at me.

"Look, just promise me you guys will sit tight and wait for me to get back. Hopefully, I'll have good news."

"Do what you gotta." Ben spins around in his chair to watch the camera. "Don't like you dealing with other vamps, though. We don't trust 'em."

"Do you trust me?" I tilt my head.

Cody nods. "Yeah. We know you. You saved our asses in the weird place. You could've killed us or erased our brains multiple times, and didn't. So, yeah, we trust you. But we don't know any others. Can't just go trusting every bloodsucker we see because we met *one* who's cool."

"What he said." Ben points his thumb over his shoulder at his brother.

"You guys saved my ass too in there. I'm trying to return the favor now." I half climb out the window again. "Just, stay safe. I'll be back as soon as I can."

# 24

## SO MANY QUESTIONS

E xistence as a vampire has to be about more than fashion and social politics.

After all, we're powerful undead beings in possession of mystical powers and abilities, not Kardashians. Well, they're probably vampires, too. Can't think of any other reason but mind-control for why they're famous. But seriously, Aurélie is obsessed with elaborate dresses. Most of the vampires at those soirees are all dressed to the nines. The main reason anyone goes there is to be seen around the prominent people.

Here I am flying back to San Diego when I really ought to be going home. Ben and Cody would almost certainly get themselves killed if left to their own devices. Even sillier than the idea of them taking on a group of elders is me worrying about meeting Cassandra Upton in jeans, sneakers, and a T-shirt. It feels like a significant portion of my worries after becoming a vampire have been about fashion—or the lack of it.

Emerging naked from a morgue cooler feels like fate mocking me with a birth metaphor. I'm sure most vampires don't spend their first twenty-four hours among the undead naked... or locked in a tiny mausoleum. Or thinking they're dreaming it all. Yeah, so I had a nontraditional start. The majority of those who receive the Transference are aware vampires exist before they are turned, whether or not they accept the change willingly. A point could be made about Glim only being aware of vampires for a few seconds before his sire bit him, but he still had more time as a mortal knowing about them than I did.

Looking back on it, it's kind of embarrassing to have been a vampire who didn't realize vampires existed.

Maybe those remote tribes in the Amazon or whatever have the right idea. People can't be fashion snobs if no one wears clothes. It would make for a bizarre world, wouldn't it? Can you picture naked police officers chasing a naked burglary suspect down the street, stuff flapping around all over the place? Blind people couldn't tell if guys were clapping or jogging. Criminals might be too busy laughing to flee. But, yeah… the world isn't supportive of the idea. The planet itself I mean, not society. Some places are simply too cold for mass global nudity.

Yes, it's absurd. Yes, I'm stressing out and thinking of random nonsense.

Mass global nudity would, however, prevent me from having an anxiety attack over walking into what's basically the vampire mayor's office dressed like a college slacker. A more reasonable solution would be uniforms. Every country gets a different uniform. Like private schools. They do it so kids don't pick on each other for fashion choices. Doesn't help much. Kids will pick on each other for anything. Cheap, ugly, or dirty clothing is only one small part of a massive pie.

But at least I wouldn't have to worry about meeting Cassandra and feeling like a scrub.

Doesn't help I've been stuck in the same clothes since Friday. Being an Innocent comes with all the nice parts of being so close to alive as well as all the bad parts—like sweat. I haven't even taken my pants off to use the bathroom once since Saturday. Don't need to unless I eat human food. All that stuff trapped in place, no air moving. Yeah, I feel funky as hell. I don't smell anything weird, but people generally don't notice their own stink.

I'm sure if I'm rank, Jermaine will warn me.

Innocent or not, I'm still a vampire and don't generate funkiness quite as fast as a living person.

And what the hell is wrong with me? The Littles are home without adult supervision, Cody and Ben are separated from a brutal death by a thin veil of uncertainty holding back their stupidity, and I'm worrying about what to wear. Gotta be nerves.

I couldn't care less what anyone thinks of me due to my fashion sense. It's more like I don't want to wind up in 'contempt of court' for being too casual around the political leader of the area. Whatever. If Jermaine said no big deal, it's gotta be no big deal.

Roughly an hour after leaving the boys' house, I swoop in to land in the darkness behind the Delirium club. The place is obviously in operation, but there's no one else out here. I head around the building on foot and spot Jermaine hanging out by the main entrance, talking to a pair of well-dressed guys in dark suits, both of whom are also vampires—and total dudebros. At least by looks. Guessing this is Chad and Trevor. Or one of them's a Jake. Bet they used to work in sales.

Jermaine's in a clingy blue long-sleeved shirt, skinny jeans, simple silver necklace chain and snakeskin boots with elongated pointy toes —not exactly an outfit anyone would consider wearing to court.

"Hey," I say in a low voice after walking up to him.

"Sarah." He shifts to face me. "Meet Greg and Tom. They're both fairly recent additions."

Wow. For sure I thought the blond guy was going to be 'Chad.' I wave. "Hey."

Greg and Tom both give me a polite smile of greeting, a note of confusion on their faces as if it surprises them I'm a vampire. Their body language gives off a sense of distancing, like I'm their girlfriend's kid sister they'd rather not deal with or even be near. Works for me.

"Ready?" asks Jermaine.

"Yeah. Beyond ready. I'm still hoping to make it home tonight."

"C'mon." Jermaine waves to the dudebros. "Back soon. Try not to burn the place down."

Tom makes a clicking noise and finger guns at Jermaine.

Oh, douche. Yeah, he's *totally* a sales weasel of some kind. Or was.

Jermaine leads me into the parking lot to a newish black Mercedes sedan.

Okay, odd. Maybe he can't fly. I keep forgetting it's not a universal ability, merely common.

"Cassandra lives a ways off from downtown. Nice place." Jermaine starts the engine. "Take us about twelve minutes to get there. Hope you're not in too much of a rush."

"It's twelve minutes I'm not on the way home, but not a big deal if it stops—I mean helps keeps hunters away." Whew. Almost said stops the guys from being idiots.

Jermaine glances at me. "Gonna be honest with ya, honey. I'm not seein' Cassandra losin' too much sleep over it. She might send some eyes up there to check it out, but if you're expectin' the 'vampire police' to go boot heads, you're gonna be disappointed."

I let a silent sigh out my nose. Yeah, I *had* kinda been hoping the situation would be fixed right away, but he's got a point. It's like asking government to help with anything. Takes forever, may or may not actually happen, and when it does happen, the results are disappointing—or they make the situation worse.

Ugh. Maybe I should forget about this entirely and go home—after giving the boys a compulsion to stay away from 'the Klopeks.' Yeah, sounds easy to say. But, this is me after all. For the same reason I didn't leave Ava Marquez handcuffed to a post in the basement, I'm going to see Cassandra Upton.

"So… what should I expect of her?" I ask, a few minutes into the ride.

Jermaine's driving in the most casual posture I've ever seen anyone adopt inside a moving car. His seat's way back. Left hand on the wheel, right elbow on the center console, body shifted sorta sideways. Yeah, he's still mentally in the late Sixties. He's so 'chill' I can almost feel a marijuana high creeping in. Or what I imagine it would be like.

"Cassandra's a lot like I imagine she was in the 1800s when she ran a saloon out here. Lady knows what she wants and how to get it. Knows who she is and makes no attempt to hide it. Word is, it's how she caught the eye of the one who turned her. Thought a woman 'entirely lacking in social graces' deserved to stick around for a while." He chuckles.

I glance over at him. "Lacking in social graces? Was she a, umm…?"

"Prostitute? Nah. Cassandra ran a respectable place. Strictly gambling, booze, and information. I'm talkin' like they did back then." He grins. "When they said a woman's 'lacking in social graces,' it's a nice way of sayin' she didn't let men boss her around and didn't treat people better for havin' money."

"Oh, so she's strong and down to Earth?"

"Maybe. Far as I'm concerned, she's pretty much normal. But, normal for these days is radical in 1800."

"True." I nod.

Best to go into this meeting and not expect anything. Being in the car with Jermaine, I can't help but wonder how vampires who've been alive for so long process changes in social norms. Heck, Uncle Hank hasn't been alive nearly as long as some vampires but his head is firmly stuck in the racist, sexist, backward mentality of the 1950s. One thing for a mostly harmless old man to hold those views, but a vampire elder? Ack. Though, I'm guessing most vampires of a certain age feel so superior to mortal humans they tend to lose sight of ethnic boundaries and lump everyone together into a single 'lesser mortals' category.

"You know," says Jermaine in a wistful tone. "I hear she's still got the six-shooter she used to carry on her in the saloon before she… lost her mortality."

I chuckle. "You say it the way most guys say 'lost her virginity.'"

Jermaine laughs, barely moving his hand to make a lane change in anticipation of an upcoming left turn. "Situations are more or less similar. Both open the doors to a world of wonders a person's previously unaware of, and there ain't no undoin' it once it's done."

Can't help but cringe a little inside at the memory of my first experience going all the way. Wasn't ready for the pain—or the blood. Scott got mad at me 'for overreacting', stopped abruptly, and left me there bleeding. Honestly, I should've broken up with him the next day. Would have saved me months of self-doubt and anxiety.

"Yeah, I guess."

"Don't know?"

I blush a little. "No, I'm not as innocent as I look."

He grins. "You seem embarrassed. Sorry. I'll change the subject."

"It's fine. Just bad memories."

"Don't let it get to you. Virginity is a bullshit social construct." He waves his free hand around randomly as he talks. "A person's worth to society don't have a got-damn thing to do wit' how much or how little booty they get. The whole concept defies understanding. Some dude gets a ton of tail, he's virile, elevated, and respected. Girl gets a ton of tail, they make her out to be some kinda horrible person. Mofos like me, well… people just don't talk about us in polite company." He wags his eyebrows at me. "Don't matter. I don't hang out with polite company. It's just a fancy way to say 'stuck up jackasses.'"

I chuckle. "Sounds like you know a lot about the subject."

Jermaine makes 'bitch please' face at me. "Honey, I am the PhD of love."

"Heh." I kinda zone out, thinking of Hunter… and how odd it is for vampires to want or even appreciate sex.

"Don't get your hopes up though. I'm taken."

I snap out of my daydream—wait, do vampires *have* daydreams or nightdreams when we're awake? "Huh? What?"

"You've got a look to you."

"No… not going there. I'm taken, too. Just having a bunch of weird, awkward questions dance around my head. Not personal."

"You're pretty new, aren't ya? You feel like a chick right out the egg."

I shrug. "Yeah, basically. If a morgue cooler counts as an egg. It's been about nine months."

"You get any since?"

"Yeah," I say before thinking about it. No idea why it came out so easily. Don't really know this guy. "Not the question I had in mind. I mean… beyond wondering why vampires still even have those urges."

"We do."

"Obviously." I laugh. "Went almost a month without it and was totally fiending."

"You look so wholesome," says Jermaine in a sarcastic tone.

"Looks can be deceiving."

"Preach, girl." He high-fives me.

I swipe my hair out of my eyes. Oh, hell with it. He's being super casual. "Something I've been wondering for a while now. Do, umm… things work the same way for guys? Obviously, there are differences between us. I mean strictly with guys pre and post vampire."

"You're asking about a vampire's post."

I snicker. "Guilty."

He chuckles. "Nah. Way different after the Transference. Much more intense. The peak lasts a good few minutes instead of like four seconds. Also, there's no—uhh, how can I put it politely?"

"No fluids involved?"

Jermaine snaps his fingers. "Good phrasing. Exactly. It's all mental energy. A guy vampire's no longer at the mercy of physiology. Don't gotta try to make the buildup last longer so it ain't all over after a brief explosion of pleasure, an' they go straight to sleep."

"Hah."

"It's a spiritual experience after the Transference, if you believe in that sort of thing. Speakin' as a guy, it's more exhausting now, but oh, so worth it." He elbows me suggestively. "You thinkin' of givin' boys a try?"

I pause, wondering what about me made him assume I'm into women. My secondary alter ego is Oblivious Girl. Other than people who give off obvious flags, whatever subtle cues exist are utterly lost on me. And no, it doesn't bother me he thought it, merely caught me by surprise. Probably thinks because I'm clueless about vampire men I've never done it with a guy. "Already am. I've got a boyfriend, but… he's alive."

"Aww, honey. Adorable." Jermaine takes an off ramp. Looks like we've gone right out into the desert, even though we're not too far from San Diego. "Best you avoid gettin' with a vampire boi or your current squeeze won't do it for you anymore." He shakes his head. "Mmm mmn *mmn!*"

Eep. I bite my lip, kinda frightened at the idea of how wild doing it with a vampire would be. Considering the intensity of making love to Hunter now, if another vampire is *more* intense? Wow. No damn wonder Aurélie messed Ashley up for weeks. I mean, she's used to being with another girl, so having a partner who can go off multiple times and keep at it for over an hour isn't new to her. But, vampire adds a whole new level.

I can't even imagine a guy able to continue going for so long without a sudden, erm, 'explosive' loss of interest. Almost makes me tired thinking about it. Meh. Doesn't matter for me anyway. Hunter and I are in love, not merely hooking up for sex. If I ever get involved with another guy, it's going to be after he's been swallowed by time… and it'll probably be a vamp so I don't have to constantly dwell on running out of time or ruining his life.

"Oh, my bad." Jermaine smiles. "You're in love. Can feel it on ya. All good. Don't you go rushin' anything. All pleasures come in time."

I groan.

He shifts his gaze to me, confused.

"*Come* in time? We're talking about sex…" I chuckle. "Nice dad joke."

Jermaine laughs, slapping the steering wheel. "Heh. Didn't even mean it that way. You got a dirty mind, honey."

"Who, me?" I sit as demurely as possible. "I'm Innocent."

He wags his eyebrows at me as if to say, 'sure you are.' "Ahh. Here we are."

# 25

# A LADY OF FINE SOCIAL STANDING

Cassandra Upton's house looks like one of those places you see on the show where everyone's always buying houses way too nice for normal humans to afford.

Hi, I'm Amanda and this is my husband Chad. I paint bunny rabbits on seashells and my husband studies the migratory patterns of African sand fleas. Our budget is five million. Gotta agree with Dad here. How can anyone watch that show without their brain liquefying and running out their ears? I feel dumber for even thinking of it. It's like the brain-eating pablum the society in *Fahrenheit 451* pumped into citizens' houses all day to keep the vapid upper class in a permanent trance of obliviousness.

So, yeah. Cassandra's house is huge. Only one story, sort of adobe-inspired, but if authenticity in architecture was food, this is the house equivalent of Taco Bell. Still, despite being obviously modern—lots of glass—it's nice. Too much, though. Unless Cassandra has a huge family, there's no reason a single person needs a house the size of a suburban grade school.

Wonder if she uses the pool.

Oops. Wait. I need to push all these negative thoughts deep into the back of my psyche. Cassandra got her Transference in the 1800s.

She's definitely old enough to force her way into my head and see what I'm thinking. Bad form to go in there having sarcastic thoughts about how she's flaunting her wealth. And hey, for all I know, a house like this out here in the middle of nowhere is cheap. Wait, no. What am I saying? This is California. An outhouse shed would cost as much as my family's home.

Assuming, of course, she paid anything for it. Vampires cheat.

Jermaine parks close to the front door on a cute little ring road surrounding a dome-shaped mound covered in mini cactuses and an acacia tree. I get out of the car, close my eyes, and spend a minute concentrating on what I saw in the former funeral home. No way am I going to be able to hide my concern for the Peters' boys from Cassandra if she looks hard enough. Frustrating thing about true feelings is they tend to bubble to the surface on their own. Like trying to hold a mass of Styrofoam peanuts underwater using your bare hands. The harder you try to hold onto them, the more they disperse.

Kill-feeding vampires are bad news. Everyone agrees on it, though not for the same reasons. I'm the 'squishy' sort of person who thinks it's wrong to kill. But the cold ones like Paolo can also appreciate a reckless kill-feeder will attract too much attention to the vampire community. Even if a particular undead doesn't object to the concept of killing their meals, they have to appreciate the risk. It's not illegal for a person to have a baby, but there's only so many times they can throw the kid's dirty diapers through their neighbor's window before the police get involved.

Not speaking from personal experience there. Just saying. Leave too many corpses lying around and it's going to attract attention. Sure, in this particular situation, the psychos have the advantage of an easy way to dispose of remains… but eventually, someone's going to start asking questions about the smoke coming from the place.

Jermaine crosses the relatively small porch and walks in the front door as casually as if he lived here. Not sure what to expect, I follow. The doors lead to a small foyer with rose marble tile floor and another set of double doors to a large room. It's kind of a living room, but huge. All sorts of 'Southwestern' décor from cowboy hats to saddles to vases and Native American artwork give the space a vibe somewhere between a museum and a theme restaurant. Despite the enormous sectional and multiple cushioned chairs all over the place, everyone's standing, and by 'everyone,' I mean about twenty-five people.

Seems we've barged in on a party. Not the 'people drunk all over the place' sort of party I'm used to seeing, though. This is a 'people in expensive clothes standing around in small groups trying not to talk loud enough to be heard more than six feet away' sort of gathering.

Boring old person affair. They really ought to come up with another word for it than 'party,' which implies fun—and Follows Rules Girl who never liked getting drunk is saying this.

The instant we walk in, I'm on edge. I feel like the idiot who shows up at a wedding in street clothes. All the guys are wearing suits probably more expensive than most cars. Women are almost all in fancy dresses, the sort of garments celebrities wear at awards shows— to a point. No one's going super crazy. Nothing transparent, cartoonish, or made out of pork chops. Okay, maybe celebrities are a bad comparison. They tend to get weird fashion wise. It's as though I'm at a fancy ball in some country where they still have royalty or nobility.

At least I have Jermaine beside me. The two of us are in the Tex Mex Waldorf but dressed for McDonalds. He does, however, appear to be correct. No one's giving us the stink eye. They barely glance at him, but I attract a few lingering stares. Can't read any minds here, so I've only got facial expressions to work with. Either they're astonished he's brought a girl to this event, are wondering what a mortal girl's doing here, or are horrified someone gave the Transference to a kid.

Not letting it bother me. This is my reality for the rest of forever. If it gets under my skin, it will drive me insane.

We approach one of the conversation clusters, two women and three men near a giant white fireplace mantel, dormant of course. They all appear to be in their early thirties. Only the blonde woman gives off a noticeable aura of power. It's not quite as slap-in-the-face potent as the two guys I saw at the former mortuary, more on par with Wolent, if a little weaker. Of course, he's a Fury, so his presence is stronger than most. Considering Jermaine is heading right for her, I'll assume this is Cassandra Upton.

She's pretty, but not in a Baywatch 'smoking hot' way. She's part Marilyn Monroe and part one of those German girls who carry beer around. The woman's got the kind of figure they used to paint on bombers back in World War II. Guys today would say she's 'fat.' Guys today are dumb.

And wow, she definitely has a presence. The way she stands, the laugh, the expression on her face… she owns this room—probably literally since it's her house, but I mean she'd *own* any space she occupied. I've never seen her before in my life but if she asked me to help her fight off waves of invading bandits, I'd totally grab a rifle.

"Hello, Jermaine," says Cassandra before turning to face me. "This must be Arthur's new associate."

"Hi. I'm Sarah Wright." I offer a hand. "Pleasure to meet you."

She shakes hands. "Cassandra Upton, but I suspect you knew who I am already."

"Yes."

The other woman and three men regard me in silence, their expressions curious.

"Jermaine tells me you have some concerns."

Yeah, he probably called her after I got off the phone with him. I fight the urge to bite my lip. Just because I look like a kid doesn't mean I need to constantly act like one. "Yes. I stumbled on an old funeral home in Ventura. A group of vampires are staying there, but they're kill-feeders."

"I see," says Cassandra, as her four friends wince in varying degrees at the words 'kill-feeder.' "Has Jermaine explained to you about Ventura?"

"Yes. I know it's basically lawless. Still, this group is a threat to all vampires in southern California. These two boys I know, humans, think of themselves as vampire hunters. They're dorks, and kinda dumb, but cute. Anyway, these two figured out vampires are using the old funeral home down the street from where they live as basically a charnel house. If two kids can sniff out actual vampires, it's not going to take long before real hunters show up."

"Hmm." Cassandra taps her foot, eyes narrowing slightly, jaw tight.

"I haven't been a vampire for long, so maybe I'm a little too sensitive still, but it's horrible they're murdering people. I'm way too new to do anything about a bunch of psychotic elders, so I hoped bringing it to your attention could help."

"You said five? All elders?"

"Two definitely are. I saw them." I nod at her. "At least one of the three I didn't see has to be an elder. Didn't see them, but their presence was strong enough to feel."

Cassandra shifts her weight back, holding her head up slightly higher. "I see. This is a matter to be concerned about. I appreciate you bringing it to my attention and will certainly take it into consideration."

Why does it feel as though I've gone to HR and suggested changing the placemats from green to lavender at an office? Jermaine said not to expect instant fixes. Honestly, the woman was gracious enough to meet me—an outsider—at all, and on short notice. Trying to push her won't do anything beneficial. I'll end up looking like a brat and it will no doubt blow back on Wolent, which will blow back on me and probably my family.

So, yeah. I've done everything reasonably within my power to help. Dalton told me the most difficult lesson every vampire has to learn is knowing their place. I hate the phrase 'know your place,' but mostly because it's so often used against women. Cassandra has shown me nothing but courtesy, so I return it.

"Thank you for seeing me." I kinda half bow and lean as if to walk away.

Her smile broadens. Guess she expected me to have a tantrum or start begging. She nods once as if to acknowledge our conversation is over—or give me permission to leave, not sure which. "I hope you have a safe trip back north. You may want to avoid Ventura. It isn't a pleasant area for our kind."

"Thanks. I'll try." I make a 'nice to sorta meet you' face at the other four vampires who'd been talking with her, then head for the exit.

Jermaine stays behind for a moment or three to talk to them, sounds like random local matters. Once outside, I stop a few steps away from the porch, gazing up at the cloudless sky full of stars. If my head contained a metaphorical house for my thoughts, the little brain gremlins are working overtime to add a whole wing for guilt. Not being home right now, not being able to do anything about the psycho vampires, worrying about the Peters brothers... I'm filling up too many rooms. Gotta rationalize. The world has millions of problems I can't do anything about, like famine, wars, disease, the Twilight movies... There's no reason for me to feel bad about my inability to kick the asses of vampire elders.

Got a sneaky suspicion Cassandra thinks I'm a kid freaking out over nothing. She's probably not going to do anything more than monitor the situation—if even that—until or unless it gets totally out of control. In her position, I'd probably think of Ventura as lawless and any vampire there deserves to suffer the consequences of their stupidity. Hunters probably won't flood a 120-mile radius around Ventura and cause problems in San Diego, so yeah. Maybe I am a dumb kid for thinking she would do anything.

Vampire stuff has taken up more time than it should have at the moment considering I am responsible for my siblings. I need to get home. Before I go, there's one more thing necessary for me to do. The Peters brothers *will* leave those vampires alone. I can't save the lives of everyone who ends up in the basement of horrors, but if nothing else, Ben and Cody aren't going to die there.

"Hey, went pretty well," says Jermaine while walking up beside me.

"Yeah." I fold my arms. "Thinking about it, really was kinda a long shot. Nice of her to talk to me, at least."

He grins. "Cassandra's good people."

"Yeah." I chuckle. "Ironic to meet 'creatures of the night' who all turn out to be so much friendlier than the living."

"The bad ones go to Ventura... or places like it."

"So I'm finding out."

"Speaking of... be careful out there. Gets crazy sometimes. Got a feelin' you plan to go back." He holds his hands up, shaking his head. "No damn idea why. White girls always be doin' dumb shit in horror movies."

"Hah. No, nothing dumb here. Just need to do one little thing, then this dumb white girl is going straight home. Besides, I know for a fact I'm going to live... or whatever it is vampires do."

"Oh? You're so sure..."

"Yeah." I smile. "I'm not a cheerleader. I'm not cheating on my boyfriend, and I can run more than twenty paces without tripping. Also, I have brown hair."

He stares at me in silence, brow furrowed. Takes him a moment to catch my meaning. Once it clicks, he points at me, cracking up. "Nice."

"Seriously though. I'll be careful. Not looking to cause any trouble, only trying to keep a pair of well-meaning dorks alive."

"All right. You need a ride somewhere?"

"I should be okay. Unless there's some reason you didn't fly here."

"Yeah. Can't. Don't need to, though. I'm already fly enough without superpowers." He winks. "You got my number. Call if you need advice. I'll do what I can."

"Okay." I bend my knees, about to jump into the air.

"Oh, one more thing."

I pause, looking at him. "Yeah?"

He examines his fingernails—painted the same blue as his shirt. "When you eventually get yo'self a piece of vampire lovin', I want all the juicy details."

"You got it."

"Awright, honey. You be safe, now."

I totally fail the 'cool handshake' he asks me to attempt.

Both of us laughing, we part ways. He to his Mercedes, me into the sky.

This won't take too long. If I can't talk the boys into seeing reason, a mental compulsion will keep them out of harm's way. Making sure they stay alive is the least I can do here. It might not count for much in the grand scheme of things, but it'll matter to me.

Mr. and Mrs. Peters will probably appreciate it, too.

## LAYING LOW

This sucks, but what choice do I have?

Flying to Ventura gives me about an hour to think. My stupid overactive heart is trying to make me feel bad about going home and leaving the psycho vampires to continue murdering people. My functioning brain is laughing at it. The idea of those vampires harvesting people off the street like ripe tomatoes with personal electronics and generalized anxiety horrifies me, but it isn't my place to go in there and kick ass.

There's also the slight problem of me not being *able* to do so.

No one's really explained the power curve to me. I don't know how long it's going to take before the idea of fighting an elder goes from impossible to slight chance of survival. Might not be the same for everyone. Case in point: Furies—or Beasts. Their entire thing is physical strength. Furies are a bit stronger, but only in short, intense bursts. Beasts are always strong… and they look it. A Fury could be as scrawny as someone from my family yet still be able to chuck a car at someone. Most Beasts would make pro wrestlers feel average.

Good chance anyone in those two bloodlines would end up on reasonable footing squaring off in a fight against an elder a lot sooner than any other bloodline, especially Innocents. So, there is no point whatsoever to me contemplating direct action against the crazy ones any time soon. Cody and Ben will be long dead from old age before I've got the slightest chance of surviving a fight with 'Mario or Luigi.'

Another problem, there is a Mario *and* a Luigi. Two elders. Plus whatever is in the house. Yeah, combat is *not* the answer here. Nor is talking. I'm making assumptions, but a kill-feeder vampire is going to react to me asking them nicely to stop murdering people about the same way the average Texan would react to a vegan asking them nicely to stop eating beef. Probably way worse. Trying to talk the 'Klopeks' down is about as reckless as visiting Chicago and putting ketchup on a hot dog in public.

Sophia did it during one of our road trip vacations. She'd been five at the time, and too small-slash-adorable for anyone to threaten with a knife, but I distinctly remember several people (including a nun) telling my parents they failed to raise us properly and 'set their children on a path to destruction' or something suitably melodramatic.

So yeah. I'm torn.

Leaving the situation alone feels bad and there's nothing I can do about it. Cassandra's most likely going to ignore it. As Jermaine said, dog poop in someone else's yard. Only real question is where am I going to be standing when the lawnmower hits it. Some of them winced at the term 'kill-feeding,' but not all. How much effect does vampirism have on a person being insensitive to the idea of death? Does it happen in degrees? Do wolves ever feel the least bit guilty for eating rabbits?

But... vampires don't have to kill to feed. A wolf who tried to eat without killing would be nasty as hell. It's pretty damn sadistic to partially eat a rabbit and leave it alive. It's not an option for wolves— or any carnivore—to eat and not kill their prey. Have I had this debate with myself before? Vampires are human fleas. More parasite than predator. We suck out a little bit of a person's life energy and leave them to their lives, feeling a little tired and dazed, wondering how ten minutes disappeared. Basically, we're a checkout line at Walmart.

Whatever. I have to get home. My only reasonable choice here is to let things play out as they're going to play out. Not my place to make waves here. Whatever responsibility is on me for the boys being involved in this, I'm going to fix and then go home.

I'll zip in the window, explain the reality of their situation, and cap it off with a mental command if need be. Need to do something subtle and not directly against their instincts, so it lasts longer. Hmm. Should I make them afraid the vampires are too powerful? Give them a near-irrational fear of going near the old funeral home? Ugh. Might backfire. A direct command not to go there will eventually wear off and they'll realize what I did. Knowing them, they'd freak out and feel like I'd been tricking them all along and go back to thinking *all* vampires deserve to be destroyed.

The bedroom window is closed, so I divert to land on the sidewalk instead. The house next door's having a party in the front yard. Bunch of college-age people all hanging out drinking beer and blasting Spanish reggae-rap.

No wonder the boys closed their window.

I walk up to the house, stopping at the point where the little path to the porch intersects the sidewalk. The people hanging out next door don't see me in the dark. Huh, all the dreamcatchers and stuff are gone. Oops. Hang on. This place is beige, not blue—my color vision's a little weak in night vision mode. This isn't the boys' house. Drat. I'd been so distracted by the argument in my head about what to do I landed in the wrong place. I pull out my phone and open the navigation app. Yeah, I'm three streets north of the Peters' place. Guess I *mostly* remembered where to go. Not bad trying to navigate by memory for my first time in this area.

Grumbling, I stuff the phone back in my pocket.

A sudden burst of firecrackers goes off from the direction of the house party. Cringing, I look up at the idiots—and everything goes black.

# 27

# NINE MILLIMETER MIGRAINE

Ooookay. This is weird.

I'm floating in an infinite black void, unable to see my body. Trying to wave my arms around doesn't do anything, nor can I touch myself. No, not like *that*. I mean like a hand to the face. My existence appears to have been reduced to a pair of eyes in a jar of black paint.

What the hell happened? Is this astral projection?

"Aww, too damn young," says a male voice from empty space a few feet in front of me. "What a damn shame. Sorry, kiddo. Gotta cut you out of those clothes."

Aww, dammit. Not again.

My eyes snap open to the glare of bright fluorescent lights and a white drop ceiling. A man of indeterminate age (due to a teal hairnet and facemask) stands over me, lifting the bottom of my T-shirt so he can slide a huge pair of scissors under the fabric. In the span of a single second, I process my situation. I'm flat on my back upon a steel table. Still dressed except for my shoes. I've got a major headache like I've been hit in the head by a metal baseball bat or tried to explain to 'Tiffani with an I' at Starbucks she gave Sierra the wrong drink.

Before the dude can close the scissors and ruin my shirt, I grab his wrist, push it away from me, and sit up.

"Hey! Stop. I'm not dead."

Dude lets out a long high C note like the Terminator kicked Pavarotti in the nuts—and collapses.

I look down at him, feeling a little guilty for scaring the guy so bad he fainted, but the instant my brain processes a living human five feet away from me, a huge rush of hunger takes over. Completely on autopilot, I dive off the table onto the guy and bite him on the neck to feed. I've gotta look like the vampire version of some feral street kid seeing food for the first time in days.

Throbbing in my head worsens. Oh, ick. There's a small tunnel all the way through my brain. So weird feeling cold air *inside* my head.

Realizing I'm kind of manic, I concentrate on regaining my powers of reason and manage to stop myself before taking too much blood from the guy. It's a bit like going all day without food, then being given half a small hamburger. However, I can find another two people to bite. Not gonna kill anyone.

Easy, Sarah. Get a grip.

Shit. How many days did I lose this time?

Can't be too long. I'm not naked. Waking up barefoot is no big deal. I stand, but my body doesn't really want to cooperate, drunkenly swooning over to one side. Flailing, I grab the edge of the slab I'd been lying on for balance, and cling. The heck? Did they inject me with something? The room is spinning and my legs feel like jelly. If I let go of the steel table, I'm going down.

A wheeled tray cart nearby holds a cardboard box containing my sneakers, socks, and everything out of my pockets: iPhone, two tissues, like thirty bucks, keys, two Lifesavers mints I've been carrying for six months, and my cheap bracelets. Glad I left my purse at home. No wallet or ID on me, so no one here has any idea who I am.

I edge to my left, closer to the cart, and risk removing one hand from the table to grab my phone. Takes me two tries before my hand goes where I want it to. I fumble the iPhone out of the box onto the table in front of me, then swipe at the screen so the time and date appears. Whew. Still Sunday, March 11<sup>th</sup>. Alas, I did lose several hours. It's 11:19 p.m. Grr! I almost pound a dent into the steel table out of frustration. Texts from Ashley asking where I am beg me to answer, but I have to get out of the morgue—or wherever I am—first.

It's excruciatingly tedious to perform fine hand motions, but I manage to one-finger type a response to Ash.

<Can't talk. WSA. Will text ASAP.>

WSA is our secret code for 'weird shit alert.' Means vampy stuff happened I am afraid to send out there for the NSA to eavesdrop on. With difficulty, I pull myself up to sit on the slab and reclaim my socks and sneakers, then stuff everything back in my pockets. For a second it feels as if I'm going to fall headfirst into the empty cardboard box, but my sense of equilibrium comes back online.

Whoa, this is trippy.

Okay. I can do this. Walking is easy. Even a three-year-old can manage it.

I push off my seat—and crumple to the floor on top of the dude. Dammit.

Again, I reach up to grab the table and pull myself upright, trying to concentrate on balance. Bit by bit, I shift my weight until letting go of the table doesn't send me teetering. Wow, is this headache so bad it's affecting my coordination? Even moving my arms feels as if I'm playing a video game on a crappy internet connection. Everything happens a second or two after I try to do it and doesn't necessarily go in the right direction. Trying to touch my finger to my nose results in me slapping myself in the mouth.

Having been drunk only once or twice, I'm not at all used to it. Last time overdoing it, I ended up headfirst in Tiffany Hoffman's clothes hamper. Okay, nothing is impossible. I've beaten worse odds than trying to walk across a room. Also, what's happened to me can't be inebriation unless someone force-fed me alcohol-laced blood while unconscious.

Holding my arms out for balance, I begin the drunken sway for the door. Three steps veering right, four steps veering left, near collapse, two steps careening to the right—and I fall against a giant steel box.

I'm still upright, which is good. Leaning against the wall... or no. I'm leaning against a fridge or something. It's sorta reflective, but not quite a mirror. My attention shifts from trying to figure out what I'm looking at to focusing on the blurry smear of my reflection. Specifically, the red spot on my forehead.

Uh oh. Does not look good.

I pull my phone out again, fumble the camera open and flip it to selfie mode.

Right above my left eyebrow, a hole about the size of my index finger lets me peek into my brain. Physically. Not via telepathy. Wait, *my* brain. Wouldn't be telepathy there, more like introspective meditation. Telepathy is seeing into other people's brains.

Holy shitballs. I've been shot in the head. Great. I've always wanted to know what it felt like to be shot in the head... not.

The last thing I remember is being in the wrong place. Couple streets over and firecrackers. Revving engine. Oh, son of a bitch. Hi, My name is Sarah and I'm an innocent bystander killed during a drive-by shooting. Wow. Those actually happen, like in the real world?

And shit, this looks painful. Doesn't at all hurt like it appears it would. Just a headache.

I move the phone closer, examining the bullet hole. It doesn't look as big as I figured a bullet hole would be. I pat around the back of my head, expecting a horror show, but everything feels normal there. Either no exit wound or I've stitched myself back together. Healing a major wound would definitely explain my hunger.

Dammit. Well, brain damage might explain why I can barely walk. What the crap am I supposed to do here? How long am I going to stagger around like a drunken emu on high-heeled ice skates? Ugh. Whatever. Can't stay here to be found. Someone seems me walking around with an obviously fatal injury, it's going to cause a poop storm. I risk another step toward the door, lose control of myself, and go over sideways. Crashing onto the hard tiles on my side sets off an atomic bomb in my skull. Ever have a headache so damn horrible it triggered vomiting? Yeah. That's me right now except I can't throw up. I haven't eaten ordinary food *to* throw up and my vampire side refuses to part with the insufficient meal.

When the convulsions stop, I push myself up to kneel.

The guy moans.

Oh, shit. I'm a dumbass. Hey, I've been shot in the head. I'm allowed a momentary derp. Gotta fix his memory or the PIBs are gonna be all over me. Hope the bullet didn't hit the part of the brain responsible for vampire mental powers.

I drag myself across the floor to the guy, climb half onto him, and crawl around so his face isn't upside down to me. Not sure if it matters for telepathy, but he looks too funny upside down for me to focus.

Concentrating on invading his thoughts lets me into his head as easily as normal. So weird. My physical coordination is in the toilet, but telepathy is totally fine. Whatever. No time to waste analyzing it now. This guy doesn't know too much about me other than the police dropping me off as a Jane Doe. They showed my photo around the area of the shooting but no one could identify me. Good. Brown haired 'girl next door' types like me tend to blur into people's memory pretty fast.

The cops think I'm fourteen or fifteen. This guy felt horrible for me. Aww. Yeah, I'm too squishy. I feel guilty for making him sad. At least I can fix *this* problem. A minute later, the guy doesn't remember ever seeing me or any young girl come in 'dead'. As far as he's concerned, he's hasn't started his shift yet. The time he spent prepping me and lying unconscious on the floor, I backfill with a vague memory of standing around talking about random stuff with the cops.

Okay. Done. Normally, I'd put him in a chair or something, but I don't trust myself to do much more than crawl at the moment. Trying to lift this guy is going to end with his skull smashed open on the floor. Totally feel like I'm a legit zombie. Can barely stand. Can't walk in a straight line, and I'm falling over every ten steps. The headache is so bad it's giving me a blind spot, too. Ugh. This is totally miserable. I'd once been snapped in half, my spine shattered. Literally had my ass on top of my head for a few minutes. While that hurt much more than this in terms of screaming pain, my present circumstances are so miserably unpleasant, I'd rather be broken in half again.

I manage to drag myself past a pair of flapping doors into a clinical hallway saturated in creepy institutional white. It's hard to say where I am due to everything being blurry—either a hospital, medical examiner's office, or some such place. A door to my right opens, revealing a pudgy dude in a dark security uniform.

"Holy shit!" yells the guy. "Goddamned zom—"

Whack. Derp hammer time. Can't 'member this, dun dun dun.

He stares into space, drooling.

My attempt to walk closer sends me falling into him, knocking the guy against the wall and sending us both to the floor. Whatever. I can work with the floor.

Nom.

Ooh, donuts.

So dangerous to feed on blood flavored like donuts when I'm near starved. My sanity's much more secure at least, so I don't have any problem stopping before doing serious damage to him. He, too, gets a little 'forget seeing me' memory surgery. Since I still lack the physical coordination to safely move him, he's going to think he stepped on a wet spot and slipped.

The next few minutes are kinda blurry. Next thing I know, I'm crawling along a row of filing cabinets. The room has no windows. Mmm. Floor under a desk. Comfy. I flop on my face, staring across grey linoleum. Ow. Ow. Ow.

"Hey, Siri?" I mutter, my voice a little distorted due to my cheek being mushed on the floor.

My phone beeps.

"Text Ashley. Tell her I'm gonna be late. WSA."

PAIN IS GONE.

I realize I'm conscious again, still face-down on the floor. Mental clarity is back. Yeah, having a literal hole in my head made it somewhat hard to think. I'm in the mood for a snack but not proper hungry. Ugh. Is landing on the wrong street and being shot in the head a message from the Universe telling me not to leave the area yet or does my luck simply blow?

Groaning, I roll over onto my back, happy to see my coordination is normal. No more lag. No headache. Phone out. I use the camera to check the spot like a popular girl hoping a pimple is gone. Awesome! No hole in my forehead. Cool. Seems I woke up way before my body wanted to wake up due to the guy about to strip me. I'm sure my vampire nature couldn't care less about clothing. Most likely, 'tampering with my body' set off the survival instinct. Or maybe a live person coming close enough to smell woke me up so I could eat... and after dealing with the disturbance, some deep, dark part of my psyche took over and moved me to a safe place to continue sleeping.

Shit. I probably lost a day.

Grumbling, I sit up.

I'm more than shocked to see a guy in the room next to me, casually sitting on the floor, his back against the side of a black filing cabinet. He's Hispanic, around my age, wearing a Lakers jersey and cargo shorts.

"Hey. What's up?" he asks.

"Me." I swipe at my phone. Monday, March 12th, 4:53 p.m. "Aww, crap."

"Yeah. Aw crap is right, yo."

I glance over at him. The edges of his body appear hazy and indistinct. Oh, no. Ghost. "Sorry..."

"Ain't your fault. Scrawny little punk ass Miguel."

"Sorry you died, I mean. I'm Sarah."

"Javier."

"We got caught in a drive-by shooting, didn't we?" Grr. I should've been able to duck in time. If I hadn't been staring at my phone... Yeah, my luck. Most girls walk into stop signs or trip into mall fountains due to smartphone fixation. Me? Bullet to the head. Seriously? Sometimes I really feel like a character in one of Dad's movies. What can go weirdly wrong in a funny yet dark way next?

"Sarah, I need ya to do me a solid."

Why did I ask? As if I needed a side quest. Is it rude to tell a recently murdered ghost I'm too busy to help him? For most people, probably not. For me? Yeah. Ugh. "Depending on what it is, it might take me a while to get to it. I really have to go home and take care of my younger siblings."

"Cool. Yeah, no problem. Don't gotta be today. Just, this punk ass bitch Miguel Abena needs to die."

I cringe. "Umm, Javier, I'm not an assassin."

"You're a vampire. A killer." He laughs. "Freakin' a. Vampires are real. Weird damn world, right?"

"Not all of us. Not most of us, even. I'm kinda on the tamer end of the vampire spectrum. If you want me to help chaperone someone selling Girl Scout cookies and influence people to buy a ton of Samoas, I'm your vampire."

He gazes down at the floor by his vaporous flip-flop. "My little sister's only seven. She took a bullet in the arm. Miguel could'a *killed* her."

Shit. I clench my fists, half ready to storm out of here and tear this Miguel guy a new one. Hang on. He sounds way too casual. "Wait. Are you just saying that to get me angry or do you really have a kid sister?"

Javier chuckles, shaking his head. "Yeah. I really got a li'l sis. Nah, she didn't get hit, though. The bullet missed her head by an inch. She almost died, yo. Our momma gotta explain why there's a hole in her damn pillow and why she ain't gonna ever see her big bro again."

"I'm sorry." I grab my face in both hands and sigh.

"Can you make me like you? Maybe I could kill the scrawny bastard myself."

"Sorry, no. Too much time. Been hours. Turning someone into a vampire has to be done within a few minutes of death. Any longer than one or two minutes, things can go *way* wrong." I shudder, remembering Glim telling me about the *sefil*. If a vampire tries to give the Transference to a body after the soul's departed it... something *else* moves in. They still make a vampire, but it's nothing even close to the person who formerly belonged to the corpse. Basically, a demon.

Intentionally making a *sefil* is one of the few ways to get the entire vampire community wanting to destroy you. Glim also shared some horror stories about seeing those creatures. Apparently, some vampires in the Middle East make armies of *sefil* they control like minions.

"Seriously, yo. Isabella almost died. One inch." Javier frowns.

Sigh. I really don't want to cross the line of death. It's one thing to kill in self-defense. It's another thing to have a sun freakout and kill when I'm not even consciously in control of myself. It's a completely and totally different wrong thing to hunt down and assassinate someone. Even though Javier is right in a sense. Vampires are basically the deadliest assassins on the planet. Barring magic or a sealed underground bunker, there isn't much an ordinary person could do to protect themselves from a vampire determined to kill them. Mind reading, mental control, superhuman strength and reflexes. Some of us have claws. *If* they can even hit us, bullets are usually only annoying—except for head shots.

Ugh. I am totally going to have bad dreams about the migraine.

"Umm. Will you settle for me making him go to the cops instead of killing him?"

Javier waves dismissively. "Whatever. As long as he goes down for bein' a chickenshit. He could've killed Isabella. My mother's never gonna be right. She watched me die. He killed Juan, Luna, and Joey. Fernando's got a bullet in his spine. Dunno if he's gonna walk again."

"No one saw him but you?"

"Nah. No one saw him at all. Just a dark truck. Didn't know who did it 'til I went all ghostly and shit. I don't even know how the hell I know. But, it was definitely him."

"I've heard ghosts know stuff sometimes... especially who killed them if they're murder victims." I stand. Weather looks a bit gloomy today so I'm going to get started early. "Okay. I'll mind-control him to go confess to the police for the shooting."

"That works." Javier holds up a fist to bump.

I do the best I can to tap knuckles considering his hand isn't solid. "Gotta wait until dark, though."

"Yeah, figured… on account of you being a vampire." He points at me. "One more thing. You gotta make sure he knows I'm the reason he's either dead or in jail. Javier Oquendo. Burn my goddamn name into his soul."

Eep. Not sure about soul-burning, but I can definitely make sure Miguel knows why the karmic boomerang came around and got him in the balls. I take a step toward the closet door before realizing I have no idea where the heck the guy is. "Know where I can find him?"

"Yeah. *Vato's* usually hangin' with his crew, 'cross the river in Oxnard. House off Camino Del Sol. Julian Street or some shit.

I nod. "Okay. I'll do what I can."

"Pff. Crazy shit. What kinda vampire don't wanna kill no one?"

"We're not like the ones in the movies." I put on a fake harmless face. "I'm Innocent."

He laughs.

I start laughing, too—but stop at a weird tickling sensation deep inside my head. Feels like I've stuck an entire pencil into my nose to prod the underside of my brain. Ugh. My left eye closes involuntarily; my whole body tenses up, cringing into a twist at the severe tickling. Before I can even make a noise of discomfort, my sinuses explode in a series of violent sneezes. After five or six in a row, the tickle's gone but my left nostril's plugged up.

"Got somethin' hangin' outta your nose." Javier gestures at me.

I cover my face and exhale forcefully. A small hard nugget falls into my hand. Umm… a little concerned and a lot disgusted, I open my fingers and stare at a slightly mushed copper-jacketed bullet.

"Damn, yo." Javier whistles. "That's a neat ass trick."

"Well," I deadpan. "Explains the headache."

# 28

# HOW TO GET KIDNAPPED

A m I lucky or unlucky?

Somehow, I managed to take a bullet to the forehead and *didn't* end up a blood-soaked mess. Found a bathroom here at the medical examiner's place and checked myself over for any obvious problems before going outside. I look normal. Feel frumpy, but it's Monday and I've been wearing the same clothing since Saturday. A little frump is to be expected.

Vampires don't quite bleed as much as live people, but head wounds are usually kinda juicy. Whatever. Not looking a gift horse in the mouth. I don't need a new shirt. Works for me. And crap. I really need to call Ashley, but I'm worrying about the boys. Gotta get there ASAP. Being on the phone with Ash is going to take hours. Aww, dammit. I can't just leave her hanging.

I make my way outside via a circuitous route to avoid being seen by anyone working here. My powers are offline at the moment and I'm not feeling the urge to get into an awkward conversation about what I'm doing here. Somewhere, there's definitely a police report about an unidentified teen girl brought here. Bad idea to let anyone see said Jane Doe get up and walk away.

A woman in a lab coat comes around the corner up ahead, forcing me to whirl back and go the other way. I don't get far into the next hallway before a security guard emerges from a doorway. Trapped between them, my only choice is to duck into a small office. Luck is with me. No one is in here *and* it's got a window.

Good enough. Doors are so overrated.

It's bakey outside but not smokey.

I'll take it.

Ow. Ow. Ow.

The ME's office is fairly unassuming, big, squarish, and beige on the outside. I stiff-leg it along the side of the building, heading up a bit of a hill to the nearest road. Houses across the street tell me I'm in the middle of a residential area. Hmm. I head left to the corner where a blue street sign tells me I'm at the intersection of Hillmont Ave and Foothill Road. A sorta-beige slab type sign behind me reads 'Ventura County Medical Center.' Not entirely an ME's office. Maybe I didn't need to be so paranoid about being seen after all if it's a treatment center, too.

Doesn't matter. I'm out.

According to my phone, I'm nearer the coast on the west side of Ventura. Bit far to walk to the Peters' house. Grr. I request an Uber via the app, then call Ashley.

"Sarah!" she shouts.

"I'm sorry. Some asshole shot me in the head."

"What!" shrieks Ashley. "Are you serious?"

"I'm fine. Just knocked me out for a few hours. Cost me the rest of last night though. Believe me, I wanna be home. Working on getting there. Is everything okay?"

She exhales. "Wow… uhh, yeah, more or less."

Crap. "More or less? Is anything on fire, glowing, or in the wrong dimension?"

Ashley emits a tired giggle. "No… just stressed. I called out of work not to leave the kids alone. Megan's mother came by and picked Sophia up to take to dance class. Sam went through the mirror to karate."

"Taekwondo!" yells Sierra in the background, making fun of the guy at the dojo.

Ashley chuckles. "Yeah, so it's just me and Sierra at the moment. I'm studying while she's blowing people up."

"In the video game, I hope."

"Yeah. Sierra lost her mind last night because she thinks a monster followed her when she took the garbage out."

"A monster *did* follow me!" yells Sierra. "There's something in the yard."

Ashley sighs.

"Oh, yeah," I say, turning to put my back to the sun. Damn, it's hot out. "We probably have a hell hound in the yard."

"For real?"

I'm not sure if I should be worried she didn't flip out or expect her to take bizarre things in stride by now. "I'm guessing. I can't see it either. Found a footprint the other day from a huge dog. Something ate Sam's sneakers a couple days ago, but he didn't seem at all worried, like he knew it only wanted to play."

"Wow. So, Sophia's upset you didn't come home."

"Figured. Please let her know I didn't mean to be this late. Ugh. I shouldn't have made the trip down here until after Mom and Dad came home."

"Don't beat yourself up. It's fine. I don't mind covering for you."

"Thanks. Going to deal with one little problem and I'll be home tonight."

"Little problem?"

I chuckle. "Not so little. They're teenagers. The Peters brothers. Need to stop them from winning a Darwin award."

"Oh, wow. Hang on. Sierra wants to talk."

"Hey. I'm still alive," says Sierra a few seconds later. "Where are you? You didn't come home last night."

"I'm really sorry. Not planned on. Got hit in the head and knocked out. Just woke up."

"Are you fighting in vampire wars without telling Mom? Did Dalton ask you to blow someone up?"

"Nah. Just an accident. I should be home tonight. If not, someone's going to have claws where they don't belong."

She laughs, not fully able to hide her worry under humor. Dammit. I screwed up. My 'tough' sister is scared.

"Sierra, I'm sorry. I should've put this off until Mom and Dad returned."

"I know why you didn't. You're trying to protect us from the butthead vampires. I know you didn't wanna be down there for three days, but please hurry back, okay?"

"Working on it. Little bright out for me to fly yet. Gonna hop on a plane to save time. If you want to stay up late until I get home, I won't tell Mom."

"Deal. Okay, here's Ash."

Ashley takes the phone back and fills me in on the weekend I missed. Nothing major happened, though it's starting to sound like my best friend might be insane. Chasing after three-to-six tweens— Littles plus their friends—all weekend hasn't made her reevaluate her desire to have kids. In fact, she rambles on about looking forward to chasing her own kids around. Apparently, being sleep-deprived with a loud-child-induced continuous headache is fun for her.

Admittedly, the Littles aren't *too* bad. Unless Sierra's having a bad time of it in *Call of Duty*, none of them are too noisy. Especially Sophia. Half the time, she doesn't even speak at full volume. Part shyness, part not wanting to seem rude.

A pale blue minivan approaches from Hillmont Ave, stopping at the corner.

"Ack. Here's my Uber. Let me get going. Faster I deal with this, faster I'm home," I say.

"Okay. Be careful."

"Will do. Try to stay sane." I wink even though she can't see it.

"Too late," she chirps.

Hah.

THE UBER DROPS ME OFF OUTSIDE BEN AND CODY'S HOUSE.

Thanks to the sun being so ouchy, it didn't even occur to me to be nervous while riding in a car with a fiftyish dude I didn't know while my powers are offline. The guy seemed nice enough, if a bit patronizing. Didn't believe I was 'going to a friend's house' or eighteen, and spent the whole—relatively short—ride trying to talk me into not running away from home. Not entirely sure what made him think I was running away from home. Don't runaways usually go to airports or bus terminals, not houses in the suburbs? And really, how many runaways take an Uber?

Since flight isn't working at the moment, I do the normal thing and ring the bell.

Mrs. Peters answers, peering at me in confusion.

I probably should say something first, but I'm stuck staring in baffled astonishment at her six dreamcatcher pendants.

"Yes?" asks Mrs. Peters after a moment of silence. "Can I help you?"

"Hi. Not sure if you remember me. Sarah? We met at the Lewis & Clark Caverns? Are Ben and Cody home?"

"Oh, yes! No wonder you seemed familiar. You're a long way from home."

I wince-laugh. Ouch. Damn sunlight. "Yeah, just a bit. Happened to be in the area. The boys are expecting me."

"Oh, they said something about going out to work on their little project." She leans out the doorway, peering left and right. "Not sure if they're still here. They ought to be home soon for dinner. Are you okay, dear? You look a bit off."

Stupid sun. How chipper would anyone seem while being microwaved? "Something in the air I think setting off my allergies."

Mrs. Peters peers past me. "Did you walk here, hon? Where are your parents?"

"They didn't go to California. I'm only here for a few more hours. Figured I'd stop by to say hi to the boys on my way to the airport since my flight's not until later."

"Oh, well. They should be home any minute. Why don't you come in and wait?"

"Thanks."

I step inside and close the door behind me. Whew. Having a house between me and direct sunlight is freakin' paradise. The world goes from feeling like 140 degrees to about 105. For a few minutes at least, it's awesome. Mrs. Peters asks me to 'make myself comfortable,' then goes to the kitchen. To take her suggestion literally, I'd have to borrow their shower and laundry machines, then sit in the basement out of the daylight. Not gonna go that far. Don't want to be here for hours.

Once the sensation of boiling where I stand wears off, it hits me I'd been outside in serious sunlight. 'A little gloomy' for California is still the kind of bright where I stay in my room all day back home. No smoke, which is a shock. Didn't even think about it being so bright, my mind too focused on rushing here to stop the boys from getting hurt. Huh. Is an Innocent dealing with sunlight similar to going swimming in a cold river? Don't think about it, just do it? Extreme worry surely played some part here. Seems as though I'm able to temporarily buff my sun tolerance the same way my flight speed responds to high levels of emotion.

Interesting.

Bigger issues to think about at the moment, though.

Ben's startled yelp comes from upstairs.

Mrs. Peters is still in the kitchen, so I creep upstairs to Ben's room. Got a bad feeling they've gone to spy on the funeral home despite me telling them not to. What else could their 'little project' be? As expected, they're not here, but the boys' voices are coming from the computer thanks to their remote spy camera. I walk closer, moving around to get a view of the screen.

The boys are both in view of the camera, their backs facing it. The old man—obviously a mortal as he doesn't appear to be the least bit bothered at the bright day—frowns at them. He's wearing the bastard offspring of a groundskeeper's outfit and butler's suit, totally looks like the murderous servant of the undead he probably is.

"Bird watching?" asks the old guy. "I don't believe you two are really bird watching."

"Uhh, yeah it's a school project," says Cody. "Sorry, didn't think anyone owned this place."

"We thought it was empty." Ben flaps his arms.

Wow. I've seen more believable stories told by guests on Jerry Springer. Okay, good. Come on old guy, chase them off.

Alas, the man pulls a handgun out of his pocket. "I don't think you two are really bird watching. Move."

Shit!

Cody and Ben stand there in panic paralysis for a few seconds. Ben's leg tenses like he's about to try jumping on the dude, but he changes his mind. Two boys their age should have zero trouble winning a fistfight against an eighty-year-old dude, but it doesn't take much strength or time for a finger to travel one-eighth of an inch. The old man forces them across the small parking lot and into the same door the vampire brothers carried their victims.

Again, shit!

I pace around the bedroom. Stupid. Dumbass... what were they thinking? I told them to leave the place alone. Yeah it's broad daylight, but it's still not safe. Calling the police doesn't sound like a good idea. They're not equipped to handle elder vampires and they might not believe me in the first place, at least not without revealing the spying and getting the boys in trouble. Planting a camera on someone else's property to observe them—vampire or not—is probably illegal. Showing the police the video of the man kidnapping the brothers would definitely get them to raid the funeral home... but five vampires are sleeping inside, probably in the basement. Would be a massacre. I can't be responsible for the slaughter of cops.

The old man emerges from the door. He walks back to where he found the boys, looks around for only a few seconds, and stares straight at me. Well, straight at the camera.

"Ahh. Gotcha." He reaches out. For an instant, his hand fills the screen, then it goes black.

Crap. The guy found the camera. He has to suspect the boys have been watching for a while and have seen things they shouldn't. Why? I stare at the ceiling. Why does everything always have to be complicated?

Cody and Ben are in deep shit.

Cassandra's people aren't going to help. None of my 'people' are close enough to make a difference. No way can I take on a bunch of elder vampires myself, especially while offline. Realizing I've probably just watched the last few minutes of the boys' lives go by, I choke up. I hate feeling so damn helpless. It's like I'm seven years old again, being forced to watch my mother order pizza with pineapple on it, powerless to stop her.

I bow my head, trying to cope with the storm of fear, guilt, and anger swirling around. My gaze falls on a patch of sunlight making the pale blue rug glow. Yeah. Right. Mortal me would have had better chances of doing something here. During the day, I end up being slightly weaker and less functional than before death. More than the simple lack of supernatural strength and speed, my body kinda protests being awake. Little slower and weaker, like being mildly hung over. I'd be marginally better off as a live, non-vampire doing anything in the daytime—except for minor injuries healing as soon as I go online.

However...

Being a little stiff and distracted by glare is a whole lot more functional than other bloodlines are at this hour. I stare at my hands. Ordinary. No claws right now. Not impressive in the least. Who cares? I don't need to be a force of nature. What I need to do is *something* before those psycho vamps wake up. If the boys are still in there at sundown, it really is going to be a funeral home for them.

Everyone—well, most vampires—makes fun of Innocents as more or less the 'underarm dogs' of the undead world. No one's too concerned about an upset Pomeranian or Chihuahua. What's the guy in the comics who can breathe underwater? The other heroes pick on him for having a wimpy superpower. My wimpy superpower, being functional in the day, might not be so laughable.

Okay, think, Sarah. Maybe I can do something. I'm pretty harmless at the moment, no more dangerous than any other teen. However, I bet the old man took the boys to the same room where they had Ava locked up. The cell didn't have any windows, and it's underground. All the casement windows in the crematory room have tint on them, too. Good chance of going online down there. Definitely will go online in the cell. All I need to do is get the old bastard to kidnap me, too. Once downstairs away from the sun, I give him a first-class ticket on the derp express, make him forget the boys, and get them out.

It's not going to be as simple as it sounds, though. Sleeping vampires are a lot like sleeping infants—or overly sensitive land mines. You think you're safe, but make one noise a little too loud and they explode.

If they wake up, they're going to be out of their minds due to the daylight. I won't even have the chance to fail at lying to them before I'm shredded. Not sure if being 'fully awake' will offset the vast difference in our ages and give me enough speed to get out if things go wrong. I gotta at least try though.

I start to hesitate, worrying how my family would react if I vanished, but catch myself. Can't think about this too much. Just like tolerating the sun earlier today, it works better if I simply do it. Overthinking is death, and not only mine. Cody and Ben will die, too. Can't call Aurélie for advice since she'd be asleep now. Hopefully, the boys aren't in *immediate* danger. The old guy isn't going to kill them. If he did, the vamps couldn't use them for food. Sunset is a lot more than five minutes away. No need for me to give in to panic yet. I have time. Not quite two hours, but it's still time.

If Ventura, California is the vampire Wild West, then it's time to go full cowgirl.

Wait.

That doesn't sound good at all.

Sounds kinda perverted actually. Or stupid. Yeah, stupid. My brain's spinning.

Bah. Whatever.

Mrs. Peters appears in the doorway. "Sarah? What are you doing up here?"

"I thought I heard Ben, but it came from the computer. I think they have a camera set up outside where they are. It shut off though."

"Oh."

"Sorry. Didn't mean to go roaming around your house."

"You seem worried. Is something wrong?"

"Hope not. Cody said 'look out' and the camera shut off." I force a smile. "I know where they are. Gonna go tell them to come home, okay?"

She smiles, half shrugging. "All right. They should be on their way back by now anyway. Tell them dinner's ready."

"No problem."

I follow her downstairs and head out the front door, clenching my jaw at the heat. Either by sheer force of determination or the sun not being as intense as it seems, I don't catch fire or start smoking. Wish I had a hoodie or something to cover my arms. No big deal. Only feels like going for a swim in a pool of hot needles, but as long as I don't see charring, not a problem. Merely discomfort. Totally handled.

No other choice, really.

Let's see. I could stand around the same spot watching the house until the old man sees me. No guarantee he will, and it could waste time. The window I climbed out of last time could still be open, or at least unlatched. Depends on how thoroughly the vampires investigated Ava's disappearance. Bet it confused the hell out of them how she shattered handcuffs.

I approach the funeral home from the opposite side compared to the camera's former position. Gonna try the basement window first. If I can get in and out unnoticed, even better. All I need to do is—.

"Hey," calls the old man. "This is private property."

"Uhh." I stop short, only like six steps into the small parking lot on the side of the building. Wow, the old dude's like a human radar system. Reminds me of Mr. Niedermeyer. Dude can sense a kid on his lawn out of a dead sleep. "Sorry."

Footsteps approach from my left and a little behind. I pivot toward the old guy, who's taller than he seemed on video. He doesn't look as angry as he did earlier, probably because he doesn't suspect me of spying on his vampire masters for days. He is, however, giving me a creepy sort of 'sizing up' look. Not pervy, more like 'is anyone going to miss her?'

"Umm, can I maybe use your phone? I, uhh..." I exhale hard, raking a hand up through my hair. "Feel so stupid. This guy was giving me a ride, but he turned out to be a creep. He kicked me out of his car when I wouldn't let him make out with me. I'm not even from California. This is California, right? Ugh. I guess running away was a really stupid idea."

"Yes... usually is," says the old man, eyes narrowing.

"I get it. Really. I wanna go home now. My parents have no idea where I am." I fold my arms across my chest, trying to seem frightened and vulnerable. "Can I please use your phone to call them?"

He smiles, but it's far from a reassuring smile. Only a complete idiot would do anything other than run as fast as they could directly away from this guy. "Sure. Shame you being so far away from home all alone."

I can't help but glance at the pocket he pulled the gun out of before. "Thanks. So dumb of me. You think my parents are still going to be mad?"

"Nah. If you've been gone a few days, they'll be happy to hear from you." He waves for me to follow and walks off toward the side door the camera had been watching.

Pretending to be oblivious to how overtly creepy this guy is, I follow. Easy to act scared since I don't really have to fake it. Not afraid of this guy, though. I'm worried about messing up. People don't get a second chance to sneak across a field of land mines.

The old man opens the door and steps back out of my way so I can go in ahead of him. Yeah, he's up to something... or he would've gone in first and let me follow him. His smile makes my skin crawl. Dark veins crisscross the almost translucent skin on his face, pale blotches and brown spots making him seem closer to 110 than his probable eighties. Dude definitely is not a vampire, but the elders might have made him into a thrall.

I smile nervously at him and go through the door, down a short stairway to a basement-level corridor.

Yeah, I'm every stupid girl from every lame horror movie walking right into the trap…

Or so Mr. Old and Creepy thinks.

# 29

# A LITTLE CRAZY

S peaking of lame horror movies, the hallway in front of me is right out of *Death Asylum IV*.

No, not a real movie. Just saying. Dingy white tiles, rusty metal doorframes, a couple old gurneys, and enough dust to choke a shop vac are definitely not going to win any Good Morguekeeping awards. Place might get an honorable mention in Better Haunts and Dungeons.

"Whoa," I whisper. "Do they film movies here?"

"No," says the old man. "Keep going straight."

We pass four rooms, two per side. Three contain piles of junk—chairs, folding tables, old-timey wheelchairs, and such—artifacts from the building's prior life as a hospital. One has a giant body cooler with drawers for ten occupants. Thankfully, all are open, revealing they contain no unfortunate remains. Honestly, I don't think the refrigerator unit has been operational since the late Fifties.

The door at the end of the corridor opens to a square room containing two steel tables and a counter with a bunch of cabinets. Jars of old cosmetics and various tools—some mundane, some creepy and bizarre—litter the countertop. Swaths of blackish mold mar the white tile walls and stain the remains of thick rubber surgical tubing dangling from hooks on the ceiling. Looks like where morticians did the actual work preparing the dead for burial. So damn eerie.

Annoyingly enough, I'm kinda getting numb to being in morgues.

This is, however, the first time I've *entered* one fully conscious. Go me.

Runaway teen girl would probably not be so indifferent though. Not sure it matters if I keep up the ruse at this point, but might as well.

"What is this place?" I ask in a breathless whisper. "So creepy."

"Just a funeral parlor." He gestures past me at a door catty corner to the one we entered from.

Looks darker in there. Fine by me. I head around the embalming tables and make my way into a short hallway with only one way out, the door at the opposite end. Electric breaker boxes hang from the wall on my left, so dusty it's unclear if they're still in use or relics. Mr. Old and Creepy follows me close.

"Uhh, your phone's in the basement?"

"Faster going in the side door and up the stairs than walking all the way around to the front door. Keep goin'. Cross the next room, out the other side. Stairs aren't too far."

The room at the end of this hallway is pretty big, packed with more hospital junk. Mr. Creepy wants me to keep going straight to the door, cutting across the narrow of the rectangular area. All the way to the right, five coffins—four brown, one white—are arranged in much the same way one might put beds in a shared room. In addition to all the junk left over from this building, a ton of other old crap is stacked up around the coffins. Wardrobe cabinets, bureaus, two desks, some paintings, weird art objects. The stuff looks super old, like 1700s type old. Gonna go out on a limb here and guess it belongs to the vampires. Probably some heirlooms they owned while alive.

Yeah, they're the exact opposite of young. Message received loud and clear. Not messing with them.

As soon as we entered this room, I came online thanks to the heavily tinted windows. Fortunately, I'm gawking at the coffins all the way to the right, so nothing's close enough to me to catch the brief red glow in my eyes for the old guy to notice. He probably thinks I stopped short to gawk in horror at coffins, but the joke's on him.

I'm not horrified. More about to laugh at these vampires for being so damn stereotypical.

Not even stereotypical. Like, seriously... *who* does this? Vampires sleeping in coffins is movie bullshit. This is the undead equivalent of walking around with a mullet and parachute pants in 2018 and thinking you're cool. I can tell the caskets aren't 'inventory' from the funeral home, sitting around empty, since they're way too nice and un-dusty. Also, the entire end of the room gives off 'thar be elders here' vibes.

"Don't worry about those." The old guy nudges me forward. "Funeral home. We got lots of coffins." He emits a wheezy chuckle.

I cross the room to the indicated doorway, entering another corridor leading to the crematorium chamber. Aha. Familiar surroundings. I don't bother pretending to be freaked out by a giant horror movie body-incinerator. Wow, this is almost too good to believe. He's leading me right to the boys. Yes, I can smell them. No, they don't stink. My nose is only slightly less sensitive than a bloodhound's when online.

"It's not my fault this time," whispers a boy.

"Shut up, Ben."

"Sarah was right."

"Shut up, Ben."

Handcuffs rattle.

"We have to get out of here before the sun goes down or we're in big trouble," whispers Ben.

"We're *already* in big trouble. Shh. The old dude's coming back. I think I hear something moving out there.

The old man directs me to the other side of the room, pointing me at the door to the room where I found Ava. "Stairs are right on the other side of that door."

Wow, this guy thinks I'm seriously stupid, doesn't he? Guess I kinda sounded it—on purpose though. Okay. Plan worked so far. I've found the boys and they're still alive. Time for phase two: getting out.

I open the door.

Cody and Ben sit on the floor, each with their hands cuffed behind their backs around a different metal support column. Duct tape binds their legs together at the knees and ankles. Wow. Guess the bad vamps got upset at Ava disappearing and didn't want any more 'food' running away.

At the sudden opening of the door, the boys freeze like deer in the headlights of an oncoming truck. It takes them a second to realize it's me, at which point their expressions shift from worry to staring at the old man behind me the way little brothers might look when their much older sister shows up to throttle the school bully who's been picking on them.

Pretty much what's about to happen here. I just need to do it quietly. If those elders wake up, I'm screwed. Fortunately, they're far enough away in the other room where it's fairly safe. And I mean 'fairly safe' as in a bomb technician handling nitroglycerin is 'fairly safe.' Still wouldn't take much to irrevocably screw up.

"Umm. This isn't a stairway," I deadpan.

The old guy pulls the gun out of his pocket and points it at me, then tosses another pair of cuffs to the dusty concrete floor by my feet. "Lock your hands behind your back around one of those empty posts."

I twist to look back at him. "Wow, a gun? And I have to tie *myself* up? Really? What happened to full service? This isn't one of my better kidnappings. Sorry, but I'm going to have to post a bad Yelp review."

The old dude's right eye twitches. Guess he's never heard of Yelp.

His thoughts are open to me, confirming my suspicion he's not a vampire. I'm also not seeing any compulsion. The old bastard is abducting us gleefully, fully aware the vampires he works for intend to kill us. It doesn't even bother him he thinks I'm about fifteen. Well, it does, kinda. But only because I don't have as much blood as a larger person.

Great. I'm the runt in the order of chicken wings.

*What are you doing in here?* The old man's eyes widen as he realizes I'm inside his head.

We stand there staring at each other, mutually stunned. He's freaked I'm reading his mind while I'm caught off guard by a mortal human noticing. He wonders how a vampire's awake during the day, assumes I'm here to assassinate his masters, and is about to shoot me in the face and/or sprint down the hall to rile them awake.

Crap! Can't let that gun go off—way too loud.

As fast as I can make myself move, I spin into a crossing punch—think they call it a right hook or something, what do I know about boxing? My knuckles mash into the side of his jaw, the bone giving out on impact with a splintery crunch like a box of spaghetti snapping in half. His head whips around, almost pulling an Exorcist. The dude emits a faint gurgle and crumples to the floor.

Whoops. I think I killed him.

"Whoa," whispers Cody.

"Shit," I whisper, crouching to check on the guy. I pat his cheek. Nothing. Lift his head a little, then let go.

Plop.

Yep. Neck is smashed. Head's all floppy and stuff. Spine's got less consistency than a politician.

"Dammit." I heave a sigh and stand. "Why are old people so brittle?"

"Holy shit! You killed him," whispers Cody.

"Umm, yeah. Didn't mean to, but the guy's actually evil, so, umm… oops."

"Dude…" Ben gawks at me. "You like teleported. One sec you're standing there looking at us, the next, you're three steps away with your arm out."

I crouch by him. "Yeah. Had to take him out before he made too much noise. Guy was about to shoot me and go wake up the vampires. Keep your voices down."

"Right on." Ben nods. "Dude's a murderer."

"And a kidnapper," adds Cody.

"But not a vampire." I extend the claws on my index fingers and slice the duct tape on the boys' legs simultaneously.

Ben shakes his head. "Doesn't matter. He's responsible for probably thousands of murders."

"Millions," says Cody.

"Millions?" Ben chuckles. "Let's not get crazy."

"Dude, we're locked up in a vampire nest, about to be killed at sundown. I think we can go a little crazy."

I pull Ben to his feet, spin him around the metal post, and break the cuffs off his wrists. "No, you're not. We are leaving right now. *Before* the sun goes down."

Cody kicks his legs away from the sliced duct tape and wriggles upright, turning to show me his handcuffs. "You were right. Sorry. We should've stayed home."

"Oh… I'm supposed to tell you guys, your mom wants you to come home. It's dinner time."

They look at each other—and say, "Crap" at the same time.

# WHEN IN DOUBT, GO BIG

Cody hugs me after I snap the handcuffs off him.

It's a small break in his 'tough guy' vampire hunter persona. Perhaps proof he really is fifteen—or maybe sixteen by now.

"Guys," I whisper. "What I'm about to say is extremely important. The vampires in this place are at least 200 years old. If they wake up before we leave, we're going to die. Do not make any loud noises or go anywhere near the hallway on the left. We're going to leave this room, walk past the crematorium oven, and go out the nearest window."

Ben starts to nod, but stops when Cody says, "We have to destroy them."

"No, we don't," I whisper, trying to sound like Mom commanding Sierra to go to bed. "We are leaving."

"Yeah." Ben points at his brother. "We gotta destroy them."

I slap myself in the forehead. "Are you guys for real? Do you realize what almost happened to you?"

"Yeah. Exactly why we have to destroy them." Cody narrows his eyes. "As soon as they wake up, they're gonna come straight to our house and kill us anyway."

"Ugh. You don't know that." I point at the old man. "How much chance do you think he had of killing me?"

"Uhh, less than zero." Ben smiles at me while ripping a piece of duct tape off his jeans and tossing it aside.

"Okay." I set my hands on my hips. "The old man had more chance of killing me than I have of killing *one* of those elders. There are five of them. The idea you're going to destroy elder vampires is even dumber than the flat Earth BS."

"No way," mutters Ben.

I sigh. "Okay, fair point. Nothing's dumber than the flat Earth BS, but one baby vampire and a pair of teenagers attacking five elders is damn close."

"We have to at least try." Cody flails his arms.

"Try? Do you have any specifics in mind beyond 'try'?" I glare at him. "Look, even if you somehow manage to defy the one in two billion odds of actually destroying a vampire as old as them, the instant you start messing with one, the rest are going to wake up—and they *will* rip us into shredded meat. There won't be enough left between all three of us to fill one taco."

"You had to go there, didn't you?" Ben scratches his stomach. "Dammit. Now I'm really hungry."

Cody turns green. "Dude! She's talking about people meat. Not beef."

"Oh." Ben shrugs. "Never mind."

"Sorry. I'm still kinda hungry. Had a bad night, err, morning. Anyway... these vampires are super old. The only thing we can do is get the hell out of here before sunset and hope they don't come looking for you... or me."

The boys reluctantly nod.

I hate the idea of them possibly being right. If the old man knew about the camera, it's possible the vampires are aware someone has been spying on them. They *might* come after the Peters family. Not too hopeful a pack of kill-feeders would be merciful enough to simply erase their memories, even if it would be less hassle than having to relocate years before they likely planned to. We're not exactly dealing with rational creatures. Perhaps they're not nuts, but they definitely consider themselves above mortals.

"Hey," whispers Cody once we're out in the main basement.

I twist to look back at him.

He's staring at the crematorium oven the way most boys his age would ogle a Ferrari, Lamborghini, or Bree Swanson in a swimsuit.

"No," I whisper. "Won't work. We *might* be able to roast one of them, but the others will kill us. The crematorium isn't big enough for five coffins at the same time. Besides, they're in nice steel ones. Cremation uses cheap wooden coffins or even big cardboard boxes. Gotta give you points for creativity. The oven wouldn't really care how old a vampire is. But... we'll never pull one of them out of their steel coffin and stuff them into the oven fast enough to do anything other than get ourselves killed."

Ben looks down, deflated.

Cody keeps on smiling.

"I don't like that look on your face."

He pulls out the flare gun. "This doesn't care how old they are, either."

"Dork. We went over this. You have one shot."

"I have ten more shells in my jacket." He pats his pocket.

Sigh. I hold my hands up as if framing a movie screen. "Picture this: you open the lid of one coffin, fire point-blank into a vampire's chest. He goes up in flames. Four other coffins pop open and you explode in a flash of claws before you can even open the breach to pull the spent shell out of the gun."

Cody grimaces.

Ben snaps his fingers. "Idea."

"Is your idea something other than leaving right away? No? Don't wanna hear it." I plod over to the window. "Come on."

"Put the flare away for now, but we're gonna need it in a minute or four." Ben runs across the room to a workbench and starts rummaging around.

Cody appears to be as confused as I am, but stuffs the flare pistol back in his pocket.

"What are you doing?" I rasp.

"Looking for a big pair of wire cutters," says Ben.

"Why?"

He points at the oven. "It's got a huge propane line. We cut it. Let the gas out… wait like ten minutes. Fire a flare in the window from outside. Kaboom." He mimes an explosion. "That's how you kill five vampires in one shot using a flare gun."

"Genius," whispers Cody, eyes wide.

"Ugh." I face-palm again. "You guys aren't serious."

"Deadly serious," says Ben, his expression grim. "The gas is heavier than air. It'll stay in the basement unless it fills completely, but still, the explosion will mostly go upward because this is a basement and the walls are braced by earth. This house has plenty of open space around it. Not gonna burn anyone else's house down."

"Awesome. Let's do it," says Cody.

"I dunno…"

Ben pulls on my arm. "You gotta know they're onto us. You said you weren't a bad vampire. Do you want them to keep killing people?"

"Of course I don't. But we can't—"

"We can." He points at the oven. "If I can find something big enough to cut the pipe."

This is so effing crazy, but the last thing I want is to stand here arguing with them while the vampires hear us and wake up. I've got two choices: go along with it or mind-control the brothers. Option one is crazy, but option two has zero chance of stopping murder. Also, I'm not going to get in trouble with Cassandra for doing it. This is, after all, the vampire Wild West. In fact, she, Jermaine, and their entire group would probably find it hilarious. Got the feeling they didn't much care for any vampires who chose to live in Ventura. Total 'wrong side of the tracks' vibe.

And a gas explosion is something any reasonable person could pass off as an accident. Or arson, but arson doesn't make anyone think of vampires.

"Okay, fine." I walk over to the oven. "Which one's the gas line?"

"Need a tool," whispers Ben.

"You *are* a tool." Cody grins.

Ben gives him the finger.

I hold up my hand and sprout claws. "Got it covered. Which one?"

"You can scratch metal?" Cody tilts his head at me.

"I can cut metal if it's thin enough."

"Whoa." He blinks.

"Uhh, your fingernails aren't harder than copper. How the heck can you cut metal?" asks Ben.

I shrug. "Probably for the same reason I have claws in the first place, live forever, and can mind-control people. Science has left the building... or at least hasn't found the light switch yet."

The boys grin.

Ben walks over, giving me this mildly awestruck look. He continues studying my clawed fingers, pointing without looking at a half-inch-diameter copper pipe running down from the ceiling into the side of the oven near the back end.

"Are you sure?"

"Yeah."

"How do you know so much about crematory ovens?" I raise an eyebrow.

He points at the pipe. "Says propane on it."

I shift my gaze to the copper tube. Sure enough, 'danger – propane – danger – propane' is stenciled along the entire length.

"Okay... you two get out the window."

The boys dart around from window to window, peering outside to find the one offering the most distance from which they can shoot a flare while taking cover in a place of concealment. Finally, they pick one and climb out.

I'm going to regret this, aren't I?

Sigh.

Guilt makes me hesitate, at least until I remember the one bitch saying she hopes the little girl character in *GoT* dies. Grr. I stop breathing, then press my thumb claw into the pipe, slicing the thin copper about as easily as pushing a knife into thick plastic. After making a huge gash down the pipe, I retreat from the loud hissing. A few feet from the open window, the damn sunlight shuts me offline, forcing me to climb—rather than fly—to the outside. It's an ungainly position with little leverage, but the boys grab my arms and pull me up into an inferno of daylight, greatly speeding the process of me getting out. Muscles are a bit stiff in the California sun. Figure we've probably got about an hour and twenty minutes of daylight left.

Honestly, my plan worked far better than expected. Didn't take long at all to find the boys and get them out. Project Big Boom is an unexpected layer of madness, but too late to chicken out now.

We run across the parking lot, across the dirt field separating it from the road, and take cover in the heavy bushes where the boys had placed the camera before. The three of us hunker down out of sight and watch the building. Hopefully, leaving the window open won't let all the gas out. Shouldn't be a problem if he's right about propane being heavier than air. It couldn't possibly escape outside until the entire basement filled to near the ceiling. Plenty to incinerate the kill-feeding elders.

Cody and Ben breathe rapidly, throwing off a ton of nervous energy like they've just egged a house and think they got away without being identified. Pretty sure blowing up a building is illegal, vampires or not. This is kinda going way beyond eggs. It's the most illegal, dangerous, destructive thing I've ever been part of. The only reason I'm not throwing up is not having any solid food in my stomach. Follows Rules Girl is losing her damn mind. Relax. I *can't* get in trouble for anything. Mind-control makes problems go away. Committing a little mild arson is a small price to pay for saving the lives of everyone these bastards will prey on in the future.

Cody pulls out the flare gun.

"Wait." Ben puts a hand on it. "Not yet. The fiends are down a hall in another room. Need to give the gas a chance to spread."

From here, I finally notice the giant propane tank outside the building. It's bigger than a Smart Car. Might even be bigger than my Sentra.

"Did I ever ask you why you're carrying a flare gun?" I whisper.

"Because we're vampire hunters." Cody grins.

"Why are you whispering? We're outside." Ben smiles.

"We're still in the middle of doing something highly dangerous and illegal." I smirk. "Whispering feels appropriate."

Cody's confidence falters. "Umm. Are we gonna get caught?"

I look around. Don't see anyone watching. Don't hear anyone nearby. "Probably not, but this is for a good cause. I got you covered."

"Huh? How?" asks Ben.

"Wow, you guys can be dorks. Mind-control works on cops, too."

"Wicked." Cody grins. "You must get away with anything."

"Nah. I can't mind-control myself." I fake pout. "I'm the good girl."

Ben snickers. "The good girl about to blow up a nest of evil vampires."

"Well, they are evil." I speak from a position of total certainty. The old man's thoughts confirmed my assumptions. They've been abducting and kill-feeding for a long damn time. *Not* nice people. Not even people anymore. Monsters.

"Dude, we need to get home. Mom's gonna be pissed if we're too late for dinner," whispers Cody. "Gonna take the shot."

"Few more minutes." Ben looks up from his cell phone. "I just texted Mom to say we're on the way home. She thinks we're farther away than we are."

"Cool." Cody points the flare gun generally at the funeral home.

Four minutes later, Ben nods once.

Cody aims...

*Pop!*

A streak of orange zooms out of the barrel of the plastic pistol, flying in an arc before hitting the parking lot about ten feet short. The flare skitters off to the side, missing the window and lodging against the wall.

"Dammit." Cody opens the pistol's breech and stuffs in another shell. He snaps it closed, aims again.

"Aim higher. It's not like a normal gun," whispers Ben. "Arc it like an arrow."

"Yeah." Cody raises his arms a bit, as if he's trying to shoot at the roof instead.

*Pop!*

The flare zooms across the road. Looks good for a second, but corkscrews into the wall next to the window.

"Crap!" Cody reloads so fast he almost drops the gun twice.

"Good aim, bad flare." Ben pats him on the back. "Stupid thing curved."

I look around in case someone's come out to see what the noise is. This pistol isn't quite as loud as a 'real' gun, more like a firecracker, but it still might make curious neighbors come looking. Still don't see anyone, but privacy won't last much longer. Also, I pick up the two spent shells he dropped. Do *not* want police finding those.

Cody fires again.

All three of us hold our breath, watching the tiny orange spot cruise across the dirt field in a graceful arc. Even without my powers online, time seems to hang still. The little glowing spot sinks... sinks... and sails through the window without even hitting the rim. Perfect three-point shot.

Nothing happens.

Cody lowers his arms, mouth open. "Aww, what the heck ha—"

*Boom!*

One second I'm staring confusedly at the window, the next, I'm flat on my back feeling like a speeding garbage truck hit me. Can't see much due to having a face full of sunlight. Faint clonks and cracks occur randomly in the distance. Oh, the place must have exploded. Guess we were a bit too close and ate the concussion wave. At least nothing hurts. Merely a full-body stun.

A moment or two later, the boys crawl over to me.

"Sare, you okay?" asks Ben.

"I think so..." I sit up.

The funeral home is gone.

Like, *gone.* A couple pieces of the outer wall stick up around an enormous hole—the former basement. Ninety-eight percent of the building disintegrated into toothpicks and flew mostly upward like a giant shotgun blast fired out of the earth. Bits of wood, scraps of metal, and other fragments rain around us. For an instant, I think I hear the anguished scream of an older woman being burned alive. Kinda reminds me of Grandma Sheridan when the network interrupts Jeopardy for an emergency news broadcast.

"Holy shit," I whisper. "You still have the flare gun?"

"Yeah." Cody holds it up.

"Good. Don't drop it to be found."

"We gotta get out of here *now*." Ben pulls me to my feet.

The three of us run like hell.

# BONA FIDE

Mrs. Peters invites me to have dinner with them.

The boys' father apparently got stuck at work late. She thinks I'm here alone in California—which is true—and doesn't want me 'wasting money' by having to buy food out somewhere. I humor her and sit at the table. Talk about surreal. We just legit destroyed an entire building with a propane gas explosion and the boys are having dinner at home like nothing crazier happened than they played a winning game of football or soccer at school.

This can't be healthy.

Mrs. Peters made enchiladas—enough to feed a small army. Over dinner, she tells me all about how much she loves Mexican food and always makes it in huge batches so she can freeze it for quick meals. It's also bizarre to watch the boys lie to their parents, claiming they were out hiking along the Santa Clara River east of the city. They're acting like we didn't walk past a car with a smoldering toilet bowl smashed into its roof on the way here.

For the most part, I keep my mouth shut—except for eating—and try not to let my guilt show. I'm forced to muddle through a mostly believable lie about my reason for being in California—Helping a friend Cassandra move into a dorm.

After dinner, the three of us go upstairs to Cody's room. I'm itching to get to the airport—probably LAX since it's much closer than San Diego—but it wouldn't feel right to just zoom out the door after something like what we did. Plus, I still need to wait for sunset. Can't influence my way onto an airplane during the day.

Cody's room is similar to Ben's, only he's got more 'military' decorations and only a single computer monitor. We went to his room because one of his windows faces the direction of the former funeral home.

The boys cram together by the window, both using binoculars to survey the blast site.

"Wow. I've never seen this many cops in one place," says Ben.

"Lots of fire trucks, too." Cody whistles. "It's like apocalyptic."

"Are they gonna find us?" whispers Ben.

"No way, dude." Cody fiddles at the focusing knob.

I half sit on the desk beside the window, arms folded. "The cops are probably going to be more confused why the tank had propane in it at all. You said no one's operated the funeral home officially for like twenty years, right?"

"More than twenty," whispers Ben. "Closer to forty."

"And we don't even know if those vampires even officially bought the property. They might've simply moved in." I fidget. "Ehh, probably had the old man's name on the paperwork if anything."

"Remember, we weren't anywhere near the place, hiking the riverbed." Ben whistles in awe. "Check it out. The basement is wide open. Don't see the coffins, though."

"Three houses left, on the roof. There's one. I think. Kinda looks like it used to be a coffin. Nothing in it."

I cringe.

Cody shifts to look. "Whoa. Whoever was in that got freakin' *launched.*"

"Umm, all those houses there, the windows are busted." Ben peers over at me sheepishly. "Didn't think it would blow up this big. We're going to get in a shitload of trouble."

"Dude." Cody lowers his binoculars, faces his brother, and raises a hand. "We did it. We finally got confirmed kills. Five fiends dusted!"

"Righteous!" Ben high-fives him.

What have I done...?

"Guys..." I shake my head. "Do you understand how lucky you got? You *can't* keep being so reckless. You're going to get yourselves killed."

Cody wags his eyebrows. "We almost did. You saved our asses."

"Yeah." Ben sighs. "We should take it easy until we're older."

"Take it *much* easier." I smile. "Don't want you guys to get hurt."

"Cody?" asks Mr. Peters from the hall. "Is there a girl in your room?"

"Don't worry, Dad," calls Ben. "It won't happen again—like... ever."

Cody slugs him in the shoulder and they both burst into laughter.

Mr. Peters looks in, spots me, and waves. "Oh, hi. I remember you. The caverns, right? Aren't you from Washington?"

"Yeah. Had to visit California and decided to stop by. Can't stay long. I'm going home tonight, actually. Gotta leave pretty soon to catch my flight."

"All right. Nice to see you." He smiles.

"Oh, Dad!" Cody grabs his phone and tosses it to his father. "Take a picture of us?"

The boys stand on either side of me making goofy faces. Apparently, 'unimpressed smirk' doesn't make for a good photo. Multiple goofy—and one or two serious—pictures later, the sun is down enough for me to slip the boys a tiny mental compulsion to feel satisfied at being bona fide vampire hunters and not go out of their way to get killed until they're over twenty-one.

They hid it well, but old dude abducting them at gunpoint kinda scared them. I'm fairly confident they'll think twice before doing anything reckless in the name of 'destroying fiends' again. Well, at least for a few years. Who knows? Apparently, Ventura has a ton of vampires in it, and not the nice kind.

I finally bid my farewells and head out the door at 7:14 p.m.

After sending <OMW to airport> to Ashley, I take off... though I do make a quick stop to feed from a middle-aged guy jog-walking his dog. It's a friendly goldie who doesn't mind me biting his—or her—master. Good dog. I erase myself from the guy's mind and add a little nudge for him to give the dog an extra treat.

Finally... on the way home.

Swear, if anyone else tries to get in my way, I am going to claw the shit out of them.

# TRADITION

O kay, I kinda lied to myself.

Got halfway to LAX before I remembered promising to help Javier. Whenever—*if*—being a vampire ever starts to feel like something bad, I'm going to remember him. Ending up as a ghost sucks way more than vampires. Wait, no, not really. They don't drink blood. Being a ghost *stinks* more than being a vampire. We kinda have the 'sucking' part monopolized.

Gah! Without Dalton, I'd probably have been a ghost haunting my house and having to watch my family fall apart. Especially Sophia.

To make a long story short, I couldn't find Miguel Abena, but it didn't take me too much mind reading to find his crew. Well, I probably *could* have located him, but I didn't feel like spending hours hunting. I was able to locate six of his associates, all members of a small gang. Four of them happened to be in the SUV at the time of the drive-by. Couldn't tell which one shot me since none of them saw me in the dark at the fringes of the party. They'd sprayed full-auto wildly, not caring who they hit. While Javier did belong to another gang, he hadn't done anything to antagonize them. The shooting had entirely been Miguel's people doing some 'rite of passage' bullshit to prove they had the balls to kill someone.

I'll trust Javier, as a ghost, to know for a fact Miguel's the one who killed him, even if Miguel himself has no idea who he hit. Anyway, I gave each one of them a mental compulsion to go to the cops and confess, thinking if they did 'real time,' they'd be 'legit.' All six of them are going to mention Miguel killing Javier Oquendo. Maybe I embellished a little, making them believe Miguel wanted to kill Javier specifically.

Perhaps it's a bit extra of me or even unethical, but I'm a little pissed at him for shooting me in the head and keeping me away from home for an extra day. Because of him, I'm missing my Monday classes. Bad enough I've kind of cheated on my responsibility to my family while the parents are away. I wasn't about to let Miguel steal even more time from my life, so I settled for sending six of his 'friends' to the cops instead.

Either way, I hope Javier's satisfied.

Worked out, too. Without the detour, I would've ended up waiting around at the airport for the next flight. Skipped the cockpit thing this time, helping myself to an unclaimed seat in coach. The flight is almost three hours, but it's a third of the time it would take me to fly myself.

At 10:21 p.m., my feet finally make contact with the deck behind my house.

Feels like something big and nasty is watching me from the yard, but I don't see anything.

Don't sense danger, either, so... yeah.

"Thanks for keeping an eye on them," I say.

Something emits a *mrff* noise.

Wow. Sam's got a hell hound, even if he doesn't know it. How am I going to explain *this* to Mom? Ehh, I'll stay out of it. Let him explain it. I head inside.

"Lucy, I'm hoooome!" I yell.

PlayStation music in the living room stops. Sierra, already in her nightgown, sprints into the kitchen and crash-hugs me. She squeezes with surprising desperation, but lets go the instant the thumping of the other two Littles coming down the stairs rattles the living room.

She doesn't want to be seen acting scared or clingy. Wait, whoa. Sierra actually hugged me. Not merely leaned against me. Shit. I messed up.

"Hey," says Sierra. "You're late."

"Sarah!" squeals Sophia. She runs into a hug, utterly unconcerned at being seen happy-crying.

Sam walks over and hugs Sophia into me tighter.

"Yeah. I'm back. Didn't mean to be gone so long."

Ashley appears in the archway connecting the kitchen to the hall. An explosion of wild red hair surrounds her face. She's wearing one of Mom's pink bathrobes over one of my long T-shirts, and looks fried.

"Ash?"

"They're yours now!" she rasps, then cackles. "Freedom!"

Uh oh. "Are you okay?"

Ashley's cackling morphs into normal giggling. "Yeah, just messing with you. Though, I did come pretty close to taking them to the vet clinic and putting them in kennels."

The Littles laugh.

"So, umm, why are you late?" asks Sam.

"It's too close to bedtime for me to start explaining." I pat him on the head. "Promise I will tell you guys about it tomorrow after you get home from school."

"The story's *that* long?" Sierra whistles. "Wow."

"Let's do something together." Sophia hits me with her weaponized pleading *Les Mis* stare.

"Yeah." Sam nods.

"Let's do something together and we won't tell Mom and Dad you left for three days." Sophia raises an eyebrow at me.

Hah. I ruffle her hair. "You guys won't rat me out anyway, but sure. What do you want to do?"

"Cheesy Eighties movie?" asks Sam.

Sophia shrugs. "Don't care as long as we're all doing it."

Sierra shifts her jaw side to side. "I dunno. Feels kinda wrong to touch 'the stash' without Dad here."

"Umm... cheesy newer movie then?" Sam scratches his head.

"Cool," I say. "But… give me a few minutes. I *really* need to shower and change."

"Yay!" cheers Sam. "I'll make popcorn."

"It's like a half hour 'til eleven." Sierra blinks at him. "Too late to eat."

"We're staying up late for a movie." Sam grins.

"We don't have to." Sophia flashes an innocent smile. "I could pause time."

"No!" yells Ashley. "The last time you monkeyed with time, you turned me into a little kid!"

"And you were adowable!" I grab her in a headlock, rocking her side to side. "Soo cute."

Ashley sighs.

Sierra and Sam crack up laughing.

"Oh, shit," I whisper, letting go of her. "Is Mom's Tahoe okay?"

"Yeah." Ashley nods. "The tire's replaced and looks new."

I stare at her.

"Hell hounds pee fire." Sam whistles innocently.

"You guys are messing with me." I point at Ashley. "You are an even worse liar than me. Especially when you're lying for a prank."

"Aww." She snaps her fingers.

"Wait." I look at Sam. "You know about the hell hound?"

"Ashley told me. He's nice."

"He's huge," says Sophia.

"You can see him?" I tilt my head at her.

Sierra looks a touch jealous, but doesn't yell.

"Yeah." Sophia grabs popcorn from the cabinet. "We don't have to worry about feeding him. He consumes fear, avarice, and the spiritual energy released during human suffering."

"So, if we bring him to one set of first-round auditions for *America's Got Talent*, he's good to go for a year." Ashley wags her eyebrows.

Laughing, I hug her, then hurry downstairs to clean up.

Three damn days in the same clothes.

Ugh. Never again.

# 33

# A LITTLE MORE THAN SLIGHTLY CHARRED

**W**ednesday, *March 14th, 2:52 p.m,* says voiceover guy in my imagination. *An ordinary late afternoon in an ordinary Pacific Northwest town, only today, the sun decided to be a bitch.*

Ashley's probably just getting out of class now and going straight to her job at the vet clinic. Otherwise, I might've asked her to drive. I'm presently in the Tahoe on the way to the airport to pick up the 'rents. I almost made the Littles stay home due to the brightness.

The Universe decided to give me the middle finger. And it's not being subtle about it. One knuckle is touching my nose. Seattle isn't supposed to borrow California's sun. It did. And gave it some Tabasco. Maybe because I dared to relax and feel happy about spending Tuesday at home doing what I should have been doing all weekend—watching my siblings.

Yes, I cheated. Cut class Tuesday night to stay home with them. Going to mind wank the teachers tonight to make them think I was there and figure out what I missed. Sierra decided to skip her sword class, too, for the same reason. Unlike taekwondo, the place charges by session. So, her not going once doesn't technically make her miss anything permanently. Dad paid for forty-eight sessions, not six months of twice a week.

Anyway, relaxation, or not being terrified, or whatever... the sun is frying me unlike it did in California when I shouldn't have been out in it. I wanna say it had been brighter in San Diego as I left the medical examiner's office and it didn't bake me this hard, but I'd been totally distracted by my situation at the time. There *is* some relationship between my mental state and my sun tolerance. Going to have to figure it out. If it's a power I can develop, seems like a good idea to do so. How crazy cool would it be for me to be able to go outside during the day and act normal? Still wouldn't let me wake up any earlier, but I'll take not bursting into flames if possible.

Because I'm nervous about getting into an accident while driving the Littles around, they are keeping relatively quiet and not distracting me.

Everything's going reasonably well—right up until a cop comes out of nowhere behind me with his lights on.

Shit... what did I do?

"Sare, there's a cop behind us," says Sierra.

"I know."

"Why?" Sam twists around to look. "She's driving like a little old lady."

"They pull people over for going too slow sometimes." Sophia shrugs.

"No, they don't." Sam shakes his head.

The two of them serenade me with a 'no they don't/yes they do' back and forth like something out of a Bugs Bunny episode as I make two lane changes to the right—signaling both times—and pull over on the shoulder.

We sit there in nervous silence for a while, the cop staying put. I watch him via the side mirror. Probably running the plate. Shouldn't be an issue. Registration is good. Insurance is good. Mom's driving record is spotless.

"Make him go away," whispers Sam.

"Can't. In case you haven't noticed, it's thermonuclear today."

"Oh, crap." Sierra gasps. "We're going to jail."

Sophia 'eeps.'

"We are not." Sam rolls his eyes. "She didn't even do anything. Besides, *we* wouldn't go to jail. We'd end up in foster care until Mom and Dad can get us back."

Sophia 'eeps' again.

"No one is going to jail, foster care, or anywhere else," I say, trying to calm Sophia down before she erupts in Mount Tear-suvius. "I'm legal, didn't break any traffic laws, and have permission to use the truck. The absolute worst-case scenario right now is the cops arrest me and drive you three to the airport to get Mom and Dad. But there's no reason for it. I don't even know what the heck he pulled me over for."

Cars keep whizzing by for a few minutes. It's tempting to text the 'rents and tell them we're going to be a little late, but I don't want to touch my phone while a cop's sitting behind me. Don't want to give him any ideas about ticketing me for cell phone use while behind the wheel.

Finally, the guy gets out of the patrol car and walks up beside the Tahoe. I roll my window down. He gives me a weird look for wearing sunglasses. "Afternoon."

"Hi, officer."

"This your parents' truck?"

"Yes. Mom's."

"She know you have it?"

"Yes. We're going to pick our parents up from the airport."

"You're old enough to be driving, right?"

"Yes, officer. I'm nineteen." I don't bother saying 'I have a young face.' Sounds like a lie even if it's true.

He glances to his right. "Know why I stopped you?"

"Honestly... not a clue. Was I going too slow?"

The cop jerks his thumb to his right. I look—and notice smoke wafting out the window of the door behind mine, which Sophia had cracked open a little. Oh, shit. Total *Cheech & Chong* moment. Cop probably thought he'd found a busload of stoners.

"Thought you might've been smoking a little of the ol' hashish. Course..." He leans closer, sniffing. "That's not weed. Something's on fire. C'mon, get on outta there before it catches."

What am I supposed to do here, tell him *I'm* what's on fire? Pretending to be worried, I open the door and jump down to the street. The cop shoos the Littles out, telling them to all exit via the passenger side to stay away from passing traffic.

Once the Tahoe is empty, the cop half climbs in, looking around and checking between the seats and whatnot for the source of the smoke. A minute or so later, he backs out, seeming confused—until he looks at me.

Smoke's wafting off my body. Not a ton of it, but it's kinda obvious. I look like someone trying to conceal a dozen lit joints under my sweatshirt. He doesn't seem to know how to process what his eyes are telling him. I can practically hear the gears in his brain jam to a stop.

"Craaaaaap!" yells Sophia, her voice as loud as if she'd screamed into a microphone connected to a concert sound system.

"Gah!" I clamp my hands over my ears—but gasp in shock at a sudden, awesomely pleasant coldness washing over me.

"Whoa," whispers Sam.

"Why is it dark?" asks Sierra.

"Sare!" whispers Sophia, her voice part grunt as if she's holding up a heavy object she can't lift for too long.

I glance around. Looks more like I'm in the shade than darkness, but then again, I have vampire eyes. A totally sealed room with no light sources appears to be ordinary lighting to me. I can't see the dark. I'm online and not roasting. The area of shade forms a perfect circle about as big around as our living room.

Oh shit. She conjured a sphere of darkness. I'm about to freak out at the idea every driver going by probably sees this enormous orb of infinite night on the side of the road when I realize all the traffic is frozen in place.

The cop, too, is standing there like a mannequin, not even breathing.

"Giant ball of night. Niiice," says Sam. "Not very subtle."

"Dork. She paused time, too." Sierra elbows me. "You do realize our sister has become the kid from every Stephen Spielberg movie the government tries to abduct or destroy."

"Max will eat them," says Sam.

"Max?" Sierra and I ask at the same time.

"The dog." Sam grins.

I peer at Sophia. She's going gradually red in the face, standing behind me holding her arms out to either side, her lips curled in an adorable snarl. Her eyes are somewhat less adorable, fiercely locked on me with a 'hurry the hell up' glower.

Right.

I dive into the cop's head, erasing his memory of seeing me on fire. He's going to remember thinking he saw smoke coming from the brakes but it turned out to be a plastic bag stuck to the catalytic converter. No big deal. We're good to go, have a nice day, drive safe, and so on. Since I'm probably going to resume smoking when Sophia drops her magic, I give him a compulsion to disregard it.

"All set."

"Whew." Sophia slouches.

In an instant, I'm being microwaved again and traffic resumes.

"Aha, plastic bag on the catalytic." The cop smiles at me. "Thought you might have had a fire issue. Have a nice day, miss. Drive safe."

"Will do. Thank you, officer."

We scramble back into the Tahoe. Like Follows Rule Girl would, I signal and pull into traffic as soon as it's safe. The Littles and I spend the rest of the ride to the airport discussing if Sophia is going to piss off some kind of time guardian if she keeps tinkering. Sophia rather calmly says they only care about big changes. Altering the course of world history or something. Avoiding a ticket or stopping a police officer from becoming awakened to the existence of paranormal beings is relatively minor.

"Besides, I only stopped time in about a two-mile area."

"Oh, only," I say.

"You are scary, Soph." Sierra shivers. "And wait... what happens at the edge? Do people outside the stop keep moving until they crash into cars stuck in time?"

"Most likely," says Sam, "the border of the temporal disturbance has a compression effect where time feels like it slows down progressively the closer an observer gets to the event horizon where time experiences a full stop."

"Okay, Carl Sagan," says Sierra.

Sophia shrugs. "Sounds reasonable to me. I don't really know."

"Hang on…" I make eye contact with her via the rear-view mirror. "Your magic is strong enough to stop time in a two-mile radius while simultaneously shielding me from daylight, but you can't fix the air after Dad blows up the bathroom."

"Yes." Sophia nods. "I can't use magic when I'm unconscious."

We're still laughing when we arrive at the airport twelve minutes later.

MOM AND DAD ARE WAITING FOR US AT THE CURB IN THE PICK-UP LANE.

Mass hugs ensue.

After helping them load luggage into the back, I face Mom and offer the Tahoe's security fob with all the ceremony of a samurai gifting a katana to their warlord. "As foretold in the writings of Azmordac, I return this great relic to its rightful master."

"Wow, you remembered." Dad grins.

Yeah… Azmordac was a weird little Nostradamus like prophet from the D&D campaign he ran for us last year.

Mom calls me a goofball with her eyes as she takes the fob. "Is it in one piece?"

"Yep." By some miracle, but yeah.

"We actually destroyed and repaired it four times," says Sophia in an entirely serious tone.

Mom gives her side eye, unsure if the girl's kidding or serious.

"It is unscratched," says Sam. "But it smells like Dad tried to grill steak again."

Mom raises an eyebrow at me. "You burned my truck to dried-out cinder?"

"Little bright today." I make a pinchy gesture. "Not intentional. It's me burning."

"Oh…" Mom cringes. "Sorry, dear."

Dad rolls his eyes. "I did not burn those steaks to a cinder."

"I liked them." Sam raises his arms and lets them flop to his sides.

"Says the boy who thinks demons are normal," mutters Sierra. "You don't have taste buds. Steak exists in three states: not yet cooked, perfectly rare, and charred to a cinder. Any state other than the first two is the third state."

"Meat is evil." Sophia makes a 'blech' face.

The rest of us laugh. We're laughing *with* her, not at her. Mostly.

We hop in, Mom behind the wheel. I surrender the passenger seat to Dad as per our usual protocol and end up in the middle of the back seat, Sierra on my left, Sophia and Sam on my right.

"So," asks Dad once all the doors close. "Anything go crazy while we were gone?"

"Kinda," I say. "But not here. Blew up some psycho vampires in Ventura, California."

"It was on the news, too." Sam bounces in his seat. "But not the vampire part."

Mom twists around to look at me. "What were you doing in California?"

"Made a bad call." I explain Wolent wanting me to bring a message down there in a gesture of officially joining vampire society as an associate of his, and being afraid using my family as an excuse for delaying it might get Paolo and Stefano plotting even harder to do bad stuff to us. "If anything like this ever happens again, I'm not going anywhere until you guys are back."

"Fair enough," says Dad.

Mom looks at him.

"The kids aren't *little* anymore, and she had Ashley helping out." Dad doesn't seem thrilled, more accepting. He sighs. "We're in strange territory now, Allie. I think Sarah's gotta trust her hunches sometimes."

"She is lucky nothing happened." Mom starts the engine.

"Yes, I was. You're right, Mom. I learned. Won't roll those dice ever again." Ooh. Distraction time. "Check this out…" I take my phone out and pull up the photos of child-i-fied Ashley. "Found a photo tweaking app."

Mom squeals like Sophia seeing a kitten. "Oh, my. She is *so* cute."

Sierra and Sophia exchange a surprised glance at Mom believing me.

"Not sure you rolled dice. You made a decision based on calculated risk." Dad reaches back and pats me on the knee. "Maybe you overestimated the risks, but you did what you thought had the kids' best interests at heart."

"Trying." I flash a cheesy smile.

"So, I really have to hear this story. How did you blow up five elder vampires?" Dad wags his eyebrows. "Did you bring the headband?"

"No, I didn't. Was not expecting to get into a fight at all, just Fed-ex a scroll. Thought it would be simple."

"Adorable." Mom hands my phone back.

"The pictures, or Sarah thinking something she had to do for vampires would be simple?" asks Sam.

Mom sighs. "Both."

Sierra examines her fingernails. "Nothing is ever simple for the drama llama."

"I'm not the drama llama." I point at Sophia. "She is."

For an instant, it seems Sophia's about to stick her tongue out at me, but she presses the back of her hand to her forehead and drapes herself across my lap as if fainting. "Everyone is so unspeakably wicked to me. I simply cannot bear the torment any longer."

"See!?" I tickle her exposed sides.

"All right then." Mom pulls away from the curb to begin our ride home. "Let's hear the story."

"Right, so… you remember Ben and Cody?"

# 34

## TOO NORMAL

My head hurts.

No, not because of a bullet. Freakin' schoolwork. It's so damn tempting to compel my teachers to simply give me a passing score and skip the rest of their classes. How is it I'm a vampire who can stay up all night—who *has to* stay up all night—and I *still* end up feeling like there's not enough time in a day to get everything done? Even being able to type at superhuman speeds only helps so much. College work is more than writing essays. This surge is mostly due to make-up work for the classes I missed on Monday, but Professor Connolly in Tuesday's bio class hammered us with a project paper.

Since the parents are home, I can retreat into my cave and throw all my waking time at homework.

By Friday night after class, I'm all caught up. Except for another philosophy paper Dr. Heath assigned last night. It can wait for the weekend. Happy to be out from under the burden of school work, I end up staring blankly at my computer screen, not doing anything for a few minutes.

Sometimes, doing nothing is awesome.

The brain needs blah time.

Sierra walks into my room, knocking on the door without slowing down as she enters. "Hey, Sare."

"Hey." I swivel the chair around to look at her.

Typical Sierra, dark blue T-shirt, jeans, barefoot. She's also holding two plastic-and-foam swords. "Wanna practice a bit?"

"Yeah, sure. Why not?" Been meaning to suggest it, but... distractions.

We head upstairs to the kitchen and go out the patio door to the yard. Sierra tosses me one of the swords. Feels like a wooden core wrapped in PVC and a layer of dense foam. A hard enough wallop from one of these wouldn't be comfortable, but it'd never kill or even seriously hurt someone. Well, *I* could probably break someone's face with it. But I'm not going to whack my sister any harder than a friendly bonk.

Perhaps attempting to exploit my hesitation to 'hurt' my siblings, Sierra goes on the attack right away. It's truly weird how Dalton shared his knowledge with me. I react on instinct, parrying her strike and flowing smoothly into a counterattack—which she expects and ducks. Wow, okay.

Again, she comes in, faking a gut shot. I know the move; this is going to end up poking me in the face the instant I try to defend the feint. I ignore the low blade and 'stab' her in the chest.

"Gotcha."

"Grr." She grins.

We reset and go at it again. The soft *thwap* of our fake swords bouncing off each other fills the backyard for a few minutes. I'm holding her off from hitting me back for the most part, and not putting too much effort into tagging her. She's surprisingly adept, stopping every one of my attacks. Her constant smile—like she's having the time of her life—prevents me from really trying to smack her. I don't mean 'really smack' in the sense of hurting her, more like putting genuine effort into scoring a point. If she taunted me or boasted, I'd bop her a few times.

She's surprisingly good for an almost twelve-year-old, but it would take an enormous amount of skill for a human to defend against vampiric speed. If I really wanted to bop her, boppage would happen.

Her technique is also alarmingly familiar. Too familiar.

Hmm. As a test, I stop holding back. For a few rounds, I put sincere effort into trying to score a hit on her, but don't resort to superhuman reflexes. She *still* holds me off, but is definitely working for it. Purely out of curiosity—I swear I'm not mad at her—I cheat, speeding myself up a bit faster than humanly possible.

She does, too. Blocking my next three attacks, barely, but still blocking them. What the hell. Finally, I try a feint as fast as I can make myself move. Any normal person would see me do some *Matrix* level blurry crap. Sierra grunts, but manages to get her foam sword in the way before my 'blade' bounces off her chest.

We stand there, swords crossed, staring at each other. I'm the picture of total resting calm while she's sweating and gasping for breath. Her expression is obvious. The girl might as well have 'busted' written on her forehead in black Sharpie marker.

"Sierra?" I ask.

"Hmm?"

"How did you learn Dalton's style so well?"

She blushes a little. "Uhh, what do you mean?"

"You shouldn't have been able to block this."

"I know."

"But you still did."

"Yeah."

We remain there in the same pose our swings ended in, swords crossed, for another few seconds before relaxing and standing like normal people. She's still breathing way hard. It's obvious she *really* had to work to keep up with me the last few rounds. Sierra's sorta favoring her left leg. I hope she didn't pull a muscle straining to block my last shot.

"I asked Dalton for help."

"Umm…" I tilt my head. "He said he could only transfer knowledge to me because he's the one who gave me the Transference. We have a mental link due to his being my sire."

"Yeah, probably."

"So… how did he manage to teach you so fast?" I blink. "If he turned you, I'm going to rip his balls off."

She laughs. "No… he didn't. Look at me. I'm still alive."

True, she's not a vampire. Whew.

"He's a good teacher."

"What are you hiding?" I ask.

Sierra raises both eyebrows. "You think I'm hiding something?"

"Yes. You're making *that* face."

She looks down, raises and lowers her toes. Shifts her weight on to her right leg, then sighs. "You're gonna freak out."

I tuck the foam sword under my left arm and take her hand. "I promise I won't."

"Really?" She looks up at me.

"Really."

"Okay." She lets all the air out of her lungs, takes a breath, lets it out.

"You're delaying."

"Yeah. Let me delay."

I tap my foot.

"So, umm. Dalton gave me a tiny sip of his blood. The night the blunt sword broke off and broke the window on the Tahoe? Yeah… I was a little stronger than I should be."

Ooh… I shiver in a brief surge of freakout anger, but let it go. "He made you into a thrall?"

"No. It's totally different. C'mon. You know Dalton. He wouldn't set aside some of his power for me."

"Yeah, he actually would. You're a kid whose life is kinda in danger because of something he did."

Sierra blinks. "What did he do to put me in danger?"

"Turned me."

"Oh." She gives me this blank look like she can't decide if she should laugh or feel sad. "He didn't though. I'm not like his slave or anything. It just gave me some of what he knows… and made me a little stronger and faster. He said it won't last forever… or even very long. Maybe a month or two. I'll still remember what he taught me, but won't stay boosted unless I keep getting blood from him."

I pull her into a hug. "He *did* thrall you."

"No. He's not gonna control me. Besides, it's ickier than kissing a boy. Tasted horrible. Not like you where it tastes like food."

Her revulsion is both cute and authentic. Okay, I don't think she plans to continue begging him for supernatural favors. "Why did you ask him to do it in the first place?"

"It's not gonna hurt me." She jabs her big toe at the grass. "Sophia's got magic. Sam's got pet demons. And I'm just normal ol' Sierra."

"You're not jealous?" Crap. Dalton said she's jealous, but not in a 'I hate my siblings for being cooler than me' way. She's feeling vulnerable and frightened.

"Correct." Sierra nods once. "I'm not jealous." She lowers her voice. "I'm scared. We're in a world of evil crap now, and... I really don't wanna be defenseless."

There are a few things I am completely certain will never happen: an end to global warfare, national healthcare in the USA, someone inventing microwave food that doesn't stay frozen in the core, and Sierra ever admitting to being afraid of anything. Like, no way. She'd never even lie about it to get something she wanted.

I hug her tight. She squeezes me back.

We have a sincere moment... at least until she whispers, "Can anyone see us?"

I laugh.

She giggles, pulling back from the hug, wiping tears on her arm.

"Please be careful."

"I will. Being careful is the entire point." Sierra holds her fake sword up. "Are we done for now or do you wanna go a few more points?"

"Up to you."

"Feeling like movie or games now." She exhales hard. "I'm wiped."

"Cool."

"Oh, by the way... Sam's got a hell hound."

"Yeah, I know." I hang my head. "Has Mom discovered him yet?"

Sierra cocks her head back, eyebrow up. "Is she screaming and losing her mind?"

"Good point." Sigh. "How do you think we should tell her?"

"Uhh, do we have to? He's invisible unless he wants someone to see him."

I look around the yard. "Really?"

A shimmer near the fence all the way at the back end catches my eye. For a few seconds, a huge dog fades into view. Looks like a cross between a Doberman and a German Shepherd, only much hairier, shaggy even, and about the size of a pony. Oh, he's got little horns, too. His eyes glow an eerie shade of dark crimson, yellowish smoke peels out from between teeth I'm sure could snap a man's leg off in one bite.

Somehow, he manages to be utterly terrifying and still cute. I mean, a doggo is still a doggo, right?

He rests his chin on his forepaws, and fades away.

"Wow…" I glance at Sierra. "You know Mom is eventually going to find out."

Sierra starts walking back to the deck. "Yeah. But we can enjoy the quiet before she does."

Hah. True. "Yeah, enjoying some quiet sounds *really* good about now."

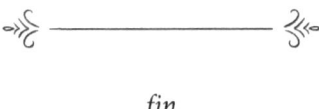

*fin*

# ACKNOWLEDGMENTS

Thank you for reading *A Vampire's Guide to Adulting!*

I am truly humbled by the reaction this series has gotten from readers. Never imagined it would be so well-received when I started it on a whim. I am beyond thrilled so many of you enjoy being part of Sarah and her family's world. Hoping to continue this series for as long as I can.

Additional thanks to Lee Hargrove for editing and Alexandria Thompson for the cover design.

# ABOUT THE AUTHOR

Originally from South Amboy NJ, Matthew has been creating science fiction and fantasy worlds for most of his reasoning life. Since 1996, he has developed the "Divergent Fates" world, in which *Division Zero*, *Virtual Immortality*, *The Awakened Series*, *The Harmony Paradox*, *and the Daughter of Mars series* take place. Along with being an editor at Curiosity Quills press, he has worked in IT and technical support.

Matthew is an avid gamer, a recovered WoW addict, Gamemaster for two custom RPG systems, and a fan of anime, British humour, and intellectual science fiction that questions the nature of reality, life, and what happens after it.

He is also fond of cats.

Visit me online at:
Facebook: https://www.facebook.com/MatthewSCoxAuthor
Amazon: https://www.amazon.com/author/mscox
Pinterest: https://www.pinterest.com/matthewcox10420/
Goodreads: https://www.goodreads.com/author/show/7712730.Matthew_S_Cox
Email: mcox2112@gmail.com

# OTHER BOOKS BY MATTHEW S. COX

Divergent Fates Universe Novels

Division Zero series

- Division Zero
- Lex De Mortuis
- Thrall
- Guardian
- Harbinger
- The Shadow Fixer
- Neuroshock

The Awakened series

- Prophet of the Badlands
- Archon's Queen
- Grey Ronin
- Daughter of Ash
- Zero Rogue
- Angel Descended

Daughter of Mars series

- The Hand of Raziel
- Araphel
- Ghost Black

Virtual Immortality series

- Virtual Immortality
- The Harmony Paradox

Prophet of the Badlands Series

- Prophet's Journey
- Prophet's Mercy

Divergent Fates Anthology

(Fiction Novels - Adult)
The Roadhouse Chronicles Series

- One More Run
- The Redeemed
- Dead Man's Number

Faded Skies series

- Heir Ascendant
- Ascendant Unrest
- Ascendant Revolution

Temporal Armistice Series

- Nascent Shadow
- The Shadow Collector
- The Gate to Oblivion
- The Queen of Discord
- The Burning Alchemist

Vampire Innocent series

- A Nighttime of Forever
- A Beginner's Guide to Fangs
- The Artist of Ruin

- The Last Family Road Trip
- The Phantom Oracle
- How Not to Summon Demons
- Ordinary Problems of a College Vampire
- A Vampire's Guide to Surviving Holidays
- An Introduction to Paranormal Diplomacy
- A Vampire's Guide to Adulting
- How to Stop a Vampire War in Six Easy Steps
- Ancient Vampire Death Cults and Other Annoyances
- Hunting Vampires for Fun and Profit
- A String of Seriously Unlucky Events
- The Summer of Completely Usual Strangeness
- Demonic Crisis Management for the Modern Vampire

Standalones

- Wayfarer: AV494
- Axillon99
- Chiaroscuro: The Mouse and the Candle
- The Spirits of Six Minstrel Run
- Sophie's Light
- The Far Side of Promise anthology
- Operation: Chimera  (with Tony Healey)
- The Dysfunctional Conspiracy (with Christopher Veltmann)
- Of Myth and Shadow
- The Girl Who Found the Sun

Winter Solstice series (with J.R. Rain)

- Convergence
- Containment
- Catalyst
- Catacombs

Alexis Silver series (with J.R. Rain)

- Silver Light
- Deep Silver
- Silver Quarrel
- Silver Crucible
- Silver Heart

Samantha Moon Origins series (with J.R. Rain)

- New Moon Rising
- Moon Mourning
- Haunted Moon

Vampire For Hire series (with J.R. Rain)

- Moon Master
- Dead Moon
- Lost Moon
- Vampire Destiny
- Infinite Moon
- Vampire Empress
- Moon Elder
- Wicked Moon
- Moon Blade

Maddy Wimsey series (with J.R. Rain)

- The Devil's Eye
- The Drifting Gloom
- Dark Mercy
- Primal Wrath

Samantha Moon Case Files series (with J.R. Rain)

- Blood Moon

Immortal Operative (with J.R. Rain)

- Broken Ice
- Broken Wing

Four Elements series (with J.R. Rain)

- The Elementalist
- The Black Rose
- The Wakefield Curse

Witches series (with J.R. Rain)

- The Witch and the Hangman

Zeb Clemens series (with J.R. Rain)

- The Beast of Devil's Creek
- Wanted: Undead or Alive

Young Adult Novels

The Eldritch Heart Series

- The Eldritch Heart
- The Cursed Crown
- The Sapphire Soul

Evergreen Series

- Evergreen
- The World That Remains

- The Lucky Ones
- Nuclear Summer
- The Nuclear Frontier
- The World We Make
- The Threat Unseen

Progenitor Series

- Out of Sight
- Out of Mind

Diary of a Teenage Fey

(Short story series)

- Elder Horror
- The Hag of Barrow Falls
- Babysitter's Nightmare
- Lharakki
- Bauble for a Soul
- Simulacrum
- Amorphous
- Manticore

Standalones

- Caller 107
- The Summer the World Ended
- Nine Candles of Deepest Black
- The Forest Beyond the Earth

Middle Grade Novels

The Adventures of Ubergirl series

- My Dad is a Mad Scientist
- Aliens Ate My Homework
- The End of all Halloweens
- Dr. Infinity and the Soul Smasher

Tales of Widowswood series

- Emma and the Banderwigh
- Emma and the Silk Thieves
- Emma and the Silverbell Faeries
- Emma and the Elixir of Madness
- Emma and the Weeping Spirit

Standalones

- Citadel: The Concordant Sequence
- The Cursed Codex
- The Menagerie of Jenkins Bailey

www.ingramcontent.com/pod-product-compliance
Lightning Source LLC
Chambersburg PA
CBHW032149190626
46814CB00005BA/1907